SWORDSMAN

Book 3 of
the *Fellowship of the Mystery* trilogy

by Terry L. Craig

SWORDSMAN
Published by Wild Flower Press, Inc.
P O Box 2532
Leland, NC 28451
www.wildflowerpress.biz

First edition printed November, 1987
Second, expanded edition printed 2005
Third edition 2017
Copyright © 1985, 1987, 2005 by Terry L. Craig
All rights reserved.

ISBN 13: 978-1-946549-01-3

Scripture quotations are from the following versions:

Dedication

Dedicated to my beloved Bill
and my favorite sister, Jo Ann

Author's Note

In the late 1970's, I began scribbling notes for a book and sending them off to my sister. I described images of a future world where war precipitated the loss of much of the global oil supply, and acts of biological terrorism had taken many lives. But in this world, all hope wasn't lost. A new source of energy that traveled through fiber optic strands was hailed as the means by which humanity could move beyond mere survival mode. This technology made a cashless global economy possible, and aided in the enforcement of controlled population zones. Every person could be tracked via the use of microchips (containing a person's entire history) imbedded under the skin. To ensure the survival of the majority during the transition, governmental policies were implemented to limit resources spent on caring for the elderly, the handicapped, and those who resisted necessary changes. In order to guarantee peace, there could be no "exclusive" belief system or culture. With all this in place, mankind's need for order and for material gain would be kept in perfect balance.

I could only write late at night as I juggled the responsibilities of work and family, so it was a slow process. In 1987, I thought I'd finished the tale of this future world and published the first edition of SWORDSMAN.

That novel was the skeleton of this one, but virtually all the scientific advances and cultural trends in the book you now hold were in the original novel. Although I have added some new characters and more details, this version remains true to the original storyline.

To illustrate how we might arrive at the world portrayed in SWORDSMAN, I later wrote two prequels: GATEKEEPER and SOJOURNER, which contain the history of events and characters in this final book. These three books make up the *Fellowship of the Mystery* trilogy.

As of this (3rd) printing, it's been nearly forty years since I began mailing those first notes to my sister. Amazingly, nearly all of the inventions and technologies described in SWORDSMAN are in everyday use or within reach. Time has taken that which might have been considered a farfetched story and turned it into a plausible scenario.

However, I want readers to note that—while I believe the Lord has given me views into some future events and what may precipitate them—neither this book nor the others in the series are intended to give people a timetable for future events.

SWORDSMAN is a story . . . written to show the potential fruit of ideologies and attitudes that are blossoming in society today. It's an opportunity to see how our small, daily decisions (or compromises) foreshadow the decisions we will make concerning larger, more difficult issues. This is a tale about the impact of accumulated choices on our lives, on the lives of those around us, and possibly on the generations to come. And, most of all, it's a story about faith.

First off, you need to know that in the last days, mockers are going to have a heyday. Reducing everything to the level of their puny feelings, they'll mock, "So what's happened to the promise of his Coming? Our ancestors are dead and buried, and everything's going on just as it has from the first day of creation. Nothing's changed."

Don't overlook the obvious here, friends. With God, one day is as good as a thousand years, a thousand years as a day. God isn't late with his promise as some measure lateness. He is restraining himself on account of you, holding back the End because he doesn't want anyone lost. He's giving everyone space and time to change.

[2 Peter 3:3-4, 8-9 in The Message]

Chapter 1

A suburb of Dallas in the former state of Texas

"What are we doing here?" she whispered. She could see their breath blowing away in the cold wind.

"Shhhh!" he said, waving his hand down and creeping toward the house. When he reached the window, he slowly straightened up, raising his eyes just above the sill.

After a while, she began to think he'd frozen there. He hadn't moved as much as a finger in several minutes. She crawled over to where he'd pressed up against the building and she could hear singing. It reminded her of something, but she couldn't think of it right then and wanted to go. She reached over and jiggled his arm.

"Michael," she said in a hushed voice, "what in the world are you doing?"

He'd been so carried away watching the people in the house, the start of her touch made him lose balance and fall backward onto the ground.

"Someone's outside," a voice in the house said.

"Let's go see," said another.

A woman's voice said, "If someone's out there, invite them in!" and laughter followed.

Michael jumped up, grabbed Linda by the hand, and started running as hard as he could. He dragged her around the side of the house, then through the yard and up a street, his long legs taking great strides. He ran so fast, Linda could hardly keep up and nearly fell several times.

When they got to the corner she managed to call out, "Michael! Stop! Are you trying to kill me?"

He leaned against a signpost and gasped, "Sorry . . . I thought they were going to catch us spying on them."

"What do you mean 'us'?" she asked, slightly indignant. "I wasn't spying on anyone. You were the one peeping in the window." Her eyebrows came together. "What were they doing anyway? . . . It sounded like they were just singing."

"They weren't just singing," he said, starting to walk.

Linda trotted a few steps to catch up with him. "Then what were they doing?"

"I don't know exactly."

"Who are they? Do you know them?" Her curiosity started to roll.

"Why? Planning on doing one of your 'in depth' reports on them?" He made little quotation marks in the air.

"Don't be a jerk, Michael. I mean, were they doing something weird or what?"

"Just forget it, okay?"

"Drop dead," she said, coming to a halt. She waited for him to notice she'd stopped and come back, but he kept walking. "Okay. Okay," she called. "You keep going, I'll come home when I feel like it. *If I feel like it!*"

Did he hear her? He didn't even slow down. What was with him anyway? She felt insecure and she didn't like it. Men chased her not the other way around. At least, that was the way it was supposed to be.

A surprising thought shot into her brain. *Wow. Maybe I've started to wrinkle or something. I'll definitely have to think about this.*

When Michael arrived home, it had begun to get dark and he could see the soft light of candles in some of the windows he passed. He entered the apartment through the kitchen and saw a light coming through the door to the living room. Stopping only momentarily to pick up a piece of dried fruit off the table, he walked into the living room to find two people sitting on his couch, kissing. He could see the backs of their heads.

"Party's over, folks," he said, continuing past them on the way to his room. . . . Just what he thought. Two guys.

"Hey Michael, what time is everyone getting here?" one of them called.

"Everyone who?" Michael stopped and looked out of his room at the couple.

"You know. Everyone. Zac, Linda, Jody, John . . . everyone."

"That's funny, I don't remember inviting anyone." He wanted to say something else to make them feel unwelcome but changed his mind. Linda must've planned a party. Maybe it would cheer him up. But first, he needed to find the box. He tried to remember where he'd stashed it last. . . . Under the bed? Too obvious. Anyone could find it there. In the closet maybe. He scavenged around in the closet, beginning to sweat. . . . Where had he put that box? He pulled the drawers all the way out of his dresser and left them on the floor.

"Looking for this?" Michael turned to see Martin, the feminine half of the couple, standing in the doorway, holding the small, black box.

"Where was it?" he said, grabbing it.

"Under your bed," Martin said.

"Well, just stay out of my room and keep your hands off my things." Michael started searching for the wire now. "You got the wire, too?"

"No. We couldn't find it."

Wanting to end the conversation, Michael closed his bedroom door. Bending down, he reached between his mattress and box springs and soon located it. He sat on the bed and plugged the wire into the box. He felt very little discomfort when he put the other end of the wire up into his sinuses and worked the electrode into just the right spot. He sat for a moment with his thumb resting on the toggle switch for the box. When he flipped the switch the jolt sent him back on the bed where he lay perfectly still, allowing alternating waves of numbness and pleasure to undulate over him.

He felt a floating sensation for a time and then as though he'd been drawn down into something. Suddenly, he became aware of sights and sounds around him.

Where am I? Michael thought, looking around. He could hear music playing and see many people sitting in rows around him. . . . Church. He was in church and he was only ten years old.

His little sister, Jill, sat farthest down the pew. Next came Father, Mother, brother Ben, then himself, and finally, older brother Zachary.

When they all stood to sing, Michael's vision zeroed in on a particular man in the choir. Every time the song got to the word "Emmanuel," the old guy got almost half of it out before yawning. Michael finally succumbed to the suggestion and yawned.

"Ouch! Stop pinching me!" Ben said loud enough to be heard several rows away.

Heads turned.

Mother leaned down and whispered, "Then stop picking your nose!"

Michael giggled.

Without her even looking over, Mother's radar hand came around Ben and found its mark. Michael heard a snap and felt a simultaneous sharp pain as Mother thumped him right behind the ear.

The hymn finally wound down, and the usual coughing, book closing, and foot shuffling could be heard.

Pastor Ted raised his hands for silence in the sanctuary.

"Father," Pastor Ted began, "thank You for this glorious day. We are so happy we could greet it together with You this morning. . . . We are so grateful to be in Your house, partakers at Your table . . ."

Father coughed. Mother nudged him.

Pastor Ted continued ". . . and as we gather today, we will remember in our prayers those who are ill or in need. Sister Margot, who underwent surgery this past week . . ."

Michael looked at his fingernails, then at his shoes. Ben started fidgeting with something he'd taken out of his pocket, then showed it to Michael: A small race car he'd gotten with his allowance.

"Bet it could do a hundred." Ben whispered to Michael.

Mother's radar hand found Ben's ear.

"Ow!"

Pastor Ted paused a moment too long for more breath.

"AMEN!" Father said, seating himself.

Pastor Ted looked around for the disturbance, "And for these flowers on the altar today. . ."

Father stood up again.

"I gotta go to the bathroom, Mom." Ben said without whispering.

She glared down at him and said under her breath, "You'd better be right back!"

Ben smiled triumphantly at Michael as he started past him toward the aisle.

"I gotta go, too, Mom." Michael said quickly, getting right behind Ben before she could reply.

Pastor Ted had about run out of prayer now.

"In the name of your Son, Jesus . . ."

"Thank God." Father said and sat down.

In the back, Ben tried the bathroom door. An usher quickly approached.

"Sorry. You boys will have to use the one in the balcony section. This one isn't working right." As the boys headed for the stairs, he added, "And no fooling around up there, you hear?"

Ben and Michael donned their most angelic faces and replied, "Yes, sir."

When they got to the top of the stairs, they looked around. Hardly anyone sat in the balcony. They went over to the corner near the bathroom door and stopped.

"You go first." Ben said.

"I don't need to go." Michael said.

"Me neither," Ben said before spotting the usher coming up the stairs. He quickly went in and closed the door. Michael stood outside, trying to look honest. The usher glanced over at him and then returned down the stairs.

Ben opened the door a crack. "He gone yet?"

"Yeah."

"Look what I found!"

Michael looked at the object in Ben's hand. It was a large, midnight-blue felt-tip marker. Michael's eyes got wide and he said, "What are you gonna write?"

Ben leaned forward and whispered, "How about 'Pastor Ted loves Mrs. Furguson'?"

Michael stifled a laugh. Mrs. Sue Furguson, the church organist, was a huge, middle-aged woman, who wore enormous glasses and warbled when she sang. "Yeah!" Michael whispered back.

Ben closed the door and didn't open it for quite some time. Standing outside, Michael got rather bored before he noticed the usher walking toward him.

"Why are you still up here?" the man asked suspiciously.

He suddenly had second thoughts about Ben's activities in the bathroom. "My brother is . . . sick," he said, leaning against the door.

Ben heard Michael outside and thought for a moment. Then he started making what he thought would be believable throwing-up noises.

"Does he need help?" The usher showed concern now. It sounded as if Ben might be dying in there.

"Oh no!" said Michael. "He throws up all the time at home! He'll be okay in a minute."

Ben stopped the noises. "Well, if you say so . . ." the usher said. "I'll be back in a few minutes to see if he's okay."

As soon as the man disappeared down the stairs, Michael knocked on the door. "Ben. Ben, it's me. Open the door!"

Ben opened the door and his brother entered the restroom. There, neatly drawn above the toilet, an arrow-pierced heart proudly stated, "Ted 'n Soo."

"Ted 'n Soo?" Michael said. "I thought you were gonna write 'Pastor Ted loves Mrs. Furguson.'"

"Well I was. But after I thought about it, if they were in love, he wouldn't call her 'Mrs. Furguson' now would he? . . . Besides, I don't know how to spell Furguson."

"You're such a dummy!"

"Then *you* fix it!" Ben said, jamming the marker into Michael's hand.

They heard a knock on the door.

"Are you still in there?" the usher asked through the door. Michael and Ben's eyes grew wide.

"Yes . . . I'm in here with my brother. He's okay now. I'm just washing his face and stuff," Michael said loudly. Then he reached over and turned on the water.

"Do you want your mother?" the voice asked.

"Oh no!" he quickly blurted out. "She hates to miss church. We'll be out in a minute anyway. Thanks."

"Okay," the usher said, "I'll come back in a minute and if you're still in there, I think I'd better get your mom."

"Ben," Michael said in a panicked whisper. "If he comes back and sees this," he pointed to the blue Ted 'n Soo heart, "we'll get killed right here in church! . . . Help me get it off!"

They used wet toilet paper, and blue ink ran down the wall in rivers. As they finished with each glob of paper, they put it in the toilet. Eventually, they ran out of toilet paper and used the tissues near the sink. Finally, the letters were barely visible.

Ben peeked out the door. "He's comin' Michael! *Hurry!*"

Michael flushed the toilet and turned out the light as they hurried out, meeting the usher at the top of the stairs.

"Hi," Ben said, walking past the usher with a large smile. "I'm feeling just fine now."

The usher shrugged and followed them down, not noticing the water beginning to soak the carpet in front of the bathroom door.

Ben and Michael found their way back to their pew, squeezing in with sighs of relief. Mother gave them a look, and they both smiled, happy to be safe in her presence again.

More than fifteen minutes passed. Michael and Ben had all but forgotten the whole thing when it happened. Pastor Ted had somehow compared a fishing trip to being a "fisher of men." He'd gotten to the climax of his sermon when a thin stream of water began pouring off the balcony and down onto the hat of Mrs. O'Brien.

At first, Mrs. O'Brien sat in stunned disbelief as two, three, and then four more little strings of water came down on her shoulders and the seat on either side of her. Then, one large stream poured over the edge of the balcony. It danced briefly on the wide brim of her hat which promptly collapsed in her face, allowing the water to pour directly down the front of her dress. She stood and screamed.

Then, Michael saw himself and Ben in their old home on 22nd Ave. Father towered over them, holding in his hands a bill totaling $705.26 for repairs to the plumbing, cleaning of the carpets, and replacement for Mrs. O'Brien's hat and dress. Mother, once summoned to the room, knew enough to stay out of arm's reach.

Father glared at her. "Going to church is 'good for business', huh? *Whose business? The carpet cleaner's? The plumber's?*"

Mother looked down and said nothing.

"And *you,*" he said, glowering at Ben, "you worthless little twit . . . You always have been useless and always will be! . . . *Worthless idiot!*" He bellowed, raising his hand to strike Ben again and again.

Mother covered her face and ran from the room. Their little sister wailed and grabbed Michael by the arm. "Mikey, Mikey! Make him stop!"

Michael, only slightly larger than Ben, moved between them. "*Look,* I did it too! Don't hit him anymore!"

Father, drunk and enraged beyond reasoning, turned on Michael full force. "I'll teach *you* to interfere!"

Everything in Michael cried out, *Run! Run!* but he couldn't seem to move fast enough. He strained every muscle to get out of the way, but found himself only capable of the slow-motion run of nightmares. As the first blow struck the side of Michael's head, searing pain shot through him, and he sat up.

He looked around, grateful to be awake. Sitting in his dark room, he could hear the sounds of people laughing and talking in the next room and saw light coming under the door.

He got up and, on the way to the door, tripped over one of the drawers he'd pulled out during the search for his black box. He kicked another drawer out of the way before opening the door.

While he'd been unconscious, the living room had filled with people. Michael knew most of them, but there were a few he'd never seen before.

"I sure hope someone brought something cold to drink," he called out, stepping over and around guests sitting on the rug.

Just then a loud burst of laughter came from the kitchen. When he walked in, he found Zachary sitting in one of the chairs. A small group of people gathered about him while he told one of his stories. Zac could make almost anyone comfortable in any situation by telling them a joke or a story. Sometimes Michael wondered, *Would Zac blow up if someone taped his mouth shut?*

"Do you ever give that silver tongue of yours a rest?" he asked.

"It's better than sleeping my life away, brother dear." Zac said in a funny voice.

Michael could tell by the look his brother gave him the statement had serious implications. "I plead guilty, your honor," he said, trying to keep things light. "But if you'd stop stealing all the girls away from the party, maybe I could stay awake for a minute or two."

He found the beer and tried to get one open. It hadn't been chilled so he displayed a distinct lack of enthusiasm in the endeavor. The cap finally came off in his hand, allowing the warm beer to fizz out the top and plop onto the floor. He stepped out the door and stood outside watching the foam erupting from the bottle.

Zac came out and sat on the top step near Michael. He made no attempt at building up to the subject. "Aren't you getting a little carried away with that box?"

Michael put the beer on the railing and sat down. "I don't know. I think I can handle it. I mean, I don't need it, but it sure isn't bad, you know?"

"No, I don't know, Mike. Why do you do it? You say you don't need it; and yet, as each day goes by, you're slipping away a bit more. And you don't seem any happier for it. In fact, you've been in quite a mood lately."

"Look, if I need a Father Confessor, I'll let you know, okay? I just need to work out some things. I can do it."

"I know you can," Zachary said quietly. "Just look out there." He pointed to the section of bright lights in the city. "We're all going to make it. Why, we can even see *real* lights over there. Soon the whole city might be wired again and it could be better than ever. I was afraid for a while, too. It's been scary at times, but lots of us have made it through all these transitions without getting coded. If we all stick together, they'll have to compromise with us eventually. Just look how little time has actually passed, and here we sit," he hesitated a moment, "almost back to normal."

Michael shot his brother a sideways glance. "Spare me the pep talk. It will never be 'normal' for us again, Zac. You know that as well as I do. What amazes me is how people can lose so much and forget it so quickly. They're ready to line up and start the whole mess over again on a handful of promises. . . . Maybe I can make it all come into focus soon, but I need to put some more space between myself and what's happened. I guess I'm still hoping this is all a dream."

"*Aha!*" Zac exclaimed, "Dit you zay *dream?* Vot vus da dream about? You can tell da Doctor." Zachary rubbed his hands together and leaned toward Michael with his best "crazed psychiatrist" look. Michael couldn't help laughing.

"Are you ever serious, Zac?"

"Never for periods exceeding five minutes. Serious gives me warts."

"Don't change. I need someone like you in my life. I guess I take everything too seriously."

The kitchen door opened, and two girls peered out. "Are you guys coming in, or is there something about the two of you we don't know?"

"Jealousy will get you nowhere, girls," Zac said before he jumped up and ran after them.

Michael remained on the steps. Although he occupied a first-floor apartment, the hill-top location afforded him a view of the city. He scratched the stubble on his face and peered out at the lights.

He had to admit, when everything went so wrong he thought the whole human race would be canceled. A series of disasters spilled across the globe in rapid succession. An explosion on an international space station took the lives of all personnel before debris damaged numerous strategic satellites. Within minutes of reaching an agreement averting war with Russia over the incident, U.S. President Cole was assassinated. In a matter of days, his successor faced yet another crisis when thousands of people in the Northeast U.S. began dying of a fast-spreading contagion. While the eyes of the world were focused on these calamities, war broke out in the Middle East. Overwhelmed by the loss of satellites, ground equipment, and news crews, television media could only provide updates regarding bombed oilfields and the populations of several cities wiped out by nuclear blasts. Humanity let out a trembling sigh of relief when leaders signed a cease-fire agreement.

But the reverberations from these cataclysmic events were just beginning. Without a steady supply of oil, most forms of heat, refrigeration, lights, and transportation disappeared. In a bid to save as many lives as possible in America, the government ordered all persons in the northern half of the U.S. to submit to martial law, quarantine, and relocation away from the cold and contamination. Michael remembered his own forced migration south. Did anyone know how many million people died during that winter?

Now, except for the land around the Mississippi River, where almost no one dared to venture, the south had become densely populated. News reports said most of the empty land to the north wouldn't be useable for several generations to come.

Despite extreme predictions by scientists, survivalists, and religious groups, technology *didn't* completely crash and the majority of Americans *didn't* perish. Discovered before the disasters, an oil-free source of energy, transmitted through fiber optic cables, would soon do more than anyone ever dreamed. Instead of being reduced to cave-man status, mankind might actually take a gigantic leap into the future.

Michael looked out at the city again and marveled, *How can all this turn around so quickly?* His eyes found the area of bright lights again. Real lights. To his amazement, the new technology continued to expand everywhere. Soon, if they chose to, all people could have lights again. . . . Did he, Zac, and so many others want to acquiesce to governmental requirements in order to get those lights? If enough people held out for a compromise, would it happen?

He got his beer off the railing and took another sip. *A year ago, I thought each day might be my last. I thought if I didn't catch the disease, I'd starve . . . or freeze to death. Yet, here I am, with something to drink, clothes on my back, a place to live. Maybe Zac is right. Maybe, if we all stick together, life could have meaning again.*

He shivered. The night had gotten chilly so he decided to go back into the house.

Chapter 2

A suburb of Dallas

When Zachary awoke Sunday morning, he knew he'd need a whole day to recuperate. Even his mouth felt fuzzy.

Had his companion for the night departed? He opened his eyes and found himself alone. Something written on the mirror over his dresser attracted his attention, but he couldn't make it out from his current angle. Eventually, his curiosity got the best of him and he got up to look.

The girl had scribbled, "Very Funny!" with lipstick in big scrawling letters. He couldn't think for the life of him what had been so funny. He'd have to ask her the next time he saw her. If he ever saw her again. . . . Had he met her at work, or at the party at Michael's house? Did it matter?

When he started walking toward the bathroom, he saw someone on the floor just beyond the door. He froze for a moment, then rushed down the hall to find her lying in a tight, fetal position. Only her arm stretched out beyond her contracted frame with a reaching hand, now resting lifelessly on the rug. Zac leaned down to touch her. Cold. He sank to the floor and gently stroked her hair as if she were only crying or sleeping and his touch might make her look up and smile at him.

###

Hours later, a friend of Zachary's came by Michael's house and woke him to tell him the news. At first Michael had trouble unfogging his mind enough to understand what had happened.

"No. Just some girl Zac found dead in his house. They took him to the hospital to answer questions, but he got so shook up they had to sedate him."

Michael pulled on his pants and began scrounging around for a shirt to wear. "Okay. Hey, thanks a lot, Allen, for coming by and all. Help yourself to some food, if you can find any."

###

Several miles away, Linda tiptoed out of an apartment and closed the door. She pulled uncombed hair away from her face and hurriedly descended a flight of stairs. *What on earth was I thinking?* she asked herself. She praised herself for not giving her real name or address to the lunatic inside the apartment she'd just left.

Let this be a lesson to you, she admonished herself. *Even if we've had some difficulties, Michael's worth the effort.* She hurried home, a bit more grateful for her situation. With men in such short supply, competition over guys not mutilated by war or contaminated had gotten fierce.

###

While Linda found her way home, Michael walked the short distance to the hospital. When he arrived, he found himself at the front desk, confronting a truly nasty human being.

"Look, Ms., uh," he said, reading her tag, "Anderson, I don't know where my brother is. I just know he's here. He came after he found a dead girl in his house."

Anderson raised an eyebrow. "Would he be in quarantine then?"

Michael panicked a moment before he remembered what Zac's friend said. "No! They just have him sedated somewhere."

"Does he have a code?" she asked, quite unimpressed.

Michael rapidly lost his patience. "Just what difference does that make?"

"Look, little person," she said leaning down from the six-foot-high level of the desk, "I don't need this from you. I have things to do. If you can't make up your mind whether you want to see your brother or not, kindly let the others come forward to be helped."

Michael stepped back. He knew he'd punch her if she said one more word. After looking around, he decided to try the doorway marked "EMERGENCY." A large sign on each of the double doors said "NO VISITORS ALLOWED," so he leaned against the wall next to the doors and tried to listen to any conversation inside.

". . . so then they prepped her and sent her on up to surgery, but she didn't look good to me and her vitals were pretty shaky," a woman said.

". . . Yeah, she did look bad . . ." a male voice answered. Michael could only catch parts of what the man said. " . . . and what about the guy . . . brought in?"

Michael moved closer, pressing his ear against the door.

"Which guy?" the woman asked, "The old man with the cut, or the young one with the dead girlfriend?"

"Your choice. I just wanted to know where everyone went."

"Well, Carlton treated the old guy while you were in surgery. The young guy with the dead girlfriend is in the hall on the fourth floor until they either find some room for him or release him."

Without warning, the man from the emergency room walked into the lobby with a cup in his hand, almost smacking Michael with the door.

"Excuse me," Michael said, catching up with him, then turning to look down at his tag, "uh, Dr. Donner, I was walking in there when I heard you talking about my brother. He's on the fourth floor—in the hall. Is there any way I can see him?"

"Sure, just get a pass from the desk over there and—"

"No dice. That lady wouldn't let me in if the building were on fire and I had a bucket of water."

Donner didn't even look. "Anderson must be on duty. Isn't she a real love? One of my favorite people." He paused a moment. "Okay, tell you what. You take this cup and find some bottled water. I'll brave Anderson for a pass."

Before long, Michael found himself climbing the stairs to the fourth floor with Dr. Donner.

"Why is he just in the hall?" Michael asked.

"Well, not only is this hospital crowded, but your brother doesn't have a code."

"What does *that* have to do with it? He can pay the bill. If you ran a credit check on him, you could verify that."

"Paying the bill is only part of it. When patients don't have a code, it really complicates things for us. The chip that comes with a code has all past medical history on the patient, where they live, next of kin, etc. already stored. Patients with codes can be plugged into and monitored by the computer. When a patient doesn't have a code, all of that must be taken from them by a staff person and verified before the patient can be linked into the system. Until then, he has to be watched by people—and people are in short supply around here."

They'd reached the door to the fourth floor, and Donner unlocked it. When they got inside, he strolled down a corridor which had at least ten people on cots along one wall.

"Let's see now, he should be right around here somewhere." Donner said before stopping beside a lifeless looking form.

Michael moved closer to the man on the cot. It was, indeed, his brother. Zac looked so pale, it frightened him. Visions of their father, mother, and sister lying silently in a single hole in the ground, flashed through his mind.

Michael looked up at Donner. "Is he dead?"

"Of course he isn't . . . although he does look a bit green around the gills." Donner bent down and tapped Zachary on the chest, then leaned closer. "Wake up. You have a visitor."

Zac's eyes opened and it took him a moment to focus on Michael. "How did you know where to find me?"

"That was easy. Getting in to see you wasn't. Are you all right? What happened?"

Zachary seemed somewhat disoriented. "I'm okay . . . I just found this . . . girl. She was lying on the floor in my bathroom and I . . . and I don't remember her name . . . pretty girl. . . . She wrote something on my mirror with her lipstick. I was asleep" Zac closed his eyes and tried to recall. "What was her name?"

Donner broke in at this point, reading from a piece of paper "Her name was Janice Emory, and it appears she worked at the same factory you do. I briefly examined her before they took her down to the morgue. She had massive tumors, probably from exposure to contaminants. Judging from the quick look I got at her, she must have been in incredible pain all the time. Probably died as the result of drinking alcohol—which was more than her already-failing system could handle."

"She never mentioned pain." Zachary seemed puzzled. "We didn't drink that much."

"It wouldn't have taken much. Her system was on the verge of total collapse. . . . Don't feel guilty. It really was only a matter of weeks or days before she would've died anyway. Take my word for it. She should have been in a camp."

"Isn't that a bit coldhearted?" Zachary said, getting a little color back in his anger.

"You couldn't even remember her name, and I'm coldhearted? Look, I was only trying to make you feel better, that's all."

"I'm sorry," Zachary's said solemnly. "When can I leave here? I want to go home."

Dr. Donner looked at his watch. "Well, I suppose you could leave now if you'll sign a release. But you need to do it in the next half hour, before the shift changes, or you'll be charged for another day."

"Are you sure you want to go home?" Michael broke in. "I mean, you don't look so great. Maybe you should spend the night at least."

"No. I want to leave. I'll sign anything, just get me out of this place." Zachary got to his feet, but wavered a bit, so Michael caught him by the arm.

"If you insist on leaving, maybe you should stay with me for a day or two. Just till you are feeling better, okay?" Michael offered.

"I might take you up on that. But first, let's just get out of here." Zac said.

Getting checked out took twenty-five minutes, during which Michael had another run-in with a nurse. Finally, they made their way to Zachary's house to get some of his personal things. They walked there in a silence so uncharacteristic of his brother it unnerved Michael.

Once inside, they decided that Zac could shower and change clothes while Michael went out to purchase some food for the evening. When Michael returned, the door to Zac's apartment stood wide open, and he cautiously went inside. At first, he feared something terrible might have happened and ran around the house calling his brother's name. No Zac.

On the way back out through the bedroom, he saw the writing on the mirror. "Very Funny" he read aloud, surmising the girl wrote it.

He went back into the living room and searched for any sort of note from Zac. Nothing. After a few minutes passed, he felt torn between being furious and worried to death. Had troops come and taken Zac away because they'd decided he was under suspicion in the girl's death? After checking with the neighbors, he came to the conclusion his brother probably left the apartment on his own. How dare Zac pull a stunt like this? Michael finally decided to go home. By the time he got there, the food in his bag had gotten warm.

###

After spending the day sorting through the wreckage of the previous night's party in their apartment, Linda forgot her earlier gratitude for Michael. The moment he walked in the door, she confronted him.

"Just where have you been?" she asked. "You know it is only common courtesy to leave a note when you're going to be gone for dinner."

Michael thought this rather an odd thing for her to say since she'd disappeared for the entire night. He didn't mention it. He'd grown too tired and too worried for another one of their knock-down-drag-out fights. He set the bag of groceries on the table and walked into the living room.

Not willing to give up that easily, Linda followed him. "Don't you walk away from me again" She grabbed him by the arm and pulled him around. "If you ever turn your back on me again and walk away while I'm talking to you, I'm packing my bags. Do you hear me?"

"Look, Zac was in the hospital and I went to get him out. Sorry I didn't take time for a ten-page letter."

"What was Zachary doing in the hospital?" She didn't want to drop the argument, but her inquisitiveness forced her to ask.

"He found some girl dead in his apartment and it really shook him up. They sedated him. Shortly after I got there, they released him, and I wanted to bring him here for a few days."

"That's it!" she exploded. "That tears it, Michael. I am not a nursemaid! I have a hard enough time with my job and doing work around here without having to deal with your brother around the house."

Michael grabbed her by the shoulders and shoved her up against the wall. "You are a selfish, disgusting person, you know that? All you ever think about is yourself and that job of yours. Zachary is *missing*—he's *disappeared*, and for all I know, they could have taken him away, or he could have killed himself somewhere." He wanted to shake her until her teeth rattled. He closed his eyes and took a deep breath before letting her go and walking to his room.

Knowing Zac, she thought, *he'll show up in a day or so with stories of some woman who took him in. Michael will have gotten all upset over nothing.* She started to say something but decided to keep quiet. She could hear him rummaging around and knew the object of his search: His little, black box. *Oh well,* she thought. *Maybe it will put him in a better mood.*

Chapter 3

Northwest of Dallas

Sara looked down to see the thick mud squishing up and over her shoes. Now her shoes and ankles would bear the purple stain of the awful neutralizing/sterilization chemicals used to dust the camps every few days.

She'd been told she would not have to undergo further quarantine. As a precaution, however, soldiers took her old clothes and burned them before forcing her to walk through a long wooden building where she'd been sprayed with a foul-smelling substance. Before exiting, she received a wrinkled, baggy dress to wear along with her leather shoes, which had been ruined in the wash.

After handing her a flimsy raincoat, they permitted Sara to leave the decontamination building—one of two buildings straddling the fence between the inner and outer camps. Everyone went in through the *other* building. Few ever came out.

Now this, she thought, looking down at her purple-stained shoes.

Then the smell came to her nostrils. Every morning, workers burned the dead along with all their effects, and the smell filled the air. Sara would never forget that stench. She'd smelled it every day for weeks.

Yesterday, they'd cremated Sara's mother along with other victims. By now, people in special suits would have sealed the ashes in cans before placing them on shelves in large steel and concrete rooms alongside hundreds of other cans. Sara shuddered.

She'd reached the large outer gates and now stood in line. The cavernous grief inside her made her hurt all over, and she could see similar pain reflected in the others who waited in line. Most of them had come to spend the last few weeks, days, or even hours with someone they loved so much, the danger didn't matter.

Sara had been traveling with her mother at the onset of the illness and *had* to accompany her to the camp. After transport here, Sara dictated a letter to her father telling him what had happened, *begging* him not to come. Noel, Sara's sister, was too young to be without both parents. . . . But, she wondered if *anything* could keep him away. He would have gotten her letter by now, and might even have started the long journey on foot. But it didn't matter now.

At this moment, Sara could only think about leaving this place of death. She wanted to get far, far away, to breathe the air, to feel alive again.

A soldier holding a rifle approached, looking straight at her. He stood head and shoulders above her, had a square jaw, and dark eyes.

"Certificate please," he said without any introduction.

She fumbled in her raincoat and removed several papers she'd folded together. Printed on them was her life history: Birth, inoculations, diseases, height, weight, marital status, religion, and—most importantly—her health status as of this moment. If ill, she would have been forced to stay.

He let go of the rifle, letting it hang from the shoulder strap. "Well," he said, skimming the papers, "Miss Sara Reisling, how do you feel today?"

She resented his misuse of authority, but replied as calmly as possible, "Fine, thank you."

He stared at her over the top of the papers. "Let me see your hands, Miss Reisling."

Certainly he could read the papers. She considered this another form of harassment. Obviously, if she'd shown any signs of contamination, they wouldn't have let her out of the inner camp.

"Your hands," he said again. She removed them from her pockets and held them up under his nose, confident this would settle the matter.

"Come with me."

"Why?" she quickly asked, starting to feel a little alarmed.

Her heartbeat quickened when he folded her papers and stuck them in his pocket. She couldn't leave the camp without them. She tried to keep hold of rational thoughts.

He grabbed her arm, squeezed firmly, and then quietly commanded, "Come."

"I . . . I," she said as he pulled her along. She dug in her heels and resisted before they came to a halt. He turned and gave her arm a jerk, making her fall to her knees.

"*Get up!*" he barked.

Sara looked to the others who'd been in line with her. She couldn't believe it. They all looked away!

"You can't do this to me," she said in a small voice, "I'm not sick."

"I said, *get up!*" He hauled on her arm and then, just as suddenly as he'd shown barely controlled rage, he became nearly civil—subdued again—and said, "Now do you wish to come along quietly or do I have to drag you?"

"Where?"

"I want your medical release verified," he said, eyes half closed. "This way."

Very well, she thought. She didn't want to get in trouble for non-cooperation. She'd go. They'd have to release her . . . eventually.

There is no need to panic, she told herself over and over. *No need to panic . . . no need to panic . . . no need to . . .*

They walked by the open door of a guard shed and he suddenly shoved her in. She fell on her side, unable to move. The fall had knocked the wind out of her.

The soldier quickly stepped inside and bolted the door. Only tiny threads of light sliced into the darkness from between warped wooden walls and boarded windows.

Sara opened her mouth in an effort to get some air. He leaned down and slapped her hard across the face. She coiled up and pushed herself back into a corner, trying desperately to force air into collapsed lungs.

Stripes of light and shadow bent around him while he paced back and forth—like a tiger in a deep forest. "You thought you could change the world didn't you?" he said in an agitated tone. "But you lost."

Sara sat in the corner shaking. She could taste blood in her mouth. Once her eyes began to adjust to the darkness, other things took shape. A desk and chair in the far corner. He tossed her papers on the desk, and her eyes darted back to him.

"Come now," his voice sounded almost soothing, "I can't believe a woman as beautiful as you doesn't possess at least some intelligence. Can't you see you've made the wrong choice?"

Now she knew. She cleared her throat and tried to sound calm. "But it's *my* choice. Aren't we all free to choose?"

She saw a flash of teeth. "You fanatics should have disappeared, like you wanted to . . . while you still could."

She prayed silently the only words coming into her mind. *Lord, give me courage . . . help me.* She pushed herself further into the corner when he crouched down. The smell of his rancid sweat permeated the heavy air in the room.

"Have I caused you trouble?" she asked quietly. She didn't know if it would keep him talking or infuriate him.

"Trouble? If you people had cooperated when the movement first started, *none* of this would have happened! We all suffered, and it's your fault!" he said, jabbing his finger at her. "Now you'll pay . . . and your God *still* won't help you. He didn't come for you then and he won't come for you now. You made us suffer . . . " he leaned forward and whispered, "Now it's *your* turn."

The soldier saw fear in her eyes. This pleased him. She knew he meant what he said. He paused for a moment to savor it all before he said, "Unless you'd like to change your mind."

"My mind," she said, echoing his tone.

"You could agree to get coded, right now. Here. Before you left the camp. Or," he stood and stepped close to her, a towering shadow, "you could be like the others. . . . Some of them scream while they burn."

Many times she'd imagined she would be so brave, so defiant in the face of such a threat. Like Rosa and Ricky and so many others. Instead, she sat there shaking—praying she would die quickly. She wasn't brave or defiant. Just scared that in a matter of moments this man would kill her, or worse yet . . . have her burned alive. Who would ever know? They could send a letter to her family saying she'd been contaminated as well and had succumbed to the illness.

Almost as if he'd read her mind he said, "No one ever suspects. We could even send your family a letter speaking of a marvelous *recovery* in your mom . . . asking them to come and see for themselves."

"No!" she said quickly as the implication took shape in her mind.

He laughed. "You wanted a choice," he leaned closer, "now you've got one!"

"You couldn't—"

"How many lives is it worth to you?" he asked, bending over, clamping an iron hand on her jaw.

She tried to raise her body up to relieve the pressure on her jaw. Tears burned in her eyes and she struggled to speak. "It has been worth . . . the lives of many, many . . ."

"*Yes!* But now we're talking about you and *your* family!" His forehead touched hers now. He let go of her face and grabbed her shoulders with both hands. Squeezing hard, he shook her and almost shouted, "Give it up! You can do it! You saw how He deserted your old woman. *Give it up!*"

His fingers dug into her shoulders, making them burn unbearably. "No!" she managed to call out. As soon as she said the word, time froze in her mind. She remembered many experiences, the last and most vivid memory being the Presence filling the room when her mother died. The Presence of the Lord. Her mother had not been forsaken. . . . In fact, Sara realized, the same Presence was in the room with her now.

Although she could still feel the searing pain, calm flowed through her. "I have only one place I wish to go . . . and if I deny Jesus, I've lost it. You can make my heart stop beating, but you cannot take my life unless I give it to you."

"Is that so?" he spat out through clenched teeth.

She looked at what seemed myriads of eyes glinting from inside his eyes as his large hands closed around her throat. He started crushing her windpipe, and she could no longer breathe.

The door rattled before someone knocked hard.

"Open up! Colonel Tobin is conducting an inspection of the camp. Open up!"

The soldier threw her back into the corner and moved to the door. He unbolted it and stood at attention. The door flew open, and an almost blinding light filled the room.

Unable to move at first, Sara remained in the corner when the soldiers entered.

The colonel said, "At ease," once he entered the room. When he saw Sara, he asked, "What's this?" He noted all the marks on her face and neck as he helped her to her feet. "Are you hurt?" he inquired, letting go of her hand.

She had trouble speaking so the colonel turned to her attacker. "Look, soldier, you can get leave to do this sort of thing in the city, but you can't do it here. Clear?"

"Yes, sir."

The colonel looked at Sara again. "Young lady, get off this compound within fifteen minutes, or I will have you incarcerated. And remember to have your good times in the city after this."

She moved quickly to the desk and grabbed her papers. "These are mine," she said in a hoarse voice.

"Are those hers?" the officer asked the soldier.

"Yes, sir."

"Sgt. Fredericks, see this woman off the grounds."

"Yes sir." Sgt. Fredericks saluted. "This way," the sergeant said, pointing toward the door.

She swiftly moved past the soldier, the colonel, and the others. After exiting the door, she looked up and smiled. "Thank You, Lord. Thank You."

The sergeant shook his head as he walked along and muttered, "What's it comin' to? . . . Religious prostitutes . . . nothin' normal anymore."

Flooded with relief, Sara didn't care *what* the soldier thought. They walked the short distance to the gate; he escorted her out, then returned inside the camp to close the gate behind her.

Just at that moment, it started to rain, and she could hear the wail going up in the center camp. It came from the tents and shacks where those left to die cried out in fear of contaminated rain.

Sara's gladness evaporated in an instant when she turned to look one last time into the camp. She could see a small child behind the barbed wire of the inner camp. A girl of six or seven. Most of her hair had fallen out.

All of the grief and rage she'd felt for so long welled-up and she could no more contain them than a mighty river. She beat her fists on the gate and cried out, "Father God! HEAR THIS SOUND . . . SMELL YOUR CHILDREN BEING

BURNED . . . SEE THEIR SOULS BENEATH THE ALTAR! MY VOICE CRIES OUT WITH THEIRS, LORD. . . . HOW LONG UNTIL THE DAY OF RECOMPENSE? LET ME SEE THAT DAY, LORD. LET ME SEE JUDGEMENT COME TO ALL WHO HAVE DONE THIS. . . . Let it be soon!"

Chapter 4

A suburb of Dallas

For months now, life at home for Michael varied between total oblivion and raging battles with Linda. Zachary had disappeared without a trace. Reporting it to the police had been a waste of time.

Uncounted myriads of families suffered separation in the great move south, but only coded people had much chance of finding each other through the system. Police and governmental agencies no longer searched for missing persons. Private "locator services" charged prices few honest people could afford. Family members became responsible for following leads, checking hospitals and morgues. Due to the massive number of suicides, so many new bodies turned up every day, the grisly task eventually became too much for even the most determined seekers.

Zachary's name could only be added to a list that would be put in an information bank and never looked at again. Meantime, Michael made so many trips to the hospital (and the morgue) he'd gotten to be on a first-name basis with Dr. Donner (Albert) who promised to keep his eyes open for anyone resembling Zachary. But Albert never found him. Michael finally succumbed to the hopelessness of it all and gave up looking.

Some days Michael got so upset over Zac's disappearance, even the mention of it gave him a terrible sinking feeling inside. Zac had to be dead. Other days, Michael told himself he didn't care. If Zac wanted to vanish without a word, so be it. Whichever mood Michael was in, however, the only solace he found was in his little black box.

Black boxes weren't illegal, but pretty much shunned by society as a whole. People who used them occupied the same class heroin and crack addicts once occupied. Authorities expressed alarm, but had a hard time with the legal aspects of it. Although users, technically, put themselves in a drugged state, their own bodies created the drug when certain nerve endings in the brain were stimulated by an electrical shock. Use of the box often rendered the user unable to move or communicate for several hours. In very few cases, erratic or violent behavior occurred. Side effects ranged from minor cell damage (caused by scar tissue from electric burns at the point of contact) to instant death if the user misplaced the electrodes. Prolonged, heavy use could result in seizures, coma, vegetation, or death.

Late one afternoon, Michael found himself returning to consciousness after a "ride" with his black box. Sights and sounds once again began to filter through the gauzy haze surrounding his brain. He could hear Linda whistling and humming. He sat up on the bed for a few moments to get his bearings, then walked to the kitchen where Linda busied herself unpacking groceries.

"Wow, that's an awful lot of expensive food," he said, watching her. "You get a raise?"

"No, Michael, I got something better." She opened a cabinet and pulled out a large bowl. She began filling it with all sorts of fruit, most of which Michael hadn't seen in ages.

"What's better than a raise? Where on earth did you get all this?"

"To answer your first question, a code. To answer your second question, with my code."

Michael's mouth dropped open. "You're kidding . . . not really."

"Yes, *really*. And stop backing up as if I were contagious or something. Why shouldn't I have? Good grief, Michael, you sound like one of those fanatics. Have you decided to become superstitious or something?"

"Linda, I thought we'd decided not to do this unless we had to. I thought you at least would've *discussed* it with me first," he said, confused.

"And just *when* could I discuss it with you? When are you *awake*?" she said, throwing up her hands. "It's really none of your business what I do with my body, anyway. What makes you think, even for a moment, I would like to live like this permanently when everyone else is getting on with life? Why would I want to eke out an existence with candles and powdered food when I could have *this*?" she said, picking up a frosty-purple plum. She set down the fruit and pretended to knock on a door. "Hello inside! Wake up Mr. Gordon! While you were sleeping, the rest of the world has been signing on and *living* again. It's time to join society and breathe, Michael."

"But, what about—"

She gave him an exasperated look. "None of the dark predictions have come true. The world did not spiral down into darkness. There are no goose-stepping storm troopers beating down our door. People with codes don't each have an 8-by-10 inch glossy photo of a red-horned anti-Christ on the wall next to their viewer screen. No one is being forced to do anything other than to live in peace. Just *get over it,* Michael."

She glanced around the room, disgusted. "This place is a dump. And although we won't be able to get anything nicer for a while, when this place is wired, there are all sorts of things we can do with it."

"Excuse me," he said, leaning forward, "did you say 'wired'? I thought this was *our apartment.* Or did you just assume that would be none of my business, too?"

"Crap, Michael, you aren't going to have another one of your tantrums are you? Why don't you just go and shock your brains out with that *thing* in there and leave me alone? I can't believe you! You're trying to look down your nose at me when I have almost single-handedly rescued us from a life of dismal poverty. You! A man who finds life so delightful he has to stay unconscious half the time. Well that's fine by me. And here I thought you'd be glad we'd be hooked up to the real world soon. That's just great," her voice trailed off as she turned away from him and looked out the window.

Michael moved closer to her and put his hand on her back. "I'm sorry. I guess I should be getting used to all the changes, but they just keep coming so fast. I can't seem to catch up to this world. I'm still caught up in the old one."

"Don't you see?" she said, facing him again. "That's the dangerous thing. You can't cling onto the 'old' world. It doesn't exist anymore. I was scared of getting a code, too, but refusing one didn't benefit me one iota. Then, going day after day and seeing the full lives of people with codes really made me think. All the old ideas and ways are *gone.* If we want to go on, we have to make a new world. We *need* to embrace the

Global View. If we do, life can be greater, more satisfying, more . . . " she stepped close to him now, searching for words to describe how wonderful it now seemed to her, "more magnificent than anything anyone has ever seen before."

"You know, you sound like a video commercial I saw downtown. Not that that's bad," he added hastily.

She looked up into his eyes and pulled his arms around her waist. "Come on. Come into this world. Come with me. We can enjoy everything again. Wouldn't that be fun?"

Before he could reply, they heard a gentle knock at the door. Michael went to open it and felt a jolt when he looked out and saw his brother Zachary standing on the doorstep.

For months, he'd wondered what he would do if this moment ever came. He leaped out the door and hugged Zachary tightly. Then he pulled away and punched his brother right on the jaw. Zac went over the railing and landed on his back in the tiny patch of grass Linda called "the yard." Stunned for a few seconds he just lay there.

Michael jumped over the railing and pointed a finger at him, "Don't you *ever* do that to me again!"

Zac sat up and tried to work his jaw with his hand. "I know I deserved that," he finally said. "It's a long story, Michael, but I hope you'll hear me out. I know you must have worried . . . and I'm sorry."

Michael paced a few steps, "I was worried at first, and then I was angry because I couldn't find you." He walked back toward Zac and pointed to himself, "You're all I've got left."

Linda stood in the doorway, watching the two brothers staring at each other in silence. Then, slowly, Michael's hand reached down to Zachary. Zac took it and pulled himself up, and they hugged once again. When they turned to face Linda, Michael said, "We were just about to celebrate! Right, Linda?"

She smiled, knowing his anger had blown over. Even though she felt no fondness for Zac, this might be just the boost Michael needed. She'd gotten over the hard part of telling him about the code, now maybe they could just get on with the business of living again. As Linda fixed a feast in the kitchen, Michael and Zachary sat in the living room and talked.

"So where have you been anyway?" Michael asked. "I thought you'd disappeared right off the face of the planet."

Zac sat leaning forward with his elbows resting on his knees. "Well, it's kind of hard to express," he said, looking down at his shoes. "After you left my apartment, I went into my room and saw the words the girl . . . Janice . . . wrote on my mirror, I just sort of flipped out." Zac stared into space for a moment. "Michael, do you remember Stephanie?"

Michael looked up at the ceiling, pondering the question. "That girl you loved so much in high school . . ." he said, then slowly added, "the one who died of cancer."

Zac exhaled deeply. "Yeah . . . that's the one." He closed his eyes, and Michael imagined that perhaps his brother was picturing the girl he'd lost so long ago. Zac opened his eyes again. "You have no idea how determined I was to never let another person touch my heart the way Stephanie did. And how did I accomplish this? By doing what I did best—I made everything a joke.

"I've spent most of my life entertaining people. Not for their sake, but for mine. If I made them laugh, I could keep them from seeing inside me . . . I could disarm and use them, and they could never hurt me." He shook his head. "And so I'd put on a little act of some sort and gotten this girl to come home with me. I spent the night with her and let her die in my own house without ever even learning her name."

Michael broke in at this point, thinking to comfort Zac, "She would have died anyway, and you gave her a little pleasure before she went. After all, it wasn't as if you dragged her into your house by force."

A pained expression filled Zac's eyes. "That's exactly the point, Michael. She was so desperate and so lonely she settled for a one-night romp with me. Me—a man who didn't care who she was or how much she hurt. I told myself it was a fair exchange. I'd use her, she'd have fun. She could share my food, my booze . . .

"I was so angry at God for so long for taking Stephanie away. I never stopped to think how destructive it made me. I wanted to believe I never hurt people, but in a flash I saw what a user I'd become. In that moment, I realized that my life was totally meaningless. I ate, I drank, and I made merry, because tomorrow I could die. But tomorrow always came and, for all that, I was so empty. I told myself that, since God and I were at odds, I might as well live it up. I tried minute by minute to fill the vast loneliness in me." He paused and looked at Michael. "And, in that moment, I finally understood you and your black box."

Michael looked away, and they sat in silent acknowledgment. For the first time Michael could remember, they understood each other.

Zachary came back to the subject of his disappearance, "I had to get away from the way I felt inside. At first, I thought I might go insane. I walked and walked not knowing or caring where I was going. When night came, I found myself at the dump. I never realized before how many people actually live there—mostly children, sleeping in makeshift tents and old cars and stuff.

"It was dark, and I decided just to sit there. I guess I wanted to die, and I almost got my wish when a gang of teenagers came and robbed me. That's all I remember . . . but, apparently, they beat me until I was unconscious, took my money and my clothes, and left me for dead. Some people came to the dump to leave food and found me delirious, so they took me home with them."

"Why didn't they take you to the hospital?"

"One of the people happened to be a doctor. He did everything that could be done for me. They figured if they took me to the hospital, and I was wanted by the police . . . I would receive no more care and would probably die. They had no idea who I was or where I'd come from, but something made them want to save me.

"Anyway, I woke up days later in a bed with clean clothes and clean sheets. I had no idea where I was. I heard voices in the next room, so I got up and opened the door. There was some sort of meeting going on. . . . The people were so absorbed in what they were doing, they didn't notice me for a while. They were worshiping the Lord with faces raised . . . some with their hands up . . . some singing in a beautiful harmony. The sound was like water spilling out, with a voice."

Michael felt a chill go down his spine. He'd been to such a house and heard singing like this. He remembered the day he and Linda sneaked up to it. Zac continued speaking and Michael refocused his attention.

". . . and they were all so happy to see me awake and walking around. I was amazed they cared so much for me without knowing me." Zac looked down again. "In a short time, I was strong again but the dark feeling didn't leave me.

"The people asked me to stay on. I could stay as long as I wanted, no questions asked . . . and I'm sorry, I know I should have found a way to contact you . . . to tell you where I was, but I couldn't. I was a dying man who had come into a place where there was life. I didn't want to leave it—or even think of anything else.

"And one night, when we were just sitting together, they talked to me about the Lord. I realized I knew all this stuff . . . I'd learned it a long time ago, but I'd locked it all away. And, suddenly, I understood. God loved me, like those people did— more than they did . . . even knowing just *exactly* who I was and all I'd ever done. The knowledge exploded in me. I *could* touch God. He *could* speak to me. He *did* care. . . . Surrendering was easy after that." Zachary looked at Michael now, his eyes alive with a special radiance. "And the darkness in me fled away."

"The feast is served!" Linda said, hurrying into the room with a platter.

Michael looked up, grateful for the interruption. "Oh great! I'm starved. How about you, Zac?" Although his brother's words had an almost electric quality, Michael felt squirmy about them. Zac was trying to dig up something very uncomfortable here, and Michael didn't think he *wanted* it dug up.

The rest of the evening passed pleasantly with most of the conversation being of the "light" variety. Linda, to her horror, had heard some of the conversation between Zac and Michael. She'd have to do something very quickly to counterbalance the effect Zachary might have on him. Perhaps she could invite a Living Witness to come and speak to Michael. Meanwhile, she would be friendly to Zachary and keep the conversation neutral. She knew a lot more about coding now, but was no expert. She knew even less about fanaticism so she did not want to risk an argument she could easily lose.

As the next few weeks rolled by, Michael and Linda started to enjoy a little more tranquility. Michael stopped using his black box and, for the most part, seemed more optimistic. Zachary showed up at the house every few days and encouraged Michael to keep up the progress. Linda tried never to leave them alone.

Chapter 5

Atlanta, in the former state of Georgia

"My highest goal in life," James Hart said, "is to be remembered as a first class journalist."

Sitting in his cramped, stuffy office, James tried to think back to a time when his surroundings were much more spacious and refined—and to remind himself that it could happen again if he succeeded in his current endeavor.

His every inflection would be preserved by the recorder not five feet away from him. He could decide how much or how little of this to write later. The important thing, at the moment, was to get inspired.

James hesitated, wondering if the idea of having his secretary give him a pretend interview would get him in the mood to write. Certainly, nothing else had worked. Perhaps the whole "interview" concept would prove to be a waste of time—especially with Mia doing the interviewing.

Although Mia could transcribe notes, answer phones, and send out correspondence, no one would ever accuse her of thinking very far outside the box or of being a brilliant conversationalist. Basically, Mia was little more than a human data organizer. And there she sat—with her wiry salt-and-pepper hair, wearing the nappy, gray sweater he hated so much—waiting for her next cue. He tried to ignore her blank expression . . . and the fact she had a huge run in the left leg of her smoke-colored stockings. It looked like an anemic gash running over the top of her bony knee.

James closed his eyes and moved both his hands in a come-on-and-give-me-the-next-question maneuver.

Mia blew her nose on a wad of tissue then stuck it back in the pocket of her sweater before reading another question from the list in her lap. "How long have you been a writer?"

"Twenty years . . . and in that time, I've seen the world go from frivolous self-indulgence through disasters, through war and into the Transition—a process destined to take humanity to a new level of civilization. I've reported virtually every moment of it." He stopped himself from adding, *and I wanted to be the one people believed in, the one they trusted.*

He cleared his throat and continued. "I've tried to never let the corrupt decide what I write. More than once my life has been threatened if I dared to tell the truth."

"And did you?" She'd set down the list. "I mean, did you always tell the truth."

"Yes, Mia," he sighed. "Next question."

"Oh." She picked up the list and found her place. "Why are you writing your book now?"

He'd been asked to write his autobiography. Many in authority hoped it would prove a useful tool in changing the very fabric of society. Could James help humanity find a common voice?

"Well, I think . . ." He put the palms of his hands together and touched his chin with the tips of his fingers, "they hoped that if someone like me could put what has happened into an honest perspective, it might be a source of comfort and courage to many who simply don't know where to turn. My words might connect people with a sense of overcoming in a world where so many have experienced disillusionment."

James swiveled around in his chair and stared out the window. "Skip the rest of the questions about the book for now, would you Mia? Next topic."

"Tell me about your childhood."

"Hmmm. I was very frail as a child. I spent most winters confined to my bed. . . . I filled many hours reading books and magazines." At a sudden memory, he swiveled back to smile at his secretary. "Most of them were smuggled in through my bedroom window by the girl next door. Gina DePalma. I'll never forget her as long as I live. She had dark, brown hair that she wore in a long braid down her back. She'd pass me things through the window. And I'd hide 'em inside a big Bible, like this, see?" He reached over to two books on his desk and opened them. He put the smaller book in the middle of the larger one and held them up with a sly look. "Through those books and magazines . . . I lived other people's lives, and saw the world through their eyes. Even now," he said, looking at the hundreds of books on shelves which lined his office walls, "I still love to read." James slowly set the two books back on the desk in front of him.

Mia, warming up in her role as interviewer, moved on to the next question. "What about your parents?"

James frowned. "They were both very religious. . . . Oh, the long hours I spent on hard wooden pews in that small, church building. As far as my mother and father were concerned, *everything* had to be offered to God. No silliness, no distraction could be allowed. God was serious and required strict adherence to the rulings and traditions handed down. My mother worried over me and constantly warned me about the burning fires of Hell—although I can't imagine it would be any hotter than that little church in the middle of summer. . . . To this day, I can't understand what drew them to such a hard life or what caused them to cling to anything so dismal and repetitive."

He straightened up in his chair before continuing. "When I grew up and left home, I almost never looked back, certainly not with any sense of the 'good old days.' I can still recall the sweetness of the first days I lived in the world outside my parents' dominion. I loved being on my own! At nineteen, I got a part-time job working at a newspaper. Once I finished college, I landed my first full-time job there as a reporter."

James stopped and considered how his young life had shaped his career. If he'd learned anything from his childhood, it was to search relentlessly for impurity. Although small in stature, he'd discovered words were weapons he could use to whittle the corrupt down to size. He'd stopped talking, so Mia figured she needed to move on.

"Dr. Cliff Edison," she read, then ad-libbed a question. "What about him?"

James straightened at the mention of the name and thought, *Did I write his name on the list? I must have.* He searched her face, and wondered if it were possible that she didn't know or didn't remember, and he asked himself, *Why does it still haunt me so?* James let his mind return to a time before the collapse of the old life in America and said softly, "I knew him."

When James had already achieved much as a journalist— awards, honors, and what he wanted most—the respect of his peers, an international news magazine asked him to do a "piece" on Dr. Clifford Edison, the famous television evangelist.

Should he let himself visit this again? He couldn't help himself. Almost forgetting Mia's presence, he started talking. "I'd seen Dr. Edison on T.V. a few times and I have to admit I had a certain fascination with the man. Edison was gutsy, quick-witted, and a good story teller. Back then, the man was famous—not only for his diamond rings and fancy cars but for the message he preached. He attracted followers from around the world."

James placed a hand on the two open books sitting in front of him. "Dr. Edison insisted if the principles of his teachings were followed, people could attain anything. He said that laws governed every facet of life. He taught there was 'a purpose for every principle and a principle for every purpose.'

"The difference between this and the religion of my youth was what first attracted me. My parents believed the closer one got to God, the harder it was to live in this world. Perfection meant denying any pleasure. But, according to Dr. Edison's teaching, the closer one got to God, the greater the rewards in this realm. The path to this was merely a matter of knowing and using certain principles Edison extracted from the Bible. Simply put: The rules of my past had been all in the negative realm. I'd learned the things I was not permitted to do. Dr. Edison's principles consisted mostly of things to do— keys that could open any door.

"Edison's 'Envisionary Faith' appealed to possibly millions of people who'd never seriously considered using the Bible to achieve the lifestyle they wanted to lead. But here was a man who was neither ashamed of what he was nor afraid to embrace good things. People *wanted* to identify with him." A glimmer of triumph momentarily lit James' eyes. "He was one of the ones who promised Jesus was coming back before any real trouble started, you know. He said *real* Christians would never suffer in the coming darkness."

James stopped speaking and the glimmer dimmed. Could he bring himself to write about his personal entanglement with Edison?

"You know what, Mia? I'm tired. I think we'll call it quits for now. Let me think of some more questions, and we'll do this again tomorrow."

She reached for the recorder.

"No," he said, "leave it there."

Accustomed to his moods, she quietly slipped from the room.

James got out a pencil and began drawing on a piece of paper. He slashed across the page with long, sharp lines as he thought.

He could still remember his first time at a Dr. Cliff Edison Revival. Going in, he'd looked around and noted most of the other attendees wore expensive clothing. No doubt they were professionals in their fields of endeavor. None of the religious "pseudo-humility" that James hated so much exuded from them.

When Dr. Edison was introduced, the place came alive with sound. Not the polite applause so many speakers get, but the entire group of people stood on their feet, shouting and clapping and raising their hands. It was more like a rock concert or a football game than a religious gathering. The electric atmosphere itself had given him such a rush.

James stopped drawing. Why was this still stuck inside him? How could he purge it out? He rubbed his jaw as he considered the problem. *Maybe if I just sort the whole thing out—honestly and completely—I can let go of it all and get on with my life.*

James closed his eyes and considered what happened so long ago. Thoughts came together, as they often did, just like the words of a story, and in his mind, he saw them appearing on a computer screen.

> This became the first of many meetings I attended in an effort to get a true reading of the spirit and the life of the people who followed Dr. Edison. Each meeting proved to be powerful, riveting, compelling; and for a time, fearing I'd be swept up in an emotional current which would destroy my objectivity, I quit attending.

> Finally, I asked to interview the man himself and found Dr. Edison didn't want to be interviewed by anyone, especially not me. But over the course of several weeks, I relentlessly pursued contact with him and eventually convinced the man I had no plans to write sensationalistic slander in order to sell magazines.

I remember the first meeting we had in his beautiful home. To my surprise, I found we actually had much in common. Both of us felt we'd been strangled by rigid religious upbringings. Both of us left home as soon as possible to start lives of freedom . . . although Cliff admitted to being a real "hell raiser" for a time.

"It was when I got to the bottom of the barrel I realized that I'd done little more than switch from one dark barrel to another," Cliff said to me. "I knew there had to be more somehow. I decided if there was some ultimate attainment, some ultimate God, I wanted to know who He was and what He was all about. As I turned to the Bible, I soon discovered there was more to knowing God than self-denial. When I looked, I realized that He owned everything, He existed everywhere, and He wanted to share it all with me! Not just things mind you, but power— the anointing. . . . Then I found that <u>everything</u> I could creatively envision was within my reach! I learned that everyone could vision themselves into a supreme moment when the universe would unfold for them . . ."

James tightened up in his chair. Could he bring himself to admit his own foolishness? He inhaled slowly, knowing it had to be done. If only to himself, he had to admit it. It would be a cleansing experience.

How can I be objective about others, he decided, if I'm not honest about myself? He continued his mental "story," sickened by his own gullibility.

Over the course of a year, Cliff and I became fast friends. We admired one another and shared personal parts of our lives. During this time, I wrote several articles reflecting the respect I had for him. I saw him as a man of power, of vision, and (most importantly) a man of integrity. I began to see him as a mentor of sorts, and sought to hear the truth from him. It seemed to me the message Cliff brought only got more and more dynamic as time went on. His teaching underwent an ever-expanding metamorphosis. It got more powerful, more encompassing each time I heard it. And, as I submitted myself to the principles bringing an explosion of success in Cliff's life, I found a greater measure of success in my own. I became convinced I'd found the path to abundance.

When Cliff's ministry seemed greater than ever, some Christian groups began to question both his motives and his methods. He launched a counter-attack, accusing them of petty jealousy. He declared it was only too typical of their "sorry party" attitude. If he'd taken some of their followers (or more pointedly, their followers' tithes), maybe they should consider it for what it was: God's judgment against their hypocrisy and misinterpretation of Scriptures. If they were truly Christians, they would share his concern about corruption in their own churches. He, in the meantime, would continue to bring light to the sheep.

During this time, Cliff seemed to blaze his way around the globe, either in person or on television, and his popularity grew. Everywhere he went, he preached with such conviction, many believed. It wasn't that old guilt-trip sort of stuff that made people slobber and cry, it was a liberating gospel—leaving all guilt behind, focusing the mind on the reality you really wanted, accentuating the positive, and leaving the negative behind.

At the close of that year, during a season when people didn't know what lurked just beyond the horizon in world events, the scandal broke.

James went to the place in his mind where he preserved his bitterest memories. He began to pour out some of the words and pictures that had been fermenting there for years.

Cliff confessed he'd run over and killed a small child, then left the scene of the accident. And there was more. He'd been under the influence of drugs and alcohol at the time of the accident and he'd only come forward with the truth when another man was charged in the case. As the media dug for more, other things came to light. Adultery and financial irregularities had also taken place before the accident.

James recalled the shock of hearing the first news of it. Within days of the revelations, Cliff held a large press conference.

Of course, I wasn't asked to cover the story and watched it on television at home. I sat there staring at the screen when Cliff came outside his house for an interview, mobbed by scores of shouting reporters. Thin and pale, he almost looked like a different person. In his hand, he held a piece of paper from which he read.

"I wish to make a statement. . . . In recent days I have confessed to wrongdoings which I committed during the course of my ministry. I led a life unworthy of a Christian, a husband, a pastor. I wish to express my sincerest apologies . . ."

At this point, Cliff stopped reading the paper and looked up, "Words cannot express the remorse I feel for taking the life of Bradley . . ." his voice broke with emotion and he stopped to clear his throat, "Bradley Hausman. I know there is nothing I can do to ease the anguish I have caused his family. I have resigned as pastor of my church, and I have turned all information pertinent to my case over to the authorities." He found his place on the paper once again, "I know I must face criminal charges and will be punished for what I have done."

"What is your wife's reaction to all of this?" one reporter shouted.

Cliff looked up at the crowd. "My wife is a woman of uncommon faith, and although I do not deserve it," he said, straining for control, "she has forgiven me and remains by my side in all things."

"Don't you feel you have compromised Christianity by your actions?" another voice called out. For some reason, as Edison considered the question the tension left his face.

"I am the 'chiefest of sinners' . . . but had I studied the <u>whole</u> counsel of the Bible, I wouldn't have veered into such error. If I had really been walking with Christ, I wouldn't have run to do all the things I stand here today to confess. I wouldn't have made promises I had no authority to offer. If I had really loved Jesus, I never would have brought such shame upon His name."

"Are you saying you weren't a Christian?" several reporters said at once. The face of the newscaster appeared on the screen, "This, once again, for those of you who are just joining us, is the scene outside the home of the self-deposed minister Cliff Edison . . ."

As I sat and watched this exchange, an incredible sense of rage and shame came over me. I felt so stupid to have been used by a consummate actor who, apparently, was no longer in possession of his faculties. There I was, one of the most respected newsmen of the day, writing sappy, inaccurate, testimonials about a man who was a total fraud.

I have to admit it, James thought as hatred rose up in him afresh. As far as I am concerned, Cliff stole the thing I treasured most: my credibility.

James now recalled a chance meeting with Cliff in a restaurant waiting area shortly after he was indicted, but before the trial. He saw Cliff before Cliff saw him. Their eyes finally met.

"Cliff! My old buddy, Cliff!" I said, my voice stinging with sarcasm, "It's me! James! You know, the idiot who furnished your propaganda for a year!"

We stood face to face for a moment before Cliff gave an almost imperceptible nod—as if he agreed with my statement. Then he went on to answer the question he knew I wanted to ask: *Why?*

"At first I told myself" Cliff said, "it didn't matter what I did as long as the people got what they wanted out of it. Everyone followed me as long as I gave them permission to pursue their desires without guilt. Most weren't looking for the truth, just a way to fulfill their greed or to satisfy their pride and feel good about it. My disciplines gave them a sense of religion without having to deal with God or what He might really want from them.

"While I started out with some basis of truth, my vanity led me into delusion. I was the guru on top of the mountain who thought he'd discovered the key to knowledge. I knew the rules that would make me the master of all. I knew the Unbreakable Laws of the Universe that supposedly even God had to obey when I quoted them. It was so popular, I told myself, it had to be right. . . . I chose not to linger on the scriptures contradicting my point of view. I chose not to think that, possibly, I was being used as the devil's pawn to get people's eyes off God. I chose to forget I'd be held accountable for what I taught."

Cliff seemed lost in thought for a moment, then continued. "Once, after a service, some guy really let me have it! And I went through a time when I started to feel convicted about it. But when I thought of throwing away MY empire—vanity, pride, and greed let delusion strike again. I started to think I could just confess my mistakes to God, as I made them, and leave it at that. As long as my sins were secret, I could go on being the idol of thousands. The teaching was still sound, wasn't it? It must be, I thought, for the people came in droves and fell at my touch. I tried to fool myself into thinking it would destroy the faith of so many if I told them. Finally, I realized that many of my followers didn't have any faith—in God that is. They were like the pubescent children of an indulgent father, caring only for what they could receive not how they got it or where it came from. I saw my own sins being reproduced in their lives, and then I knew . . . and it all crumbled."

He looked straight at me. "I did a lot of terrible things, James, and I'm sorry. You know, I almost told you once. But I knew the admiration you had for me would disappear and you'd look at me the way you are looking at me now, and I just wasn't man enough to face it . . . 'Sorry' is not enough, but it's all I've got now."

All the contempt I felt sprang up in me and I backhanded Cliff across the cheek as hard as I could.

"There!" I said loudly to him, "When you're ready to offer up the other cheek, let me know! The only person you're sorry for is yourself." I turned to walk away but halted when Cliff spoke.

"Funny thing I've noticed," Cliff said, wiping blood out of the corner of his mouth, "there's a lot of 'righteous anger' around these days. The people have found out that they were following me instead of God. And to call me a liar is to admit they believed a lie. . . . They can't feel righteous anymore . . . and they're angry."

I returned to spit on him, then walked away.

Cliff was found guilty of several charges and received a short prison sentence. I know he served his time and got out, but no one knows what became of him. Soon after, the world was overtaken by events so intense and that the whereabouts of any one person lost significance.

James stopped his mental interview. Actually, this *could* be the opportunity he'd been hoping for. Although the public had soon forgotten he'd ever even known Cliff Edison, rarely a day passed when he did not recall it in some way. Now, perhaps, the chance to finally vindicate himself had come.

He would write about Cliff. *Yes,* he quickly thought. *I'd call the chapter, "The Rise and Fall of Dr. Clifford Edison." I could expose the flaws of Bible thumpers—their hypocrisy, their manipulation.*

James rotated around to his keypad and quickly typed a few notes.

"Yes," he said aloud. "I can finally lay all this to rest."

Almost immediately, his creative side began to revive. The next topic he'd want to address? He typed, "A Lesson in Chaos."

It seemed as if the entire generation had somehow known there would be a cataclysmic event in their lifetime, forever altering life as they knew it. He bit his lip. *Perhaps this,* he considered, *was what drove so many to such excess. His fingers pounced on the letters as sentences poured out of him.*

> Just how or why the events in America started when they did, or who caused them, was never really clear. First, biological and chemical contamination sprung up in multiple locations. Was it bio-terrorism? Was a foreign power behind it . . . or was it just the counter-attack of spores and germs which had become resistant to man's continuous overuse of antibiotics and sterilization? Could it have been judgment from God? Was it Mother earth re-aligning the forces of nature, as she did when the dinosaurs disappeared? Everyone had a theory. No one could prove any of them.

James now remembered the time when, not so much in belief as in desperation, even he had looked up a final time and said, "God, whoever, whatever you are . . . please, let all this stop. . . ." But of course, it didn't. There was war, and although the horror of it was felt in the U.S., it was far worse in other countries. Then came no oil, famine, riots, no electricity . . . no normalcy.

James placed his fingers on the keypad again and let his thoughts flow through them.

> We no longer clung to thoughts about jobs, cars, houses, Monday Night Football. We wondered where we would get food, medicine, water.

Some had stockpiled food, but if they weren't prepared to defend against sustained attacks by mobs of people with guns, grenades, bricks and clubs, they died before they ate it. Those who survived civilian onslaughts lost what they had to military confiscation.

'Resource Management' became a key function of the government. Nothing could be used or consumed unless it was determined to be in the long-range interest of society as a whole. At first, there were many horror stories, but as the population completed the exodus south, the number of dying peaked out, and things began to improve.

James stopped typing. The largest single problem now, he'd been told, was getting people who had been thinking of individual survival to see themselves as a corporate group again, to think in terms of long-range common goals.

This is when Fibertronics, to James' thinking, became the key piece of the puzzle for the salvation of civilization. Without it, humanity would have been reduced to living in caves again and many more would have died; with it, civilization could not only grow but leap forward in development.

James wrote "Global Resurrection." For the first time in ages, his thoughts were flowing freely and ideas were taking form.

James had experienced all of it. He'd seen the evolution of thought and events. Now he would describe all the sights, sounds, people, and emotions of the last few years in great detail: How he felt when he buried his best friend. How he managed to cope during the first months and his move south. How he made the decision to get a code and how his life was better for it. . . . He would interview top national representatives, he would try to get access to more information on Mr. Kressman—who had done so much to mend the wounds of a dying world. If the book was good enough, it would be translated and used as part of the Living Witness program worldwide.

Yes! This book won't really be about ME, it will be about all of us. He became filled with happiness. The real purpose of the work suddenly crystalized in his mind, and he wrote it out.

> Although almost every being, institution, or thing has failed us . . . there is hope once again. If we have learned the lesson of Brotherhood . . . if we can make friends with nature, if we agree to build together, if we relinquish the past and all the error of its thought, there will be many tomorrows—and those tomorrows will all be better ones.

When he finished the book it would be called *Changing Times, Time for a Change.*

Chapter 6

Northwest of Dallas

Sara Reisling looked out the upstairs window of the house that doubled as a neighborhood store. It had rained for a day and a night without stopping, dashing all her hopes of receiving supplies. The roads and storm drains in the area hadn't been repaired in years. Even though much of the standing water had finally drained away, several inches remained in the street.

Just as well I didn't get supplies, she told herself. *People may have trouble getting to the store for the next day or so.*

With no refrigeration, she had to be careful not to overstock perishable goods.

Leaving the portion of the house where the family lived, Sara descended the stairs to the store. She unlatched the shutters on the windows facing the street and swung them open. When she did so, she noticed the night's flooding had left a deposit of mud on her porch. Frowning, Sara moved to the front door, unlocked it, and stepped outside to secure the door in an open position. She couldn't avoid treading on the layer of slick soil. When she looked down at her shoes, an unwanted memory flashed in her mind. She remembered the day she stood ankle-deep in purple-stained muck . . . waiting to be released from the camp where her mother died.

A persistent humming sound brought her back to the present. At first she couldn't be sure. Was it an engine? She looked down the street and saw some of her neighbors looking out their windows as well.

They must hear it too, she thought. An engine hadn't been heard in this area in four or five months so it attracted a great deal of attention.

A jeep fish-tailed around the corner, followed by two men on horseback . . . they had to be military. Few private citizens had use of vehicles or horses.

The jeep slid to a halt in front of the store. The men on horseback brought their horses right up onto the sidewalk before Sara stepped back into the doorway.

"This must be one of 'em," one man in uniform said.

"Yeah," said another, "Go on in, I'll be there in a second."

A terrible sense of dread came over Sara. Soldiers could requisition everything in her store, and pay her with a credit slip. A credit slip of no value to one who had no central-computer account to be credited.

She quickly walked to the back and called up the stairs to her sister.

"Noel?"

"I'm coming, Sara!" came the reply. But, as Noel stood at the top of the stairs, she saw the urgent expression on her sister's face. "What's wrong?" she asked, in a hushed voice.

Sara spoke slowly and quietly. "Stay upstairs. Soldiers are here . . . with a requisition. Stay with Daddy . . . and pray."

"Okay." Noel understood.

Sara turned quickly and went back into the store to find the floor already covered with mud where the soldiers walked between the shelves. With clip screens in hand, they quickly inventoried all the items in the room.

The man in charge said, "Where do you keep the grain?"

"I'm out," she said.

"Dairy items?"

"Out."

"Meat products?"

"Sorry, out."

"Isn't that convenient?" he said.

She thought a moment, then smiled inwardly.

"I challenge your recollection of inventory," he said, moving to the counter, "and I demand to see your stockroom." He pulled out a badge. "I can do that, you know."

"Oh, by all means. This way please," she said, leading the way back to the cellar stairs. He searched the boxes in the room for quite some time before demanding to look throughout the entire building. Sara accompanied him on his tour and by the time they returned to the store, most of her canned goods were in cloth bags, ready to be toted away.

She tried to keep her composure and said, "Is there anything else you'd like?"

"No. Not that you have," said one of the soldiers with a clip screen. He turned to their leader. "I've almost got a tally here, sir. If you'll just sign it, we can . . ."

"Wait," the officer interrupted him.

"Yes?"

"Well . . . think about it, Hobbs!" he said in an exasperated tone. "Why send a truck for a few cans when we'll have to find yet another store for the other things we need." He pointed to the clip screen. "Use your head. And look for the next store marked on your index." He then turned to Sara and spoke in a mocking tone, "I *know* this breaks your heart, but we're leaving the stuff. . . . You can put it back on the shelves, right?" He turned back to the men. "Let's go."

Before she could reply, they'd gone.

Chapter 7

Near the Gulf of Mexico of the former state of Texas

Alex Dubois moved to adjust the dials on his readout screen. He blinked widely to refocus his eyes on the symbols rapidly appearing and moving off the screen.

Forget it, he thought closing the program. The light from the screen faded, and banks of lights in the ceiling grew brighter.

The tone sounded, and he selected the "receive" option. His computer powered up again, and the ceiling lights dimmed.

"Alex?" The face of John Klost appeared on his screen. Alex's mind leaped about for a clue as to why *the* John Klost would call him. They'd met at the Institute years ago, but had never been close friends.

"Hello, John, how are you?"

"A matter of great urgency has come up and . . . well, if you're free, I'd like to meet with you now."

Things quickly jumped beyond the curious stage to all-out mystery. Why would he want to meet right *now*? Unfortunately, John's placid face couldn't be interpreted.

"Sure," Alex responded. "Where would you like to meet?"

"Here at the center. A man will arrive for you in five minutes." John nodded his balding head before the screen went blank.

# # #

Miles away, John Klost cut his transmission before turning to the workmen in the office. "How soon will you be done?"

"Just need to turn the last nut here, sir, and we're done," replied one of two men installing a basin on the wall.

"Remember, it has to look like it's always been there. Clean up every chip of paint, or whatever," John added.

"Yes sir," the workman replied.

# # #

In his office, Alex scratched about in his mind for anything he'd read about Fibertronics lately. Total blank. But it had to be something important for John to call this late and request a meeting at such short notice.

After the turn of the millennium, many corporations sought shelter in places which could be secured against the ravages of man and the elements. Some hoped to build labs in space, some burrowed underground. E. E. Kressman, multi-conglomerate CEO, topped them all with his "Neptune Project." Renamed the Strategic Underwater Fibertronic Center after the disasters, it had been built under the Gulf of Mexico and was virtually a sovereign state. Why would Kressman's right-hand man want a conference at this hour?

Wide awake now, Alex swirled around in his chair and sprang up. He went to his bathroom and looked in the mirror. Not bad for a man of thirty-seven. No gray hairs. Near-perfect vision. He stood sideways, then turned and moved closer to the mirror. He could use a shave maybe; but he didn't have the time, so settled for running a wet comb through his hair.

Coming out of the lavatory, he dipped both hands in the bowl attached to the wall on the left. He did it without even thinking about the act and dried his hands on the little towel hanging beneath the bowl. He'd performed the ritual hundreds of thousands of times since boyhood—upon entering his home or after being in the lavatory. It was an automatic reflex. He'd been trained since boyhood to automatically do things the "right" way. For example, all of the floors in his house were wood and all his carpets were wool. His shoes had always been made of real leather. He'd been taught to never touch man-made materials with bare feet.

He also didn't work at the hour of sunrise or the hour of sunset. Although he'd stopped meditating on the "beginning of power or the need for protection" during those times, honoring the tradition still had a place of importance in Alex's life.

He'd just about finished up the work on his desk when Klost's man arrived at the main door of the building. Alex told the guard, an oldie, he'd be right down.

When Alex approached the main door, he could see a man of large stature with close-cropped dark hair and a well-manicured beard. The man had an amused grin on his face as he stood looking down at the guard. Alex thought perhaps the oldie had done or said something amusing. When he got closer, however, he saw the oldie was merely staring off into space. Alex looked back at Klost's man, who stopped smiling.

Personally, he had no overpowering love of the procedure which turned some people into "oldies," but he did see its absolute need in society. With the labor force so decreased, and an abundance of aging people to support, the government had nearly floundered.

Before the disasters, scientists developed a procedure, called "regeneration," which often made old people useful again. As with many forms of progress, there was a price: While the procedure made great strides in revitalizing the bodies of elderly people, as often as not, a severe loss of intellect resulted. A man of seventy with all his mental faculties and a deteriorated body, could regain his strength, but might lose his intelligence in the process. The people who experienced the negative side of regeneration became known as "oldies," and could do little more than menial labor. Alex considered this a fate preferable to rotting in some facility, using up valuable resources.

Older people were "encouraged" to fulfill a "duty to society" and undergo the process around the age of sixty-five, so they wouldn't become a drain on family or the state. In the meantime, scientists continued to tweak the procedure in hopes of better results.

Alex started to say "What's so funny?" but, before he could open his mouth the man introduced himself.

"Alex Dubois? I'm George Smith. We'd better hurry. Mr. Klost is waiting for you."

As Alex followed Mr. Smith, they wove their way through the crowds. Despite the late hour, people filled the walkways in this part of the city. Finally, the two men came to an unimpressive building with an oldie out front. As with most oldie guards, it only involved itself when the person trying to enter couldn't get the door open. If asked, it would buzz someone inside to open the door.

George Smith walked right by the oldie. When he got to the door, he didn't get out a key or a card as Alex expected, nor did he push a series of buttons on a keypad or wait for a scan. He just opened the door.

"Don't you lock this place?" Alex couldn't help asking.

"Of course we do. It's the latest thing . . . activated by codes. Only the right people get into the right doors this way. It'll be on the market in a coupla months, I think." Smith gave him an annoyed, *don't-you-know-anything?* look.

Once past the small foyer of the building, Alex marveled at the space and beauty within its inner chambers. He hadn't seen its equal in years. Warm lights glowed everywhere. And, could he hear water splashing? They turned a corner and entered a huge room with a magnificent, lighted fountain. They walked around the fountain to a corridor with a wide, arched ceiling. Once they entered it, he couldn't help staring at a myriad of ancient artifacts behind huge display windows lining both sides of the corridor. They appeared to be from every civilization and time period: Golden gods, jeweled headpieces, spears, stone tools. Incredible! He'd be willing to wager many of these objects had never been seen—even in museums. Each display contained items more beautiful than the last.

Busy looking at the artifacts, he hadn't noticed the gentle downward slope of the passageway. When they stopped walking, he looked back and realized they'd come down quite a distance. Next, he noted they'd come to a dead-end.

Smith moved closer to the wall and a crack appeared in the surface. It opened wider before they stepped into a square, wood-paneled room about ten feet wide and long. Once they did so, the wall closed behind them. Alex stood next to his escort, waiting for the man to do something, but he just stood there.

"Are we being scanned?" he finally asked.

Smith rolled his eyes. "We're in an elevator."

Alex resented the patronizing manner, but managed to say, "Oh."

He experienced no sensation of movement while they stood there for an eternal minute. A door behind them finally opened. Determined not to appear disoriented, Dubois whipped around and started to charge out of the elevator like he'd been there at least a dozen times. Instead he nearly knocked over John Klost. Alex turned to see Smith stifling a giggle.

"Thanks, George, I'll take him from here," Klost said.

"He's all yours," Mr. Smith said, before the elevator door closed between them.

Alex started to apologize to Klost for the collision, but John said, "Let's hurry while we have an air lock available."

Klost grabbed his arm and strode off down a corridor at a great pace. Alex felt like a school boy being dragged off to the principal's office.

At last they came to a round portal. When Klost drew close, it opened and they stepped into a cream-colored, tube-shaped room about eight feet in diameter and twelve feet long. The doors closed before Alex sensed forward motion.

Klost pushed a button on the floor two times with his foot, and two hatches popped up out of the floor, across from one another, with a three-foot aisle between them. Alex watched the hatch lids moving upward and noted they were attached to cushioned seats (the inside of the hatch lid being cushioned for a seat back). When the seats had risen about three feet out of the floor, they stopped.

"You might as well be comfortable, the trip takes a few minutes," Klost said, motioning to one of the chairs. "Watch a metagram if you'd like." He pushed another button, and the round wall they faced became lit with projected patterns of concentric stars, triangles, and circles in kaleidoscopic colors with movements gently pulsating to soft rhythms—the latest form of "elevator" music.

Alex sat down and tried to appear "comfortable." The room started to tilt down at the front, but his seat stayed level. He looked at Klost.

"That's right. We're going down through the tunnel. This is nothing more than an underwater subway car," Klost said before pulling a clip screen from the case on his lap. "If you'll excuse me, I just have a few last-minute notes to make before we arrive." He busied himself with it for the remainder of the ride.

A tone sounded, and Klost put the clip screen back into a case, closed it, and stood up. Alex stood before Klost tapped the foot button again, and the chairs descended back into the floor. The door on the car opened, and they walked through a short tube to a room of unbelievable dimensions.

Alex couldn't remember ever being in a room this size. It appeared perfectly square, and along each wall were possibly a hundred round portals like the one he'd just stepped through. The walls, decorated with thousands of beautiful hieroglyphic designs and pictures from ancient cultures, rose to dizzying heights. The ceiling, also covered with beautiful designs and pictures came down steeply to a point in the center of the room, like an upside-down pyramid. A transparent point on the pyramid held a dazzling ball which cast myriads of beams of light around the room while it slowly revolved.

Alex just stood there, trying to comprehend its enormity.

"I felt the same way when I first saw it," John said, bringing Alex back to the present. "It's just so spectacular. . ."

Alex, still at a loss for words, nodded. He followed John across the room, looking around, mesmerized by the grandeur of it all. When he became aware again, he realized he'd stopped in front of an open portal, and John was standing inside, waiting.

"Sorry," Alex said quietly. They proceeded down a hallway to a large, lavishly furnished office which Alex assumed was John's. An ornate sculpture in the corner appeared to be Mayan, and the painting on the wall might well be a Renaissance piece.

"Sit down, Alex." Klost motioned to a chair.

Once seated, Alex noticed the basin on the wall. "I didn't know you were—" Alex started to say, pointing to the basin.

"Actually, I'm not. It's for the president when he's here."

"You mean the president of Fibertronics is—?"

"Well," John interrupted, "it's a personal thing. He doesn't want to advertise it, so just keep it to yourself, okay?" He'd been leaning forward and speaking quietly, but then straightened and said in a business-like manner, "Now, as for why I've called you here. You may know Chester Crowne, our VP of Public Relations."

Alex nodded.

"Well, Chester died this morning. By the time we got him to the hospital, it was too late to have anything done for him." John paused for a moment and sighed. "Anyway, the show must go on so to speak—so to make it short, we want you to be our new VP of Public Relations."

Alex sat in stunned silence. The largest corporation in the world wanted him, a virtual nobody in world affairs, to be a VP!

"We've looked over your history, Alex, and we feel you're the right man for the job. If you are wondering why we picked you instead of some big name, frankly, it's because anyone who's well known may have alienated some segment of the public already. We wanted someone new. Someone with enough brains and diplomacy to really get out there and change minds about what this whole shift in society is all about. The world is in the most crucial stage of the Transition. It's imperative that people embrace the universal truth of the Global View and recognize that encoding is the personal means of validating a commitment to it. We believe you're the man who can communicate the ethics and the needs of this new age in a campaign that will be a defining moment in history. The president himself made the final decision."

Klost pressed a button, and a screen popped up out of the desk facing Alex. "I took the liberty of having this ready for you. It's our offer to you. If you want to accept, you can do so now."

Alex read the salary offer and about all of the fringe benefits, already formulating his letter of resignation to his employer. He scanned the entire document before reading the last lines:

> Offer made subject to release from current contract and effective immediately upon termination from previous employment. Code and imprint here.

"If you'd like to sleep on it . . ." John offered.

"No need, John, I'd have to be insane to turn this down! Keypad please." A keypad popped up in front of Alex, and he began to punch out a message of resignation to his company with an "urgent" assignment (which meant it would appear immediately in the readout at his company). Then, he brought the Fibertronics offer back to the screen. He keyed for a tone to add his code and imprint. The tone sounded, and he placed the fingers and palm of his right hand upon a panel to the right of the keypad. His prints and code appeared briefly on the screen followed by the word "verified."

"I believe that takes care of it," Alex said.

A beeping noise sounded, and the screen flashed a priority one message. John pushed the incoming button, and a message appeared on the screen:

Resignation of Alexander Rubin Dubois Approved

Record transfer accomplished
Due salary credited
Link complete for deposits
New debit line moved up ₮500,000
All locks below priority 2 activated

Alex's eyebrows came together. "What's all this about locks?"

"All locks in this building and other Fibertronics buildings have one of ten security ratings. One being the highest and ten being the lowest. Your code will now open any lock with a priority two or below in any building anywhere in the world belonging to Fibertronics, our affiliates, or cooperatives. In six months, you will be upgraded to priority one."

Alex knew he must be in a state of shock. He'd just quit his job and been hired as a vice president of Fibertronics and he felt numb. Not happy or exhilarated or anything. Just numb. He rubbed his temples, thinking, *I must be in some sort of shock. I feel . . . nothing. Maybe tomorrow, when I realize . . .*

"Now," Klost said, "the next thing to decide is where you want to live. In the future, you'll be doing quite a bit of work in Dallas. Will you want to find your own apartment there, or would you like one of ours? I must tell you that, in either case, almost half of your time may be spent traveling to other regional offices; so, you won't be spending a lot of time at home—wherever that is."

"I'll have to think about it." As Alex said the words, he realized how tired he was. "Can I let you know tomorrow?"

"Of course! I realize it's late, but we needed to get this settled as soon as possible. Can't let anything lag for long, you know. I'll see you get home safely."

They both stood and walked toward the door.

"By the way, Alex, this is your office."

When Alex settled into bed that night, those were the last words to pass through his mind before he fell asleep.

Chapter 8

Northwest of Dallas

After threading their way through the crumbling neighborhoods, the two young travelers approached the house-turned-store and entered through the front door with other customers. Jason hoped one of the members of the family who owned the store would recognize him.

An older man behind the counter greeted them, then kept an eye on the two as they slowly browsed, waiting for a lull. Before the other patrons left, a woman entered the store from a back room and asked the old man if he'd like to break for lunch. It had been a long while since he'd seen her, but Jason recognized her. Jason signaled Troy to linger a bit longer. They'd wait for a private moment to speak with her. The remaining customers finally exited the store, but the old man remained, hesitant to leave his daughter alone with the two young men.

Jason set down the jar of home-made apple butter he'd been holding and approached the counter. "Excuse me," he said, "we're in the area to attend a memorial and we need directions." The young woman's sad blue eyes showed no recognition of Jason or the coded statement he'd made. "Oh?" she said, "Who passed away?"

"We're not sure it's our relative," Jason replied. "We'll need to identify the Body first. . . . My parents sent me to represent them in this matter and said possibly the woman at this address could direct us to the proper location for the memorial." Once he'd said the whole thing, he could see he'd connected with her. The old man looked at his daughter before she replied, "Yes, I may be able to give you help."

"You're Sara aren't you?" Jason asked outright. "We met a long time ago. . . . In Oklahoma. Perhaps you don't remember me. Anyway," he said, producing a folded piece of cloth and sliding it across the counter toward her. "Rosa, sent you this."

When he took his hand off it, Sara reached out and grasped the cloth tightly, pulling it close to her body, as if it somehow contained a treasure she'd longed to find. She slowly opened it to see the writing inside. At one glance, she knew it was authentic. Refolding the piece of cloth, she tucked it up the cuff of her sleeve and looked at Jason again.

Reaching out and gently placing a hand on his cheek, she studied his features. Her countenance slowly softened into a gentle smile when something came back to memory: A younger version of this face. . . . "Oh, yes," she said, quietly. "Now I remember. You're one of them . . . one of the nine. You're Jason aren't you?"

"Yes," he said, relieved. "Only there's lots more than nine now. There's twenty-six of us." He suddenly remembered his companion. "And this is Troy. He came south with me, and we'll both be going back in a few days."

Sara and her father both came around the counter to greet the visitors. "I'm Pete," the old man said before embracing them. "Welcome."

"Please tell me Rosa and Ricky are both well," Sara asked.

"Yes. They're doing fine. Rosa wants very much to see you, but it isn't possible for her to leave all the little ones."

"I'm grateful even for the letter," Sara said. "I bet you're tired and hungry. Go back inside with Daddy, and eat some lunch, then we'll talk."

Although still pretty, Sara didn't seem as animated as Jason remembered her. "Yes, ma'am," he answered. "Thank you."

"Yes. Thank you." Troy echoed.

"Hey," Sara called to the two young men as they walked toward the back of the house. "I do hope you planned on staying with us."

Jason nodded. "We were hoping to be here a couple of nights. We don't mind sleeping on the floor."

"Nonsense," she replied. "We have cots in the storeroom and we're happy to have you."

After the boys and her father went to the kitchen, she asked her sister, Noel, to watch the store for a while. Climbing the stairs to the family's private rooms, Sara entered her bedroom and sat on the bed before pulling the letter from her sleeve. She unfolded the soft, tightly woven cloth, and let her eyes slowly drift along the words, wanting to savor every word.

Dearest Sara:

I was so happy to get your last message . . . was it nine months ago? How I long to see you, but, unless things change, it's doubtful we will be able to come south. We have so many children now! Some were found, some wandered in. Little Daisy continues to improve. She's turning into such a beautiful little lady, and freely chatters with everyone now. How it blesses my heart to see her prosper.

How are you, dearest friend? Is all well with you? How is your little store doing? How is your family?

Sara stopped reading. Rosa didn't know yet. If it had happened a couple of years ago, Rosa would've been the first person she called. . . . It still seemed so odd to think this was no longer possible. Odd and sad. She couldn't reach out over the miles to share about the loss of her mother and hear the comforting voice of her friend. Sara leaned her head against the headboard for a moment and thought. Being strong for her father and sister had been so hard. Perhaps, in a letter to Rosa, she could share her deep sorrow. In the next couple of days, she'd have the opportunity to compose a letter to send back with Jason. Yes, this would be good. She found her place on the cloth and began to read again.

We are getting a bit gray around the edges ☺ but we're blessed. Life here is not easy, but we rest at night knowing God is with us. We continue to see His intervention in the lives of many desperate people. Wonderful things are happening elsewhere as well. (Jason will fill you in.)

Winter was sooooo cold! We're grateful for the beginning of spring. We've even dared to begin planting a garden. If you have any tomato seeds, could Jason buy some from you? I have such a craving for tomatoes—not only for their taste but for their delicate smell and bright red color, too. Enough of that! I'll make a separate list to put with this letter. Jason has so many things to carry. . .

While Sara pored over her letter, Jason and Troy ate soup and shared some conversation with her father. Even though this was a "safe" place, they were careful not to give detailed information about where they'd been or whom they'd seen during their time in the south. The fewer people who knew such things, the better.

After they finished eating, Sara appeared in the kitchen. She looked as if she'd been crying.

Her father got up and stood beside her as she put away the clean dishes on the counter. "Everything okay?" he asked softly.

She patted his hand. "Yes. I'm just happy to hear from her."

She turned around and smiled at the two guests. "Tell you what. Why don't we get all the things you'll be taking and set them aside, then Noel and I will decide what we can sew into your clothes.

"We know how to do it," Jason offered, "they taught all of us how to sew last winter."

"Then maybe," Sara said, "we can sit around the next few evenings and have a quilting party with your clothes. First, let's go down to the cellar and see if we can fill Rosa's list." She headed for the stairs. "Bring your gear. You'll sleep down here."

Once they gathered in the store room, she had them collect the items they'd need to carry back to Ricky and Rosa. Tomato, squash, and cucumber seeds, yeast, a couple of tiny pairs of scissors, skeins of colored threads, safety pins . . . . The list contained nearly a hundred small items and several bulky things.

She looked at Jason and asked, "I know you have so much to carry, but is there some small thing Rosa would love? Something she wouldn't ask for? I want to send her a little gift."

"Maybe a piece of cloth," Jason answered. "You'd have to pick it, though. I don't know about things like that. . . . Troy and I want to take presents home, too. Something from us."

"Sure," she said. "Just tell me what you have in mind."

Jason's eyes swept around the room before they lit on a jar containing a rare treat: Candied orange slices. "I overheard

Rosa saying to Ricky she wondered if she'd ever get to taste an orange again."

Sara quickly got the jar open. "Good thinking! How many pieces?"

"One."

She stopped, her hand still in the jar. "Only one?"

Jason nodded, then looked at his companion. "You know Rosa. If there's more, she'll give them to the kids and not keep a bite for herself. One is more like a gift just for her."

Troy's head bobbed up and down. "Yeah."

Sara looked at Troy. About five foot ten, he had a round face and small eyes. She could imagine him taking calculus classes or building computers in days gone by. "You don't talk very much, do you?"

He shrugged and shyly smiled. "Jason usually talks enough for both of us."

Chapter 9

A suburb of Dallas

Michael sat looking blankly at the screen, watching the news, of course. He'd developed an addiction to television again. Today, some long-lost citizens got repatriated somewhere. Big deal. He switched channels. A man with a well-trimmed beard stood in front of an audience.

"What we men, as the minority, must do," he said in an ever-so-soft voice, "is learn to celebrate our manhood in respectful, edifying ways. . . ."

Michael hit the selector button again. The picture showed a now-familiar figure, former First Lady Edith Todd sat, curled up and cozy, on a white-sand beach with three other women.

"Yes! Exactly," she said with a warm smile. "I still believe in angels, and spirits, and the warmth of the Christmas season. It's one of my favorite times of the year. But I want to celebrate *all*–"

Michael grunted and turned the channel again spent a few moments pondering one of the new dramas cranked out by the studios—shows written to be "more relevant in the new world."

On the screen, a teenaged girl looked around furtively before trading some household goods for food with a woman at the back door of a store. After witnessing the exchange, a handsome teen boy approached the pair.

"Man," he said, "that's so viral of you." Expressions like "viral," and "toxic" were *coolspeak* terms aimed at selfish, greedy, or survivalist behavior.

"Don't you know," he continued, "that you're stealing from all of us when you barter things outside the system?"

Michael rolled his eyes and changed the channel.

The next scene showed a female reporter standing in front of a twenty-foot-tall bronze sculpture of the globe.

". . . and while the lighting ceremony won't take place for another week, we're able to bring you an exclusive, sneak peek at this breath-taking sculpture by the renowned bronze artist,

YanYan." The view changed to an angle above the piece while the reporter's voice continued. "As you can see, the top quarter of the globe is gone. The jagged edges depict the violation of earth's dignity by acts of man. And, if you look closer, inside the globe are likenesses of men, women, and children whose faces are etched with the horrors we've all endured."

Michael's face scrunched up in disgust when he saw the haunted faces of the people whose arms and hands extended up beyond the jagged edges of the blown-apart globe—as if they sought to capture the pieces and pull them back in.

"At the official unveiling next week," the reporter said, "representatives from the UN will take the ceremonial torches and light the eternal flame, which will burn inside the sculpture around the victims within." The camera pulled closer for a tight shot of the plaque as she read it aloud. "The inscription underneath it reads . . .

'Dedicated to Mother Earth
and in memory of those
who died so senselessly
in Earth's final conflict.

Let us never forget
without RESTRAINT, there was chaos
without REASONING, there was war
without JUSTICE, there was no peace.'

"The original will be lit here next week," she continued, "but, within a year I'm told, duplicates of this sculpture will stand in every major metropolis around the world.

"Next up, our medical reporter, Lonnie Shue explores the world of addictive behaviors . . ."

Michael shook his head and touched the button before the screen went blank. Yawning, he looked at the clock and realized he'd managed to stay up past midnight again. It became so easy to do with real lights and television. With the dim glow of flames or chemical lamps, he'd rarely been able to stay up past nine-thirty.

Linda should be home soon, he thought.

He heard a knock and went to the door. When he looked through the peep hole, he saw Zac standing in the cold, rubbing his hands.

"Hey, Zac," he called, opening the door. "Come in. Isn't it a bit late for you to be wandering the streets?"

His brother stepped inside the newly refurbished apartment. "Sorry to bother you. I saw your lights on and decided to drop in for a moment."

"No bother. I was just starting to get bored. You thirsty? Hungry?"

"No thanks," Zac said, taking off his coat before dropping into a chair.

Michael sat on the sofa. "So how's life? I haven't seen much of you lately."

"Pretty good. I've been busy." Zac paused and looked around. "Isn't it hard to believe that last spring we sat outside here in the cold wondering what was going to happen to us? Who'd have thought back then you'd be the one to have all the 'conveniences' of life right in your own house."

"All you gotta do is get an old lady with a code, Zac." Michael said it to be funny, but regretted it when he noticed the expression on Zachary's face. "Hey look, sorry. I know how you feel about codes—like they're evil. I used to feel spooky about 'em, too. But you know, I kinda like living like a real person again. I've even considered taking the plunge myself."

Zachary leaned forward in his chair. "Tell me you will never do that. I'm serious, Michael, promise me."

"Oh Zac! Don't be so dramatic. What would happen if I did? Would I get filled with demons?" Michael put two fingers behind his head to look like horns. "Come off it! Nobody believes that stuff anymore. Next, you'll be shouting the world's coming to an end. . . . Well, in case you forgot, that already happened, Zac. Too bad we survived it, because that sure kills your theory."

Just bringing it up reminded Michael of the months just before and during the disasters. So many preachers seemed to be shouting, "This is it! Get right or get left!" Yet the horror of day-to-day living continued—with no evidence of a rescue. And, when each day dawned, even more horror had arrived.

"I've lived through it all and I want to know—*where is your God*, Zac? Where was He when Ben died like a rat in a cage? Where was God when all those people were suffering? Where was He when Mom and Dad and Jill were dying? Why didn't He show up? Why didn't He at least help us? I can't live on fairy-tale promises of being whisked away to some never-never land, Zac. I want to be a part of the real world. A world that is living and growing. . . . Even if that means living without your God." Michael finished almost in a whisper.

Zachary looked down during the tirade, but now looked straight into his brother's eyes. "I'm sorry men used threats or false promises to get you to seek God, but let me say this: He *did* help you. I *know* you can look back over the last two years and see where He saved you . . . where you should have gotten infected, you should have starved, you should have frozen to death . . . and the only reason you *didn't* is because He put His hand on you."

Michael felt a deep chill come over him.

Zac's gaze didn't waver. "And now men are promising you prosperity if you'll *deny* what Jesus did to save you. . . . Never trust your soul to the promises of men, Michael. The Lord is the only one worthy of your faith. Don't look at what men say about Him. Don't even take *my* word for it. . . . Look at what He says about Himself. Every promise *He* makes, He keeps."

Zac reached into his back pocket, pulled out a small Bible, and pressed it into Michael's hand. "The people who picked times and dates for the return of Christ set themselves up for a fall and took multitudes of people with them. . . . But what they did doesn't change what God will do! He's alive, Michael. He lives. Don't let Satan snatch that from you. All these events were written down thousands of years ago so we could have a warning and take it to heart. Don't let bitterness harden you till you become deaf to the truth."

Michael didn't know what to say. He stuck the Bible in his shirt pocket, but only to stop the sermon.

The door closed, and they turned to see Linda standing in the kitchen.

"Hello, Linda," Zachary said quietly.

"Hello," she replied coolly.

"Well, Michael, I must be off," Zac said, standing up. "I really only stopped in to say goodbye."

"Are you going somewhere?" Michael asked, surprised.

"Yes, I'm leaving in the morning—I mean, in a few hours from now—and I wanted to say goodbye this time," Zac said with a slight smile.

"Will you be gone long, or is this just a short trip?"

"I don't know. But I hope you'll remember what I've said before you make any changes." He paused. "God bless you, Michael." They hugged, then shook hands. There were tears in his eyes.

"Goodbye, Zac." Michael said, a bit baffled.

Zac looked at Linda and said, "Goodbye," before picking up his coat and leaving.

As soon as the door closed again, Linda turned to Michael. "I think he's gone crackers."

Michael didn't want to discuss it and headed for his room without comment.

Zachary stood outside in the cold and prayed.

Chapter 10

A suburb of Atlanta

Deana and Leon Newsome sat on the park bench. They'd just eaten an excellent little lunch and now rested in the shade before returning to their respective jobs.

Deana studied Leon for a moment. To her, he still looked as handsome as the day they'd married 24 years ago. She felt so lucky to be the one he'd chosen. She felt even more fortunate to be with the same man after all they had been through.

She vividly remembered the day they married. Due to vast religious differences in their family backgrounds, they opted to have the ceremony performed by a judge. She wore a beautiful dress; he, a spectacular suit. They both cried. After the ceremony, they ran down the courthouse stairs and into a life most people envied. He worked as a lawyer; she became an accomplished commercial artist. They traveled, danced, and dined away the first two years of their marriage. When she became pregnant, they were both thrilled at the prospect of a child. And when Leon Jr. was born, it all seemed as if they lived in a dream. They had a beautiful baby boy.

Leon Jr. embodied all the things most parents really want in a child. He did well in school, seemed musically gifted, and by the time he turned ten, could've been the dictionary definition of a child who had everything.

Then, Deana became pregnant again. They hadn't really planned another child, but decided they wouldn't mind having another one. Deana knew another baby might set her career back a year or two, but figured she'd still be able to take up where she'd left off. So what if she became the world's most successful artist a few years later?

But when Jessica came into the world, the fantasy came to an end. The little girl was beset with many problems at birth—the only visible one being a withered hand. Doctors soon discovered evidence of brain damage and heart trouble as well. For the Newsomes, the first three months of Jessica's life became filled with worried nights and tear-filled moments in hospital waiting rooms.

As Jessica grew older, testing revealed mild retardation. Physicians surgically corrected her heart defect, but they could not fix the crippled hand—the only thing marring Jessica's otherwise lovely features. She had long, dark hair and huge, sad, brown eyes.

Even though their lives took a turn for the worse, Leon remained as solid as a rock. A tenacious person, he helped take care of Jessica and remained very protective of her. The girl adored her father and spent many hours just sitting on his lap while he pored over law books or prepared cases.

Both Leon and Deana decided early on they would not let this tragedy alter the way they lived. They encouraged Leon Jr. as much as they could and tried to spend "quality" time alone with him.

Two years after Jessica's birth, Deana went back to work and again enjoyed success in many arenas. Although her work sometimes kept her away from home for long hours, she kept a full-time housekeeper on duty at all times to take care of Jessica and to provide the home atmosphere both children needed.

When the disasters came several years later, they counted themselves fortunate to be living in the south. Because of this, they escaped the contamination, loss of family, and the need to move that so many others endured. They did, however, suffer in the financial crisis accompanying those events.

Leon and Deana had been at the top for so long, neither of them could imagine what life would be like if they were forced to live in poverty. Leon never doubted they could manage, but did they want to "just manage?" Although being able to send Leon Jr. to private schools ranked high on their list of priorities, Jessica's welfare concerned them more. What would become of her? What if she needed surgery or medicine?

When the government introduced codes, it seemed the only logical solution to most of their problems. Indeed, it gave them a temporary edge over people who wasted time deliberating the matter. (Uncoded people could rarely compete for the best jobs.) Although both Leon and Deana balked a little at signing the Notice of Allegiance, they decided to sign anyway. In the final analysis, they admitted old religions and super-patriotism of any sort didn't mean much. To them, getting coded remained their best option.

And now here they sat, on such a glorious day, enjoying life once again. Deana patted his leg. "It's about time to go, honey. Give me a kiss, and I'll see you later."

Leon opened his eyes. He'd almost fallen asleep. Just as he looked at her, a ray of light shot through the leaves and landed on her dark, shiny hair.

"Okay." he said, kissing her lightly. "Remember, I'll be late tonight. Eat without me. Love you."

The rest of Deana's day went quickly enough, and she soon found herself at home once again. Edwina Grant, the new housekeeper, met her at the door. Although Leon Jr., now 21, had been going to a military academy for two years, Jessica, at 11, still needed supervision and couldn't be left alone. How happy Deana felt to have gotten Ms. Grant to work for them. She also found a secret satisfaction in the fact that Ms. Grant was black. It gave her a sense of elegance—of old-style status.

With her education, the woman, had she been coded, would still be a nurse practitioner. Deana saw this as a prime example of silly superstition ruining a person's life. Ms. Grant, an impoverished widow, probably was a religious fanatic. What kept people like that going? . . . Deana didn't much care. She just appreciated the advantage it gave her in getting such a qualified person for so little.

"You've got a big surprise upstairs!" Ms. Grant said, taking Deana's case and jacket.

"Is anything wrong?" Deana said with some alarm.

"Oh no! Nothing like that! Go upstairs and see!"

Deana quickly climbed the stairs and looked around. First, she opened Jessica's door. Once she saw Jessica sleeping soundly in her bed she quietly closed the door and looked further down the hall. As soon as she saw the light shining under Leon Jr.'s door, she ran down the hall and opened it. There sat her only son.

"Hello, Mom." He said it casually, as if he had been there all the time and had just seen her that morning.

"Lee!" she exclaimed, running to hug him. When he stood, she realized he'd grown even taller. Her boy had become a man. "Just look at you! You've gone and grown up," she said. "I can hardly wait until your father sees you. I think you might actually be taller than he is! And look at these muscles! They really make you work out, huh?"

"It's a total program, Mom. We develop every area of human potential."

"You sound like an advertisement." she said, laughing. Then she added more soberly, "Have you seen Jessica?"

"Yes. I got here just after lunch . . . that Ms. Grant, put her to bed a while ago. . . . What do you know about that woman anyway?"

"What do you mean? Did she do something wrong?" Deana asked.

"Just a feeling. . . . Is she legal?"

"Leon! You don't think we'd break the law do you? What a thing to say to your own mother."

"I wasn't trying to offend you, Mom; just save you some grief, that's all. I'll bet she's not coded."

"You know as well as I do, Lee, anyone with a code doesn't need to work as a housekeeper for a living. What am I supposed to do?"

After a few seconds of silence, she broke into a smile. "Look at us! We should be celebrating your homecoming and here we are discussing domestics! Come!" She grabbed his hand and led him out of the room toward the stairs. "We'll open the best bottle of champagne in the house!"

He stopped. "Mother?"

"Yes?"

"I don't drink alcoholic beverages. They are bad for you."

"Then we'll open the best bottle of ginger ale in the house!"

"No sugar, either."

At first she felt a bit miffed. Why did he have to make such a big deal out of everything? Then she decided she should just be happy to have him home and said, "Then we'll run out to the store, and you can show me what you'd like. Okay?"

The two hurried down the stairs and out of the house as Leon shared about a recent honor he'd been awarded.

###

Upstairs, Edwina Grant sat in the darkness of the little girl's room. She stroked Jessica's hair and said quietly, "Don't worry, precious, I love you."

Edwina wondered how different her life might have been if she'd adopted children. Would she have ever met Jessica?

Many years ago, Edwina met and married Dr. George Grant. Eventually, they ran a very successful clinic in New York City and planned, someday, to adopt. But after the riots in New York almost took George's life, something unexpected happened which changed their course. They made a commitment to God and decided to wait for His direction in all things.

Two years later, the disasters struck, and a whirlwind of activity overtook them. George helped others until he would drop, and Edwina stayed right by his side. When they had to move south, like everyone else, they'd been forced to leave most of what they owned behind. They promised each other to stay uncoded and together—no matter what it took. They would trust God.

When they'd been in the south for only three months, George had a heart attack and died. Devastated at first, Edwina soon found she had no time to wonder why or even to feel sorry for herself. She needed to find a job. It was the one time she had actually been glad she had no children. At least she didn't have to look at hungry little faces every night.

One of the hardest decisions she'd had to make was to become a housekeeper. But Edwina had always been a realist; she could do that or take a code.

Eventually, she landed the job she had now, with Mr. and Mrs. Newsome. Of course, since they had codes, they didn't pay her with cash. Instead, she received food, clothing, shelter, and other goods to compensate for her work. Had it not been for the little girl, Jessica, she wouldn't have stayed with them.

Jessica came at a time in Edwina's life when she needed to be needed by someone and needed to have someone to love. Almost from the moment she first saw those huge brown eyes, her heart had been captured. White and black, servant and served made no difference to either one of them. She loved Jessica as if she were her own child.

Edwina reached down and stroked Jessica's hair again.

Mr. Newsome loved her, but seemed to live at work. Mrs. Newsome just wanted to see that the child got "quality care." They kept the girl in the house and almost never took her out.

It was their son, Leon Jr., who'd been their pride and joy. Pictures of him were everywhere along with trophies, awards and certificates he'd won for different achievements. Edwina had never met him until this day. He had treated her rudely— like a little, black slave.

With total clarity, the reality of her status in life rose up and smacked her. How cheapened, how low she felt. All evening, she'd struggled with pride and remained cordial to the boy, but when he looked at his sister, it became almost more than Edwina could bear. He hated Jessica, her little angel. He made no attempt to be nice to the child and actually made fun of her when he noticed she'd put her shirt on backwards. Crushed, the little girl went to bed early. Edwina wanted so badly to retaliate, she made herself retreat to the kitchen until he went to his room.

"Lord," she said, almost inaudibly, "if my pride has to die a lot more, then so be it . . . but, please don't let him hurt her. She's not a piece of junk. Help me to show her how special she is to You."

She sat in the darkness a while longer, listening to Jessica's rhythmic breathing, and then went off to bed.

Chapter 11

A suburb of Dallas

Michael held onto the machine with a conscious effort. The vibrations of the compactor he used to pack the asphalt made his hands go numb. He shut off the motor, and it gradually wound down until the rattle of the plate against the pavement ceased.

"Hey you!" a woman called to him from down the street. "If you're done, put it inside and lock the door!"

"Okay!" he shouted back. He pulled a lever to make the wheels come down and rolled the machine into a nearby doorway. He'd exited and started locking the door when a man ran into him, knocked him down, and fell on top of him.

"Hey!" Michael said, trying to untangle himself and get up, "Get off me!"

The man looked at him, eyes full of terror. "I swear, I've done nothing! Help me. Please . . . I'm hurt." When he tried to stand, he fell again.

"Sure, sure. What's wrong?" Michael caught him under the arms and propped him against the wall.

Out of breath from running, the man groaned with each exhale. Soaked with sweat, his curly brown hair stuck to his face and neck. His torn shirt and blood-soaked pant leg testified to his desperation.

"Hide me," he gasped. "Please hide me!"

Michael didn't know what to do or say.

"Please," the man said again, closing his eyes.

Michael put the man's right arm over his head and held on around the man's waist. He had no idea why he wanted to help this guy; but, for some reason, felt compelled to do it. Fumbling with keys in one hand, he managed to hold the man up with the other. His pulse now racing, he got the door open and laid the man on the floor near the machine. He quickly ran outside and closed the door. Before he could lock it, he heard people running so he moved away from the door and leaned against a nearby light pole, trying to look as if he were waiting for someone.

Two men and a woman in uniform, carrying rifles, slowed their pace as they drew close to him. The woman had her weapon strapped over her shoulder. She held a small box in one hand, and in the other, she held a disk resembling a dark, flattened egg.

"Wait!" she called, and they all stopped.

She looked at Michael and walked near him. "No, not him. He has to be nearby, though, or they'd have caught him at the next checkpoint."

She began scanning nearby structures by pointing the ovoid object at them, then moving it up and down as she watched the box. She pointed it at the building two doors down and found nothing of interest. She scanned the building next door. Nothing. She pointed the egg at the top of the building where Michael had hidden the man and gradually moved it downward. Michael had to call on every ounce of courage not to run.

She got to the bottom of the building. "There he is!" she said in hushed excitement. "In there, in there!" She pointed to the door.

The two men, rifles ready, approached the door. One aimed at mid-door level, the other lay flat against the building, grabbing the knob. They silently counted to three before the man holding the knob threw open the door.

When nothing happened, they cautiously entered the room. Moments later, they emerged, dragging the injured man by the arms. Michael tried to look like a shocked spectator when they hauled him out. The man didn't say a word but kept looking at Michael until they dragged him out of sight.

# # #

Three miles away, Linda finished up the last piece of business in her old assignment. She pulled up all the necessary documents for a recommendation and made sure they were in order. A small photo of a little girl appeared in the upper left-hand corner of her screen. Linda eyed the skinny, blond child, and a wave of sorrow washed over her. She had to admit her main attraction to this particular little girl was identification. She could see herself at the same age when she looked at this child. Starving for better things, but trapped with parents who didn't care about the indignities of living with less.

"Things will get better for you, Teresa," Linda said, lightly touching the picture on the screen.

She finished filling out the forms which would result in a school transfer for little Teresa. The girl would soon be attending a gifted school specializing in media presentation. With creative mentoring and intervention, who knew how far this girl might go once liberated from the bondage of her parents' dead beliefs?

Linda pushed the "send" key, then slowly spun around in her swivel chair, savoring the moment. Helping this girl really *did* satisfy her soul. She looked at Teresa's picture again, and the warm feeling inside grew. To her great surprise, she felt a small inkling of something maternal. She stopped spinning and got a grip on herself. *What happened to all the vows to never marry, to never have children?*

She instantly looked around the office, as if others might have somehow read her thoughts, then gave a quiet chuckle and smoothed her clothing.

How silly, she admitted to herself. *Still . . . would I marry Michael if he asked me? I'm getting older and there are so few viable men. . . . When he gets coded, I'll consider an offer.* A feline-like look of satisfaction graced her features as she stretched. *The other women around here would be positively eaten with jealousy.* The thought almost made her want to purr.

###

When they met at home that evening, Michael still felt very shaken by the incident he'd witnessed earlier in the day. After one look at him, Linda realized her plan for the evening wouldn't materialize.

"What's wrong with you?" She asked in an irritated tone.

"The strangest thing happened today—" Michael began.

"You think *you* had a strange day," she cut him off. "My bosses have decided to move me to the Office of Public Information."

"As opposed to Educational Services?" he asked.

She gave him a dirty look and squared her shoulders. "I think I did a good job in Educational Services." she said, defensively. "I'm the one who singled out that little girl for media classes. I'm the one who polished the 'think inside the grid' campaign for the youth. I'm the one who came up with the Earth Day idea. Are you ridiculing me?"

Michael remembered her Earth Day idea. It involved children from around the city writing the names of family members lost in the disasters on little slips of paper. In addition, they could write about the possessions or situations they missed most since the war and the disasters. The messages were collected city-wide and, in a televised event, thrown into the Dallas copy of the YanYan sculpture of the burning people inside the broken globe. The idea got picked up in several large cities and even received mention on the international news. Both the sculpture and the idea revolted Michael beyond words. He wiped the image out of his mind before he looked at her. "What gave you the idea I was trying to ridicule you?"

She studied him for a moment. "Maybe I just need to unwind. I don't know. . . . Anyway, this new job is a promotion of sorts. I'll be working with adult topics again." She looked up at the ceiling and tried to console herself. "I suppose I should be flattered, but the whole place is just a mess! The last reporter kept really sloppy files, and it will take weeks just to get everything in order. And, to top it all off, I have to help them kick off another campaign on coding."

"Oh really?" Michael said. "What can be said about coding that hasn't already been said? How about, 'We'll get you no matter where you hide'?"

"Well, actually," Linda broke in, "It's not necessarily saying more as it is saying it to the right people. You see, present ad campaigns are mostly on viewer screens, and the people who have viewer screens at home already have . . ." she stopped talking when Michael's words finally soaked in, then looked at him. "What did you just say?"

"I said, 'We'll get you no matter where you hide.'"

"That's great Michael! Honestly! That's just exactly what we need to say!"

At first, Michael thought *she'd* decided to get sarcastic as well, but soon realized she meant it.

Her mind filled with ideas, and she started saying them out loud. "I mean, that's where it's all headed . . . perfect order. Your mail can get to you wherever you are, your phone calls . . . everything. You can buy or sell anywhere, because it's all going through the same place. . . . But your life can be as simple or as low tech as *you* want it! The system will meet you where you're at! What a great idea! And all I have to do is place the idea in front of the people who need it. On billboards, in schools . . . this is fabulous! You've made my whole day, Michael. In fact, I'm going down to the office while the idea is still hot." She kissed him. "See you."

The door closed behind her, leaving him alone.

"We'll get you no matter where you hide," Michael said to himself.

Chapter 12

West of New Orleans, in the former state of Louisiana

"Are you ready?" the older man asked.

"I guess I'll never really know until I step out. . . . I feel ready. Here goes."

The younger man walked out of the room where he and the older man had been praying for quite some time. He strode down the corridor with a book under his arm, passed through another door and out onto a stage. When he looked out, he could see several hundred faces.

The crowd grew silent when he walked across the stage. He cleared his throat, feeling a bit intimidated as he stepped up to the podium.

"Good evening," he said into his microphone. "I have to admit to being surprised at seeing how many of you came this evening. The grapevine must work pretty well in this neighborhood." A ripple of laughter passed through the audience.

"I want to start off by saying I know almost everyone here must think of themselves as 'spiritual' or they wouldn't have come to hear some nobody talk about God. The first, and most important question, though, is: Are we thinking of the same God?

"You might be thinking, 'What's he mean by that? We gather regularly with others for a shared spiritual life, we pray, we sing.'

"What I mean, though, is just that. Do you and I worship the same God? I don't know what you believe . . . I'll tell you what I believe.

"I believe in the Father, the Almighty. I believe in His *only begotten, resurrected son, Jesus Christ.* I believe in the Holy Spirit. I believe what this book says." He held up a Bible. "Not just part of it, all of it.

"Now I know many, in an attempt to rationalize the events of the last few years and still 'hang onto' their faith, have come to think of this as a book of stories, or past history, or a symbolic book with mystical but not literal meaning . . . .

"If that were so, then I would say it was a piece of trash." He tossed the book down, startling the audience. "I mean, think of it logically. Why order your life around something unless it's true? Why revere a book claiming to tell you about the only Way to life, if it doesn't?

"You might say it has rules we should all follow. . . . Why? To be enlightened? . . . To have a better life next incarnation? To be socially acceptable?"

He looked out at the people before slowly leaning down, picking up the book, and holding it out to them. "Look at this book. Read it. The whole thing points to *one* man. Not one of 'many enlightened men,' but *the* man who came as *God wrapped in skin.* Not one in a line of men who were possessed by a 'Christ spirit' as some would say. . . . Not merely one of God's messengers, but a man who claimed to be one-of-a-kind. No *honest* student of this book can mingle it with anything else. Either you believe Jesus came to us as God with eyes and ears and hands—the way this book says it—or you don't. Either Jesus' words are true, or they have no value in *any* religion. . . . There really is no middle ground. . . . Jesus asserted His deity, lordship, and kingship. He claimed to be the visible image of God—the same in nature, authority, and power. The leaders in the temple demanded Jesus' blood because He said these things.

"Jesus was more than one who just *showed* the way, He said 'I *AM* the Way!' He didn't claim to merely be a *light bearer,* He said 'I *AM* the Light.' He didn't say He would help us figure out life, He said, "I *AM* the Resurrection and the Life.'. . . These are huge claims. If they are false, the man was a megalomaniac on a major scale. If he was so deluded, why would you listen to *anything* he said? Why keep a book which points entirely to Him and says all His words are true?

"In the Universal Global Wholeness Church, domes have fused the identity of the Living God with the gods of other people. And their description of this . . . generalized 'god' can be as encompassing as 'the Universal Oneness' or as simple as 'self.' Whatever works for you! It's okay! . . . Even Jesus, the prophet, or Jesus a temporary 'aspect' of the conglomerated god is welcome . . . just as long as He isn't the Jesus who said, 'No one comes to the Father except through me.'

"Consider this a moment," the speaker said, setting down the Bible and slowly pacing around the stage. "What is the point of homogenized religion anyway? They say, 'It's all the same . . . the different beliefs are like spokes on a wheel . . . all going to the same center. It's all the same, essentially. . . . Well, okay, it's sort of the same, even if the writings of these religions go in different directions. . . .'" The speaker shrugged. "'Well, maybe it's not the same,' they admit, 'but this way makes everything equal.'"

"So, the central purpose for homogenized religion is *equality,* is it? . . . Let's explore that idea for a moment. *Is* making everyone say that 'all religions are the same' a way of making all religions equally *valuable,* of raising them to the same height?" He raised one hand, then the other. "Or is it," he said, lowering both his hands, "a means of making all religions and gods of NO value, all equally *de*valued? . . . Think now. You're being encouraged to have a 'spiritual life'— as long as your god isn't supreme—as long as he, she, or it— isn't a cut above the rest.

"If you believe the claims of Jesus, if you accept His resurrection, you make Him singular, extraordinary . . . unique." The speaker raised an eyebrow and smiled. "The problem is that the 'tolerant' can't allow that which is unique or above the rest."

The man stood silently for a few seconds before saying, "But, Jesus' claims, His life, and His works *are* unique . . . so that leaves you with a choice."

"Tonight I say what Joshua said to the people thousands of years ago: '. . . choose this day *whom* you will serve. . . . But as for me and my house, we will serve the Lord.'"

There arose shouts and applause. To his great surprise, only about fifteen people got up and left.

He held up his Bible again, "And that brings me back to this book. How many of you have read it? All of it?" About half of the audience responded.

"How many have read it in the last . . . oh say . . . two years?" Many of the hands went down.

"Well, if you want to believe what something says, I suggest you not only read it, but start trying to remember it. Dig around in your books and find it. If you don't have one, *get* one. Because soon it will disappear from stores and your dome."

A lady in a front row seat stood and said, "I've been a Christian since I was a young girl and I've belonged to my dome since way back when it was a church. . . . Are you telling me I have to leave it?"

"I can't tell you where to go—or not to go. But if you are hungry for the God I speak of, look at your dome and ask yourself if He is Lord—and I mean *Lord*—there."

A man in the back of the crowd called out a question. "Do you think that the code they want us to take is the forbidden 'mark' spoken of in Scripture?"

All eyes riveted on the speaker. Would he dare say it?

He didn't flinch. "Well, sir, what I *think* isn't the issue here. Although I *think* it is, I *could* be wrong. The anti-Christ might not show up for another thousand years! All this could just be a shadow of things to come. The real issue, though, is what you have to say in order to get a code. You must say that Jesus is not the savior of the whole world, that you don't need Him to be *your* savior . . . in essence, that you are willing to classify Him as a famous myth among all myths. Code or no code, threat or no threat, a believer should never be willing to deny Jesus."

There was silence as he opened his Bible and said, "Will you please turn with me to John 3:16?"

After a short pause, the man began reading, "'For God so loved the world that He gave His one and only Son, that whoever believes in Him shall not perish but have eternal life.'

"Sadly," the speaker interjected, "Most people never read the next verse: 'For God did *not* send his Son into the world to condemn the world, but to *save* the world through Him.'"

The man let his eyes sweep over the people. "You see, the world and everything in it was already engulfed in death when Jesus stepped into time. This world and everything in it was already doomed to destruction. Jesus didn't come here to bring death, He came to rescue us! *Jesus is Life!* To accept Him is to accept everlasting life, to reject Him is to remain in the grip of the world . . . in the grip of death."

So began the first night of a two-week engagement for the speaker. Each night, he came out and saw larger crowds. He had no idea so many people were so hungry to hear the message he'd been given.

At the end of each evening, he would say, "The Word of God can divide light from dark, life from death. The Word of God is living and active and sharper than a double-edged sword, penetrating even to dividing soul and spirit, able to judge even the thoughts and attitudes of the heart. Remember, *the Word of God* is your sword!"

In the days to come, his real name would be unknown to many who heard him speak. Most would know him simply as Swordsman.

Chapter 13

Little Valley Refuge, southwestern region of the former state of Missouri

In the Northern Zones

Hundreds of miles from the nearest inhabited city, three women stood in the fading light. The sun would soon set behind them, but a signal from a lookout said the travelers would make it home before dusk. The women stood at the base of the incline talking quietly, their eyes constantly scanning the rocky ridge above them. Two of the women had dark hair, the third member of the little group appeared much younger and had long, strawberry- blond hair.

"I see someone!" Amanda, the youngest one, exclaimed quietly.

"Oh, me too!" Rosa said, squinting. "Several people." She willed her eyes to focus farther, to catch more detail. Was one of them much taller than the rest? Yes. Even though he'd lost 60 pounds, his large 6-foot-4-inch frame and dark skin made him easy to spot in a crowd. She could clearly make out her husband walking along with the rest of the travelers. "I can see all of them now," she said.

"Mandy, would you go tell everyone?" the other woman asked the girl.

More than anything, Amanda wanted to welcome the travelers. Jason had been her closest friend ever since they'd both been adopted into Rosa and Ricky's family at a quarantine camp. In fact, up until Jason left on this trip, she'd spent time with him every day for more than a year. How glad she would be to have him back.

Rosa saw the look in the girl's eyes. "See? He's okay. They'll all be down here in just a few more minutes."

Amanda nodded, then turned and sprinted toward the main camp. At least she'd be the bearer of good news. The two women, Rosa and, Jen, started up the slope to meet the approaching group.

Earlier in the day, a guide ran into the camp with word that Jason, Troy and the other travelers had encountered trouble about fifteen miles away. Rosa's heart skipped around in her chest when the guide told them the story.

"Yesterday morning," he told Rosa and her husband, Ricky, "two rangers up in the hills spotted a pair of blinkers tracking us. The rangers lost sight of them in the steep terrain and trees, so they decided to join us, thinking they might protect us from a possible ambush. About a half hour after that, it happened."

The guide said he didn't know who shot first. During the battle, both blinkers were killed and one of the rangers, a woman, suffered two gunshot wounds; one bullet went clear through her right calf, the other grazed her left arm. Within minutes of the battle, the uninjured ranger headed into rough country, saying he'd try to draw off any other blinkers who might be in the area.

"Jason and the rest of us," the guide told them, "carried the injured woman to a cave, where Jason tended her wounds. We all waited in the cave for the rest of the day and last night, hoping to stay hidden from any immediate surveillance sweeps of the area. This morning, the group sent me on ahead to tell you they're on their way, but it'll be slow going with the wounded ranger."

Upon hearing this, Ricky and another man, Bill, quickly threw a few supplies together and set out with the guide to find the travelers. They hoped to bring everyone back before dark.

Now, with the sun completely below the rim of mountains behind them, Rosa and Jen continued their climb to meet the returning group. They kept a rapid pace, even on nearly vertical parts of the landscape, grabbing onto roots and rocks along the way. At forty-five, nearly fifteen years older than Rosa, Jen could still match her friend stride for stride. Rigors of life in the wilderness had made them both very fit.

Although hurrying, neither woman wanted to appear panicked. Children, waiting to welcome Jason and Troy home from their first journey south, might be watching from a distance.

As soon as she thought she could be heard, Rosa called out to her adopted son first. "Jason? Are you all right? Troy? Are you okay?"

Jason nodded and gave her a tired wave.

"Yes, we're fine," Troy answered.

She could see the faces of everyone but the woman on the stretcher now. All of them looked haggard and her husband looked concerned. Was it the seriousness of the ranger's injuries, or was it something else?

Ricky hastened ahead of the small group and closed the distance to the women, skidding on the steep terrain several times before reaching them. He took no time for a greeting. "We may need to consider hiding the woman in the tank," he said quietly.

"You sure?" Jen asked.

He turned to look at the approaching group. "I'm not so much concerned with her injuries. She'll recover. I just don't know how much we can do for her, other than hide her." He took his eyes off the approaching travelers to look back at the pair of women. "You'll see what I mean when you meet her. We may need to get her completely out of sight. Only God knows." He looked directly at Jen. "Meanwhile, can you run ahead and get the lights going? We'll need a full kit, and anything you have for wound care."

She began her descent. "I'm on it."

Ricky turned to his wife. "Make sure all the little ones are in."

Rosa nodded, and he started to move away, but she grabbed his hand. Ricky turned to face her, and she gazed up at him for a moment. Silver hairs at one of his temples zigzagged like lightning bolts through his black hair. *He shouldn't have silver hair so soon, she thought.* She reached up and smoothed one of the lightning bolts. "It will be well, *mi amor,*" she said to him.

The expression on his face relaxed, and he leaned down to kiss her on the forehead. "Yes. You are right. It will be well."

At the bottom of the hill, Jen hurried toward the refuge, an encampment consisting of several small cabins, one larger cabin, and a number of tents sprinkled around an open area in the center. When she passed by one of the tents, she called to Amanda and Dori to come help turn the cranks on the small lights in the "hospital tent."

While she moved along, Jen considered what might happen with the wounded fighter. Would they need to keep her in the tank? Only the oldest teens and the adults—all permanent members of the group—knew about the bunker they called "the tank."

When they first migrated into the area, just before winter, Jen discovered a woman near death in the woods. A tree had fallen on the woman in a sudden storm, trapping her in a running stream of melted snow for hours.

After dragging her to dry ground, Jen wrapped a coat around the dying woman and held onto her. The woman spoke of a husband who had been killed by foreign soldiers months before, leaving her to survive by herself in this vast wilderness. Years ago, the couple had buried a huge survival bunker not far away in the side of one of the hills surrounding a shallow, cup-shaped valley. They had every intention of hiding there when "the end of the world" came, and believed they'd become pioneers in the times to follow. What a bitter irony, the woman observed, to have survived the worst, but end up alone. Before breathing her last breath, she told Jen how to find the hidden entrance to the bunker.

When the group located the large, buried cylinder, they found its chambers stocked with canned goods and preserved foods which would have lasted the couple for as many as ten years. Along with the food were weapons, ammunition, medical supplies, a small library of how-to books, water purifiers, bags of seeds for future planting, and items such as hand-cranked radios and lamps which never needed batteries. Deciding to keep the location of the bunker a secret, the group set up their camp down in the valley below it. During the winter that followed, supplies from what they dubbed "the tank" had made a huge difference in their quality of life.

Jen frowned. Now they'd have to be willing to hide the wounded woman there. Once the ranger felt well enough to leave, might she bring others back to loot it? Within seconds, Jen scolded herself. Neither the tank nor the provisions in it were the result of their own labors. Only the One who had brought them this far could decide how to use the tank or the things in it. Tonight, they'd ask Him what to do.

Elsewhere in the refuge, Rosa tried to settle the children down for bed in a cabin crammed with sleeping mats. Unaware of their adopted brother's troubles, they'd all excitedly anticipated Jason's return from the South. Most of them had been fantasizing for weeks about the little surprises the travelers might be bringing home.

"Did Jason bring anything for *me*?" four-year-old Angela whispered to her mother.

"It's late now, *mami*," Rosa said softly. She knelt and opened up the covers so her daughter could snuggle in next to a sleeping toddler. "Tomorrow we'll open everything up and have a look."

"Why can't we do it now?" Angela asked, large brown eyes shining in the dim light.

Rosa gave her a slightly scolding look. "It's late now. Those things will wait until tomorrow."

Angela's lower lip hovered near a pout. She reached under her pillow to find the remnants of a rag doll and nestled it near her chin. She didn't love old Molly Dolly as much as she used to, but her interest in the toy was rekindled recently when her little brother, Daniel, started clinging to it. Alternating between taunting him with the doll and snatching it out of his grasp had been her main preoccupation the past few days.

"Big girls," Rosa said, tucking the covers around her daughter, "learn to wait . . . and they learn to share." She leaned close, "Now, give me *un beso* and go to sleep."

After Angela kissed her, Rosa roamed the room looking for other children who needed a last tuck in or one more good-night kiss. She knelt down to cover up 6-year-old Dylan.

"Tell me the five-egg story," he pleaded in a whisper while holding up five fingers. "Tell me how the eggs fed lots and lots of people."

Several little heads turned expectantly. Their eyes focused on Mama. She suspected a ploy to remain awake. "I can tell you. Tomorrow."

"In the morning? First thing? Will you tell us then?"

"Yes, will you tell us then?" small voices repeated.

Rosa smiled and looked at them. "Why?"

Dylan sat up. "What if Jason's packs were too small to carry everything? What if he *forgot* somebody? Would God put more things in there? Enough for *everybody*?"

Many of the little ears in the room now strained to hear the answer. She had to admit, he had a point. How much could be in those packs? Yet, little Dylan had already connected this with what he'd been told about five eggs during the great migration.

"It's late," Rosa said. "Tomorrow, I will tell you all the story of the five eggs. But, we can pray right now about Jason's packs because Father God cares about *everything*."

Several children sat up.

"Everybody lie down, first," she admonished. They all complied before she continued. "Okay. Dylan, you pray."

"Oh Lord," he said in a fervent tone. "Help Jason's packs to have things for *everybody*. Just like the eggs You made into more for everybody to be able to eat them. Amen."

Rosa and the other children added their amens to the prayer. After giving a few instructions to fourteen-year-old Eli, she left the cabin.

A few small solar-battery powered lamps, obtained a month ago via a barter, enabled her to thread her way through the encampment. She stopped to speak with several adults before she located Jason, who sat with Amanda on the ground near the "large" cabin where more than half of the people from the refuge had spent the past winter. When he saw Rosa, he stood up and let her hug him.

"I'm so grateful you made it home safe," she said.

"Yes," he answered, in a tired voice. "Me too. . . . The things we brought back are over at Troy's. Do you want to go and see them?"

She could see Jason and Mandy wanted to catch up on current events. After giving him one more quick squeeze. she said, "Tomorrow will be soon enough. Tonight we'll just be happy you're home."

Stepping away from them, Rosa could hear Jason saying, "You wouldn't believe how hard and sad most of the people look. And they're still afraid to spend too much time out-of-doors . . ."

In the hospital tent, Ricky and Jen finished dressing the visitor's wounds. Bill, a quiet man in his late fifties, sat nearby, observing the activities.

The ranger held her jaw clamped shut through the entire procedure. Her wounds were banging away like sledgehammers, even *before* they'd been touched. She'd been around and experienced enough injuries to be concerned about her leg.

"Sorry," Jen said to her. "All we have is a topical painkiller. I packed some around the wounds, and it should start helping a bit."

"I'll do okay," the ranger answered grimly, fearing if she looked at all vulnerable, they might want to pray—*again.* She'd had enough praying and talk of God in the past two days to last her into the next century.

At the same time, Jen noted the hard countenance of the woman who had chosen to live the life of a resistance fighter. "I'm sure you'll do fine," Jen said softly. "Jason did an excellent job of stitching you up."

The ranger exhaled and nodded. "Good kid. Kept a cool head. We could use someone with his skills in our outfit. Our medic got killed about a week ago."

"Excuse us for a sec." Jen said before she and Bill went to confer in the corner of the tent about the mixture of the ointments and poultices they would use. While they did so, Ricky hoisted the ranger up and placed her on a cot. Next, he eased several pillows behind her before carefully propping up her wounded leg. He asked her to lie still while he took her pulse. Much to her surprise, the throbbing pain soon began to ebb.

Having finished his consultation with Jen, Bill moved to the end of the cot, took the boot off her good foot, then placed it with its mate. Looking at her footgear made the ranger wonder where the rest of her gear had gone. Did they have her pack and her rifle? Would they give them back?

Jen approached her with a cup of warm liquid saying, "Here's a little tea. It'll help your immune system."

The ranger eyed the cup and sniffed the steam wafting over the rim before taking it. Cautiously, she took a sip, then another, before chugging down the rest of the cup. "Thanks," she said, wiping her mouth and handing back the cup.

Looking at Jen's clean, soft hand grasping the cup, the ranger realized how grime, pressed into the creases of her own weather-beaten face and hands, probably made her appear centuries older by comparison. Even Ricky and Bill, still wearing the same clothes they'd trekked in all day, didn't have the sweat and dust of a two-hundred-mile-forced-march on them. She also noticed Jen's clean brown hair, cut just above the shoulder. It made her want to rake fingers through her own oily, blond crew cut. She looked at Jen and said, "Maybe I could wash up tomorrow?"

Jen set the cup on a nearby stand. "Sure. We probably have a spare set of clothes for you, too."

Bill leaned forward. "I forgot to introduce you two earlier. That's Jen—short for Jennifer. Jen, this is Sam."

"Hey," the ranger said.

"Is Sam short for Samantha?" Jen asked in a friendly tone.

"I'm just Sam."

Jennifer nodded. "Sure."

More out of habit than mistrust, Sam's hazel eyes swept over the tent at regular intervals. Her caretakers, while thin, all appeared to be in good shape. The oldest one, Bill, had the air of someone who had been in an upscale profession before all this. The tall guy, the one they called Ricky, was missing half a finger and she wondered how he'd lost it. Fighting perhaps? The man's sheer size and sinew would make him a formidable opponent in hand-to-hand combat.

The ranger cleared her throat. "I'll be out of your way as soon as I can get around. My partner will probably come for me in a week or two."

"How does he know where to look?" Bill asked.

"He knows. We figured you were up here somewhere, and he's the best tracker there is."

Bill sat on a stool, resting his forearms on his knees. "Do you think troops will be looking for you?"

Although she'd normally want to minimize the danger, for some reason, Sam felt compelled to warn them. Perhaps hearing the sounds of children in other tents made her more aware of the group's vulnerability.

"It's possible. They may decide to do a big sweep. . . . They've been nailed in this vector twice in the past week," she said. "My partner took all the precautions he could, though. He plugged out the two blinkers—" Sam stopped, and reassessed her words. Who knew for sure what might offend these people? She scrounged for terms which wouldn't seem so crude. "My partner took the chips out of the dead soldiers and buried the bodies before he took off. That may or may not work."

"What do you mean?" Bill asked.

Sam thought a moment. However unlikely it seemed, perhaps these people had somehow eluded troops all this time. Maybe they weren't up on the latest technologies.

Ricky sat quietly, watching the exchange between the ranger Jen, and Bill.

"Internationals," Sam explained, "implant their soldiers with special chips. *Their* chips emit longer-range signals. That's why we call 'em 'blinkers.' Global positioning devices can locate the signals anywhere on the planet. If we left the chips in the bodies, their buddies could track in on them in no time."

Jen frowned. "But, if your friend took the chips, won't they know where to find *him*?"

Sam closed her eyes and pictured it. For a moment, it was as if she were moving right alongside him. She lost all thought of her predicament or even her hosts. The satisfaction of revenge and the thrill of frustrating the enemy's search began pulsing through her veins, overriding any other sense. A smile came to her cracked lips.

"That's kinda the point," she said. "Any technicians who might be scanning for blinkers would see continuing movement and, hopefully, think those two were still alive and on patrol. Once my partner gets to some really inaccessible spot, he'll disable the signaling devices, then leave. If troops are dispatched to investigate, they'll go to the location where the signals stopped. It might take 'em a couple days to get to the area, then search it."

Sam opened her eyes, but they remained focused far away. "Even if, for some reason, they decided to devote some satellite time to the search, it could give us an advantage. Whenever we can get their satellites looking in the wrong spot, it gives us a window to do *other* things undetected."

"This is a game to you?" Jen asked.

Sam's reverie came to an abrupt end, and her weathered face hardened. "No ma'am. This is war. We do whatever will give us an edge. *Somebody* has to fight them." Once again, her eyes swept over her caretakers. How stupidly naive they'd been to bring her here. They could all be killed for helping her.

Perhaps her luck would hold, and the best-case scenario would play out. Didn't the other guys in her unit always say she was like a cat with nine lives? Besides, if troops actually showed up, she could crawl out into the forest and survive for days without *anyone's* help.

She tried to soften her tone. "Don't worry. The two we bagged didn't have radios with them, so they weren't in voice contact with others. While they may have been on some sort of patrol, it's more likely they were looking for personal opportunities. When they saw your little group, they probably decided to ambush them and keep whatever they could stash or carry for themselves. It's something they wouldn't do if they thought they were being heavily monitored. And, if things have gone according to plan, their superiors are just now figuring out somebody's missing. Chances are fifty-fifty they'll assume these two deserted and just stick their names and descriptions on a 'wanted' list."

She'd said all there was to say. She closed her eyes, hoping they'd take a hint and leave her alone.

"It's been a long day. You must be hungry," Ricky said. "Someone will bring food to you shortly. Then you can rest."

"I'd appreciate it."

Ricky stood up. "Good night."

Jen and Bill stood with him and stepped outside the doorway of the tent. As they exited, a woman entered with a piece of bread and a wooden bowl containing soup for the ranger.

Once she'd received it, Sam eagerly downed the hot food—a rare commodity for someone on the run. Heat, smoke, and scents of warmed food could be detected for miles. A ranger wouldn't often take the risk of cooking.

Was it the soup? The tea? The warm blanket? The long days and nights with so little rest? Soon, despite her pain, the ranger could barely hold her eyes open. Would she be safe if she fell asleep? Could these people fend off an attack with so few weapons? Her training and discipline mattered less with each passing moment. She finally succumbed to exhaustion and fell into a deep sleep.

Fifty yards away, people gathered for their nightly meeting in the center of the camp. Most of them sat on stools or on the grass. Hand-cranked lamps on poles gave them a bit of light under the big dipper, which hung directly above them in the sky. Dreaming of tomorrow's treasures, small children slept nearby, serenaded by crickets chirping in a continuous open-air concert. Of all those gathered, none of them questioned the decision to bring the injured woman to the refuge. They did, however, need wisdom in deciding what to do with her.

###

Hours later, Sam slowly opened her eyes. How long had she been sleeping? Her arm and her leg felt as if hot coals rested on them. Someone had doused all the lights in the tent, but she could see something very bright outside the opening. What was it? An immense column of flame, rotating like a blazing tornado from the open area of the camp. She could hear the roar of the fire. And something else. Different voices, taking turns, talking to someone.

Sam's thinking abruptly shifted from curiosity to alarm. *Are they all* crazy*? The light of such a bonfire would reflect on clouds and be visible for 50 miles or more! Satellites are probably tracking onto the heat signature even now! Every blinker within five vectors will be coming to kill us!*

She needed to get off the cot. She had to get away! "They're not going to get me," she managed to mumble. She tried to sit up, but a firm hand on her shoulder gently held her down.

"You're okay," a voice said. "You're okay, Sam. No one will harm you. Be at peace."

The words seemed to strike her like shock waves. She couldn't fight them. She lost consciousness.

###

Out in the open area of the encampment, people stood with arms and faces uplifted—laughing, crying, calling out, wanting to be completely engulfed by the presence which had become visible, tangible, and consuming.

Chapter 14

A suburb of Atlanta

The three Newsomes, Leon Sr., Deana, and Leon Jr. sat around the table and talked. Jessica and the housekeeper, Edwina, had gone to bed, allowing the three of them to linger into the early hours of the morning.

Home on leave, their son had only three days left before he would return to the academy. His first few days in the house had proven to be quite a strain on his parents. Leon Jr. seemed so different, so distant. He felt he "had to" be brutally frank about their faults and habits, which created more than a few tense moments. But after Leon and Deana talked it over, they realized some of the tension came from the fact their little boy had grown up. They were having trouble seeing him as an equal with his own views and rights. After they recognized this, they tried to give Leon Jr., or Lee as they'd always called him, as much respect as they would another adult, and things seemed to flow easier.

They felt a tremendous amount of pride for Lee. He'd gotten honors at school again this year and been selected out of thousands of others to be in an elite branch of a new, multination military force called the Universal Legion.

Leon Sr. sat back for a moment, watching his son and wife in the midst of an animated discussion. They were so much alike. Both were opinionated, zealous, and very intelligent. They even looked alike and had many of the same expressions and gestures. Somewhat amused, Leon Sr. only shook his head.

"Mother," Lee said earnestly, "you can live your life in a spiritual void if you want to, but there is so much more to be had if you would only grasp it. I mean, sure, you have all this, and you even have your own . . ." he said, then leaned in to whisper in her ear.

"*Lee!*" she said. "You don't have to be quite so explicit. Besides," she said more quietly, "she might hear you."

"So what? I'm not trying to be racist, Mom. But anyone who is willing to grovel around and eat the crumbs of life when they can have so much more is either sick or hiding something. We have black people at the academy, but they're different. They've made something of themselves. They'd call that woman the same thing I do."

Deana interrupted him. "It took me a long time to find someone as good as she is with Jessica, and I don't want her to quit, so please indulge me by keeping that opinion to yourself."

"And that's another thing," he took a breath as if waiting a moment before reciting a prepared speech. "Look at Jessica. Why do you let her stay like that?"

"What do you *mean*?" Leon Sr. said in an irritated tone. "What are we *supposed* to do with her?"

Ignoring his father, Lee directed his reply to his mother. "Here is the essence of what I've been talking about all evening, Mom. If you deal with everything on a strictly physical plane, you're going to have to cope with a lot of failure. . . . More could be done for her."

"In what way?" Deana asked.

"Mom, think back to when you were a girl. Your family belonged to the Transpersonal Thought Church didn't they?"

"Yes."

"Didn't you ever see miracles happen? Wasn't there any power in what you believed?"

"Well . . . I don't know. I saw things, but I never quite believed."

"But it's *true*," Lee broke in, "It can happen. There's power to be had. It works, Mom, I've seen it. It may be somewhat different from what you were taught, but it works on the same 'thought-power' principles that have been present throughout the ages."

"So what are you saying? That Jessica could be healed by this?"

Leon Sr. stood. "If you'll excuse me, I'm getting really tired and I have to work tomorrow. . . . Good night." He leaned across the table and kissed Deana. Their eyes made contact for a brief moment and she saw a warning look in his eye.

"Good night, Dad." Lee said.

"Good night, Son." he said, rubbing him on the shoulder. "See you tomorrow."

Once the door closed, Lee looked at his mother. "It's mostly his fault, you know."

"What a thing to say! We've tried to give you some room for your opinions, but we can't turn our lives upside-down just because you're convinced of this or that. How about giving us some room?"

"But why should you live in a spiritual void simply because he's blind? Admit it. Isn't there an emptiness in your life sometimes? Especially when you look at that girl upstairs?"

Tears stung Deana's eyes, and she shook her head yes.

"Come out with me tomorrow night, Mom. We'll go to a dome. . . . Have you been to the one near here?"

"No."

"Then come with me. What've you got to lose? It can only enrich your life as a person, as a mother, and as a world citizen. After all, you signed the Notice of Allegiance. This is what it's all about. Striving for the benefit of humanity, helping the government to function, becoming a part of everything, affirming the new life, and dedicating yourself to what is to be. Come with me and you'll see. . . . Okay?"

Chapter 15

Little Valley Refuge in southwest Missouri

Sam's eyes popped wide open when she heard people passing by the tent, talking. She jolted before she recognized her surroundings, then relaxed again. Judging by all the brightness, the sun had been up for hours. She swallowed a few times before saying, "What a weird dream."

Jennifer moved closer to the cot. "What?"

The ranger rubbed her forehead with her good hand. "Oh. Sorry. I was talking to myself. Had a really strange dream last night. I saw a . . . never mind." She looked suspiciously at Jen. "Maybe it was that strange tea you gave me."

Jen smiled and sat down next to the cot. "Not likely. We don't make 'strange tea' here."

"Are you going to move me someplace else today? I heard some of them talking about me yesterday."

Her caretaker exuded cheery assurance. "Nope. You're safe right here with us." She pointed to Sam's bandages. "Change of subject. How are the arm and the leg?"

Sam held still for a moment, thinking, then looking confused. "Actually," she said, "they don't hurt." She slowly lifted her bandaged arm and flexed it. Next, she moved her leg slightly and rotated her foot around. She sat up and stared at Jen. "This is really weird."

"Let's see. Give me your arm"

The patient held out her arm while Jennifer removed the bandage layer by layer. Once the last of the dressing came off, they both surveyed the poultice Jen made the night before. The brown glob completely covered the wound Jason had stitched together.

Jen approached it with a large pair of tweezers, Sam turned her face away and steeled herself for the pain. Jen slowly eased the glob away, then said, "Well, will you look at that!"

Sam turned to see the poultice and noted rows of threads sticking out of it. "What are those?"

"Your stitches."

Sam's eyes shot down to her arm. Only a stripe of new, pink flesh revealed the location of her wound.

Sam whispered, "Is that possible?"

Jen's eyes shone. "Obviously it is. Let's see the leg."

When the last wrap came off her leg, Sam leaned forward to look. The swelling had gone down, and the wound appeared nearly healed. She hadn't planned on being able to move the leg, much less walk on it, for quite a number of days. Certainly not without a great deal of pain.

"Both of these injuries look like they've been healing for a week or more," Jennifer said.

"What's *in* that stuff?" the ranger asked.

"The same ingredients I always put in it. . . . But that's not what healed you. No poultice does this," Jen said. She studied the wound before looking back up at her patient. "Do you want to know what's really happened?"

Sam immediately stiffened and said, "I don't think so."

"Okay. . . . Stay here a minute and I'll go get you some clothes."

"Sure." The ranger rested her head back on her pillow, feeling a little scared, wanting to think of something else.

Elsewhere in the camp, Rosa pulled small objects out of the bags. Occasionally, Jason and Troy would consult each other before declaring the owner of the little prize. The atmosphere in the tent felt like Christmas. Of course, Rosa reminded herself, the little ones wouldn't remember Christmas like it used to be. And, to her, this seemed even better.

"*Ooooooooos*" and "*ahhhhhs*" went through the children as each gift– a finger puppet, a tiny toy frog that hopped, a plastic ring– was handed out to a happy recipient. Lastly, the older children, as a group, got a baseball—along with a surprise gift from the adults: Hand-sewn leather gloves of various sizes and a home-made bat. Everybody got something.

Once the children were allowed to go squealing out of the tent to play with their new possessions, Jason and Troy showed the adults the rest of the haul. The items from their packs included a ream of artificial paper, a box of pencils, a box of pens, 6 bolts of cloth, 100 skeins of thread, 3 packages of needles, 2 small pairs of scissors, 5 packages of assorted safety pins, 4 boxes of salt, 2 small tool kits, and 8 pairs of reading glasses.

In addition, the young men had small gifts for adult family members. Jason gave Ricky a thin, plastic magnifier to use in reading or for surgery. To Amanda, he gave a pretty, gold hair ribbon. To Rosa, he gave the candied orange slice, wrapped in a piece of gift paper and tied with a silver chord.

Although many of the things Jason and Troy lugged home were of considerable value, the packs carrying these items would have been ditched if, in dire circumstances, the boys had been forced to run. The young men's clothing, however, contained the most vital, valuable, and dangerous things. As the seams of their coats and vests were opened, letters from friends in the south and ninety-six very small Bibles were extracted. Many of the adults waited with as much anticipation as the children had shown.

After savoring the message from her dear friend, Rosa wiped her eyes, tucked the letter away and walked beyond the edge of the camp. Inside the little valley, adults moved with less caution than they'd use if they trekked over the hills into the dense wilderness surrounding them.

Behind a small stand of trees to the west of the camp was a good-sized pond. Occasionally, Rosa would go there alone when she needed a few moments of total privacy to think or pray.

From a distance, Jason saw Rosa slipping into the trees. Was she going to sit by the pond and savor the candied orange slice he'd given her? Her eyes had gotten a little sad when he gave it to her. What did that mean? Was she disappointed? Maybe the idea to get her just one slice had been a stupid one. Maybe he should have gotten her something else. Something better.

How could he ever thank Ricky and Rosa for all they'd done? Even when the disasters threatened to devour all life, they adopted him and the others, showing them how to face whatever might come.

Now seeing Rosa walking toward the trees, he had a strong urge to follow her. Part of him didn't like her going into the woods unescorted, the other part of him wanted very much to see if she liked her present.

Several times, he lost sight of her in the trees, but continued walking in the same general direction she'd taken. He slowed his approach to be as quiet as possible once he could see the water. Where had she gone? He stopped just short of a large tree. Perhaps, he decided, it was wrong to follow her anyway. He started to leave when he heard her voice and realized she was standing in front of the very same tree!

"I wanted to come and talk to You alone," she said. "Lord, You know my heart."

Now Jason felt like the worst kind of lowlife. He closed his eyes as his head slumped forward. Should he just let her know he was there so she wouldn't go on? Could he move away without her knowing? He chanced a peek around the tree and saw Rosa standing mere feet away, facing the water.

"Look at it," she said, reaching into her pocket. "Isn't this beautiful? Isn't it delightful? And the smell . . . oh, the smell." She held it to her nose and inhaled the fragrance. "You must have told him to buy this," she said, backing up a step.

Jason ducked behind the tree and held his breath. She remained silent for a few seconds.

"You know what Jason means to us, Father," she said. "It's hard to believe he's the same scruffy boy who gave Ricky such a hard time. He really is living proof of Your power to heal a shattered life. We both have come to love him so much, and we stand in awe of the wonderful man he's become."

Jason closed his eyes again and stood still. He wanted to move away but needed even more to hear her words. They were unsolicited, unrehearsed words. They were life, pouring into his soul.

"It was hard to let him go on this trip," Rosa continued, "but we're so grateful You led him back to us safely. . . . He and the others could have been taken or killed, but You shielded them. Thank You, Father. . . . They lugged all those things so far. And Jason brought this to me. It's almost scary—it's such a small thing . . . yet I'm holding in my hand something he risked his life to give."

Jason heard her sigh before she said, "Words can't describe Your greatness or Your beauty, Lord. Last night, You over-whelmed me. Never in my life have I wanted so much to give You something." She inhaled the fragrance of the orange slice one last time. "This isn't money or diamonds . . . but it's all mine—and it's very precious to me. And I'm giving it to You, Lord, with my prayer for Jason. May he love You all the days of his life, may he walk where You lead, and know a great reward in Your kingdom."

With those words, she threw the small gift out into the pond, then stood watching the ripples from it gently move out along the surface of the water. Jason pressed up against the tree when she turned and walked back through the trees toward the camp.

"Is everything okay?" Jennifer asked. She'd been standing outside a stall in the women's bath house for quite a while. "Do you need any help?"

"No!" came the terse reply. After that came several muffled remarks.

Jen started to speak again but stopped when the little door suddenly opened. Sam emerged, scrubbed, brushed and wearing a blue tunic with pants. Seeing the ranger like this left Jen speechless.

Sam shrugged and grunted, "I know. I feel as awkward as a cow with a crutch in this stuff." She clomped out of the bath house in the loose leather-and-wood clogs, leaning on a wooden cane they'd given her. "When do you think I can get *my* clothes back?"

"Uh, it may be a while. You remember they had to slit the leg of your pants and the sleeve of your shirt, don't you? Plus the bullet holes. And blood all over them."

"I had two other sets of clothes in my pack. Where's my pack?"

"It's in the tent. Nobody touched it other than to carry it here. If you want to get your things out, we can wash them . . . but it would be better if you didn't wear your uniform until you're leaving."

"I understand," Sam said before she stopped and wriggled around. "It's just that this stuff is so . . ." She couldn't seem to think of a term to describe her discomfort.

Jen nodded. "You've been a soldier for a while. Anyone would feel different. But, really, you look great. Ready for breakfast?"

"Yeah. I'm starved."

A beautiful day beckoned, so they sat on stools outside the large cabin eating a small breakfast while they talked.

"Been here long?" Sam asked.

"Since late last fall."

"You going to make this a permanent settlement then? Gonna build more cabins as the population grows?"

Jen looked around. "No. I don't think so. The cabins you see were built for the winter. Once the weather got better, we started spreading out into the tents. . . . It's funny. Years ago you couldn't have paid me to live in a tent. But now," she smiled, "as soon as the really cold weather stopped, I couldn't wait to get into one."

Sam squinted. "If you're not fighting the government and you're not making a settlement . . . what exactly *are* you doing out here?"

"We're raising a lot of orphaned children, we're finding people who need help, and giving them hope for the future."

Sam wanted to say, *What future?* but decided against the idea. Instead, she asked, "What made you want to do this?"

"Not what, but Who. For one reason or another, none of us made it south. We believe God let us escape the forced migration so we could serve Him up here."

Sam wiped her mouth with her hand, then almost wiped her hand on her pant leg. She looked up, frustrated.

Jennifer handed her a square of cloth. "Here's a napkin. Why are *you* still up here? Why are you a ranger?"

Even though she remained seated, Sam's body seemed to come to attention. "The blinkers and their whole . . . stinking government. Everyone should fight 'em."

"But why do *you* fight them?"

"During the disasters, they took my husband, my oldest son, and my sixteen-year-old daughter. I was out of the house searching for food when it happened. They took everybody but Chris, my youngest. I came home to find him alone." Sam vacantly stared into the distance. "After that, a survivor from a squad told me both my husband and my oldest son had frozen to death working over in Ohio. Later, I heard my daughter died of a fever . . . while locked in a brothel." The wooden plate slid off her lap, knocking over her cane. "Nothing I can do will ever finish paying them back for what they've done to me."

Jen leaned down and picked up the plate. Sam took a few deep breaths before looking at her and asking, "You ever been married?"

"Yes."

"Ever have kids?"

"No," Jen said softly. "When Carl and I found each other, we were already in our 40's. He was in the Army, I was a pharmacist. We were only married for 18 months when he was sent overseas. He died in the war. Syria. His remains were contaminated, so I never got them back."

Sam shrugged. "At least the government didn't *steal* him from you."

Jen sat motionless, obviously stunned by the remark.

"You can't know how I feel," the ranger explained. "I'll die fighting 'em and that suits me fine. All I want to do is kill as many of them as I can before I go."

"How sad," Jen said.

Sam glared back at her. "You holy people really frost me. It's rangers who make areas safe for you to live in. . . . What good has all your praying and singing done anyway? I don't think you're truly aware of how bad it's getting out there. . . . And stop looking at me like that!"

Jen leaned forward and spoke very clearly. "*God* is the one who has kept us alive, Sam. He's the one who's kept *you* alive. *He's* the one who's healing your wounds. Won't you just consider–"

"Oh please," the ranger said, grabbing her cane and rising to her feet. "I need some exercise and some air. Am I allowed to walk around?"

Jen looked down. "Just stay in the camp."

"Not a problem," Sam said, limping away.

###

An hour later, Jason spotted Rosa carrying a basket piled high with clothes of all sizes. She halted and set it down in order to pick up a small shirt she'd dropped.

"I'll carry that," Jason said, hurrying over and hoisting the basket. "Where are we going?"

"Now that I have more thread, the first order of business is repairs. The weather's so nice, I thought I'd sit under the canopy by the commons."

"I'll help you," he offered.

She tried to take the basket from him, saying, "Today's a day off for you."

He tightened his grip. "Today's supposed to be a day off for *everybody*. Remember?"

Rosa shrugged. "Well, the girls said they'd play with the children. I thought I'd *enjoy* sitting under the canopy and sewing."

"Okay. But let me carry this over for you." They started walking before he said, "Later this afternoon, Amanda and I are going to become coaches. We have to show our team how to play baseball. That'll be *my* fun for the day. . . . We've divided the kids into two teams. Ricky's team has already challenged us to a game before sunset."

She laughed. "You have no idea how Ricky has waited for this," she said, putting an arm around Jason. "You're the best, kiddo."

They arrived at the little canopy, and she seated herself before he set the basket near her chair. He got a stool for her feet while she extracted a skein of white thread from one pocket and the package of needles from the other. She chose a small needle and pinned it through her tunic before stowing the rest of them. Once she'd measured out some thread and bit it off, she looked over at Jason and said, "I haven't really had a chance to say thanks for the gift you brought me. You'll never know how much it meant to me."

He looked away and faltered, "Oh. I. . . . You're welcome, Rosa."

###

Late that afternoon, almost all the residents of the refuge gathered in the large open area they referred to as "the commons," hoping they'd see some baseball before dark. By the time the sun started inching toward the rim of the western peak, a tied score added to the first-game excitement. Jason's next batter was Daisy. The bases were loaded.

Rosa sat next to Ricky and his team on the right-hand side of the field, Jason and Amanda sat with theirs on the left.

Jennifer and Sam came to watch the game, seating themselves in the "spectator section" nearest to Rosa, but Jen cheered for both sides. Although no one forced her to attend, Sam sat on a small stool, looking about as happy as a truant who had been dragged to school.

"Strike two!" Bill called out.

"That's okay!" Jason yelled to his batter. "You'll get this next one, Daisy! Just keep your eyes on the ball."

Tiffany threw the next pitch underhanded, and Daisy swung at it. To everyone's amazement, she actually connected with the ball. It flew about thirty feet before it hit the ground, bounced once, and started rolling."

"Run! Run!" Jason and Amanda yelled in unison.

"Get it Kyle!" Ricky shouted. "Get the ball!"

As Daisy neared first base, Eric closed in on home. Infielder Kyle ran forward to scoop up the ball and missed it.

Jason jumped up and down waving his arms. "Run! Everybody, Run!"

Kyle kept chasing the ball, only to accidentally kick it further away. Eric made it home, Daisy looked at Jason who motioned her on, so she ran for second base. Nearly all the spectators rose to their feet.

Kyle finally caught up with the ball, then dropped it before tossing it toward first base. It fell short and bounced. As the first baseman made a diving catch, Tanya, from Jason's team, rounded third and continued toward home.

"Go! Go!" Amanda said, running alongside the girl.

"Throw it home! Throw it home!" Ricky shouted in the growing din.

Paul threw the ball to second, in time to snag Daisy.

Even though they couldn't hear him for the noise, Ricky continued, "Throw it home! Throw it home!"

Tanya crossed the home plate just before the ball arrived. Jimmy, the catcher, threw it to third where the baseman tagged Virginia out, ending the inning. Everyone cheered.

Kyle, the clumsy infielder, dejectedly walked toward the rest of his team. Ricky ran out to the boy. "That's okay! It's your first game! You're doin' *great* for your first game!" The huge smile on Ricky's face was so convincing, the boy brightened. Ricky scruffed up Kyle's hair and said, "That's it! Go get ready to bat!"

With his hundred-watt smile still glowing, Ricky gave instructions to his team, then trotted over to his place and sat down. Unable to contain his excitement, he gave his wife a quick squeeze and said, "Is this fun or *what*?"

She gave him a peck on the cheek. "Are you still a big kid or what?"

"Ohhhhh yeah. Wanna be a kid with me?"

"Sure. Where's my cotton candy?"

Eight-year-old Keesha, sitting on the ground in front of the couple, became filled with astonishment. She leaned between her adopted parents and asked, "You can make candy from *cloth*?"

"No," Rosa laughed. "It's a kind of candy people had in the old days. It was made from sugar but it *looked* like thread, spun round and round in big fluffy wads, and it came in pretty colors– like pink and blue."

"Really? What did it taste like?"

"Like a sweet cloud. But we don't really have any. I was just being silly with Papa."

"Oh. Then, can I have some cotton candy, too?"

"Of course you can!" Ricky said, pretending to hand some to Rosa, then to Keesha. "Just make sure you eat it slow. I wouldn't want you to get a tummy ache."

Keesha took a bite from her imaginary treat and chewed slowly. Ricky leaned close to his wife and whispered something in Spanish. She looked into his eyes and nodded.

Feeling like an eavesdropper, Jen leaned back and turned to her guest. "Do you think–" she began before noticing the stool next to her had been vacated. She stood up in time to see the ranger hobbling back toward the tents. Jen wove her way out of the surrounding crowd and trotted after Sam. "Are you okay?" she called out when she got closer.

Still limping toward the tent, Sam didn't turn around but answered, "I'm fine. I just need to lie down and put my leg up."

Concerned, Jen closed the gap between them. The ranger heard footsteps and stopped. Once Jen caught up, Sam said, "How do you stand it?"

Jen knew exactly what she meant. "You mean the pain of seeing couples, and children, and fun?"

A cheer went up in the field behind them.

Sam turned to face her. "Yeah. How do you stand it?"

"Everybody here has had to learn something," Jen responded. "No one has the right to be the shadow of death on someone else's joy. . . . Everyone here has lost parents or children or spouses or friends or all of them. Some have been tortured. Some of us have been raped. Should we punish each other and the children for these things? Should the kids feel rotten all of their days because the past hurt so much?

"*All* of us used to have so much compared to this. But it was never enough. Before the disasters, we were free to pray, or vote, or speak out against things we knew were wrong, but did we? When near-obliteration was right around the corner, some of us didn't care because we thought we'd be outta here. Others only thought about style and getting more stuff. . . . Now we're all stuck with the results of our selfishness and our mistakes. So what are we going to do about it? If the world goes on, what will we have given to those kids?"

Jen slowly stepped closer to Sam, continuing to express a lesson she'd learned in the midst of her own sorrow. "Life can't revolve around our pain, our losses, or even around the guilt of surviving when so many people didn't. Each of us has to stop being the center of a pity party and let *life* go on. It's about giving people faith and hope. . . . And, believe it or not, Sam, when you let yourself share other people's joy as if it were yours . . . it actually *becomes* yours." Jen reached over and put her hand on the ranger's shoulder. "It's not too late to– "

Sam pulled away so hard she, nearly fell down. "Stop it!" she cried, catching herself and then moving further out of reach. "You don't understand. Someone has to pay!" She moved as fast as she could toward her tent. "*Someone* has to pay!"

Chapter 16

Near the Gulf of Mexico in the former state of Texas

Fibertronics' V.P. of Public Relations, Alex Dubois, approached the door he'd first entered the night he'd been hired, and it opened. Only now, this door (and almost any door belonging to Fibertronics or its subsidiaries) unlocked with *his* code.

Always a man of means, he'd never lacked anything he truly wanted. The only way he could describe his life now, however, would be "total affluence." At first, he'd experienced fascination with the material things around him: The art, the opulent decor, the space, the food. At the same time, he had the sense it might be a bit of a waste for all this to be enjoyed by so few. Gradually, though, as the pressures of his position squeezed increasingly on his time and energy, he felt less amused and less guilty.

He'd been out of town for two weeks, so was unprepared for the change he saw when he entered the room where the fountain used to be. The fountain had been replaced by a copy of the now-famous YanYan sculpture with the despairing people inside it. Like the original, it had been lit, so flames seemed to eternally burn the occupants who reached out of its midst. Although he'd seen the sculpture on the news, he'd never actually taken the time to look at it. Doing so now gave him quite a disturbed feeling. He started reading the large plaque below it:

> Dedicated to Mother Earth
> And in memory of those who died so senselessly
> In Earth's final conflict.
> Let us never forget:
> without **RESTRAINT**, there was chaos . . .

He stopped reading and glanced at his watch. No time. He must move on. Walking around the statue, he picked up his pace and headed for the corridor on the other side of the room. Now, when he walked down this hall of artifacts, he no longer lingered to admire all the treasures behind the glass.

Gone were the feelings of gratitude and anticipation. Instead, a cloud of uneasiness seemed to abide here, waiting to settle on him, making him oblivious to the beauty nearby.

He made his way to the airlock, and blankly watched the metagram on the wall during his solitary ride. When he stepped out of the airlock, he looked around the Archive for a moment.

"Alex," John Klost said, walking toward him. "He wants you. On the phone."

Without being told, Alex knew to whom John referred and immediately felt adrenalin cascading through his body.

"Thanks, John, I'll head for my office now."

Once Alex stepped inside the door to his office, indirect lights behind screens along the walls came on, simulating early morning sunshine through curtained windows. Putting his briefcase down in a large leather chair, he walked around the desk, seated himself, then reached over to touch the pad activating his system.

He stopped and took a deep breath before allowing his finger to make contact with the pad. Was he ready? Yes. The computer screen and keypad lit up before he punched in his code for a direct linkup to the president's office.

It rang once. "Hello." Only the sound of the voice came through his speakers, no picture appeared on his screen.

In the six months he'd worked for Fibertronics, they'd never met or talked, but Alex would know this man's voice anywhere. The sound of it was forever imprinted upon his mind. On the leading edge of the disasters, and then in Earth's darkest hours, the media mogul regularly came on the air to appeal for restraint and reason. Throughout that horrible season, he became the common-man's advocate—unafraid of governments or threats—working to end the insanity that nearly blew everyone to bits.

"Hello, Mr. Kressman. Alex Dubois here. How may I help you, sir?"

"Oh good. Dubois. I would like to meet with you in two hours if your schedule permits."

"Certainly, Mr. Kressman. Two hours. No problem." Alex said, glancing at his watch.

"Then it's settled. I'll see you in two hours. John will bring you. Goodbye."

"Goodbye, Mr. Kressman."

The next two hours proved to be agonizing for Alex. He had scores of things to do, but he couldn't concentrate. He would be meeting and talking to one of the most . . . or maybe *the* most powerful man on earth.

As the time drew near, his stomach began to tie itself into knots. He actually feared he might vomit.

He heard a tone at the door, and John came in. "Ready, Alex?"

"Sure. Just let me get my briefcase."

"Sorry. If he wanted you to bring anything, he'd have said so."

"Oh," Dubois said lamely, "I see. Well, then I guess I'm ready."

Once they'd exited the office, John made for the air locks. Alex couldn't help asking, "Isn't his office here?"

"Actually, his office is anywhere he is. Right now, he's on land, so that's where we're going."

They passed through the air lock, occasionally making small talk until the ride ended. Upon exiting, they went in a direction Alex hadn't walked before, through a labyrinth of corridors. When they arrived at an elevator, John let Alex enter while he remained in the hall.

"Aren't you coming along?" Dubois asked.

"No. I have urgent work elsewhere. When you get to the top, you'll see which way to go."

John walked away as the elevator door closed.

As usual, Alex had no sensation of movement, but when the doors opened, he found himself looking at greenery of all kinds. He briefly considered how all of Kressman's elevators seemed to have the potential for this "Oz" effect. Until the doors opened, you couldn't be certain of your destination. He stepped out into a spacious room and looked high above him at the frosted acrylic ceiling, which let the light of day pour into the room, yet insured privacy.

He lingered a moment to admire the beautiful, tropical foliage and couldn't resist touching several plants. The cool, slick feel of the leaves said they were real. How long had it been since he'd seen a garden? He remembered why he was there and hurried down the path in front of him.

Once he began working his way through the plants, he realized he could hear the sound of water. Plants gave way here and there to stones of larger and larger size on either side of the pathway. Eventually, he walked between two good-sized boulders. He started to wonder how in the world they'd been transported to the top of the building when he heard Kressman.

"Good afternoon, Dubois."

To Alex's surprise, the corporate mogul stood there, very casually dressed, in a white turtleneck, loose-fitting white trousers . . . and white slippers. He was a bit older and smaller than Alex had imagined him.

In a protocol briefing for new employees, Alex had been told to *never* initiate physical contact with his employer. A "respectful, verbal greeting, offered in lieu of a handshake," would be expected.

"I'm honored you sent for me. How do you do, Mr. Kressman?"

"Quite well, thank you. Come sit down with me," his employer answered. He pointed to a footstool-sized rock, "You may sit there, if you'd like."

The rock had been placed near a spot where water washed over a large boulder into a pool of water. Alex seated himself, feeling a bit awkward. Kressman sat, Yoga style, on the sand floor near the edge of the pool, facing Alex. Although exquisitely landscaped, the space around them had none of the artifacts or works of art so prevalent in Kressman's other buildings.

"I come here to get away from it all," Kressman said. "It's one of my favorite places. It's tranquil and uncluttered. . . . And since—for obvious security reasons—I can no longer disappear into remote, unpopulated places, I allow myself this one luxury."

Alex noticed the slight accent in Kressman's near-perfect English. He wore no watch, but did have a sizable gold ring on his right hand, engraved with three interlocking triangles.

"I want to tell you," Kressman said, "at the outset of this meeting, that you may ask questions later. First, however, I want to tell you a bit about the past few years. It will give you a greater understanding of the goal for all my endeavors. Fair enough?"

Alex took his cue and nodded. "Fair enough."

His employer shared a brief time line. Several years before the disasters, he had purchased Global Viewcon

Systems, which owned Universal Information Group—the planet's largest news-gathering organization.

"Prior to the outbreak of the last war," Kressman said at one point in his discourse, "I sensed the coming danger. It was then I made the difficult decision to forsake my simple, private life to reach people with clear, basic guidance. It was either this, or know the guilt of un-involvement during Earth's darkest hour."

Among other things, the international corporate mogul recalled how he'd used television to spread his message of restraint, reasoning and justice. Why not use his vast influence for good?

"Then," Kressman continued, "during the horrors of all the contamination and the great carnage of the war, I decided to commit all of my skills, strengths, resources, and connections to unite the world in peace. . . . A lofty goal, but worth any price, no?"

Kressman stopped speaking, but Alex sensed this was not his opportunity to respond. Somehow, he knew the man wanted him to take a moment and ponder what had been shared. Only the sound of water cascading into the pool kept total silence at bay. After nearly a minute of this, Dubois watched his employer reach out over the pool of water. The man barely touched the surface with his fingertips, then closed his eyes and faintly smiled, as if he'd been softly caressed by a loved one. Alex continued to wait.

"Even before the disasters," Kressman finally said, "people had forgotten tranquility. All they knew was strife, greed, jealousy, and suspicion." He opened his eyes and moved his hand to a flat rock near the water's edge; then he touched his wet fingertips on it, leaving four distinct dots of water on the stone. Next, he dipped his index finger back into the pool, and used it to swipe across all the dots, making them a single trail of water.

"Unity of purpose and belief," he said in a soft voice, "were the only things that could raise humanity out of such a desperate situation. I'd already taken my case to the people with my media connections. Next, I'd win the reluctant governments who responded only to power. When so much of the Mid-East oil got vaporized, I seized the opportunity to use yet another tool destiny had already placed in my hand. I owned the rights to an oil-free source of energy—Fibertronics.

"The various heads of state quickly realized any nation without Fibertronics would find itself at an extreme disadvantage. To refuse it would be to stay in darkness while their neighbors obtained the ultimate in space-age technology. For governments, it became a choice of follow the path of unity, or be overpowered—if not by other countries, then by the disgruntled citizens of their own. In order to survive, they complied."

With his coat and tie on, the warm, still air and the humidity in the room were making Alex perspire. He didn't dare remove his coat though. Despite Kressman's informal appearance, it might seem too casual a thing to do. Dubois wiped a trickle of perspiration off his temple as he tried to concentrate on his employer's words.

"This was when we realized it was time for humanity to take the next step," Kressman said. "People needed to see the problems that using money creates. Money only brings about rates of exchange, which, in turn, brings about the problem of some nations regaining power over others. Why use currency at all? It's filthy, actually. Most people in civilized countries were ready for a total debit system anyway."

Alex's eyes again followed his employer's hand as it reached down to grasp the water-marked rock and drop it into the pool. "The idea isn't at all new," Kressman said. "Each person could be given a coded chip distinctly identifying him or her from anyone else. It's a flawless form of identification, buying, selling, licensing, and all record keeping. It creates order, security, and freedom all at the same time. Of course, we won't know *all* its benefits until everyone is coded and the interim cash is gone."

"And what was a dying world," Dubois dared to interject, "is finally transformed into a new era of civilization."

Kressman looked directly at him. "All in all, I think it's been a tribute to the resilience of humanity."

"And the incredible resolve of one man," Alex added.

"Well, actually," Kressman said, "I leaned heavily on the discoveries of other people and the existence, at the time, of rivalries between countries. I just sort of orchestrated the whole thing. I *am* a good organizer."

Dubois marveled at the humility this man possessed.

"And that brings us to where we are now, Alex, and how you figure in all of this; or, how I will lean on your talents."

It was almost too much to believe. E. E. Kressman wanted his help! Alex sat at full attention, waiting.

"As it stands," his employer stated in an urgent tone, "we have only about eighteen months before the full transfer date and we're a little behind schedule. We were doing quite nicely until the religious zealots started making trouble. As ridiculous as it sounds, they're claiming that getting coded is receiving a forbidden 'mark' mentioned in the Bible. After all this, after being proved wrong, they're still clinging to these obscure beliefs and fanatical practices. They're not only refusing to be coded, but are trying to convince others to refuse it.

"A year ago, there were scattered, small groups of fanatics who maintained a good deal of secrecy. They met mostly in homes and rural places. I insisted that the government slack off on them . . . I felt certain that, once they saw the world wasn't coming to an end and realized how wrong they'd been, they'd forsake their ignorant ways. Undecided people would be able to see our good intentions. . . . But now, the fanatics have taken advantage of the situation to come out into the open seeking converts." Kressman shook his head while spreading his hands in a questioning gesture. "What I find most alarming is that they're beginning to have some success!

"We've tried this past year to demonstrate patience, and appeal to reason, but obviously, this has not sufficed. We must change our tactics. We cannot allow the fanatics to create a parallel society. We must start a counter-campaign before they gain any more strength. We will take public attention away from *religion* and focus it on character and motives." Kressman stopped speaking and looked toward the path back to the elevator.

Dubois turned to see a man stepping quietly into the area where they sat. The worker handed Alex a small clip screen before silently treading away. The flat acrylic screen was not the usual 8-inch by 11-inch size. With the exception of a small metallic strip at the bottom, the screen was completely transparent. On either end of the metallic strip were small 360° toggle buttons. It was thinner than models he'd grown accustomed to using. As soon as he put his right thumb on the right toggle, the screen lit up.

"Feeding into the screen," Kressman told him, "you'll find a current list of their leaders in this country. Don't go over it now, but take the screen with you when you go. For security purposes, your code is the only one that will allow the screen to activate."

Alex took his thumb off the toggle, and the screen went blank before Kressman continued.

"First, we must gather and evaluate information about these people so we can mount a campaign, addressing specific points. You must find the areas where their ideas conflict with what can be clearly observed and then capitalize on it. Expose their failings. Fire up old rivalries. Get creative. Help undecided people see the error in the fanatic way. Let the fanatics know that, even though their false ideas have threatened our very existence, *we* want to validate life. We are willing to help them see the light and welcome them into the world family."

Kressman leaned forward. He wanted to make sure Dubois grasped the seriousness of the situation. "You *must* make them understand. We cannot permit them to unravel what we have accomplished. . . . All resources are at your disposal."

Alex felt the urgency. He nodded.

"When you return to your office," Kressman said, rising to his feet, "prepare to temporarily move your work to our central office near Dallas. You will be given access to the names and addresses of all employees who can assist you there, and the location of information banks to be tapped. Whenever your presence is needed here, you'll be given special transportation. Is this enough to start on?"

Alex stood. "Plenty, sir."

"And I want you to start today. All your other duties are to be delegated to others."

When Alex returned to his office, he read over the list of potential assistants. Most were men. At that very moment, he realized how tired he'd become of working with men. The world currently had a female overpopulation, yet it seemed as if all his co-workers were men.

He scanned the list again for female names. He picked one and typed her code into his keypad. The computer responded:

Linda Sue Posner, Dissemination Department,
Office of Public Information
Current Assignment: Coding
Specialty: News reporting

He tapped another key and waited for a response. Less than two seconds passed before she appeared on his screen.

"Posner, Dissemination Department, may I help you?" she asked.

She was beautiful. This could work out nicely, he thought.

Chapter 17

A suburb of Dallas

Michael sat in disbelief. "Why? What have I done? I've given up *everything* to please you."

Linda looked up at the ceiling. "You gave up your black box. Big deal. It seems to me more like you've been taking everything. I pay most of the rent. I buy most of the food. I got the house wired, I bought the video screen. You certainly don't contribute much to expenses."

"I work hard for my money," he said quickly. "I work outdoors so I can make *more* money. Just exactly what do you expect me to do?"

"There have to be some changes, Michael."

He stood up, hands clenched. "Look, Linda, I can see what this boils down to . . . I don't have a code and he does."

"Who does?" She asked, enjoying her new-found power. He actually looked jealous.

"You know exactly who I mean. That man you've been working with . . . Alex something-or-other!"

"You know his name as well as I do. There is a certain charm about a man with unlimited wealth and power. He's not bad looking either."

Michael stormed outside to sulk on the front porch. After a few minutes, Linda came out and stood by the railing, next to him. She reached out and tentatively touched his shoulder. He didn't respond.

"It doesn't have to be this way. I love you, Michael."

"But you love wealth just as much," he shot back.

She ignored the insult and squeezed between him and the railing. "You must admit that our life together could be," she said, running her hands up both his arms and locking her fingers behind his neck, "infinitely more pleasurable if we could live in nicer surroundings. You're so smart and such a hard worker. Within a couple of years, the sky would be the limit for us. A new beginning has been offered to us. Why not take it?"

His frown softened, so she pulled a little closer and spoke just above a whisper. "And let's face it, sweetheart, indoor jobs that pay anything decent are non-existent without a code now. How do you think I feel about you working outside—exposing yourself to the atmosphere all day? How does it look at my job when the man I live with doesn't have a code? Sometimes I think they're laughing at me. One of the girls at work said she saw you working with a paving machine the other day. She mentioned twice how tan you looked. It was embarrassing."

"Don't do this, Linda." he said, pulling away from her grasp.

Her exasperation boiled to the top. "I can't see what your problem is. It doesn't hurt . . . and the benefits outweigh any sacrifices a hundred to one."

"Yeah. You ever think about what *other* things our house might be wired for? Even in unwired places, they can hunt you down like a dog if they want to."

"What are you talking about? Sure they can find criminals easily, but that's an advantage isn't it?"

"Not if they decide you're a criminal," he countered. "You think I don't know the little games they play with non-coded people? Besides all the video surveillance they have everywhere, half our neighbors are probably spying on us as it is. All they'd have to do is say I look 'suspicious' and—despite your connections—I'd be toast."

"Oh that's *so* ridiculous," she countered.

"Oh yeah?" he asked, stepping up to the railing and leaning over it. "They're probably watching and listening right now." He turned to look at some surrounding windows, then focused on one in particular. "Hey Mrs. Nagel, you old bat! I'd like to—"

Linda retreated out of sight and lowered her voice. "*Why* are you acting this way? You aren't a criminal, so why do you care?"

He turned, and when she saw the expression on his face, she realized she'd just proved his point. She stepped back out on the porch and spoke in her normal tone. "This is just a dodge, Michael. It proves you can't think of a good reason for being such a chicken about getting a code."

She instantly regretted her last remark. His eyes flashed and for a moment she saw the man who had dared to lift the smelly, trampled, nearly-lifeless body of an unknown woman off the ground in a quarantine camp then look soldiers in the eye and say she was not sick with the fever. He'd carried her out of the camp and saved her life. For a terrible moment, she remembered being that woman. Whatever his faults, Michael was no coward. Linda blinked hard to clear the picture from her mind. She couldn't cave in now. If he was going to be her man, she *had* to press in and make him see.

"You know what you have to sign," he said flatly. "I don't want to make that kind of statement."

Moving closer again, she chose her next words carefully. "If you think of it in a different light, it's not *giving up* anything as much as it is accepting the rights and views of others as being valid—equal to—your own. That's all it is. We must be willing to open up to the Global View. The end-of-the-world predictions of the fanatics and the doomsday prophets were false! C'mon, Michael. Think of the peace and quality of life that have come back into the world already. Only those who cling to old bigotries and biases live with nothing—because they *choose* to live that way rather than admit they were wrong."

Michael scowled. "Then why can't all of you, since you're so into 'sharing,' just share it without all the strings attached? A guy around the corner told me his wife got sick last week and they refused to give her any medicine unless she agreed to get coded!"

He'd brought up a valid point, but she knew how to answer him. "It's not as if we don't care, Michael, it's just that there isn't a surplus of anything yet. Why give goods and services to those who have no intention of cooperating or helping rebuild society when there are people out there who are willing to overcome superstition, family opposition, and other obstacles for the benefit of all people. It's sort of our reward to have first option on these things. . . . That's fair, isn't it?"

Michael thought about the stories he'd heard. "What about the way the troops bully non-coded people? What about all the non-coded people who just disappear?"

She heaved an exasperated sigh. "Of course, the troops were rough with people right after the disasters. I haven't forgotten what we went through, Michael. But those were desperate times, which called for desperate measures. Sure, there are some abuses, but the more people cooperate, the freer things get. You have to see the other side. . . . And as far as people 'disappearing,' it's simply not true. It's an urban legend. People who aren't coded sneak off to avoid paying bills, or whatever, and the system can't find them. Does that mean they were kidnaped or killed? No! . . . What about your brother? He disappeared, didn't he? Did the government take him? No. Was there some big conspiracy? No. Do you personally know anyone else who has disappeared?"

Michael didn't answer.

"I'm telling you, for the most part, the persecution is imaginary. And as for the other thing, only people who *want* to disappear are disappearing. There are no wholesale abuses. I'm a reporter, Michael, I know things."

"You *used* to be a reporter," he corrected. "And I know things, too, Linda. Like how you and the 'free' media of old nearly devoured my brother Ben and our family with half-truths and rumors. Even back then, reporting was rarely about the truth—it was about agenda. It's even worse now. There's only *one* agenda. 'Facts' are limited to the daily spin the government tells you to chuck out over the airways. . . . They say nobody's getting snatched out of their homes or falsely imprisoned, you just repeat it. Maybe I can't prove what I think, but neither can you."

"*Fine!*" she said, her pulse rising. "The system has some flaws. What system hasn't had flaws? And what does it have to do with us? Come on," she pressed. "What *real* reason do you have for not taking a code?" She motioned with her hands. "Tell me. I want to hear you say it. I want you to hear how stupid it sounds."

Michael glared at her in silence.

"Then *I'll* say it. They say you'll go to Hell if you do. . . . So let me see if I have this straight," she said in a mocking tone. "You don't even believe in God, but you're afraid you'll go to Hell, is that right?"

"I never said I didn't believe in God," Michael corrected.

"Okay. But the rest of the things the fanatics say about getting coded—they just use those things to scare people because they don't have real reasons for refusing a code. They base their ideas on superstition and fear. It's like being afraid to walk under ladders or staying away from black cats. Admit it. It's silly."

Michael put his hands in his pockets and looked around. "Maybe, maybe not."

"So you're saying that *I'm* going to Hell, is that right? Just because I don't agree with someone else's concept of 'God,' I have no right to live or be happy?"

He let out a sarcastic laugh. "Well, what are you saying about fanatics? I mean, don't *you* condemn the fanatics for not conforming to your criteria? Don't your people try to force them to live in misery because they don't agree with your 'view' of the world?"

She looked down at her dress and straightened it. "We're not saying there is *no* God either. We just don't agree with the fanatics' ridiculously narrow concept of God. Their insistence that Jesus is the *only* way to enlightenment is separatist and has already caused too much grief. Remember all the panic and the turmoil they caused when they said Jesus was coming back any minute to rescue them and punish *us*? Don't you remember all those horrible 'He is coming soon—get right or get left!' ads they tormented people with? Yet the disasters came and went and the only ones who escaped did so by dying. And now, *much to their dismay,* we're prospering and they're still here!"

Michael frowned. "Zac says those ads didn't represent the thinking of all Christians. It was a misinterp—"

Realizing she'd once again let the conversation spin out of her control, she put up her hands and interrupted him. "We don't deny that Jesus existed as a *person*, or that he was a good man or even a great teacher. We just don't believe he should be promoted as the *only* 'Christ,' okay? We *have* to insist on the Global View."

"But shouldn't people in an advanced society have the right to believe what they want?" Michael appealed.

"I can see you want to get stuck on non-issues. What we're discussing here, Michael, is why *you* won't get a code."

"I'll take what you've said into consideration," he said quietly.

She turned away from him. "Okay, you have one week."

Michael's mouth dropped open. "What?"

"Well, that's better than breaking up today," she said flatly and walked back into the house.

Minutes later, she emerged with a suitcase. Not his, but hers.

"Tell you what, Michael. I've thought about it. I'm going to stay someplace else for a week, and you can call me at work if you change your mind. At the end of the week, *we'll* either be planning on moving elsewhere together, or *I'll* be moving elsewhere. The rent is paid for the next two weeks, so you can stay here until then. Afterwards, you'll have to either pay the rent or move out."

Michael stood there like a soldier at attention, watching her.

"I really do love you, Michael," she said, kissing him on the cheek, "but I have to do this for your own good. You won't make a decision until you are forced to, so I guess I'll have to force you. One way or the other." She turned and walked down the street.

Chapter 18

Near Houston in the former state of Texas

The Reverend Ike Bointon sat back in his chair and played his fingers on his desk. This would be very sticky, but manageable, he thought. The money had to come from somewhere. To open their pockets, the sermon needed to be one of his best. It would be challenging.

A smile came to his lips as he leaned back further in the chair, which threatened to break under his large frame. He heard a light knock at the door and sat up straight.

"Come in," Reverend Bointon said in a resonant voice.

The door opened slowly, and a head with curly gray hair peeked around it. "I'm not bothering you, am I?"

"No, Mrs. Weakes, come on in!"

A wiry little woman stepped into the room and closed the door quietly. Now waiting for instruction, she stood there, nervously clutching her purse.

"It's okay. Sit down, sit down." He smiled warmly and pointed to the chair in front of the desk.

She sat and started fidgeting with the handkerchief she'd wadded up in her hand. The Reverend realized he needed to put her at ease about something.

"Would you like some tea?" he offered.

"No, thank you. I don't really know how to say it . . ."

He felt a momentary panic as she searched for words.

He jolted a bit when she suddenly blurted out, "I'll be sixty-five next week."

After a moment, his face flooded with color again. "Oh! Is that what's got you worried? We all get older."

"You don't understand, Reverend. I'll be sixty-five next week," she said, continuing to wring the hankie.

Now he understood. Sixty-five. To regenerate or not regenerate. The government's new push: All people sixty-five and older should encode and regenerate. Originally advertised as a "virtual fountain of youth," the procedure now loomed as the dark duty of the elderly. As the first large wave of patients emerged, and the brain damage which occurred in a good percentage of them became evident, others became hesitant to comply. In new ad campaigns, the aging populace heard constant calls to "not be a burden," and struggling families were encouraged to make the "responsible choice" and consent to regeneration when aging members were ill or incapable of voicing an opinion.

The Reverend Bointon quickly calculated the possibilities.

"Mrs. Weakes," he said, kindly. "May I call you Charlotte?"

She nodded.

"Can I be honest with you, Charlotte?"

She swallowed hard and nodded again, eyes big and round like a little girl's.

"I've always thought of you as a person who appreciated honesty. Well, Charlotte, I don't want you to think I'm talking against the government, but I feel like you could hold out on regeneration. You're just so healthy and vibrant as you are, I wouldn't want someone to tamper with you. What do you think, Charlotte?"

Her eyes flooded with tears of relief. "Oh thank you, Reverend. I . . . I just haven't known what to do. The thought just scares me so. . . . I don't want to become a sexless 'oldie' that's little more than a machine . . . but I want to do what is right." She dabbed at her eyes. "Now, with your advice, I have the courage to hold out a while. Thank you so much!"

She got to her feet and reached across the desk lightly touching his hand. "Maker should have made more people like you." She turned and left the room.

He leaned back in his chair, smiling once again. Sometimes it was so easy he couldn't stand it. He'd said what she wanted to hear without taking too strong a stand against the government. He'd endeared himself to her and kept her from leaving his dome. It was a good thing, too, because oldies didn't attend domes. And, even if they had enough brains left to know where they were going and get there, they no longer had funds. The entire accounts of oldies were signed over to the government in exchange for a guarantee of long-term care. Maybe, with her time approaching, Mrs. Weakes would leave most of her money here rather than let the government have it.

Looking at the time, he realized he must start the Process of Readiness.

He went to the closet door and opened it. He reached for the matches on the shelf where he always put them, and found them. He lit the candle and said the words. They rattled off his tongue rapidly and without feeling.

"Blessed be this day as I am armed for battle . . ." He reached for the "helmet"—actually just a cap. He touched the top three times and put it on his head. Then came the big, baggy pants which tied at the waist. After those, came the apron which went on over the head. Next, he slipped off his shoes and put on the slippers.

Last, he took the golden cuff (gold sequins on material) and slipped it over the sleeve of his left arm. After years, of practice he could do it almost in one motion.

He stood still for a moment then made sure everything was straight and in its proper place before extinguishing the candle with two fingers, intoning a final prayer, and leaving the room.

He entered the dome through the passageway and made his way up to the mound. The mound represented a mountain and could be made of rocks stacked on one another, but in new domes like this one they'd constructed it of poured fibers painted in multi-earth tones resembling rocks.

He stood on the mound and smiled down at the people for a moment. The Circle had grown steadily since he took over the dome. Even tonight, he thought he noticed some new faces. His eyes swept over the crowd until they stopped on Mrs. Fairbanks, a middle-aged woman who had lost her son and her husband in the war. She had a plain, bony face on which she wore no makeup, dull brown hair, and a skeletal body which she generally covered with drab clothes. Even though she'd resisted getting a code, she'd managed to hang onto much of her family's wealth. With her money and connections, she had no lack of suitors; all of whom she turned away in order to devote her life—and hopefully, her wealth—to the dome.

Something about Mrs. Fairbanks looked different this evening. She didn't look as somber as usual. There was a faint hint of color in her face, softness instead of hard edges . . . perhaps a little smile on her lips. Something. Looking back, the Reverend would see this was where he made his first mistake of the evening: alluding to Mrs. Fairbanks in his sermon. His next mistake would be the subject of his sermon.

"Looking at all of you has given me such joy this evening. I know the Maker can unite us all from different walks of life into one Circle of love . . . without false claims or gimmicks."

He cleared his throat before continuing. "It came to my attention today that a man known amongst his people as "Swordsman" will be speaking in this vector for a few weeks. Doubtless most of you have heard of him.

"Don't misunderstand me, I am sure the man's intentions were probably good. At least in the beginning. And I hear the man is gifted with words. . . . But that's all they are. Words!

"It says many times in the Green Book how multitudes will be led away by voices full of guile feeding off the superstition of so many who don't know better. Better you should be deaf than to hear and follow one who speaks such words. And I believe that what this Swordsman is leading up to. . . . He's trying to revive a fanatical cult—a cult that will divide all we've tried so hard to unite—and plunge the world into darkness once again.

"Superstition is following irrational fears and beliefs which lead to chaos and destruction. *True* religion is the spiritual ascension of society toward that which is higher in unity, love, and peace—toward a realm which knows no bounds and is unfettered by restrictive terms or names. As we move forward in true religion, we don't continually hone down what God is in order to make some sort of exclusive club; but instead, we see this realm ever-expanding, as one truth bears witness to another." He paused briefly so the full impact of his words could be absorbed.

"Now let me get off that subject for just a moment. How many of you lost immediate family in the war? Were I to ask for a show of hands, I'm sure most people here would be counted. Some, more than once." He shot a sympathetic glance at Mrs. Fairbanks.

"The war and the horrors we faced were the result of differences in ideologies, different ways of life. This group says 'I can't live with you' and that group says 'I won't tolerate you' and before you know it, we have bioterrorism, contamination, war. . .

"But, for the first time, the world has a real shot at lasting peace! A peace which transcends governments and languages. Wealth and knowledge are being shared throughout the globe. Until now, governments and religions have never gotten along. But, for the first time, there's unity of purpose. We've begun working together for the new world we've all dreamed of.

"Then along comes a wave of fanatics—fundamentalists, who are breaking laws, creeping from house to house, hiding in the zones, and setting us up for a fall. They've taken a line or two from the Bible and are trying to tear apart half of the domes in this country! That's elitism and separatism! That isn't how we accomplish our tasks. . . . Even before the disasters, our denomination recognized that oneness of purpose could free the whole world. We adopted a credo: Liberated minds, emancipated hearts, unlimited access. . . . That should be our goal, even today.

"Unfortunately, the young, the confused, the helpless— the ones we should be reaching out to help—are the ones most susceptible to the dysfunctional rhetoric of the fanatics. Tonight, I'm asking you to work *with me* to prevent more tragedy. We've got to try harder, dig down deeper, give more, and do more to reach them."

Bointon took a deep breath and looked across his congregation. "I want each of you out there to think for a moment. What if your father, husband, daughter, or son had not been lost in the tragic events we've all endured. What a joy it would be! Sad to say, it didn't happen that way. But there are thousands of fathers, husbands, daughters, and sons out there who are alive, and passing our doorstep each day. Can't we, a Circle who *have*, give more to reach them? Indeed, we would be bringing blessed joy to ourselves. . . ."

He bowed his head for a few seconds and then walked down the aisle and out of the dome to his office. Mrs. Fairbanks rose also and left the dome—before the collection. A buzz went through the crowd.

Mr. Brentworth finally stood and said, "Well, I don't know about you, but I think the Reverend is right. We shouldn't let those wacky religious nuts get away with this. Let's give our dome a good name by doing something to improve our world!" And with that he went up to the keypad and made a show of punching in his donation. As he left, the others got in line and waited their turn.

The Reverend sat in his office, looking at the screen, and watching the tally going up. The readout showed the amount of each donation and the person who made it, while automatically deducting it from the person's account and crediting it to the dome's balance. People with cash donations inserted them in a teller machine which instantly tallied these contributions in a separate column.

He backed up the video to the point where he left the mound and watched the reactions of the circle members. To his great surprise, Mrs. Fairbanks got up and left without making the large donation he'd been so certain she'd give. In fact, she hadn't gone to the teller machine at all.

He quickly got the total back again. . . . Well, even so, the total amounted to a tidy sum. He went back to the study brochures he'd been browsing through earlier. Soon, he needed to begin taking more courses. There remained more to learn in this "universal incorporation of faith." Although great pains had been taken to make the Transition in each country sensitive to particular bends of culture and belief, changes would continue everywhere in order to accommodate the opening of faith to all.

Secretly, Ike Bointon felt uneasy about some of the changes. While a blended belief system did dampen the fires of dangerous zeal, it also took away from the continuity and stability of the church experience—something Bointon liked in his life. His denomination had been in the process of relinquishing "hard dogmas" for several decades, so much of the new "inclusive" thought easily slid into the pages of the green book. But the *rituals* of the church, he felt, gave people the comfort of something familiar. As long as Circle members could broadly interpret the *meaning* of the rituals, why tinker with them? His old members would balk at sweeping changes to the traditions they'd observed all their lives.

Yet all domes had to comply with certain standards by certain dates. He would have to start taking some new classes at the seminary, and even get coded. As a leader of a growing Circle, he'd be expected to fully embrace the new life he preached about. He leaned forward, scanning the brochures for different courses on his desk, and told himself, *You'll have to become more realistic. So what if the traditions have to bend a bit?*

He sighed and leaned back in his chair. As long as he was the respected leader of a dome, he could still find ways to live well, couldn't he?

Chapter 19

Dallas

Fibertronics' V. P. of Public Relations, Alex Dubois, sat behind the desk in the fifteen-by-fifteen-foot, cream-colored room, disgusted by its cheap decor. Even though he'd been given an unimaginably posh office under the Gulf of Mexico, no one would ever see it—except fellow employees whose offices either rivaled or exceeded his own. While a second office was being prepared for him in Dallas, he had to use whatever space the company provided. Today, this was it.

A secretary ushered a well-dressed man into the room and seated him. Dubois glanced again at the file folder on the desk before addressing the man.

"Tony Bensen?"

"Yes," the man replied. "Glad to meet you, sir."

Alex nodded. The sooner he could get out of this office the better. "How much have you been told about this assignment?" he asked.

Mr. Benson shrugged. "Not much. Only that it employs my mental capacities and that it's top secret."

"Correct on both counts. That's why," Alex said, tapping the file in front of him, "your identity, your purpose, and most of the information regarding your mission will be kept on paper. We don't want anyone tapping into the computer banks and discovering you." Next, he wanted to address qualifications. "I read here you are telepathically correct over 89 per cent of the time. Is this true?"

"Yes sir. Because of the time I devoted to developing the skill, I can work under almost any circumstance."

Actually, Alex wasn't completely convinced *anyone* had the power to influence or read the thoughts of others at will. While admitting the supernatural probably existed, he personally stayed away from such experiences. Mystical things made him uncomfortable. Nevertheless, according to his file, Tony Bensen was well connected and well respected. He could claim Edith Todd and other celebrities as former disciples. John Klost made it clear that their employer wanted to use psychics as part of the campaign to stop the religious fanatics. Alex wouldn't question the logic or the decision, he'd simply recruit the psychics and give them their assignments.

"Well, Mr. Benson," he said, clearing his throat. "The job we've selected for you will require you to work in almost every circumstance. We don't think there is much physical danger, but even your closest friends must not know what you are doing. You must not tell the Circle Leader at your dome or even your girlfriend. Do you understand this?"

"Yes, I do."

"You do live with your girlfriend don't you?" Alex said, consulting the file.

"We have a nice arrangement," Tony answered. "Each of us is free to do what we please. No commitments, no questions, and both of us like it that way."

"She won't pry into your work?"

"I'm certain of it. I've had to go away for months before, and she understands it's part of what I do."

"And let me be certain, you *don't* have a code, is that correct?"

"Correct."

Alex activated a clip screen. He picked one of the targeted leaders at random. A face appeared on the screen before he passed it across the desk. "Do you know who this is?"

Tony sensed a certain amount of tension coming from Alex, but remained unmoved by it. He looked at the face on the screen. After several seconds, the face seemed to radiate in his mind.

"This is a spiritual leader," Tony said. "He's within fifty miles of here. . . . I see a gleaming object. . . . It's a . . . is this the man they call Swordsman?"

"Yes." Alex said, looking mildly surprised. "You are correct. It's Swordsman. We want you to get close to this man and to stay close. Monitor his movements and, whenever possible, his thoughts. We will have telepathic receptors ready twenty-four hours a day, but always try to confirm via standard communications when possible."

As Tony sat there, something else occurred to him. He briefly considered describing a pretty blond who would be calling Alex in a few minutes . . . should he warn Dubois to be cautious about her? Looking at the man, he thought, *The job's already guaranteed. There's no need to impress this guy.*

Why mess with his personal life? Tony nodded and merely said, "I understand. You want me to confirm whenever possible."

Wanting to be certain the man understood the crucial nature of his mission, Alex leaned forward, and risked looking into Tony's sharp, gray eyes before speaking in a confidential tone. "It's important we know the minute you do about any future actions of this Swordsman. Stories about him are already the stuff of folklore. He's becoming a champion to many who are joining him in a counter-movement. He's helping to spread it over the whole continent! We cannot let this man be seen as a martyr, but we must stop him. We must lay hold of ways to influence and expose him. If our plan works, he will discredit himself. It may be the only way to bring his followers back to rational thinking.

"The people of this movement," Alex added, "could undo all of the progress we've made since the disasters. Our whole future could depend on your work. If Swordsman and others like him succeed, we could see a total collapse in the monetary system again and the return of international rivalry between the powers on this earth. It is a grave situation at best, and we'll be counting on your help."

"I'll do my best." Tony said.

Alex stood and shook his hand. "I'll have my secretary meet you outside. He'll arrange for whatever set-up you need. Of course, all of our technology is at your disposal."

When they'd finished their conversation, Alex felt quite pleased with the day's progress. As per instructions, the fanatic leader known as Swordsman would now be hounded by two telepaths. One with a code and one without. Both had equal skill and both were experienced in undercover work. In the event the coded agent was somehow detected, the uncoded operative still had a chance.

A tone sounded, and Alex turned on his phone receiver. Linda's face appeared on his screen—smiling and lovely as ever.

"Well hello there," he said.

"Where have you been hiding these last few days?" she said with a small pout. "You're a terrible man. You get a girl used to all sorts of luxurious things, and make her feel special, then you vanish."

Obviously, she'd missed him. He laughed and said, "I've been snowed under at the office, but just this minute got disentangled. How about meeting me somewhere? I'll make up for all of the neglect."

"Sure, where?"

"The Chateau . . . in half an hour?"

"Okay. See you." She hung up.

She had her suitcase and planned to be in his apartment by nightfall. It wouldn't be difficult. Although wealthy and decent looking, he didn't seem to have had many women, and she sensed his strong interest in her. Moving in with him would almost be doing him a favor.

Chapter 20

Little Valley Refuge in southwest Missouri

Rosa stood inside the crude cabin, folding a little dress and stacking it with others of similar size while she thought about the letter from Sara that Jason had brought her. Reading about the death of her dear friend's mother had revived some of her own feelings of loss. Rosa had no way of knowing what had happened to her own mother and stepfather. They'd lost contact just before the great migration. She still missed hearing her mother's voice.

Although some memories had faded, she could still recall certain moments with total clarity. She could smell the heavy scent of cologne, and see her mother sitting on the overstuffed floral-patterned sofa where the two of them often snuggled and talked. Usually, it would be morning. They'd sip thick, delicious Cuban coffee as the warm sun came through the leaded glass windows and lace curtains in the front of the house. They'd share secrets while occasionally petting the little dog, Chico, who always rested on mother's lap.

As deeply as she missed her mother, however, Rosa had to remember an important fact: Had she heeded her mother's pleas to return to Miami when war first broke out, she, Angela and Daniel might never have seen Ricky again.

"Enough of that," she said aloud before restarting the process of sorting out which shirts and socks belonged to whom. Ignoring the sound of someone entering the cabin, she continued the routine, speaking quietly to herself. "These are Kyle's, this is Bonnie's . . ."

Two hands went over her eyes.

"Guess who?" a disguised male voice asked.

She straightened up before she realized she could see perfectly well out of her left eye, even though she could still feel a hand on that side of her face. She smiled. A missing finger would explain her ability to maintain the view in front of her.

"My," she said. "I haven't a clue. Is that you, Daisy?"

"Guess again," Ricky said, in his regular voice.

"*Hmmmmmmmmm.* I give up."

He spun her around. "It's me! The kid you fell in love with last night." He put a hand to his chest and said, "I should be hurt you've forgotten me so soon, but I guess I'm too infatuated with you to let your lack of recognition discourage me." He reached over to grab some small, wild flowers he'd placed on a nearby shelf. "Here," he said. "I couldn't find a florist open this time of the morning, so I had to drive my car forever to get these from one of those annoying guys who sells flowers at intersections. The light had already turned green so people everywhere were honking and yelling." He blew air between his lips. "The things a guy has to do for a woman."

She admired the bouquet. "*¡Qué linda! Gracias, mi amor.*"

Other than Rosa and her husband, almost no one in the camp spoke fluent Spanish. Because privacy had become a rare commodity, the couple used it on occasion to create an illusion of seclusion.

He eyed the new sash tied around her tiny waist. "That's kinda nice."

She looked down, "Isn't it pretty? Sara sent it to me."

He grabbed the ends of the sash and used them to pull her close. "Oh yeah. Handy gadget." He put his arms around her before giving her a kiss. She responded, so the kiss continued longer than the standard have-a-nice-day kiss.

When it ended, she slowly opened her eyes and, in a dreamy voice, said, "Hey, you'd better watch out. There are millions of children out there who might see you."

"One of the best gifts I can give them," he said, before giving her another kiss, "is to love you."

She smiled triumphantly at him before he pulled her even closer and nuzzled next to her ear. "Sometimes," he whispered in Spanish, "I forget just how much—"

They heard a girl's voice in the distance. "Papa!"

"Busted," Rosa sighed. "Sounds like Tiffany."

Loosening his grip on his wife, he turned and called out, "In here, Tiffany."

A young teenager came trotting through the doorway, breathlessly declaring her message. "Joe spotted at least twenty unknowns moving up the south peak. . . . They don't have codes." She paused a second to look at her hand. Four extended fingers meant she had two more parts to deliver.

"Uh . . . several of them moved through a clearing, and the rest of them are climbing through the trees."

If strangers wanted to sneak up on the camp, they wouldn't deliberately walk through a clearing in broad daylight. Government troops would have codes.

Ricky let go of Rosa, then spoke to their adopted daughter. "Tell them to signal Joe that we'll go up to meet the visitors."

Tiffany hurried back to the "signal post" where the messages were relayed to and from nearby peaks via lights, flashed in Morse code. Rosa went to tell everyone to round up the smallest children and take them indoors. Ricky whistled loudly several times as he walked through the camp, signaling people to gather in the commons at the center of the refuge. He announced the arrival of visitors and asked two men to go with him toward the south slope.

Soon, the three of them began to climb, stepping through heavy morning dew. A bright sun topping the peak to their left promised another warm day, and the calls of birds returning northward for summer could be heard among the trees.

By the time Ricky, Bill, and Chen got halfway up the incline, they could see four men cresting the ridge and walking toward them. All four of the fatigue-wearing strangers had close-cropped beards and carried rifles. Extra bands of shells were slung over their shoulders. Two of them wore braces on their wrists for small crossbows.

One of the strangers called down the slope, "Good day."

"Good day," Ricky replied. The two groups continued to approach one another.

"We mean you no harm," the stranger said. "We'd like to trade goods and gather information."

Thirty yards and closing.

"It's possible," Ricky responded.

Ten yards remained between them. By this time, the men had all sized each other up. No one made any threatening moves, so the approach continued until they'd gotten within a few feet of one another and stopped. Although Ricky and the men from the refuge were unarmed, the visitors remained aware of the possibility of hidden sharpshooters.

"I'm Major Tam of the Sovereign U.S. Rangers," one of the strangers, a well-built, ruddy-skinned man with freckles said. He'd used the banned term, "*Sovereign* U.S." as a demonstration of trust. Now he let his gaze drift down to the encampment set in the niche between the peaks. "Do you give allegiance to the homeland or to the Global View?" he asked.

"I'm Ricky Ruiz. And I give my allegiance to God."

The major smiled, revealing a chipped front tooth. "Good answer." He stuck out his hand. "Nice to meet you."

Ricky grasped Major Tam's hand and shook it before taking a closer look at one of the other rangers, a young man who had taken off his hat and sunglasses. Within seconds, Ricky recalled the face of a clean-shaven twenty-year-old. A soldier in the Army. A good man. Although the young man's skin had aged from exposure, his countenance didn't look hardened, and his eyes had retained their clear, steady gaze. Ricky waited to see what the young man would do next. Lots of people in the wilderness didn't want to be recognized or called by their old names.

"You remember me, don't you?" the young ranger asked, urging him on.

Ricky grinned. "Norris?"

"Yeah," he replied, offering his hand. "Good to see you, sir."

Ricky grabbed Norris' hand then pulled him in for a bear hug before the younger man continued, "I recognized you at a distance. You're kinda hard to miss."

First contact between unfamiliar groups in the wilderness could be tricky. A certain protocol had developed over time. If individuals from the different parties recognized each other from past encounters (or had letters of introduction from mutual acquaintances) things could proceed more smoothly. Ricky and Norris would now become the spokesmen for their respective groups.

"So you're a ranger now?" Ricky asked.

"Yes," the young man answered. "All of the survivors from a big battle over in Grand Island joined up. It was either that or be absorbed by multinational forces who were killing resistant civilians."

"What about Yurich?" Ricky asked of a shared acquaintance.

"Dead, sir. Killed saving us in house-to-house fighting."

Ricky's expression saddened before he straightened his stance and visually re-inspected each of the rangers.

"There are more rangers up on the other side of the rim," Norris offered. "We connected with some of them just a few days ago. I don't know all of them, but everyone in my unit is trustworthy, and there have been no incidents with the others that have caused me concern. Major Tam is our senior officer, and he's a brother in the Lord," Norris said.

Ricky shook Tam's hand again. "We bid you welcome. Let me introduce Bill and Chen."

Norris pointed at the other two rangers in his group. "This is Dolan and that's Weston. I still go by Norris . . . and you still go by your old name?"

Ricky shrugged. "Why not?"

"Most of us were officially listed as dead anyway, so we decided to keep our names. Less confusing for all the kids."

They started down the hill, and the young man got in step with Ricky. The others followed behind them, listening to their exchange.

"Seeing you was a real shock," Norris said. "I heard all of you were killed last summer in a fire back in Oklahoma."

Ricky nodded. "Heard the story of our demise through official news channels, eh?"

"Yeah. But then, there is . . . like, this tale about the fire at the fuel depot just . . . going out. Even considering all the things I've seen happen around you guys, it seemed too fantastic to believe."

Ricky put a hand toward the sky and smiled. "Believe it. Some resistance fighters led us away after the fire blew out and helped us get away. After that, all of us felt we'd get more done if we split up. Probably fewer than 100 of the original group are in this area, and most of them are here."

The rangers behind them moved along in silence, trying to assimilate this information. They all remembered government news reports about a large group of refugees trying to steal fuel and touching off a huge blaze at a storage depot in eastern Oklahoma. According to the report, more than 500 refugees perished in the fire.

Many rangers had also heard the alternate version of the story: When hundreds of refugees refused coding, they were not permitted to migrate south. Instead, they were locked in a depot before multinational troops set several large, above-ground fuel tanks ablaze and took off. This the rangers could believe. They'd each witnessed atrocities committed under the authority of the new government. Of *course* the troops would blame it on the civilians, isn't that what they always did?

Until now, however, none of the rangers had believed the next part of the story. The next part said the fire among the fuel tanks, which should have caused an explosive inferno, blew out within seconds, and the refugees walked into the wilderness unscathed. Could this man and others in the camp truly be some of those people?

"And Rosa?" Norris asked. "Is she well?"

"Oh yeah. Still beautiful."

"How many children have you taken in?"

"All told? Twenty-six, but some of them are grown or are nearly grown now. Other people here have taken in lots of children as well."

"How is the little girl you adopted in the quarantine camp? The one who couldn't speak."

"Daisy? She's a little chatterbox now."

"Is Jason still with you?"

"Yes, he is."

"And the girl with red-blond hair. Wasn't her name Amanda? Is she with you? Is she well?"

Ricky's eyes seemed to shoot right into Norris' soul for a moment before a familiar smile returned. "Yes, that's her name. She's still with us. She's well."

When they reached the bottom of the hill, Ricky turned to Major Tam. "How many people are with your group?"

Tam told the truth. "Twenty-nine. We're badly in need of supplies, information, and a day or two of rest. Most of us will take up surveillance positions along the rim while we're here," he said, pointing toward the mountain ridges around the valley."

"If you believe they're trustworthy," Ricky said, "they can come down to shower and wash their clothes."

"That would be excellent. A few of the guys seem a bit rough," Tam responded, "so I may keep them on post up there. But we're all rangers, so no harm will come to anything that's yours while we're here."

Their host nodded. "Understood. We have some food to barter, dental and medical services, as well as shoe repair."

"We'd be most grateful. How about maps?"

Most original maps of the continent, individual states, and cities had been lost, destroyed, or confiscated. Any charts depicting current obstacles, standing bridges, caves, tunnels, contaminated regions, government troop routes, or passages through rough terrain were extremely valuable commodities. Those of accurate scale, drawn on durable surfaces such as hides or canvas, had premium value.

"If you'll tell us what you have," Ricky said, "we'll see if there's anything we could offer you."

"Again, we'd be grateful. . . . And socks. Our feet are getting in bad shape. We need socks."

Ricky nodded. "We have some to trade, but I'll have to get back to you about how many pairs we could offer."

Tam turned and nodded to one of the other rangers who spoke for the first time. "There's one more thing," the man said. "We're looking for someone. A female ranger, wounded just over a week ago. Can you tell us if you've heard anything about her or seen her?"

Neither Ricky nor the other men from the refuge gave the appearance of knowing anything about the subject.

"I'll ask around," Ricky responded.

"Fair enough," he said. "I'd consider it a personal favor if someone could get word to her that Dolan is looking for her and that Chris is here, too."

"We'll see what we can do."

###

Elsewhere in the camp, the wounded ranger, Sam, sat on a wooden stool in the tent where she'd been asked to stay when they'd received word of strangers approaching the camp. Impatiently, she rocked back and forth, considering what she might have done if she'd had her weapons and a small head start.

"It's me," a familiar voice said from outside the tent.

Sam remained seated as Jen entered.

"I've got news for you," Jen said in a hushed voice.

"What is it?" Sam whispered back.

"The people are rangers. They told Ricky they were looking for you. A man named Dolan is—"

"That's my partner." Sam pushed herself up and headed for the doorway.

Jen finished her sentence. ". . . and they also said Chris is here."

The female ranger stopped in her tracks, before releasing a heavy exhale, then standing taller.

"Is that your son?" Jen asked.

The ranger quickly rubbed her face and cleared her throat before moving again. "Yeah, that's my boy. Take me to them."

Soon, the two women approached the four rangers who had entered the refuge. Sam's leg continued to heal quickly, so she only needed the cane occasionally. One of the rangers saw her and bumped Dolan with his elbow. Dolan turned and, for a moment, he didn't recognize his partner.

"*Sam?*" he finally said, staring in disbelief at the well-scrubbed woman wearing the blue tunic and pants.

"Yeah yeah," she said, looking embarrassed, then getting angry as the men started chuckling. "Okay. Ha, ha," she said before she got close enough to give Dolan a mischievous shove. "You son of—" she stopped herself, then decided to say what she actually felt. "Glad to see you. I knew you'd come. Where's Chris? They told me Chris was here."

Dolan started to return her shove, but changed his mind as well. "Should be up on the ridge by now," he responded with a nod to one of the peaks.

"I'll send someone for him," Major Tam said. He pointed to Ranger Weston who immediately began trotting in that direction.

Jen decided to leave the rangers alone for a more private reunion and excused herself. "I have work to do. I'll see you later."

"Yeah," Sam replied. "See ya later. Thanks."

Amazed at her progress, Dolan asked, "How can you be walking around already?

She leaned forward. "You don't want to know."

He couldn't take his eyes off her. "I can't believe it's *you*. What's happened to you here?"

She gave him a stiff smile and spoke between clenched teeth. "I'll have my regular gear on when we pull out."

###

Under the canopy on the far side of the commons, Ricky and others decided what they could offer for barter.

"We have 30 pounds of jerky we could part with," one man offered.

"They're planning on pushing north," Ricky said. "We have any copies of maps to offer?"

"One extra copy. What'll they give us for it?"

"They say they have medical enzymes, bullet molds, flints, cloaking cloth, plastic tarps, knives, crossbows, chemical-tipped arrows, sugar, coffee . . . what else?" he asked, looking at Bill and Chen.

"They have new maps of Arkansas, Nebraska and Illinois. We don't have a new Nebraska, so that could be useful," Chen observed.

"They also said they had 'assorted' hardware," Bill added. "They know we're not interested in their rations."

"And they've got cigarettes!" Chen exclaimed.

Everyone laughed.

"Okay then," Ricky said. "That's pretty much the list. They're mostly looking for food, maps, oh, and socks—but I think they'll be wanting our services as well. And we might be able to do a trade for one of our hand-cranked radios, and some of our surgical supplies. Spread the word. We'll meet again late this afternoon to make up a final list for negotiations."

Just as he finished the last sentence, a child's cry pierced the air around them. Daniel, Ricky's two-year-old son, came wailing under the canopy, hotly pursued by Amanda, followed at a distance by his daughter, Angela, and then Rosa. In his right hand, the screaming little boy clutched the rotting remains of a small rag doll.

Ricky reached down to snag the suspenders of his son's overalls, then hoisted him up to eye level.

"No! No! Mine!" Daniel cried, pulling the doll close to his chest while his little legs flailed about.

By this time, the oldest adopted daughter, Amanda, had arrived. Rosa and a frantic Angela were only steps away.

Ricky cradled the boy who looked like a small clone of himself and spoke softly. "What's wrong?"

Daniel's breath came in jumpy little spurts. "Mine," he repeated before rubbing his tear-and-snot-covered face back and forth on his daddy's shirt. "Mine."

Ricky's gaze shifted to take in the arrival of his frazzled wife with daughter Angela jerking on her arm, crying for justice.

Rosa gave her husband a look of desperation. "Think of something," she said, "or I'm cutting that doll in *half*."

"Here," he said, handing Daniel off to Amanda, "go back to the play area with him."

Still in possession of the doll, the little boy made no protest. His sister, however, started to wind up for a full-fledged fit. She quickly halted, however, when her father squatted down. "Angela, look at me."

The girl complied.

"Mommy told me you decided to give your brother the doll. Is that true?"

The little girl averted her gaze. "But, but, I'm not–"

He pulled her little chin around. "Look at me, *hija*. Did you tell your brother he could have the doll or not?"

Angela squeezed her eyelids tightly to ensure the maximum amount of leakage. "Yes, but not *now*. He can have it later, when I'm done with it."

Ricky kept speaking in a calm but serious voice. "Did Mommy say she'd make you a new doll with some of the cloth Jason brought back?"

Angela made a long, sad, humming noise before getting out the word, "Yes."

"Ahhhhhh. I see," her father answered. "She thought you were a big girl so she let you decide if you wanted your old doll or a new one. That's how it works, sweetheart. You don't need a new doll if you still have the old one. So which one do you want?"

She threw her arms around her father's neck and sobbed, "I want a *new* doll."

He chuckled and picked her up. "Well that works out just right then, doesn't it? You've given Molly Dolly to Daniel, so now you can get that new doll, huh?"

She stopped crying and nodded.

"Boy," he sighed. "I'm sure glad that worked out, because Mommy really wanted to give you a new doll. Now *everybody* can be happy, huh? Good thinking!"

Angela's expression fluctuated between confusion and delight. Had she won this deal or not? She looked over at her mother who held out her arms and said, "You even get to pick the color of your new dolly's dress. Wanna do that now?"

The little girl nodded again, and Ricky passed her over saying, "That's my girl. Make sure it's a pretty color."

"Sorry for the disruption," Rosa said to the other adults under the canopy. "Dan squirted out the gate before we could grab him."

Most of the people in the group smiled and nodded. Many of them had multiple toddlers, too.

A shout in the distance diverted everyone's attention to an area across the commons. They could see a young man, probably only sixteen or seventeen, in a tattered ranger uniform, approaching Sam. She dropped her cane and rapidly limped over to him. The two embraced before she stepped back to look at him.

Ricky put his arm around his wife. "Must be her son," he surmised.

By the next morning, the two groups had agreed on a deal. Part of the exchange included medical and dental services. The rangers currently lacked a medic and several of them required attention for ongoing conditions. Ricky and Jason would split up and visit soldiers in small encampments around the rim. Female patients would be given the option of visiting with Jen down in the camp.

The major ordered Sam to stay put for the time being. The rangers wouldn't be moving out for at least two more days. Rather than packing up the mountainside, she might as well recuperate as much as possible in the refuge. She'd be returning to a rougher life soon enough. Her son, Chris, could come and stay with a small contingent of male rangers in the camp.

By that afternoon, most of the dry goods in the barter had been exchanged. Ricky moved along the ridge with Norris, intending to visit those needing minor medical attention.

A sentry acknowledged the two men before they approached several domed tents in the trees. "This group," Norris said, "isn't part of my unit. They're mostly Sam's people. They lost a medic and several others about 200 miles south of here when they tried to take a small convoy of supplies from government troops. After things went sour, they split up and planned to rendezvous in several days on safe ground. That's when Sam and her partner came across Jason and the others being tracked."

Norris and Ricky entered the camp. While Norris made small-talk with some of the rangers, Ricky treated others with medicines pre-mixed by Jen, and stitched up a cut on one man's hand. During each private consultation, he offered to pray for the patient. One man took him up on the offer. One woman, who looked even tougher than Sam, laughed in his face.

Within an hour, Ricky and Norris moved on toward the next camp.

"There's something I need to ask you," the young ranger said.

Ricky kept looking ahead. "It's about Amanda, isn't it?"

"Oh, man," he said, disgusted with himself. "Is it that obvious?"

"Only about as obvious as daylight," Ricky responded. "When you saw her yesterday, you looked positively sick. Whenever she got out of sight, you looked even worse."

Norris blew air between his lips. Even now, the thought of her green eyes and the strawberry-blond hair, draped over her shoulder in a long, thick braid made him almost crazy. He had to ask. "Is there something between her and Jason? I saw them walking together several times."

Ricky smiled. "No. But they're every bit as close as a real brother and sister. The things we've all been through have really cemented their relationship. They'll always be important to each other."

Somewhat heartened, the ranger moved onto the next thing. "I know I'm a ranger right now. I'm not talking about now. But, next year, my commitment is up and. . ."

"She's barely eighteen, Norris."

He put up his hands and quickly added, "I know that. I know that. We're both young. And she doesn't really know me. I just want," he paused and calmed himself. "I want to know if I can come back and be part of the community. If there's going to be a future, I want to live it with all of you. Even if she decides she doesn't like me, I want to start my civilian life with you guys."

Ricky slowed his pace and considered the request before responding. The young man had demonstrated genuine faith and integrity when they knew each other in the Oklahoma quarantine camp. Although Norris must have harbored some attraction for Amanda in the past, he'd never acted on it when she was younger.

Ricky finally nodded. "If you show up, you'll be welcomed. But remember, Amanda will decide whether or not she wants any sort of friendship—or more—with you. I pray neither of you would pursue a deeper relationship without asking the Lord first."

"Yes, sir," he said, visibly relieved.

Ricky remembered how his heart nearly stopped the first time he laid eyes on Rosa, and the agony he'd felt for so long when he loved her from a distance. He put a large hand on Norris' shoulder. "Just remember. She's not only my daughter," he pointed up, "she's *His* little girl, too. Never forget it."

"Yes sir. Thank you, sir."

The two men continued on, and Norris quietly informed Ricky about the next group they'd visit. "These guys also joined us last week. Six men. They lost the rest of their unit several weeks ago and will travel with us until we can hook them up with another unit. They're the 'rough' ones the major spoke about. They're pretty hardened, but I understand they're skilled fighters and loyal to each other."

Soon, they could see four of the rangers playing cards around a small, flat rock serving as a table.

"We're here for medical visits," Norris called out while still at a distance.

The four men looked up, stopping their game. One of them quickly scooped a handful of small objects off the rock and poured them into his shirt pocket.

Entering the camp, Ricky moved to the nearest tent. "I'll set up shop in here. Who wants to be first?"

A dirty, dark-haired man rose to his feet. "I'll go first." He followed Ricky into the tent, adding, "I think a spider may have gotten me last night."

Norris stood outside with the others. All of them seemed ill at ease and several attempts at casual conversation fell flat. While Ricky remained inside the tent, tending to his first patient, another ranger wandered into the camp wearing binoculars around his neck. He did a double-take at Norris, then waved and said, "Hey. How's it going?"

Not waiting for a response, he turned and nudged one of the men seated near the rock and said, "I've been checking out the action down in the valley with Ed's glasses." He wiggled his eyebrows. "Wouldn't mind slipping down there and visiting a few of those *señoritas* myself. They sure aren't like our females. They look yummy," he said, making curvy lines with his hands. "Maybe they'd—"

"The women aren't like that," Norris interjected.

The ranger spun around, gave him a sly smile, and rubbed himself. "Just let one of 'em spend a few hours with me. . . . She'd convert."

Two of the others laughed.

Norris stepped closer. "Isn't your name Ulman?"

"What if it is?"

"Remember your oath, Ulman. Major Tam made you repeat it just last week."

Ulman shoved his face mere inches away from Norris'. "Get a dose of the facts, man. *If* you haven't noticed, it's about to go to pieces out there. No matter what we do, the blinkers will keep coming. Oath or no oath, how much longer do you think we're going to last? We've been putting it all on the line and, the way I see it, the people down there *owe* us something before we die."

Norris drew even closer to the aggressor. "*None* of us could have survived this long without help from civilians. If we start breaking the oath and plundering them, we'll be harming ourselves. Worse than that, we'll have become just like the ones we've sworn to fight. Take that as *your* dose for the day. Win or lose, you're supposed to be a ranger, not some animal in search of prey."

"Yeah. Right," Ulman spat out his words as he snapped to attention. "Truth, justice and the *Sovereign American way!*" He gave a mocking salute to the trees.

Hearing a loud voice, Ricky stuck his head outside the tent. "Do we have a problem here?"

The ranger with the binoculars jolted at the sight of him and backed up a step. Norris kept his eyes locked on the soldier and answered, "No."

When Ricky returned to his work, Norris lowered his voice and spoke to the ranger. "If you'd been directing your attention to your *duty* at your watch post, you'd have seen us coming. These men's lives depend on you. Don't let this happen again, Ulman."

Stony silence shrouded the group as the angry ranger sat with his friends. One at a time, three more went into the tent. The last one in said he had a toothache and a rash on his back.

"What's your name?" Ricky asked the ranger who had been playing cards outside.

"Baird."

"Well, Baird, let me have a look at your back first. Sit here and take off your shirt." Once the man removed the reeking garment, Ricky took it from him, saying, "I'll just set it back here and check my pack for ointment."

Prompted by an inner voice, Ricky stuck a finger in the front pocket of the shirt and pulled it open, to see what the man had scooped off the rock and stashed there. What had they been using to make bets? Unable to make out the small objects, he reached in and pulled one out. Now he recognized what he had: A damaged chip which, most likely, had been dug out of the hand of an enemy soldier—a blinker.

Ricky shuddered as he dropped the grisly trophy back into the pocket, quickly stowed the shirt, and went to work on the ranger. After he'd checked the man's rash and applied a salve, he asked, "What about your other problem?"

Baird turned to face him. "This tooth hurts."

Ricky looked at the indicated molar. "Looks like we may have to pull it."

The man swore, then apologized. "I just didn't want to lose another tooth."

Ricky studied the man for a moment, then said, "You'll need to come down to the valley for this."

Chapter 21

A suburb of Dallas

For thirty minutes Michael paced up and down outside the Center for Tomorrow building. Finally, he made up his mind and pushed himself through the door.

He walked to the desk marked "Information," and found it unoccupied; so he looked around, noting little booths on either side of the room with large video screens in them. Some of the booths had people standing or sitting in them. He moved to his right and walked by a few.

He came to an empty booth and stopped. When he crossed the boundary of the opening to the booth, a woman's voice said, "Have you wondered what it would be like to have a code?"

The screen lit up. Michael moved in closer and sat down on a little padded stool as the voice coming through the speakers continued.

"Recently, the world suffered the most devastating events in its history. . . . You may have witnessed the death and dying. Undoubtedly, you experienced deprivation, suffering, and pain."

A series of film clips depicting terrible scenes of war zones across the globe, contaminated areas in America, and the exodus south moved through the screen, connecting with similar pictures in Michael's past. The surround-sound speakers carried distant cries of men, women, and children filtering through layers of melancholy violin music.

The female voice spoke again. "You survived these events to see a new world emerging from the old . . . a new alignment of society, working for an end of bitterness and rivalry . . . an end to death due to contamination, malnutrition, and starvation. In this new alignment, poverty can end as the wealth of the world is shared." The voice sounded soothing, the music gradually brightened.

"To ensure our better future, there must be a guarantee of protection for all people. To date, over a billion people worldwide have joined this global society . . . they have agreed to make the transition and become part of the solution—to affirm life and embrace the Global View."

The scene switched to a busy street filled with pedestrians. The camera focused in on a building with a "Bank" sign out front before the narrative continued.

"Although there are many aspects to the transition, one of the most common concerns is money. Because our passage to a better future will take some time, a stable, global currency has been printed and is easily exchanged for all old forms of currency."

Michael watched as the video showed a man exchanging old, U.S. currency for blue bills.

"And, for those of you who are about to take the next step—getting a code—the *best* is yet to come . . . because when you do, you'll never need another wallet."

A woman came into view, wearing a bright blue outfit. She opened her wallet and set its contents on a counter. Among the items she displayed, Michael recognized a health certificate, credit cards, employee and I.D. cards, an insurance card, a medical alert card, blue bills, and a handful of coins.

When the camera angle widened to take in the room around the woman, it became evident she was in a Center for Tomorrow, just like the one where Michael now sat. A female clerk behind a desk counted the money. Then, she entered the amount in the woman's new, personal account before setting the money aside and producing two sets of scissors. The two women laughed and talked as they cut up the rest of the items from the wallet. The woman looked down at the back of her right hand, closed her eyes, and smiled as she took in a deep breath.

As if speaking for her, the video voice said, "Ahhhhhhhh. Freedom and security at last."

The picture switched to a number of different scenes while the soothing feminine voice continued.

"Now, with a code, she'll have freedom to buy where and when she chooses . . . without the worries that carrying money brings."

Michael watched scenes of a man losing his wallet, a woman having her purse snatched, and a man being robbed at gunpoint.

"Not to mention the inconvenience of cash . . ."

The next section of video showed a busy store with twelve check-out lines. Ten of the lines, for "coded customers only," moved along quickly. All of the patrons in the two "cash" lines, however, showed pained expressions as they inched forward at a snail's pace.

The camera slowly focused in on one patron in particular who stepped up to the counter with his purchase. He had sores on his face (possibly from contamination) and a runny nose. When he pulled out the blue money to pay, the sales clerk looked him over before reluctantly taking it. When he turned to walk away, the clerk cringed, got a moist towel from a drawer, and wiped her hands. The picture froze on the disgusted worker's face before a big black "X" materialized over the picture.

This scene faded to black before the newly-coded woman with the bright blue pantsuit appeared on the screen again. She looked at viewers in a store before the clerk helped her select one. Next, the woman simply put her hand on a small, enclosed touchscreen, waited a moment, then walked away with a smile.

The narrator said, "This woman has just purchased a viewer. She didn't have to stand in line, she didn't have to wait for someone to ring up a sale. She didn't even have to give the salesperson her address. Why? Because with a code, she needed only to wait a moment for a link-up to verify who she is, to debit her account, to credit the store's account, and to have the computer give the store's delivery department her current address. And, in the future, she will be able to use her personal viewer connection to order merchandise from her own home!"

The music drifted from a fast, perky tune, to a tranquil prelude.

"It has been falsely reported," the voice coming through the speakers softly stated, "that to get a code one has to give up religion. But those who've made the transition know spirituality is actually promoted as a positive force in the lives of coded people, and having a code automatically entitles one to membership in a dome, full counseling privileges, and free dispensation at death."

The lilting sounds of birds chirping in nearby trees joined the worshipful music as men and women of different ages and races walked into the doors of different domes with varying architecture.

The sounds of birds and music receded as an assortment of still photos from the past, depicting decadent wealth abiding alongside wracking poverty. Grossly overweight Americans with full shopping bags, waddling around in malls were contrasted to naked, skeletal children picking through trash for food in former third-world countries. Pictures of tall, fuming smokestacks were replaced by shots of soot-covered forests.

"Although we all know the sinful, wasteful years are gone, you can once again attain moderate comfort, upgraded housing, and latest in medical care."

More photos flashed by showing construction of new apartments, a family sitting together at a dinner table, a woman and her baby with a doctor, a couple holding hands as they walked through a park.

"And, be assured that, as the world standard in comfort goes up, so will yours! . . . But if we want the progress to continue, we must all help."

The speakers went silent, and two words materialized on the screen: "Encode Today." After this, dozens of faces of people from across the world appeared, smiling wistfully before the screen went blank.

Michael stood up, but lingered in the booth, staring at the blank screen. Thinking. Wouldn't it be great if he and Linda could be seen as equals again? Why should he settle for a crummy outdoor job? Life could be better.

Zachary's face appeared briefly in his mind. . . . But Zac was gone, and this problem involved the here and now. Michael sighed and walked back to the information desk.

A woman sat there with braids coiled all around her head in an intricate design. Her eyelids fairly glowed with eye shadow.

"Yes?" she said.

"I want . . . to think about it some more," he said and started to walk away.

"Wait," she responded.

When he turned, she produced a book. "You might want to read this," she said, pushing it across the counter to him.

"It's a book about a man's personal experiences. It's helped a lot of people . . . and it's free."

He slid the book off the counter and scanned the cover.

Changing Times, Time for a Change
One man's journey to wholeness
by acclaimed journalist,
James Hart

Michael frowned and started to say something, then changed his mind. "Thanks," he mumbled before sticking the book in his pack and quickly exiting the building.

Walking home, he cursed himself while he tapped himself repeatedly on the forehead with his fist. *Why can't I do it? . . . If I could just believe what she's been saying . . . God, just show me what's true.*

The first two days after Linda left, Michael felt sure she'd be back. . . . She'd gone off and returned before, hadn't she? He tried reading the book. Although it depicted a picture of the past that was similar to his own recollection, Michael found the author's spin on the present situation disturbing. Were all of the Christians who resisted the movement fanatical liars? Would these "fanatics," if allowed to continue, throw the entire system into chaos? Michael wasn't ready to agree with such statements, but wasn't prepared to deny them, either. He tossed the book over by the bookcase in the living room.

After the fourth day of Linda's absence, he began to worry and called her office. She refused to speak to him. Now, day six had arrived, and he hadn't eaten in two days. He wanted her back, but refused to be coerced into getting a code.

After sitting at home in the dark for nearly an hour, he decided to call her once more. . . . If she'd be willing to give him some time without ultimatums, he'd give it honest consideration.

He picked up the phone and entered the number for her office.

A man answered. He had bright red hair and a beard. In his nose, he wore a gold hoop.

"No, she's left for the day," he said, in a rather feminine tone. "Is it urgent?"

Michael thought for a second. "Yes, yes. I'm her brother. Our mom is very ill and . . . well, there is little hope mom will last the night. She keeps asking for Linda. . . . Can't you locate her?" He held his breath.

"Well," the man hesitated, "hold one sec . . ."

"The screen went blank before another man's face came into view. "This is Dubois."

Michael's heart filled with rage. "Where's Linda?" he demanded.

"Linda's in the shower," Dubois said, before looking to his left and speaking to someone Michael couldn't see. "I don't know. Some tan, bushy-looking fellow demanding to speak with you."

Linda's face came on the screen. She had a towel on her head. "I knew you'd find me somehow," she said with a look of satisfaction. "So did you work up your nerve or not?"

"Well," he started to explain, but stopped when Dubois appeared behind her and began kissing her neck. She giggled.

Michael hung up.

Chapter 22

A suburb of Atlanta

Leon Newsome, Sr. kissed his daughter Jessica, good night.

"Good night, Daddy." she said, her big brown eyes searching his. "Do you love me?"

There were times when it was as if she weren't retarded at all, when she seemed so deep and reflective.

"Daddy loves you *very* much, sweetheart," he said before giving another kiss.

Edwina Grant stood in the corner of the room and smiled. She knew he'd spoken the truth.

Jessica sat up in an attempt to delay the inevitable. She put her little hand on his face and said, "Daddy . . ."

"No more talk now," Edwina said, before moving forward and pulling the covers up to Jessica's chin. " You've stayed up too late already. It's time for sleep now. Your Daddy will still be here in the morning."

Leon moved to the door and waved to Jessica. "Night night."

"Night night," Jessica repeated as her good hand appeared over the edge of the sheet and waved back.

"Good night, Jessica," Edwina said.

"Good night." Jessica repeated.

Edwina turned out the light and closed the door. Leon stood in the hall, waiting for her.

"Thank you for taking such good care of her," he said.

"It's my pleasure. She's a precious little girl."

A light seemed to shine in his eyes for a moment before he began to walk toward his room.

"Thank *you*," Edwina said after him.

He stopped to look at her.

"For loving her."

He nodded his head before turning and walking to his room. When he got inside, he closed the door and went to sit in his favorite chair. As he sat, he noticed the clock on the dressing table. Ten o'clock. He sighed. Deana was out late again with Leon Jr. Probably at that dome again. The thought irritated him.

Since being inducted into the Universal Legion, Lee had come home more often. Instead of being happy to see his son, however, Leon Sr. had gotten to the point of dreading the visits. Whenever his son returned, the house became a propaganda depot. The boy seemed bent on making his father feel less of a citizen because he didn't share his son's overzealous views about everything. Even worse, Deana responded to Lee's presence in a much different way. Increasingly, she began to take her son's side in things. She continually asked for his advice, stewed over his critical commentaries, and changed everything to please him.

Leon Sr. heard the front door close, then the sound of Deana's laughter. He quickly got a book and pretended to be reading. He sat there for quite a while before he realized she wasn't coming up to bed. He snapped the book closed and got up. His wife and son had already seated themselves in the kitchen when he came in and sat down without a greeting. They stopped talking and looked at him.

"Don't mind me," he said, with an open-handed gesture. "Just do what you always do. Pretend I'm not here."

"Hello, Father," Lee said, ignoring the remark.

Deana stroked his arm as if she were soothing a beast of some sort. "Now, honey."

Leon Sr. pulled away. "Not that it's any of my business, but just *where* have you been?"

"We went out to– " Deana began.

"The dome again?" her husband interrupted. "Maybe you guys should just take sleeping bags, and that weird food he eats, and live down there when he comes to visit."

Lee sat up straighter in his chair.

"Now Dear," Deana said, hoping to intercede before a raging argument developed, "I'm sorry I didn't tell you where I was. It's my fault. I won't do it again."

"Stop trying to pacify me! You are *my* wife, not his!" Leon said before turning his gaze onto his son. "And *you* . . . why can't you ask some girl out on a date?"

"I don't expect you to understand, Father, but I don't intend to have sexual intercourse with a woman except if I am to procreate."

"I didn't ask you to go out and have sex with a girl. I asked you why you didn't take a girl out."

"Why should I waste my time on relationships that will lead nowhere?" Lee said with a shrug. "If I fell in love, it would be that much harder to follow my commitment and break with her."

"So what are you saying here? That you are not *permitted* to pick a girl on your own? . . . You mean *they* pick the girl you marry? . . . Or is it that you just 'procreate'? This is disgusting!"

"I knew you wouldn't understand. I do it for the world, not just for me. Someday we will be heroes for bringing about that which is perfect."

Leon Sr. looked at Deana. "Is *this* our son?"

"I wouldn't be at all surprised if I wasn't related to *you*." Leon Jr. said, rising to his feet. His hands were clenched into fists. "The only thing that's definitely *yours* is the one-armed monkey in bed upstairs!"

With surprising speed, his father struck him full force and sent him to the floor. Deana rushed to get between them before there was a fist fight.

"Stop! *Stop!*" she shouted. "This is ridiculous!" and then more calmly, "You are both tired and angry . . . nothing will be solved by this. Let's go to bed and cool off and then we'll talk about it in the morning."

Lee pushed by them and said over his shoulder, "Don't worry about it, Mom."

Her husband made a move to go after him, but she blocked his path to the door. "Please, Leon. Please!"

After a few minutes, he appeared calmer, and she hoped to reason with him. "Look, honey. He did wrong. That was a terrible thing to say. I'm sorry. But you can't change it by hitting him. You'll just give him the feeling of being a martyr that way. We'll all try to sit down in the daylight tomorrow and iron this out. Okay?"

They finally went to bed. When they got up in the morning, Lee had gone.

Over the next few weeks Leon Sr. thought a lot and decided maybe he'd been too harsh on his son. Perhaps Lee only said those spiteful things because he'd been hurt by his father's disapproval.

Deana begged and pleaded with him to contact their son, and he eventually did call Lee—more to please her than anything else. Things were patched up somewhat, but from that time on, the wariness between father and son began to grow.

Chapter 23

Little Valley Refuge in southwest Missouri

At mid-day, two rangers approached the refuge in the valley. Because these men had spent the better part of a year living in the bush, the crude buildings and tents clustered together among men, women, and a host of children seemed like a thriving metropolis.

One of Major Tam's officers spotted the rangers and walked toward them. "What's your purpose here?"

"Dental visit," Baird answered. "The big, dark fella said to come down here. Supposed to ask for Bill."

The officer rotated slightly and pointed, "Go over to that bigger cabin. Behind it is a tent where they're doing the dental work. You'll see some other rangers in line. Most importantly, stay away from the personal quarters of the civilians on the west side of the field. Those tents are off limits."

The two rangers walked slowly, willing their eyes, ears, and noses to pull in every detail of the camp. Ulman remained mostly preoccupied with women. Notwithstanding the pain in his tooth, Baird wanted, more than anything else, to eat something. Something besides jerky. Something slow-cooked and tender. Something warm, spiced, and flavorful. He could smell vegetables and meat simmering even now.

They found the tent where three rangers sat in a line on the ground, all of them holding their jaws or looking entirely miserable. Knowing this must be the right place, Baird sat down at the end of the line. Ulman stood by the corner of the cabin so he could still see the women on the far side of the field—in the forbidden area.

Occasionally, a muffled groan came out of the tent. Each of the rangers sitting in line would shift around and try to think of something else.

A female ranger emerged from the tent, biting on a wad of cloth in her mouth. A civilian man appeared in the opening of the tent and called, "Next." The first ranger in the line got up and reluctantly walked into the tent. The flap closed before the other patients scooted one slot closer.

Within moments they all heard the ranger say loudly. "Ow! Yes, that one!"

"You know what?" Ulman said, walking nearer to his partner. "I think I need a drink of water. You need a drink of water?" Before Baird could respond, his friend turned and disappeared around the side of the cabin, saying, "I'll be back in a while."

Ulman stepped quickly across the field, not knowing how far he would get, but figuring it would be worth a try. Why come all the way down here if he didn't get a chance at a girl?

Much to his dismay, by the time he got across the commons, the females had disappeared. He moved along, his ravenous eyes scouring the area. He smiled when he spotted a young woman, around twenty years old, wearing a long-sleeved yellow tunic and pants. She had to be nearly 6-feet tall—an Amazon princess—with dark hair flowing behind her as she walked behind the first row of tents. In her slender arms, she held cloth bags filled with laundry.

Ulman quickly shot along in front of one tent, then another, trying to catch glimpses of her every few seconds. After several tents, he got past one and waited. The girl did not appear. Knowing he courted bigger trouble with each step, he plunged into the little alleyway, looking for her. He turned a corner just in time to see her emerging from the doorway of a tent, minus the bags.

"Excuse me," he said, clearing his throat and smoothing back his hair.

She looked at him, momentarily perplexed. "Um. I don't know why you came over here, mister," she began.

"Truth is, I'm lost," he said, taking several steps toward her. "All I wanted was a drink of water. Could you get me one?"

Her expression said she didn't believe him. "You're lost? Then go that way," she said, stepping back three paces and pointing through the next walkway between the tents. "Go across the grassy area to the big cabin on the other side. Someone over there will give you water."

He moved closer to her. When he did so, a tumble of impressions came to him: She smelled of soap. She looked so soft. She wasn't intimidated by him . . . and she wanted him to go away. Until this moment, he hadn't realized just how filthy he was. Filthy and desperately hungry for her sublime company.

He probably had only a few more seconds to make his case. "You couldn't give me a drink of water?" he asked, hoping to play on her sympathy. "I heard that this is what you people like to do. Help others in need."

"You're not supposed to be over here," she replied.

A boy came running down between the tents, calling, "Dori!" As soon as the youngster saw Ulman, he stopped for a second, then moved closer to his sister, taking hold of her hand and saying, "Mama wants you." Despite being only nine or ten, the boy's gaze warned the stranger not to come any closer to his sister.

Dori's expression remained firm. "I'm sorry, sir," she said to the ranger, "you need to go now. They'll have water for you over there."

An old woman appeared in the doorway of a nearby tent and looked at him. He sensed others stirring, wanting to see if Dori needed help.

Ulman's expression soured. "Sure. I get it," he said to his growing audience. "I'm too dirty and disgusting to mingle with the regular people here." He pointed across the commons. "I'll just go through there to the cabin." He started walking before calling out a sarcastic, "Thanks, Dori. You've been loads of help."

He'd stomped half-way across the commons when Dori caught up to him again and said, "It's not really like that, you know."

Continuing to march along, he shot her a hard look. Whatever made him think he needed any of these people? He noted the small acne scars on her face, the stains on her tunic. What made her think she was so much better? He should have stayed up on the ridge and played poker.

"If you feel dirt is an issue, though," she said, pointing to their left, "the men's showers and a laundry are that way. Any of you men can use them." She stopped walking, letting the distance between them grow as he stepped away. "I'm sorry if your visit here got off to a bad start."

He halted and spun around. "And whose fault is that?" he asked in a snotty tone.

"Yours."

The ranger took several steps toward her, a hard glare in his eyes.

Dori looked down and said, "You went where you weren't invited and you lied about why you were there."

Ulman cocked his head to one side and threw his hands in the air. "Well, you got me there! You're just a regular fountain of discernment aren't ya?"

She kept staring at the ground. "My father says sarcasm is a way for a bitter heart to shoot poison arrows. . . . It's a way to hurt people and call it humor."

"Ooooooooo," the ranger said, "and full of such clever sayings, too!" He pushed an index finger into his cheek to make a dimple, "I guess you're just perfect in every way!"

He watched her turn and walk back toward the tents. At first, he wanted to think of something else to yell at her. He opened his mouth and drew in a breath before he realized he hadn't wanted to send her away at all. What a dolt he was! He punched at the air with frustrated fists, then stormed back to the tent behind the large cabin. Unfortunately, his partner had only advanced one place in line.

"Where's the water?" Baird asked.

"There isn't any," he snapped.

After another few moments Ulman began pacing back and forth beside the cabin, mentally replaying every stupid remark he'd made. At one point, he turned at the end of the swath he'd established, and bumped into a civilian.

"*Sorry*," Ulman fairly shouted, then subdued his voice. "I didn't realize you were behind me."

"That's okay," a young man almost his age answered before offering his hand, "Name's Jason. . . . You need anything?"

Ulman frowned before he finally shook Jason's hand and said, "I'm Ulman. Bob Ulman. I heard you had a place to clean up around here. Could you tell me where it is exactly?"

Jason took him to the front of the cabin and indicated a spot some distance away. "See that little shed-looking building there? That's the men's shower. The tent on the far side of it is the laundry."

"Thanks," Ulman replied before he began walking toward it.

He got several yards away before Jason called out, "Hey! Bob!"

Ulman turned.

"You don't have a pack with you," the young man noted. "Does that mean you don't have a change of clothes?"

The ranger shrugged. "Came down with someone who needed a tooth pulled. Didn't know I'd have an opportunity to wash up."

Jason sized him up, then said, "You could probably fit into a set of my clothes while yours are wet. I'll leave some over at the showers for you."

The ranger paused, then said, "Thanks. I'd appreciate it."

###

Thirty minutes later, Ulman emerged from the showers, cleaned, trimmed, and wearing civilian duds. A tiny old woman had taken his clothes to the laundry with a kind offer to wash them. Hopefully, she advised him, they'd be dry by dark.

Returning to the large cabin, Ulman took care to stay on the "visitors" side of the commons. Although he wore civilian clothes, everyone from the refuge knew he was a ranger. Most of them said "Hi," as they passed. When he arrived back at the dentist's tent, a man informed him his partner had just gone inside.

The big man who had visited up on the rim stopped and told him he could get some soup inside the cabin. Lured by the smell, Ulman abandoned thoughts of waiting for his friend and went to eat.

###

Inside the dental tent, Baird sat nervously in a large, wooden chair which had been leaned back and secured in position with leather thongs. The solar-powered light above him was the brightest lamp he'd seen in years.

A young man had scraped Baird's teeth and poked around on his gums. Now, an older fellow approached.

"My name's Bill," the man said, smiling. "Let's have a look at the tooth.

Baird opened his mouth wide.

After looking, Bill patted the ranger's arm and said, "Sorry. I don't think I can save this one. You've got two others that I can probably do something for, though."

The big man stuck his head inside the tent and asked, "How's it going?"

"How many more patients do I have?" Bill wanted to know.

Ricky disappeared then came back, this time stepping all the way into the tent. "Three. But only one more pull after this one."

"Good," his friend said while preparing a tray of instruments. "This is gonna take more than a couple minutes."

Eyeing the instruments, the ranger asked, "Were you ever a real dentist?"

Bill laughed. "Haven't been asked *that* in a while. . . . Well, yes, I was a dentist of sorts."

The patient looked a bit concerned. "What do you mean, 'a dentist of sorts'?"

"I was a veterinary dentist. It's pretty much the same."

Ricky stepped closer and spoke to Baird. "I remember you. I just saw your partner outside, all cleaned up. I sent him 'round for a bowl of soup."

Baird tried to sit up. "You're kidding. What kind of soup?"

Bill pushed the ranger's head back down and pulled his mouth open before sticking a giant swab loaded with ointment around the bad tooth. "This will help a bit." He packed a few wads of cloth into the man's open mouth before he looked over at Ricky. "Can you hang around a minute? I may need you."

Without being told, the ranger knew the big guy's purpose would be to help hold him down if necessary. Baird grabbed the arms of the chair and held on with all of his might.

Bill leaned over his patient. "I always pray before I do things. Mind if I pray out loud?"

"Unuh," Baird said, shaking his head slightly.

Inside the big cabin nearby, Ulman downed his bowl of soup and slice of bread. Dare he ask for another? He waited for a lull before he approached the young man stirring a pot he'd pulled off the hearth.

"Do you think I could have another bowl of soup?"

"Yes, sir," the teenaged boy replied before ladling it out.

The ranger moved to the corner farthest from the door and tried to eat this bowl more slowly. He noted several other rangers, but didn't care to sit with them. They were from Norris' unit.

The big guy entered the room and seemed to be looking for someone. As soon as he saw Ulman, he stepped around people and walked over to him. "Just wanted to give you an update on your partner. The tooth is out, but we want to keep him tonight."

"Is he going to be okay?"

"He should recover. He has a nasty infection, though. We'd like to be able to medicate it and watch him for a while before you guys leave." Ricky pulled a nearby stool over and perched on it. "He's a pretty tough guy."

Ulman shrugged and went back to eating soup. "Everybody in our unit is. That's how we survive."

Ricky nodded. "Well, maybe you can relax a little for a few hours. . . . You gonna stay here tonight or go back up the mountain?"

Ulman looked up, surprised. "Would I be allowed to stay?"

"Sure," his host said, looking over at the other rangers in the room. "Long as you don't mind bunking with *them*. We're having a baseball game late this afternoon. Want to come?"

Things got quieter in the room when Major Tam walked through the door. Ricky turned and waved, the major nodded and walked toward him.

"Pull up a seat, Major," Ricky said, pointing to an empty stool.

Tam sat down before removing his hat and sunglasses. He eyed Ulman's clothing.

"I didn't know I'd be coming down here till the last minute," Ulman explained. "Someone here offered to lend me clothes for a few hours so mine could be washed."

Ricky started to rise from his seat and asked Tam, "Want some soup?"

"No," the major said, "I've already eaten."

Ricky sat back down. "I was just inviting . . ." he said, with a question in his eyes.

"Ulman," the ranger replied.

"I was just inviting Ulman here to the baseball game we're having this afternoon. His partner's gonna be laid up in the hospital tent tonight, so I thought Ulman could hang around for a while. Is that okay by you?"

Major Tam's eyes went back and forth between the soldier and Ricky a few times before they rested on Ulman. "He can stay. He's a ranger, so I'm sure I can depend on him to be on his best behavior."

Ulman looked somber, but not angry. "Thank you, sir," he said before rising. "If you'll excuse me now, I think I'll go check on Baird."

Under the canopy by the commons, Norris sat on the grass with Jason, Amanda, and a few others he'd known back in Oklahoma. After a while, Jason said he needed to go. One by one, the others excused themselves, finally leaving Norris alone with Mandy.

She briefly studied his face. It was the same earnest face she'd liked before. Older now, but essentially the same.

Her father had pulled her aside the night before for a serious discussion. He told her about Norris' feelings for her and then said that, even if she was complimented by the thought of an outside admirer, toying with Norris would be worse than cruel. Neither, Ricky stated, could she let pity enter into the picture. This was no time to instill false hopes in others. He asked her to pray for wisdom, then hugged her, and said he'd do no more interfering in the matter.

Even now, Mandy felt a bit amused. Her dear father was so concerned about her breaking the ranger's heart. He didn't know what a crush she'd had on Norris back in Oklahoma. She'd felt like such a geeky girl back then, but had talked to him whenever circumstances permitted. She'd been devastated when his unit left the quarantine camp. Shortly after that, however, conditions became so harsh, she had little thought of living beyond each day, much less seeing Norris again. Now, a year later, he'd appeared out of nowhere and sat just a foot away, having expressed an interest in her company.

Norris saw a hint of a smile on her face and hoped it meant she felt pleased to be with him. He looked out at the scenery. "The weather's been wonderful, hasn't it?"

"Yes," she said, "after such a brutal winter, this is heavenly."

Norris nodded and swallowed. What else could he say? There was so little time. Should he say something about the baseball game so she'd invite him to sit with her?

After an awkward silence, Mandy said, "I feel silly about this, but I need to ask you something."

Norris leaned forward. "I'd tell you anything, Amanda."

"What's your first name? All we've ever called you is Norris."

He grinned at her. "My first name is Luke."

A gentle breeze blew under the canopy, lifting the edge just enough for the afternoon sun to wink across their faces. Mandy scooted into the shade a bit farther and turned to face him directly.

Somewhat encouraged, he said, "I'd like to ask you a question as well."

She nodded.

"May I go to the baseball game with you?"

"Yes, on one condition. You must root for my team."

"Done!" he said, rising and offering her a hand up.

Ricky and Major Tam had moved to the privacy of a small, brown tent. Outside, several rangers stood guard. Inside, the two men sat at a small table where maps had been unrolled and inspected before an exchange.

"As you know," Tam continued, "when most of the migration was completed, the government spent the majority of its time and energy trying to contain the populace in the south. So far, their efforts up here have mostly centered on looting abandoned cities and getting crops going again.

"Once the big scare was over, though, continued restraints of martial law only reminded Americans down south of what they used to have. Resentment over the loss of personal liberty started running high. A man who has nothing left doesn't need that much 'security,' does he? Plus, seeing the government try to strong-arm Christians and others into getting coded started making lots of Americans nervous. . . . Those were the days we felt we had a good chance of winning. But being the media and marketing specialists that globalists are, they realized they were on the verge of losing and instituted a shift in policy."

Frustrated, Tam ran his scarred fingers over a knot in the grain of the tabletop as he spoke. "They've wised up now. In the south, what they couldn't get through fear, they hope to take without firing a shot. They've stopped the open persecution of people refusing codes and are trying a different tack: They're saying a good life is just around the corner now—as long as everyone cooperates. Of course, they say, Christians and others refusing codes are needlessly slowing improvements for everyone else.

"The real issue, they insist, isn't freedom of religion. It's identification. Talk shows and editorials ask what sort of people want to live like rats in decaying neighborhoods, with minimal shelter and food rather than be identified? The answer they offer is simple: Terrorists and criminals are the only ones who need to do this. . . . And, everyone knows what being labeled a terrorist can do to you. Another huge wave of people have given in and gotten coded."

The major's chair squeaked when he leaned forward to speak more confidentially. "Despite all this, things aren't entirely without hope. We have some plans which may help to turn the tide. I can't say much more than this, but I need to know something: If we come back with civilians in the spring, would you consider helping us to temporarily hide, shelter, and feed them? Will others in the refuge network consider helping us?" Tam stopped speaking when a gust of wind opened the tent flap, and they both looked over at the doorway.

Ricky took a sip of water from one of the two wooden cups on the table, then asked. "People from the south?"

Tam leaned over the table now. "No. Slaves from farms and factories up here in the zones."

Ricky took a deep breath as he considered it. Rumors had turned into persistent stories about "non-cooperative" people in the south disappearing, then being used as forced labor on huge farms and in factories in the north. While Ricky had no doubt the reports were true, he knew that even "video evidence" of these slaves wouldn't convince many people in the south. The government would merely claim they were computer-animated fantasies.

The major sensed a need to press his case. "If we could get a good number of these missing people to re-appear in the south, word of it would spread like fire. Personal accounts of real people who had been captured and forced to labor as slaves would create quite a stir amongst their acquaintances, friends, families, and others. Not to mention how it would blow the myths about the land up here being contaminated. Multitudes of people who have remained undecided about coding might yet see the truth."

Of course, anyone helping Tam pull this off would become a prime target for retribution. For nearly a minute, Ricky stared at a patch which had been carefully stitched onto the fabric of the tent, then said, "I must warn you that we will be moving from this place before winter. We've all felt we're to migrate elsewhere soon. That's our short-term plan. If Jesus isn't going to come back in our lifetime, however, we *must* make a way for future generations. . . . If He allows you to do this, and we're along your way south, we will help you."

###

The remainder of the day passed quickly. The baseball game ended with only an hour remaining till sunset. Most of the rangers came to the game and sat among the families, watching the match between adults and teens from the refuge. Ricky stood up at the end of the game and asked for everyone's attention.

"Food will now be served in the big cabin," he announced. "After the food, we will be gathering back here to pray. Anyone is welcome to come."

People in the crowd stood and began milling toward the cabin. Norris and Amanda started walking together across the field. Jason hung around with several rangers and talked.

Sam, the wounded ranger, got to her feet and looked around for her son, Chris. She'd already changed into her uniform and shorn her hair to a mere half inch long.

Dolan, her partner stretched before asking, "You sure you want to go up on the rim tonight? This is your last chance at comfort for a while."

"Listen," she quickly answered. "I just want to get out of here. I'd even take over a watch post if somebody else wanted to come down. Just let me get out in the wild where I can have gas and talk like a regular person. I'm suffocating down here."

Dolan laughed. "Did I accuse you of being a woman the other day? Let's at least grab some grub before we head up the hill."

Once again, the female ranger felt uncomfortable. "Okay, but these people are just too mushy. I hope I can get away without lots of hugging and emotional stuff."

When they got to the cabin, Jen saw her and said, "I see you're all ready to go."

"Yeah. . . . Thanks for the help and all."

Jen did hug her, but gave no indication of sadness at Sam's imminent departure. This confused her a bit. Weren't they sort of friends?

###

Back across the commons, Ulman, the ranger wearing Jason's clothes, remained seated on the grass with Dori and a mixed group of rangers and civilians.

He had come to the game earlier and seen her there. When he approached her, he noticed a small baby in her arms. Had he thought to look for a wedding ring earlier? Perhaps it was some other woman's child. This place was a virtual orphanage by the looks of it.

Dori looked up at him, but said nothing.

"Can I sit here and watch the game with you?" he asked pointing to a spot next to her?

She shrugged. He sat down.

"Look," he said, "I don't know why I said those things. Well, maybe I do know why . . . but, if I hurt you, I'm . . . sorry."

She looked at him. "*If?*"

He rubbed his forehead. "Okay. I'm sorry."

"I accept."

"Can we start off on a better foot now?" he asked.

She nodded.

"Good. I'm Bob."

"Nice to meet you, Bob. This," she said, shifting the baby so he could see her face, "is my daughter, Sherri."

"I didn't know you were married," he offered.

"I've never been married." She kissed the baby's hand and said, "He died before he even knew about her."

Ulman closed his eyes and shook his head, "God," he said, before his eyes snapped back open. "I mean, gosh. I didn't mean to say that about you being perfect and all. . . . Not that you're imperfect." He sighed. "I can't seem to get my foot out of my mouth, can I?"

She kissed little Sherri again before saying. "I made a big mistake—I suffered for it; and, sometimes, she will suffer for it. But God has forgiven me, and we'll do just fine." She looked directly at the ranger. "I need to make things clear to you, though. This is a mistake I don't ever intend to make again. I understand that these may very well be your last hours alive— so if you want to spend any of them with me, know now that we won't do anything you'd be ashamed to face God with a few hours from now."

"I understand," Ulman said soberly. He reached over and stroked the baby's cheek. "How old is she?"

"Five months. Just about to crawl."

The ranger slowly withdrew his hand and looked out at the open field. "I had a son. Lost him and his mother to the fever when he was sixteen months old. . . . I really am sorry I was such a jerk earlier. I *am* bitter inside and I say stupid things."

"It's okay," she interrupted. "I understand. Truce."

After that, Dori and Bob got caught up in the fun of the baseball game and forgot everything else. Once the game ended, the whole thing seemed surreal to him. They'd sat there, out in the middle of nowhere, all of them survivors of unspeakable horrors, all of them facing uncertainty . . . yet gathered in a field to watch baseball and nibble on carrots, of all things. Little kids had run everywhere, playing without concern. One of them even caught a butterfly. Ulman felt as if he'd entered a time warp or slipped into a parallel universe. Maybe all of this was just a dream, and he'd wake up on cold, rocky ground any minute.

Someone nearby made a joke, and Dori laughed. She had the silliest laugh. He wanted to commit the sound to memory and be able to remember it when he was far away from this place. How many miles would he be from here tomorrow night? No, he decided, he wouldn't waste his last hours here being preoccupied with tomorrow. In this parallel universe, he'd shut out all thoughts of survival or revenge.

"Are you going to go back up to your camp after supper?" one of the civilian men asked him.

"No," Ulman answered. "I'm staying with the other rangers down here tonight."

###

Slowly ambling across the commons, Amanda and Luke Norris took turns asking each other questions.

"Yes," Mandy said, "I thought the troops would kill us, but when the time came near, I wasn't afraid. I was grateful. Grateful to be with all the others, grateful it would probably be over quickly. Then, when God spared us, at first, we were all excited. It was like we were walking on clouds. In the days to follow, though, most of us became kind of disappointed that we were still here and would have to wait for Heaven. Then God spoke to us and told us we had things to do yet."

Norris didn't dare look at her. "And . . . are you like Jason? Do you feel you will never marry, never have children of your own?"

She blushed. "God hasn't told me anything about that."

Even though he couldn't see her in the darkness, he sensed her embarrassment and moved onto another topic. "I'd like to go to the meeting with you tonight. Is that okay?"

She smiled. "Yes."

Chapter 24

A suburb of Dallas

Michael could hear someone banging on the door.

"Open up!" a woman called. "I'll come back with troops if you don't open this door right now!"

Michael got up from the sofa and moved toward the sound. He tripped on debris scattered in his path and fell.

"I hear you in there! Open up!"

"Keep your shirt on!" Michael yelled. He got to his feet again and limped to the door. He left the chain on and opened it the few inches the chain would allow.

Outside stood Ms. Elliot, the landlady. Behind her waited two other women holding hands.

"Where's the rent?" Ms. Elliot said.

"Hey look . . . I haven't got it today, but I can get some money tomorrow."

"Won't do. Your rent came up last week. Either you pay today or you move today. This couple is willing to pay me right now, so make up your mind."

"Then I guess I'll leave." Michael said as he slammed the door in her face.

"Okay then!" she shouted. "Five o'clock! I'll knock down the door if I have to!"

Michael sat on the sofa with both hands on his head. Had another week passed? He went to the video screen. The news would tell him what day it was.

The screen didn't come on. He tried a switch. No lights. The power had been turned off.

He hadn't left the house since the last time he'd spoken to Linda. First, he drank every alcoholic beverage he could find. When the booze ran out, he found his black box and had only been conscious a few hours a day for nearly a week.

He tried to collect his thoughts. Where could he go?

Suddenly, he got up and walked to his bedroom. He rummaged through the closet until he found a suitcase, threw it on the bed, and started digging through the piles on the floor for whatever he needed to pack. He went into each room, ransacking it until he found two or three things to toss into the suitcase. Lastly, he found the black box with the wire still attached to it. He studied it for a while, then stuffed it into the case before closing it and lifting it off the bed.

He walked into the kitchen, carrying the suitcase, and looked around. A package of crackers appeared to be the only thing still edible. He grabbed the packet and stuffed it into a pocket before walking out the door, leaving it wide open.

Michael walked for about thirty minutes before he grew tired. Two weeks of little food had taken its toll. He found it an effort just to put one foot in front of the other. He stopped and sat down. After a few minutes, he stood again and reached into his pocket. He had fourteen blue bills and some change. It would have to do until he found a job . . . or sold his black box.

Maybe he could buy some protein packs. He found a store and went inside.

"You take money?" he asked the salesgirl.

She nodded, and he walked to the shelves containing protein packets of various flavors. He took three packages and went back to the girl.

"That will be twelve blue bills," she said.

"These only add up to ten!" Michael said indignantly.

"I'm sorry, sir," she said in a monotone as she inspected her fingernails. "The bank is now charging us twenty percent for handling money. We can't absorb such an increase and are sure all the other stores are doing the same."

Michael gave her an icy stare and handed her the money. He downed one of the packets, then headed north. Each city block he passed, the houses seemed to be in worse repair. After a few miles, homes were little more than shacks with cloth or plastic covering their broken windows. The sound of millions of flies filled the air.

He remembered a place he'd been to ages ago and tried to find it. After a tiring search he found the house, and walked across a yard completely devoid of grass. Michael stepped up on the porch, which creaked underfoot, and raised his hand to knock on the door.

"What do you want?" a male voice inside said before his knuckles made contact.

"I'm looking for Ramon," Michael said loudly.

"Ramon ain't here," the voice called back.

Silence followed, so Michael turned to walk away. The door opened, and a woman wearing a dirty satin housecoat emerged. "What do you want Ramon for?"

Michael pointed to the suitcase. "I have something to sell."

"Well, maybe we can help you," she said, moving back inside and leaving the door open.

Michael hesitated a moment, then walked to the door. It was dark inside because blankets on the windows blocked the light, but he could see the girl talking to a man. He had huge false eyelashes, bright red lips, and rouge-covered cheeks. Michael cautiously stepped inside, thinking the man looked like some sort of hideous doll.

A second man closed the door behind Michael and said, "What you got?"

Michael realized he should have stayed on the porch. "A black box."

"If we was interested, what would you want for it?"

"Four hundred," Michael answered. "It's used, but I haven't had a bad ride off it yet."

The two men laughed.

"I paid Ramon *five* for it!" Michael said.

"Well, if you want to sell it to Ramon, you can find him in prison!"

They all laughed again.

"How much will you give me for it?" he asked.

"One hundred," the man by the door said.

Michael stepped back to the door, opened it slightly, and stuck his foot in the space before responding. "You give me the money, I give you the box."

"Hey, don't be tense, man," the guy near the door said. "We ain't gonna hurt you." He looked over at his grotesque friend. "Right?"

The two of them laughed, and the woman began a slow retreat to the back of the room.

The man near the door reached into his pocket and pulled out a wad of money. He peeled off some bills and handed them to Michael. "Here. Gimme the box."

Michael took the money as he opened the door further with his foot. He unzipped the case and reached in while backing out the door. He tossed the box on the floor and, as he started to run, he heard the man yell, "I paid for it! It's mine!" followed by a slapping sound, a girl's scream, and a loud crash.

It'd been more than eight years since he'd been on the track team in school, and he was definitely out of shape; but he was certain he made record time for at least several blocks.

Chapter 25

A few miles north of Dallas

Michael prepared to spend his first night out in the open since he'd left the apartment. Last night, he'd stayed with a friend. From here on out, though, he'd be on his own.

He'd purchased an ancient bicycle for fifty blue bills and rode it where the streets weren't too cluttered. Now that the sun had nearly set, he walked along holding the bike.

He looked about cautiously. No one appeared to be walking around. Maybe it would rain. A small twinge of fear ran through him as his eyes shot up to the sky. Hazy, but no ominous-looking clouds. Since the contaminations, people feared rain, snow, and even wind. For almost a year, a sudden shower or gust could have been filled with spores, chemicals, or gasses that could coat the skin or burn the lungs. Michael remembered all too clearly being covered with blisters after a walk in a passing shower.

Darkness continued to grow until he could no longer see to walk with safety on the streets. The shabby neighborhood revealed the status of its occupants. Obviously, the vast majority had opted against coding, so their neighborhood would continue to decay. The solar and chemical lights placed here after the disasters had broken long ago and never been repaired. No government funds would be wasted here.

He spotted the glow of a fire and stopped to open his knife. Cautiously walking toward the blaze, he held onto the knife inside his jacket pocket. Stepping closer, he could see quite a few people had gathered near the fire, standing or sitting around its light. As he drew closer, one of the men at the fire said something, and they all turned to face him.

"You are welcome if you come in peace," a deep voice said behind him.

Michael turned to see a rather large man stepping out of a ground-floor window about ten feet away. The man had huge gnarled hands which, to Michael's relief, carried no weapons. He let go of the knife in his own pocket and put his hand up.

"I'm not looking to hurt anyone. I just came because I saw the fire."

"Come on, then," said a small man near the fire. When Michael got closer, the man offered his left hand. The empty right sleeve of the man's coat had been tucked into his belt.

"The name's Tom."

"Michael," he said, taking his suitcase off the bike and resting the bike on the ground.

They shook hands and walked closer to the fire. Most of them wore torn clothing, and Michael noted a badly cracked left lens in Tom's glasses.

"Got any substance?" Tom asked, eying the suitcase.

Michael didn't know what to say at first. He looked at Tom for a moment. "What makes you think I'm not a Sammie?" he finally asked in measured tones. Sammies were *ex*-US soldiers or "Uncle Sam's men" who signed on with the new government. They'd taken over many policing duties in the post-disaster South once resentment over international troops became a problem.

Tom reached into his pocket and pulled out a "flattened-egg" looking object like the one troops used to find the man Michael hid so long ago. Tom held the disk in front of Michael.

"No light. Means you haven't got a code. That makes the chances of you being a Sammie or a cop pretty slim. And it's obvious *I'm* not a Sammie," he said, pointing to the empty sleeve on his coat.

A woman called out, "*Troops!*" from a nearby rooftop.

Within seconds all the people around the fire disappeared into the darkness. Michael wanted to run but had no idea where to go. In the pitch-black streets he didn't have much chance of doing anything other than breaking his neck.

A spotlight hit him, and he heard the noise of boots on the street. Two female soldiers ran up and held him at gunpoint while a third searched him. They found his knife and took it before handcuffing him.

"My bike and my suitcase," Michael said, "don't leave them here, someone'll take 'em."

"Okay," a soldier said, "We'll bring them along. Now get going!"

One of them kept shoving him forward into the darkness causing him to trip on unseen debris. By the time he'd walked several blocks to a stone building used for a station house, he had a bloody nose and had torn the left knee of his pants. Compared to the darkness outside, the lantern lights inside seemed bright.

Stepping inside the station, Michael remembered his black box and was thankful he'd sold it. Although it wasn't illegal to have one, it would make him suspect for all sorts of things.

"Looks like another bonfire bunny," one of the female officers said.

They made him sit in a three-legged chair they'd leaned against a wall. Trying to keep his balance on the chair with his hands cuffed behind his back proved to be quite a feat.

"So whatcha doin' in these parts?" a male officer behind the desk in front of him asked.

"Nothing. Just walking. . . . It got dark, and I saw the fire. I came to the fire, and the people there said I was welcome as long as I meant them no harm."

The officer held up Michael's knife. "That why you had this in your pocket?"

"Well, I had to make sure they weren't going to harm me either."

"So you didn't know any of them?"

"No."

"Why are you out wandering around?"

"Is that against the law now, too?" Michael asked.

"What's your name?"

"You want to charge me with something?"

"Yes, 'non-cooperation' if you want to give me a bad time."

During the massive migration south, the government made sweeping changes in the law. Soldiers and police had more power to control people who resisted the necessary re-alignment taking place.

Michael thought for a moment before he spoke. "My name is Michael Gordon."

The officer looked to another soldier who said, "No code."

"Where do you live, Michael?"

"I'm sort of between apartments right now."

"Well, where do you work?"

"I'm sort of between jobs, too."

"Why aren't you rooming?"

During the exodus, a system of putting people up in government buildings evolved. Referred to as "rooming," this "positive answer to homelessness" became the worst existence possible. It consisted of a smelly mattress in a cold building where every movement could be monitored. This way, no one wanted to stay long. People found jobs and housing as fast as they could.

Michael knew his rights. "The law says I have two weeks to find alternative accommodations before I have to room, and this is only my second night out."

"We'll just check on that. What was your last address?"

He gave them the address of the apartment he and Linda had shared, and hoped the owner hadn't filed charges against him for damages.

The law allowed them to detain him while they looked into his status. A female cop ushered him to a cell inhabited by several women who huddled in a corner and ignored him. He made sure to roll out his blanket near a wall and lay with his back to it. Eventually, he fell into a fitful sleep, dreaming on and off about contaminated people, yellow air, and being chased.

When he awoke, the sun had come up, and the women were gone. He just lay still for a moment, collecting his thoughts before he got up and looked through the bars.

"Hey, when do I get out?"

The officer who had questioned him the night before walked to the cell door with the keys, saying, "Right now if you wanna go." He looked as if he hadn't slept. His hair stood up at odd angles and he needed a shave. "We've contacted your last landlord. She's not too thrilled with you; but your roommate already covered what you owe, so you're free to leave."

The officer unlocked the door and stepped back before speaking again. "Your things are on my desk, and your bike is against the wall over there. One word of warnin' though. Start south. There's nothin' north of here but the zones. The only people north of here are outlaws and wanderers with contaminated brains. We've already been out all night chasin' your fire people. The one missin' his arm is an escaped convict from Darby's Institution. He and his guys killed—and possibly ate—one of my soldiers last night. We've been lookin' in every crack for them and can't find 'em. Take my word for it. These ain't friendly parts. All you'll get up here is trouble. Head south."

Michael collected his things and put them on the back of the bike. When he stepped out into the sunlight, he could barely open his eyes. Once they adjusted, he looked around. In the darkness the night before, he hadn't seen much. What he saw now shocked him. Many of the buildings (or parts of buildings) showed evidence of fire. Some had been reduced to rubble. It looked like a city after a war.

He got on his bike and rode. The few people walking the streets kept clear of him, eyeing him suspiciously as he passed.

After midday, he stopped and sat in the shade of a wall left from a fallen two-story building and realized his last protein pack had disappeared. He had no idea whether it had fallen out of his suitcase the night before or if one of the Sammies had taken it. He did, however, have the crackers from his apartment. They were more than stale. They were limp. But he ate all of them.

He decided to take the soldier's advice and head in a more southerly direction, but because of impassable areas, he ended up going more west than south. After an hour or so, the condition of the houses improved slightly. When he found a neighborhood store that took money, he bought some food, ate it, then rested.

Sitting in the shade of a tree, he realized how quiet it was. Only the sound of an occasional insect buzzing broke the silence. Almost no one moved about. The day had grown hot, and most people wanted to be out of the sun.

A dog ran down the street and into the store where he'd bought the food. The old man proprietor chased it out with a broom, then began sweeping the front porch of the home that doubled as a store. He stopped and leaned his frail body on the broom, in need of a rest. Michael got up and walked toward the man, but before he could offer help, a woman with light brown hair opened a window on the second floor of the home and leaned out.

"Daddy! What are you doing?" she called. She couldn't see him beneath the roof of the porch. "Are you sweeping?

That's my work. I'll be right down," she said before she disappeared from the window.

Michael slowed his approach when she stepped out of the front door. She was trim and tan, and he considered how pretty she looked.

"Now Daddy," she scolded, "I said I'd do this. You aren't feeling your best today and here you are, out in this heat, sweeping up clouds of dust to breathe . . ."

The old man straightened. "I'm not a little boy, you know."

"Oh, I'm sorry," she said, hugging him. "I'm not trying to hurt your feelings. But you aren't well today. Come on, there are things inside that need pricing, and you're much better at remembering prices than I am. . . . Please?"

The old man kissed her on the forehead and walked into the store. She waited for a moment and then began to sweep.

Michael stepped onto the porch. "Can I sweep that for you?"

She stopped sweeping and studied him. He noted the tiny wrinkles around her ice-blue eyes—probably from constant squinting in the harsh sunlight. For an uncomfortable moment, those eyes seemed to have X-ray capabilities, looking beyond his frame, into his soul.

She came to some sort of conclusion before she said, "Sure," and handed him the broom. "How much you want for doing this and other icky chores around here today? My sister is gone for the day, and I've got my hands full."

"Can you cook?" Michael asked.

"Sure," she said again.

"I haven't eaten anything cooked in weeks. How about I do this, and the other things, in exchange for a hot meal?"

"Deal! What's your name?" she asked.

"Michael."

"Nice name. I like it. I'm Sara." She turned to go inside. "Come on in when you're done there, Michael" she said over her shoulder.

When he finished, she had him weigh flour and other grains to bag up, then let him stack cans and wash two remaining windows. While wiping the outside of the windows, he could see his own reflection and he realized how thin and ragged he appeared. What bothered him the most were the large, dark rings under his eyes. He couldn't believe how old he looked . . . and he suddenly felt old.

"Dinner's almost ready," she declared, interrupting his thoughts. The time had gone quickly.

Just then a girl came around the corner, pushing a hand cart loaded with large bags.

Sara ran to meet her.

"Noel! Look at all this. . . . You shouldn't have done it. You must be exhausted."

Michael came to help. Noel, who appeared to be in her late teens, had a dark tan and looked a lot like her sister. He marveled at the weight of the cart when he started to move it. "How far have you come with this?" he asked.

"About two miles, I guess," Noel said, giving him a quizzical look.

Sara realized her sister had never seen this man before.

"Oh. Michael this is my sister, Noel. Noel, this is Michael. I hired him to do chores today while you were out. Daddy was trying to do too much again."

Michael thought of the two girls with the frail old man and wondered how they could survive without constant fear of attack. Destitute people lived not far from here.

"Weren't you scared coming that far with all this food?" he asked Noel.

"Sometimes," she looked down, "but then I remember all any of us have is God's protection, and who could ask for more?"

Sara put an arm around her. "We've had to do it. Daddy can't anymore. We just go day-by-day."

When they sat at dinner that evening, Michael felt tired but really good about himself and the day. He looked around the table. The simple food smelled good. Few of the dishes matched, but all of them gleamed.

He started to reach for a biscut when they bowed their heads. Embarrassed, he lowered his eyes.

Noel spoke. "Thank you for this day and this food. Thank You for giving us strength and courage. Help us to serve You and work in Your name until Your Son comes. Amen."

The meal tasted delicious, was accompanied by light-hearted conversation, and there was lots of laughter. Sara and Noel were very animated despite the hard day both of them put in. By the time they finished eating, darkness had fallen, and the girls got up to light candles.

Michael helped them clear away the dishes while the old man retired to a rocking chair which creaked with each backward sweep. When they'd finished in the kitchen, Sara and Noel sat on a sofa near their father, and Michael sat on a chair he'd pulled away from the table.

"I know what we need," Noel said. "Play us a song, Daddy."

"I don't know, girl. I'm gettin' so old that I don't know if I have the air." He turned and winked at Michael.

"Oh Daddy!" she said with a scolding look.

He tapped his shirt pockets with his hands and eventually produced a small harmonica. He put it to his mouth and played. The skill the old man had with the instrument impressed Michael. After he'd played for a while, he put the harmonica back into his pocket and just rocked.

"Well, it's time to turn in," Sara broke the silence.

They all stood, and Michael realized he had no place to go. He'd felt so at home, he totally forgot his need to find a place to sleep.

Sara looked at Noel and nodded. "Noel, you and Daddy can mosey on to bed. I'll be up in a few minutes."

Noel circled her arm in her father's and said, "Looks like it's time to go."

"I can get up the stairs without a woman on my arm," the old man protested.

"Then you help me up the stairs," she said smiling. They left the room arguing in a friendly fashion.

Sara spoke softly. "If you'd care to stay, Noel and Daddy and I have decided you could sleep in the storage room downstairs. It's not fancy, but it's clean and dry. . . . In exchange for your labor, we could provide your meals, a cot, and ten blue bills a week."

Michael didn't need to consider it. He only needed food and shelter right now. He stood and said, "Deal," before extending his hand.

She laughed and offered her own hand. Her eyes sparkled, and he couldn't help gazing into them.

After a few moments, her look became serious, and she gently pulled her hand away. "Don't mistake our kindness for naivete," she said. "I don't know what sort of person you are, but we are Christians, and we don't steal or take advantage of people. You can have your own opinions about us or of what we believe; but if you stay here, you have to abide by the standards we live by. If you keep working as hard as you did today, you're welcome to stay indefinitely."

He felt a bit awkward. "I understand."

She took some blankets out of a closet and showed him to the storeroom in the basement. It was cool, and it smelled of dried apples.

"What a heavenly scent!" he said, trying to sound saintly.

"It is nice, isn't it?" she replied, setting the blankets on the cot then looking up at him. "This is it. . . . See you at dawn."

Chapter 26

A few miles north of Dallas

About the time Sara and her sister had started preparing Michael's first dinner in their home, Linda Posner was getting out of a jeep, feeling woozy. She hadn't ridden in a vehicle for a long while, and the road had been very bumpy. Looking around, she couldn't understand how a neighborhood so devastated could still be occupied.

A crowd gathered around the jeep, and she pushed her way through it.

"Look at that," one woman said, touching the sleeve of Linda's blouse.

"Ohhhh," several women said at once, one of them reaching out to stroke the soft cloth.

"Stop that!" Linda said, pulling away and brushing off the sleeve.

A soldier called out, "Okay, okay. Everybody make way."

Linda hurried through the opening into the building and looked around the dingy interior.

"May I speak to the officer in charge?" she said to the woman at the desk.

"That would be me," the woman answered.

"Yes. Well, I'm looking for a man you're holding here. His name is Michael Gordon."

"Michael Gordon?"

"Yes."

"Let me look at the list," the woman said, "Michael Gordon, Michael Gordon, Michael Gor—here it is." After a pause, she went to another sheet of paper and read it before she looked up. "Sorry. He's gone. We released him this morning."

Linda's heart sank. She felt weak all over and wanted to sit down.

"You okay?"

"Yes . . . Yes. I just wanted . . . do you know where he went, what direction, anything?"

"We don't keep that kinda information unless the person is under suspicion for something. You filin' charges against him?"

Linda turned and slowly walked to the door. "No. I just wanted to talk to him." She stepped outside and pressed through the curious onlookers. Climbing into the rear seat of the jeep, she said, "Driver, take me back."

The driver said nothing but started the engine and put the jeep in gear. He honked the horn twice, and the jeep roared forward as people jumped out of the way.

Broiling just above the horizon, the sun had turned the sky a brilliant red. Oblivious to its beauty, Linda clung to her seat in the jeep as it bumped over every obstacle. She wondered what she would do now. Where could Michael have gone? Why would he have come this far north? Did he know someone here? It could be as long as two weeks before he reported to a rooming center. She swore out loud, and the driver looked at her in the rear-view mirror.

Why, Linda asked herself over and over, had she tried to play that stupid game with Michael? He wasn't like other men she'd known. Why did she care what the other people in her office thought of him? Why couldn't she have just waited for him to come around? Tears threatened to spill over the rim of her eyelids, but she quickly wiped them away.

She remembered the way Michael looked the last time she saw him. He had called to ask her to come back. He looked so pale and thin. But no, she couldn't resist turning the knife just a little more. She wanted him to agree to her demands, to be jealous, to say he loved her, and to come get her.

She swore again and leaned to rest her head against the roll bar of the vehicle. *How stupid of me to think he couldn't make it without me. Isn't he the one who saved ME when we first met?* She pictured, once again, how tenderly he'd watched over her and taken care of her when she was so near starvation.

Her eyes stung with more tears as she looked out into the darkening ghetto. *He knows how to live out here. He doesn't need technology to survive. Where could he have gone?*

The jeep continued to bump along. They'd get onto some better roads soon. And then she'd have to face Alex. She'd illegally accessed his command file, and gotten the jeep to pick her up, saying it was for official business. It would've been worth it if she had only found Michael.

She began to think of all the things she would do for Michael when they got back together. She would be a better person to him . . . she would love him just the way he was.

Chapter 27

Northwest of Dallas

Despite the fact he'd been working in the store for several weeks now, Michael still had trouble adjusting to the dawn wake-up call. This morning, once he'd pried his eyes open, he'd helped Sara carry various items up from the storeroom. After an hour of lugging, Noel served them breakfast. Once they'd eaten, Sara assigned Michael some odd jobs to do in the cellar while she stocked shelves with the things they'd brought up.

In the first few days of his employment, he revamped the cellar, making modifications to shelves and storage spaces. Sara, Pete, and Noel marveled at Michael's clever changes which allowed for greater capacity and efficiency. After a week, they wondered what they'd done without him.

He'd made things so efficient that, today, Michael couldn't find much to do. He polished off his chores in no time and came up the steps. Standing in the rear doorway of the store, he could see Sara walking back and forth. He just stood there a moment, watching her take bags of flour from the counter over to a shelf.

The unbearable heat of the day made her want to slow down. Even with the shutters and the windows open, there didn't seem to be a breath of air coming in. Walking back to the counter for more bags of flour she saw Michael in her peripheral vision.

What a mess I must look, she thought.

She pretended not to see him, but pulled at loose strands of hair and shoved them back into the knot on her head. She picked up two more bags and tried to pay more attention to walking smoothly and gracefully. In fact, she became so intent on smooth and graceful, she neglected to look where she stepped and planted her foot right on a large wad of warm gum.

"Oh, no," she said, recognizing the sensation of a shoe being pulled back to the floor.

Michael chuckled and came to her rescue.

Her face flushed. "Oh, *there* you are. Can you take these bags please? Apparently, someone left a deposit here."

Michael pulled a small knife out of his pocket and set it on the shelf nearest her right hand. "Here's my knife. Hand me the bags," he said. He became even more amused as she lifted her foot and long, pink strings followed.

"*Real* cute," she said, opening the knife.

Wanting to get it over with as soon as possible, she didn't take off her shoe. Instead, she intended to simply lift her foot, scrape the gum off her shoe, and then clean the floor. But when she lifted her foot, she lost her balance, so she put out her free hand to lean on the wall. In a split second, she realized she'd been standing in front of a large, open window. She dropped the knife as she went sailing out of the store. Her outstretched hand hit the porch first as gravity continued its merciless pull on her body. Next, her hip came down with a big *plop* while her legs flew up to accommodate their slide across the windowsill. And then it was over. One foot still rested on the sill, with long strands of gum dangling from the shoe.

Had she ever done anything so clumsy in her whole life? Her eyes quickly shot up and down the street to see if anyone had witnessed the spectacle. No one in sight. Unfortunately, she could hear howling laughter coming from inside the store.

She got to her feet and leaned in the window. There lay Michael, on the floor, struggling to breathe as gales of laughter convulsed him, and tears came out of his eyes. "I'm so sorry," he kept trying to say, and, "I can't help it." He never quite got either phrase out.

After removing her shoe, Sara stepped back through the window, her face burning with embarrassment. She hurried up the stairs to her room.

The laughing didn't stop for quite a while.

About half an hour later, she limped to the top of the stairs and listened.

". . . and then," she heard Michael say, "she went *right out the window! Like this!*" followed by what she could now easily recognize as his unique form of hysteria, joined by her father's equally loud outburst. Sara quickly went back to her room and soon heard the additional sound of her sister, Noel, in stitches. She'd just about decided that she would never come out of her room again when she heard a knock at the door.

"Who is it?" She asked in a hostile tone.

"It's me. Daddy."

Silence.

"Can I come in?"

"Come in," she said, trying to sound more in control.

"Michael says you had quite a fall." Pete tried in vain not to chuckle. "Are you okay?"

Sara's face flushed again and she said nothing.

He struggled not to smile. "I'm sorry, Duchess. If it happened to your sister, you'd be laughin' too! Don't be mad," her father said, getting more serious now.

"Only if you promise not to mention it or laugh about it again."

Pete tried to look as sober as a judge. "I'll try," he said, looking her in the eye.

After holding her gaze for only moments, his chin began to quiver. Both of them burst out laughing.

Chapter 28

Austin, in the former state of Texas

He saw a flash in the audience. At this point, psychic Tony Bensen looked around and realized he'd somehow walked up for prayer at the meeting. After some confusion, a man began walking toward him . . . reaching out to touch him. When their eyes made contact, fear seized Tony's limbs, freezing him in place. The man had figured him out, and now wanted to strangle him. Swordsman wanted to kill him.

"Judas! Traitor!" Swordsman declared. Stares of hatred stabbed through him from all sides. Everyone knew. The man's hands stretched out menacingly.

"No!" Tony shouted, and sat up in bed. He looked around his room and realized it was just a dream. The same dream he'd had every night for a week. He exhaled heavily. Maybe his herbs had caused the dream. He'd have to change dealers.

Tony had been following Swordsman for weeks and had to work at keeping pace with the man who rarely rested more than a day and had meetings even on the days he traveled. Beginning tomorrow, however, the spiritual leader would be staying put for a four-day conference. Tony hoped to use the extra time to meditate during the day, thereby increasing the chances of a breakthrough.

He rubbed the kink in his neck as he tried to figure out what he'd do to armor himself against the recurring bad dream. He rotated his shoulders around and said, "So much for getting extra rest."

He moved to where he'd draped his pants over a chair and took a small phone out of a front pocket. Since he was awake, why not call in and tell them where he was? He heard a pause followed by a tone. He keyed in several numbers, then spoke slowly and clearly, "I will attend meetings in Vector 340 for several nights, beginning tomorrow. No progress thus far." He hung up and returned the phone to the front pocket of his pants. Next, he threw the rest of his herbs in the toilet and pumped them down. *What I really need is a grapefruit,* he told himself. Recent reports touted the grapefruit as "the brain food of the century." He got one out of a bag and sat at the small table in his hotel room as he peeled it. After eating half the sections, he decided he wasn't hungry for grapefruit.

"Oh well," he sighed, before placing the remaining half of the fruit in a bowl at the center of the table. *Do I feel any smarter now?* An amused smile briefly lit his face. *No.*

He went back to bed and counted down inwardly, trying to empty his mind while he breathed deeply. Soon the sensation swept over him, and he relaxed for a few moments.

In the midst of the blankness, he asked, *What should I do?*

No answer came, but after some time, he drifted off to sleep. The next morning, he awoke with a pain in his shoulder. He'd slept on it too long, and now the muscles throbbed in revenge.

As if the pain wasn't enough, he had an ominous feeling about the day. After thinking a while, he decided to spend some serious time in preparation for the evening. He needed to get his mind ready.

This is the most difficult case I've ever accepted, he said to himself. *But why? Maybe I didn't expect such a challenge. Maybe I thought I'd figured them out a long time ago. . . . But most the Christians I knew before were mere shadows of the people I see now. These people operate in a dimension of faith I've not seen before. These people have a common resolve. . . . I wonder how they keep it.*

He got out his tone recording and put it in the player. Tones poured through the speakers, filling not only the room but his mind as well. Each tone lasted twelve seconds and sounded at a slightly varying pitch. He could hum most of them by heart now and sat in the middle of the floor, with his eyes closed, modulating his own voice to match the sounds he heard.

Tonight, Tony would try to find a point of contact between his mind and the mind of another man. He'd studied the man and his habits. Nothing about Swordsman seemed overtly dangerous. Yet, as each day passed, Tony felt more and more like withdrawing. Something inside him told him he didn't want to contact, to touch, the current flowing out of this man.

Surely there will be others like me on the job. Should I just pass on this one? Tony shook his head. *I've made a commitment and I'm not going to back down now. If anyone can make successful contact with Swordsman, I can.*

He wondered if it might be the last thing he ever did.

Chapter 29

Northwest of Dallas

Having only three checkers left, Michael carefully considered his next move. Pete started to softly play his harmonica. As the time wore on for Michael to make a choice, the harmonica music got louder. Michael looked up.

"You trying to break my concentration?"

"Is that what you think your doin'? Concentrating? I thought you were going to sleep! Heaven knows I might do that very thing if you take much longer."

Michael's eyes lit up. "Too bad, Pete. I hate to see a good man go down, but this is the real world of checkers. No mercy, right?"

"I was hoping you might decide to stop a while and enjoy the music," the old man said as he put the harmonica to his lips again.

"Sorry!" Michael jumped Pete's last three checkers.

"I'm the one that's sorry," Pete said with a smile. "Sorry I ever taught you how to play checkers! Wanna make it the best two out of three?"

They both heard a familiar footstep in the hall.

"Daddy?" Sara said, knocking on the door before entering. "Can I borrow Michael?"

"Are you trying to ensure my defeat? I can't let the man get away now. You can have him all day tomorrow, Duchess. Right now, I have the family honor to think about." He winked at Michael.

"What do you need?" Michael said to her.

"The downstairs window is stuck again."

"Okay," Michael said. "Tell you what, Pete, you set up another game, and I'll be right back." Michael sprang up and left the room.

"Thanks!" she shouted after him.

Pete considered his daughter. "He's a handy man to have around. Got a lot of potential." He watched the zeal with which she attacked a wrinkle in the bed. "Uh huh."

"What do you think of him?"

She moved to the other side of the bed and pulled on the cover. "Hmmmm?"

"What do you think of him?"

She'd yanked a new wrinkle into the cover and she made an exasperated noise before she looked up at her father. "Is this some sort of trick question?"

Pete's eyes followed her as she continued to smooth out the bedspread. "There's more in his heart than we know . . . but I see things changing in him every day. I really like him. If he was a believer, he'd be . . . a good man. I hope I get to see it happen."

Her expression saddened; but before she could respond, her father put a hand to one ear and said, "Run along, Dutchess! I hear my opponent bounding up the stairs."

After Michael entered the room, she quickly stepped into the hall, but stood and watched them for a moment. "Night, Daddy. Night, Michael. Don't stay up too late. Dawn comes early!"

"In just two more games, this guy will be beaten and begging for bed," said the old man, "Unless, of course, he would rather concede defeat and hit the sack now."

"Now *my* honor is at stake. I must stay and fight to the last checker!" Michael said melodramatically.

Sara smiled. "I think I'll leave you two kids to battle it out."

Once she'd disappeared down the hall, Pete looked down at the checkers. "She's a wonderful woman."

"Uhhuh," Michael replied, making his move.

"Don't know if she'll ever get married though."

Michael put his elbow on the table and rested his head in his hand. Still not suspecting the direction of the conversation, he asked, "Why not? She's pretty enough."

Pete moved a checker. "Pretty she may be, but she's also determined to live by the word of God. Not just any man will do for her. He not only has to suit her, he has to be a Christian."

Michael looked up. "Why do I get the sinking feeling you're going to talk about getting me saved and married off just to mess up my game?"

Pete winked and leaned forward a bit. "An old man has to take victory where he can get it. . . . Besides, a little preaching wouldn't hurt you anyway. You're strong, you can take it, right?"

"Not tonight Pete," Michael said, letting his head sink down and rest on his arm. "I'm too tired to argue about that kinda stuff. Everybody claims they're right, everybody says the other guy is full of it. All they all want is for everyone to live by their rules. There's no room for the individual anymore. Why can't I just be me?"

"Okay. The old man's off the pulpit now. You wanna play or what?"

Michael smiled. "Actually, I *am* getting tired. Is it okay if we extend this until tomorrow?"

"Got ya on the ropes, huh?"

"Yeah. Let me recoup my strength." Michael stood and stretched. "Just leave it set up, and we'll take up where we left off. Good night, Pete."

"Good night, Michael. See you in the morning."

Chapter 30

A suburb of Atlanta

Jessica Newsome listened, transfixed by the housekeeper's voice. She loved it when Edwina told stories.

The little girl sat on the floor of her spacious, lavender-wallpapered room surrounded by a menagerie of stuffed animals. Mrs. Grant seated herself on top of the big toy chest. She'd gotten to the best part, so Jessica scooted closer.

" . . . but Daniel wasn't paying any attention to what they thought. He decided he'd be true to God no matter what. And you know what? Those mean old guys spied on Daniel and waited until he prayed. And when he did, they ran in and *snatched* him up!" she said, grabbing Jessica's good arm.

The girl's eyes grew wide.

"And then, they dragged him down to the king and said, 'You know what, Your Highness? This man was praying to someone else besides you!'

"Now the king realized they had tricked him into signing that law, 'cause he didn't really want to punish Daniel; but now he had to. So he sentenced Daniel to be thrown to . . . the *tigers*," Edwina said, seizing a stuffed tiger.

"Lions," Jessica corrected.

Edwina smiled. "Can't fool *you*, can I? Okay, so they took him to the lion's den and threw him in. Did the king laugh?"

"Oh, no," the little girl said. "He was very sorry. He prayed for Daniel."

"That's right!" exclaimed Edwina. "And the next morning the king ran to the lion's den and what did he find? A pile of bones?"

"No. Daniel was there. God kept him safe all night."

"Right again!" Edwina stroked Jessica's hair and smiled. "Next time *you* tell the story."

Jessica looked at her with a serious face. "I'm sure glad it wasn't me. I'm scare-da lions. How'd he know they wasn't going to eat 'im?"

"Come and sit beside me, Jessie." Edwina patted the open space next to her on the toy chest and the girl happily nestled in at her side. "I hope you understand this. Even some big people don't. . . . Think about Daniel. As far as he knew, he *was* gonna be killed if he didn't turn away from God. But he said to himself, 'No matter what happens I will belong to the Lord. If I die, it just means I get to go and be with Him in Heaven sooner than I planned.'

"And, sometimes, it's just time for people to go and be with the Lord. . . . Now, of course, all of us down here might miss that person an awful lot; but we have to know God does what's best. Faith in God means we trust Him to know what's best and let Him do it. And it's hard sometimes, Jessie. When my George died, I felt really bad inside because I missed him so much. And that's okay for a while. God doesn't blame us for loving someone and missing them. But then we have to start trusting God to help us make it without that person for a little while until we go to Heaven, too. And just look, Jessie, He sent me *you*." Edwina held her close. "You are His special gift to me, did you know that?"

Jessica smiled up at her.

"And since you took Jesus into *your* heart, Jessie, you can be just like Daniel. No one can take the Lord away from you if you don't want them to. And someday, you and me and George will be in Heaven together forever. Understand?"

"Oh yes." Jessica said before quickly shifting to, "Let's play house! You be the mama and I'll be the little girl."

The door opened, and Deana stuck her head into the room. "It's time for Jessica to eat."

"Go on now," Edwina said, helping the girl to her feet. "You go eat your dinner and I'll pick up the zoo in here."

"Wait for me," Jessica said to her. "I'll eat fast and be right back so we can play!"

"No you won't," Deana countered, "You'll eat with the rest of us and get up when you are excused."

Edwina pointed to the door. "Your mama is right. Go on now."

Jessica trotted to the door and down the stairs. She stopped and quickly checked to make sure she'd put her shirt on right, then proceeded to the dining room where her brother and father were already seated. Deana sat down with the family and they all began to pass food around.

Suddenly, Jessica stopped and said, "Dear Jesus, thank you for this good food and for 'Wina, and Mother, and Father, and Leon. Amen."

Deana dropped her fork on the floor. Leon Jr. stood, gripping his napkin in a fist. Leon Sr. choked on his water and spit it back in his glass. Jessica looked at them, oblivious to their distress.

"Why did you say that?" her father asked.

"Oh, just to say thanks."

"Who told you to say it?"

"God says we should."

"Who told you God said that?"

"Daniel."

Her father took a breath. Obviously, he'd have to work at getting to the end of this maze. "Who in blazes is Daniel?" Leon Sr. asked.

"Bal-laz-zez," Jessica tried to repeat. "What is bal-laz-zez?"

Mr. Newsome rubbed his forehead in an attempt to calm himself. "Hot fire. It means hot fire."

"Ohhhhhhhhhh. That would be the bad place. No, Daddy, Daniel's not there. Daniel prayed thanks all the time and he's in Heaven with George."

"*George who?*" her father snapped.

Tears welled in Jessica's eyes. "George Grant, Daddy."

"I told you something was wrong with that woman!" their son said accusingly. "I knew she was going to bring you problems."

"Not for long!" Leon Sr. declared, scooting back from the table and throwing his napkin on his plate. "She'll leave this house tonight!" He stood and strode from the room.

It took a moment for this to soak into Jessica's mind. When it did, she screamed, "No!" and bolted after her father.

Edwina had put the last toy in place when Jessica's father burst into the room. "Just what right do you think you have to fill my daughter's head with all this garbage?" he fumed.

"What?" she asked.

"All this Jesus and Daniel and George business. Just who do you think you are anyway?"

Jessica ran into the room and grabbed Edwina around the waist.

Edwina's pulse, pounding already, moved even faster. She knew someday they would know, but she'd always hoped it would be far in the future. She thought for a second. "Mr. Newsome," she began in a shaky voice.

"My daughter just sat at my table," he interrupted loudly, "and said 'Thank you, Jesus for the food.' You are compensated to take care of her, not to push your ridiculous superstitions on her! Pack your bags right now and get out of my house!"

"No, no, *no!*" Jessica shrieked, holding onto Edwina.

By this time, Lee and Deana had entered the room. Lee grabbed Jessica by the shoulders and tried to pull her away from Edwina. Jessica bit him, and he swore as he drew back his hand. He looked at it then said, "Why you rotten little animal!" He seized her around the waist and yanked as hard as he could.

The child, with one arm withered and weak, lost her grip. She started shrieking and tried to wriggle loose. Leon Jr. kept her from getting away by holding her good arm behind her back and placing his forearm just under her chin in a choke hold.

Jessica had nowhere near the strength of her brother, but she kept struggling to escape his grasp. Edwina latched onto the young man's arm and tried in vain to loosen it while his father shouted, "Lee! Let go of her! NOW!"

Deana stood behind her son saying, "Let go, Lee, let go!" but his hold only tightened.

"Don't hurt her!" Edwina cried as she frantically pried on the young man's iron grip. "I'll leave, I'll leave. Just don't hurt her."

Jessica stopped struggling, and her eyes rolled back in her head.

Leon Sr. shoved Edwina aside and barked, "*Lee! TAKE YOUR HANDS OFF OF HER THIS INSTANT!*"

As Lee let go, Jessica fell forward into her father's arms. He scooped her limp body up, rested her head on his shoulder, and checked to see if she was still breathing. Her eyelids fluttered, and he could feel her breath so he stroked her hair reassuringly.

After a few seconds the girl cried weakly. "Daddy, don't send her away."

Leon Jr. clamped a hand on Edwina's arm and said, "Come on, let's go."

Edwina wrenched her arm free and moved away from him.

Jessica's father turned to her, saying, "Leave now, and I'll personally pack your things tonight. You can come and get them in the morning."

Leon Jr. happily escorted her out and slammed the door in her face. Edwina ran to the home of a friend several miles away and when her friend answered the door, she found Edwina slumped in the doorway, sobbing.

It took her an hour to tell the story. Even after night fell, she wouldn't eat and she couldn't sleep. What if they never let her see Jessie again? She couldn't even think of it. What if they said she could come back with the condition she'd keep silent about her faith. What if they . . . ? And so it went for hours before she realized she couldn't change the situation by second-guessing any move they might make. For a brief moment, she even considered kidnaping Jessica, telling herself she'd be "saving" the child—her child. . . . No, she couldn't. She spent the rest of the night praying that, somehow, the circumstances could be changed by morning and she would be allowed to return as Jessica's nurse. At dawn, she felt better.

Hours later, though, standing outside the Newsome's home, fear and anger crept back into her mind, crushing all hope. She stood there, not wanting a confrontation, not wanting to leave. Finally she knocked at the door. Her heart jumped when the door opened and Mr. Newsome came out holding two suitcases. He stepped outside and set the suitcases down. He stayed on the porch and closed the door.

"The incident last night," he said quietly, "was regrettable. I am sorry this has to end on such a sour note, but it *must* end."

For a moment, Edwina felt all hollow inside. She knew what he was saying, but it wasn't making sense. "May I just see her to say goodbye?"

"No. She has become ill because of all this, and I want her to forget you as soon as possible."

"Ill?" she echoed.

"The doctor says it's nothing serious. She's just upset. She'll get over it."

Edwina felt weak. "Please."

"My son was right. You brought grief into my home."

She searched his eyes for any spark of life, of understanding, of clemency. "I just helped a little girl to have hope. I'm not sorry I did it."

Leon momentarily lost his temper. "Hope in *what?*" he asked, then regained a measure of control. He raked his fingers through his hair before perching agitated hands on his hips. "If your faith is so great, then why didn't you pray for her to be normal? All of these religions make promises. I don't see anything different."

Forgetting everything else, Edwina blurted out, "I'll tell you what's different. My God loves her and accepts her just the way she is. He's not one bit ashamed of her. . . . She doesn't have to be a 'perfect specimen' like your son . . . and maybe she's better off the way she is! In your world, she's unacceptable in the grand scheme," Edwina said, her voice cracking with emotion. "Like old people, her only possible 'use' will be as a common laborer. And, if they find she's *unusable*, they might decide to have 'mercy' on her and snuff her out like a candle," she declared, snapping her fingers in front of Leon's face.

"Oh yes," she said, nodding, "the people your son represents are all *for* liberty. Soon they'll have complete liberty to do whatever they deem necessary."

Now Edwina prayed inwardly for the strength to finish what she had to say. Her knees wobbled, but she held her ground. "And, if Jessica were 'normal,' you'd have let her become just like *him!*" she said pointing to the house. "Someday, you'll pay for what you've done." She looked heavenward and cried, "Oh God, help Jessie." With that, she picked up her bags, and walked swiftly away with her head bowed. Mr. Newsome could hear her sobs till she'd gotten out of sight.

Inside the house, Jessica lay on her bed. She'd finally fallen asleep, clutching her stuffed lion.

Down the hall, Deana and Leon Jr. sat in his room, conferring about Jessie.

"I'm telling you, Mother," the young man said, "I don't know if we can undo the damage this woman has done to

Jessie. Your best bet might be to send her to training school and see if they can teach her to do anything." He opened a drawer in his desk. "I've been meaning to show you these."

Deana took the leaflets he offered, not knowing her husband had returned upstairs. He stood in the hall, watching them through the slightly-open door.

"These are brochures for training schools?" she asked.

"Yes," her son answered.

"Where did you get them?"

"I sent off for them some time ago. I was just waiting for the right time to show them to you."

"I don't know if your father would ever go for this."

"Of course not. Why not just keep her locked up here in the house and let her continue to be worthless! He won't face facts, Mother. She's no good to anyone, and he won't admit it. He'll just get another fanatic maid in here to keep her out of everyone's sight. What good will that do?"

"Listen," Deana said, "right now he's upset. We all are. Let's just wait and see what he does. Maybe, if the time seems right, in a week or two we'll show these to him and see what he says. But, for now, let's just keep it between you and me."

Leon Sr. silently moved away from the door and into his daughter's room. She'd fallen into a deep sleep, but her eyelids were red and swollen. He sat down at the foot of her bed.

What could he do? He ran his fingers through his hair. He couldn't seem to think. All he knew was that he wanted the turmoil to stop. He'd have to get his son out of the house before he could find peace.

Chapter 31

Near Dallas

Swordsman opened his eyes and focused.

"Are you all right?" his friend asked. "For a moment there, you were so still, I thought you were dead. I've been knocking on your door and finally decided to come in."

"Sorry. I must have been in a deep sleep. What time is it?" As soon as he sat up, the dream came rushing back into his mind.

The same dream again. In it, he is standing before a large crowd. There is a flash of light, and someone is calling his name. He sees a man coming down toward him and hears a voice telling him to go on a journey. He is filled with happiness and anticipation as he starts up the aisle. Each time, just as he makes eye contact with the man, he's jolted and wakes up.

Swordsman said nothing about the dream to his friend, and they walked to a nearby home. When they entered, the smell of baking bread enveloped to them.

"Oh, can you smell it? Like heaven on earth! It almost makes me weak in the knees . . . Kristen!" he exclaimed when a young woman in an apron appeared and he hugged her. "Bread! It smells so good. But it must have cost you a mint to get the ingredients. I feel like a king!"

She smiled. "Just wait!" she said, and left the room.

Another woman fussed over the place settings, and two men looked out the window. The long table, set for six people, held plenty of food.

"Sonya, Bob, Gary." He hugged each one of them.

The five of them gathered around the table, and Kristen returned with a tray. Exclamations went around the room. On the tray were two large loaves of bread, a dish with real butter, and a bowl of peaches.

Kristen looked at Swordsman. "I figured you hadn't had real food in a while. Lord knows you deserve it."

Swordsman laughed. "And to think . . . I've been wandering all around the countryside when I could have been living like this! . . . Bob, will you say the blessing?"

Bob smiled broadly. "I'd love to."

They all bowed their heads.

"Oh Heavenly Father, words cannot express the joy You have given us tonight. It's so good to be together once again, to feast on bread and taste Your sweet fruits. I ask Your blessing on this food and all of us here. In Jesus' name we pray. Amen."

They all sat and started passing the food around.

"Oh, look at that bread!" Swordsman exclaimed. Steam rose from the slice he held in his hand and he watched the butter melt into it. "Now this is entertainment. I don't know if I should watch it or eat it!" He took a huge bite and spoke with his mouth full. "Kristen, if God has a bakery, I know where you'll be working when we get to heaven!"

They ate and laughed and talked for over an hour before they left the table and went into the living room.

Bob spoke first. "Now, you must tell us all that's happened since we last saw you."

"You first," he smiled. "I'm enjoying just *being* here. . . . Let me drink it in a while."

Each of the others shared bits and pieces of things that had happened in his absence, and he sat quietly, only interrupting for an occasional question.

Finally his turn came. They all waited. He sat in silence for quite some time before he began to tell them of places he had been and all he had seen. Small groups of believers were springing up everywhere and beginning to network. Considering the public suppression of the movement and the lack of ability for people in different regions to regularly communicate, he felt only God could be orchestrating all the things being accomplished throughout the cities.

He told of the threats and, still greater, the times of astonishment at the signs he saw as he traveled about. But as he finished the stories, he didn't show elation. Instead, he seemed to be getting depressed. They could all sense it, but it was Kristen who finally laid a kind hand upon his and said, "What's wrong?"

"Don't *you* feel the urgency?" he finally asked.

They all nodded before he continued, "Whether we leave this planet by death or at His call, I think our season here is quickly evaporating. . . . I almost feel as if our time is in months or weeks instead of years. . . . I feel such a heaviness in my spirit. . . . I can't seem to say enough, do enough. . . . There are still so many people out there. I see their empty eyes, and my blood runs cold." He put his hand on his chest. "I feel the minutes ticking away—and I can't make the clock stop. I can only pray for the strength to walk to the end of it," he said as tears came to his eyes. "I'm just so tired."

Bob looked at the others and said, "Who would have thought our young man would become Swordsman? You guys remember him? Now, here you are, and we realize once again you're still just a man. It's so easy to put someone like you up on a higher level than ourselves. Up on some mountain top where there's only God's glory and no trouble. We forget that even Moses had to come down and face real problems. But, praise God, we can share everything. The very same God who brought you to this moment can carry you right up to His very doorstep. He's not the great 'I WAS,' but the great 'I AM,' continually present and not limited by any measurement."

All of them moved to stand around their dear friend.

"Father," Bob prayed, "We adore you. Wonderful Counselor, Mighty God . . . Prince of Peace. Forgive us, Lord, for thinking only of what our brother can accomplish. Help him to carry the burden he needs to have in his heart for others in order to press on for You, but keep Satan from turning that burden into an unbearable weight. As always, we pray for Your protection of him and thank You for the way You have poured out Your Holy Spirit so richly in his life. Grant him strength, grace, and peace to walk for You each and every day of his life . . . thank You Lord."

Then Sonya spoke. "'I lift mine eyes to the hills. From whence does my help come? My help comes from the Lord, who made heaven and earth. He will not let your foot be moved, He who keeps you will not slumber. Behold He who keeps Israel will neither slumber nor sleep. The Lord is your keeper. The Lord is your shade on your right hand. The sun shall not smite you by day, nor the moon by night. The Lord will keep your life. The Lord will keep your going out and your coming in from this time forth and for evermore.'"

Swordsman let out a sigh as if released from a physical pain. "Forgive me, Jesus, forever thinking I could carry a burden You already bore." All of the tension left his face, and he totally relaxed as he said, "Father, You always know what we need most. And I needed this. To share with these most cherished people. To lay down my heavy heart. Thank you, Lord."

Chapter 32

Near Houston

The Reverend Ike Bointon put a finger under his collar, trying to stop the choking sensation. He took off his tie and put it in his pocket before unbuttoning the top button of his shirt. Squeezing between people, Bointon kept trying to get closer and closer to the man on the platform. He wanted to see this man, this Swordsman, to hear the message that had intoxicated so many listeners. What power did this man have over people? How did he do it?

Not wanting to stand among the crowds any longer than necessary, the reverend came to the meeting late and encountered a line overflowing out the doors. Some people had already settled for gathering around loudspeakers outside the building. But Bointon didn't want to just hear Swordsman, he wanted to *see* the man who'd incited people to leave his dome. He pressed into the line.

The first time that Swordsman spoke in the area, Bointon only lost two people. Mrs. Fairbanks (his largest cash contributor) was one of them. This time, in spite of his repeated warnings, at least a third of his circle had disappeared from dome services, presumably to attend this "conference."

They couldn't legally call it a crusade, but that was exactly what it was. An attempt to awaken silly emotionalism. What could be done to arrest the flare-up of a dysfunction that was such a threat to public security?

The widely-distributed book, *Changing Times, Time for a Change* would soon be released in a dramatized video format, and Bointon had already signed up for it to be shown at his dome. Other leaders told him it could be an "effective rebuttal tool" in the fight against fanaticism. He looked around at the crowd. Too bad the video hadn't arrived before this conference started.

He pushed inside the building and squeezed forward. With each step, he found the people packed closer together. When he'd gotten about a hundred feet from the platform, he could go no further. A solid wall of bodies stood in his way. He stopped and squinted at the stage. The speaker dripped with perspiration, his blue shirt stuck to his body.

"Are you drowning? . . . Not just in your own sweat." The crowd laughed. "But in a sea of pain or grief, or poverty? Are you finding that the world seems to be surviving, but you're not? Maybe you've tried Zen or T.M., or spirit-guided imagery, or booze, or drugs . . . only to find that when you are just *you*, undistracted, uncontrolled, unintoxicated, you're still drowning. Maybe you're suicidal or hostile. . . . What does the world have to offer?

"Hey," he suddenly shouted, "I heard if you put one thumb on your temple and one just over your navel, you'll see colors! . . . Nothing like red, yellow and blue as you go down for the third time! . . . Meditate on your inner self and you'll feel like you're floating . . . as you sink like a stone. Eat only bean sprouts and whole wheat bread and you'll look great when you blow your brains out! Give extra money to your dome and happiness will descend upon you like a cloud. Be a good person and you'll find 'inner peace.'" He stopped to wipe his face on a towel.

"God put a desire in each one of us to be 'right,' to be perfected. And each person striving for that end will eventually find out he's fallen short somewhere. If you're fortunate, you'll figure that out before you die. But if you let that sense of urgency, of drowning, be salved by drugs, or riches, or even your own good works, one day you'll stand naked before God, and any flaw, no matter how small, will disqualify you from eternal glory.

"You see, God lets *you* choose what you'll be judged by! And when you choose any law, any set of works—over the simple salvation of Jesus Christ, you condemn yourself. Because if you have to *earn* salvation, no matter what the religion or method chosen, you'll never make it.

"Does that sound harsh? You want to have a free will, don't you? Well, you do. So you can pick any law, any system, no matter how lofty, or pure, or selfish . . . or stupid . . . and you will have disqualified yourself."

He walked to a different part of the stage. "How about this for a credo: 'Nobody's gonna make me do something I don't want to do!'" He gave everyone a huge smile. "Okay, so you're walking down the sidewalk and lights start flashing. You hear a voice, 'Step to the side. Wait. Peacekeeper activity in progress . . .' Well, nobody's gonna tell you what to do, so you keep walking. Within moments, rifles are trained on you, and you're told to stop. If you keep walking, you get zapped with a stun gun, sent to the pavement, restrained and arrested." Swordsman shrugged. "Somebody's making you do something you don't want to do.

"And, that's just a silly, simple thing. If you choose a more detailed code or system to live by, can you see how complicated it gets, how impossible it becomes? There will always be at least one wrong decision, one wrong thought or act *according to your own rules* that will make you less than 'perfect.' Yet having chosen that law, you will be condemned by it . . . .

"You can't enter heaven through your own accomplishments, through praying, working good deeds, sacrifice, fasting, ceremony, traditions, family ties, membership to a group, or even by the working of signs and wonders! God's standard of total perfection never wavers— and that *would* seem harsh and unfair if God *Himself* hadn't paid the price for your imperfection. You need only to admit you cannot save yourself, and accept the free offer of Jesus Christ, the only One who meets the requirement of perfection."

Ike Bointon winced. *In any case,* he thought, *I went to seminary before all the incorporations . . . when they still baptized and had only the one way. . . . I don't have a code. I haven't* <u>*denied*</u> *Christ . . . just grown and expanded.* Even if a lot of this was foolish, Bointon didn't like being classified with "unsaved" humanity.

"You see," Swordsman continued, "although Satan's ego would love for you to openly deny Jesus—it's not a mandatory requirement. As long as he can get you to deny Jesus with your life, Satan's got you anyway.

"You may think you can stand on the dividing wall and jump down on the right side at the first sight of Jesus on the horizon. But that moment will come like a thief, at a time when you don't expect it."

He squatted down and took one woman's hand. "To be saved you must make a personal commitment to Jesus. And if you have truly done so, you won't keep walking in darkness."

He stood and made a sweeping motion with his hand. "You can receive the gift of eternal life, freedom from bondage to sin and death. . . . No matter if you are in the building or in the area outside. God knows who you are. He knows how many hairs are on your head!

"Pray with me . . . Father, I know I have sinned . . . I have fallen short . . . I'm sorry for what I have done, and ask You to forgive me. . . . Send Your Son, Jesus, into my whole being. . . . I accept Him as my Savior. I know He died for me. . . . I ask to be washed completely clean with the blood of Jesus Christ. . . . I renounce the works of Satan and turn away from them. . . . Help me to live a life that is pleasing to you. Send your Holy Spirit to dwell in me, to fill me. In the name of Jesus, I pray, Amen.

"If you just prayed that prayer with me, I'm going to ask you to take your first step of faith. Look around and you'll see little red and blue flags going up. For the people outside, we will be setting up special places momentarily. There will be people at each of these places to pray with you and help minister to your needs. Come and *openly* acknowledge what you just prayed."

Bointon could see dozens of little red and blue flags going up around the auditorium. *Here's where they really con all those poor suckers,* he thought. There'll be an emotional frenzy, and he'll rake in the cash.

Swordsman spoke again. "Father, as I look out tonight and see so many people, I ask that no one leave here hungry or in need." Then he stepped down off the platform and disappeared into the crowd.

Looking to his left, Ike could see a prayer station had started up next to him. An older couple prayed for a young girl of fifteen or sixteen. The girl sobbed, and the woman placed a hand on the top of her head while she prayed. Behind him, he could hear one or two people, presumably praying "in tongues." Same old show, Bointon thought. How could people be so gullible? This was so ridiculous. What had these people to gain? Only trouble.

He felt a small jolt of fear when he noticed a man walking among the people and coming in his direction. It was Swordsman. He recognized the shirt and the curly brown hair as those of the man who had been on the stage. People were trying to press in just to touch him or see him. The man slowly made his way closer and closer to Ike.

Bointon just stood there watching, no longer noticing the people in the prayer station next to him. Finally, the man stood several feet from him. How ordinary this Swordsman seemed to be. If not for the reaction of the crowd, he might have missed the guy altogether.

Swordsman moved right in front of the Rev. Ike Bointon without a glance and got several feet away before he stopped and turned. He seemed to be looking for someone in particular. Ike froze. The man's eyes made contact with his for a second and then moved over and down to a little old lady sitting near Ike in a wheelchair. Ike had barely noticed her before, but now looked at her. Her fingers were completely distorted and her hands turned sideways at the wrists. Her legs were also bent. *How revolting,* Ike thought.

"In the name of Jesus Christ of Nazareth, stand up," Swordsman said to her.

The woman's eyes filled with tears as she struggled to get to her feet. He reached down and helped her up with both of his arms and then embraced her when she stood, gently kissing the top of her head. When she straightened up from the embrace, she started shouting, the tears now streaming out of her eyes. Swordsman beamed as she looked at her hands and legs. They had become completely straight!

Bointon's mouth fell open. People all around started jumping up and down singing praises to the Lord, and Swordsman turned to walk away.

"Wait! Wait!" she cried. "Oh, God bless you!" She then produced a brown paper bag and handed it to him with another embrace and a kiss.

"Thank you," he said, receiving the gift. Without even looking in the bag, he turned to Bointon. "But if you don't mind, this man needs it more than I do." Swordsman looked directly at Ike once again. "You'll be about four thousand short . . ."

Ike couldn't pay attention to the words. What he saw in the man's eyes overrode all other perceptions. He didn't see the hatred or condemnation he almost *wanted* to see. Something else. It made him feel small and vulnerable.

Swordsman continued speaking, " . . . for the Lord is not willing that *any* should perish." He handed the bag to Ike, who stood there with his mouth hanging open, and vanished once again into the crowd of people.

Some minutes later, Bointon looked into the bag and saw it did, indeed, contain money. He went home in a state of near shock.

Later, around 2:00 a.m., Ike started to panic. He'd counted the money over and over before he realized it was about four thousand short of the money he'd taken.

Chapter 33

Northwest of Dallas

Darkness settled into the storeroom while Michael finished washing the cutting board and wiping it off. He dried his hands on the towel tied around his waist and heaved a large sigh as he sat down on an old crate in the corner of the room. He'd put in a long day and his body ached for a rest. He even felt too tired to eat. The girls' father, Pete, was ill. The many small chores the old man did around the house and store now fell onto Michael's shoulders.

Michael rubbed his eyes and leaned back against the wall.

"Hey, are you in there? You die of exhaustion or something?"

He recognized Sara's voice, and straightened up to see her silhouette in the doorway. Stray strands of her hair, which had been pinned up in a bun, hung down randomly, and the huge apron she wore had a big knot behind her neck. Her hands rested on her hips while she stood peering into the semi-darkness of the storeroom.

"Are you in there?" She said it almost as if she believed he wasn't around and was just making a last-call sort of effort.

Michael had been so busy watching her, he forgot to answer.

"Right here," he said, standing and walking to the doorway.

"Oh! I didn't see you." She fumbled in her apron pocket for a match and lit a lamp nearby before continuing. "Anyway, I'm glad I found you. . . . You look tired."

"I am tired," he said, draping his towel over a crate near the stairwell.

"I'm sorry. I know you've been doing the work of two people around here, so Noel and I decided to double the amount of money we give you."

He started to speak, but she held up her hand.

"I know that's still a lousy amount, but please accept it as a small token of our gratitude."

"What I *started* to say," he leaned down and brushed a lock of hair off her forehead, "was that I don't even spend the money you give me now. I have a place to sleep and food to eat. And it's been nice to be treated like part of your family."

She smiled. "I hope that means you'll stay at least a while longer."

"Does that mean you want me to stay?" he said, searching her eyes.

Her face flushed with color, so he quickly changed his tone and walked back toward his bed. "Are you kidding? You couldn't get me out of here tonight if the place caught fire. I just want to fall in my bed and go to sleep."

"Oh. . ." she sounded disappointed, "I'd kind of hoped . . . I mean, we wanted to invite you out tonight. I didn't think you'd want to come, but I thought I'd ask. Noel and I were going to take Daddy to see a man they call Swordsman this evening."

Without thinking, Michael replied, "You mean that religious fanat– Sorry. . . . Do you really believe all that stuff?"

"It depends on what you mean by 'stuff,'" she replied, a little defensively. "Have you ever heard him speak?"

"No, but you know . . ." he searched for something to say that wouldn't be insulting and realized most of the things he thought about religious fanatics would insult her, so he decided to forget it. "Never mind. Arguing religion has cost me too much already."

"No, really, I'd like to know what you think." She glanced at her watch. "But it looks like you'll have to tell me some other time. I've got to run if I want to get Daddy ready in time to get there."

Michael frowned. "Isn't he a little too sick for you to be dragging him around?"

She had turned to leave, but stopped in her tracks. She inhaled slowly before turning and walking over to where he stood. "First of all, Michael, we are taking him for precisely that reason. He is sick and he needs ministering to. Secondly, he asked to go. He's an old man and he might not have a lot of time left, but we'll try to spend some of it doing what *he* wants to do."

Michael looked down. "You're right, you're right. I'm sorry. I had no business interfering with you and your father."

"That's not the point, Michael. I'm glad you care about Daddy. You've spent so much time with him, just being a friend to him. He's had only us girls for so long, it's nice for him to have a male friend in the house. He genuinely cares about you, too. It's just that you don't see things from his perspective. . . . Here I go again. Babbling on when I should be getting ready. Look, I really want to finish this conversation, but I have to go." She took off her apron and handed it to him. "See you tomorrow."

He felt depressed somehow. Everyone seemed to be getting way too serious about spiritual things (one way or the other). It was bad enough that she, Noel, and Pete would regularly wander out in the evenings to meet other Christians someplace. He hoped Sara wouldn't get weird over this. He hung her apron on a hook and went to bed. He slept soundly until early the next morning when he heard a loud cry.

He snapped awake and jumped to his feet—eyes scratching the darkness for a weapon. He heard the sound again. It sounded like an anguished cry now. It came from a woman, but he couldn't tell if it was Sara or Noel. He remembered the knife he'd used for slicing dried meat and snatched it. He ran up both sets of stairs, jumping them three at a time, to the family's living quarters, ready to fight any intruder. When he reached the top, he saw the two sisters standing, huddled together. Sara stood with her back to him while Noel cried on her shoulder. Before he could speak, Noel opened her eyes and saw him holding a knife, poised to fend off a burglar. She almost fainted.

Sara turned and said, "Michael! What are you doing?"

He stopped. The hand holding the knife dropped to his side. He felt silly. "I thought I heard a scream . . ."

"Noel just had a shock," Sara said, hugging her sister.

"What's wrong?" Michael still had no idea what had happened.

"Daddy is dead," Sara said.

Noel burst into tears again and held onto Sara.

"No! It can't be." Michael said.

Sara moved down the hall a few steps, opened the door and stepped into her father's room. She held Noel's hand and pulled her gently.

Michael, several yards behind, slowly followed. *Surely,* he thought, *Sara is mistaken.* He stood in the doorway, but did not go in. His eyes took in the lifeless form on the bed, and he knew the old man was gone. The girls sat down on opposite sides of the bed, holding Pete's hands. Sara spoke to Noel.

"See? He just fell into a peaceful sleep and left. . . . Sweetheart, I know you'll miss him," her voice quavered, "So will I. But he went so quietly. In his own home. I was with him. . . . He knew it was time. Remember how he looked last night?"

Noel nodded.

"So radiant and happy. Remember what Swordsman said to Daddy? He said 'Be at peace. The hand of the Lord is on your family and will keep them safe.' Don't you see? Daddy's been hanging onto every breath for fear of leaving us. Last night, he realized he could let go; and that we would be all right. He's not suffering anymore." She reached across the bed and put her hand on top of Noel's. "It won't be long until we see him again, will it? . . . Let's pray."

Michael backed away from the door. Sara saw him through the corner of her eye but made no effort to stop him.

When he got downstairs, he sank onto his cot. He'd forgotten the knife and almost cut his leg. He tossed it over to a table and sat with his head in his hands. He spent quite a while thinking of the old man.

They'd spent so many evenings, playing checkers, talking about local politics and other non-essential matters. Only the subject of religion had ever come between them. Michael hadn't minded it so much from Pete because it seemed as if he really cared. And now he was gone.

He heard a sound in the doorway, and Sara's voice softly calling, "Michael, may I come in?"

"Door's open," he said without looking up.

She came in quietly. "Noel wanted to be alone for a while, and I thought I should come and talk to you."

He sat, still staring at the floor.

"Unless you'd rather not," she offered.

He looked up. "Oh no . . . I'm just. . . . He was a neat old guy." The numbness of the shock began to leave him, and sorrow started settling in.

Sara sat across from Michael. "Yes, he was. But I'm glad he can be with the Lord now. He's been ill for so long."

"How can you say that?" Michael said in a very serious tone.

"What do you mean?" she asked. "I'm glad he's with the Lord—"

"I mean, how can you say that? How can you be happy your father is gone when you'll never see him again? I was in Philadelphia when the plague hit. I saw thousands of people dying and begging to die. . . . Most of my family died in one day but I've never been glad they died." In his anger, he let the words he'd restrained for so long escape his heart. "You fanatics live in some watercolor little world where you deny all the things that go wrong. You're all either deluded or fakes." His hands clenched into fists. "You don't believe Jesus is coming back for you any more than I do."

Sara sat in stunned silence for a moment before speaking. "How dare you. . . . I'm not 'happy' Daddy is gone. . . . But I know I can't selfishly cling to someone—especially if they are suffering—just because I'd miss them if they were gone. And as far as never seeing him again, you're wrong." Her voice became soft once again. "My mother got contaminated helping others. She wasn't allowed to come home after it happened, so I went with her to the camp. Only it took her more than a day to die. For weeks, I changed bloody sheets and listened to her bubble as she breathed. At the end, she'd lost all of her hair and had virtually no clean skin . . . and if she felt sorry for herself, she never said so.

"In her last moment, I was with her. And if something so horrible can be beautiful, it was. She told me she could see the Lord . . . and then she died. After her last breath, when I realized she was gone, I was grief stricken. I didn't want her to leave me. I touched her one last time; and as I pulled the cover over her, I heard a sound. At first it was so soft and far away, I couldn't tell what it was or where it came from. It grew stronger, and I realized I could hear singing . . . the singing in Heaven. What a lovely sound among all the tents of dying people. I realized then she *was* with the Lord." Sara wiped the tears from her cheeks before she said, "Although I still really miss her, I *know* there will be a point in time when I will be with Jesus, and my mother and Daddy, again. If I call on Jesus to the last, I will either wake up in His presence one day, or He will come and get me."

The first rays of the sun began to light the small windows near the ceiling of the cellar. Her eyes had been focused on some distant space, but now she looked at Michael.

"You see, the Lord never promised me I wouldn't suffer or see suffering. He just offers to share my burdens and help me through these dark hours. God is the Comforter. . . . He has seen every moment of your life, Michael, and His hand is always there to help. But if you turn away, how can you be bitter when you don't feel relief? God never takes anything you don't give Him. And if you want to carry every burden around all by yourself, it will always be a heavy load."

Almost instinctively, she leaned forward and reached out to take his hand before she thought better of it. "Michael, you've spent most of your life stuffing hurt down where no one can see it. Whenever you can't face something, you press it into a corner and try to forget it's there. I can tell. You retreat somewhere else inside yourself and wait for it to go away. . . . All the things you've seen and felt in the last few years . . . you may have buried them beneath the surface, but they aren't gone. Your hostility proves it. I know you loved Daddy, but you don't dare let yourself feel his loss. You're afraid you'll crumble. You can't hide from the pain forever, Michael. Give it to the Lord. I'm not saying it will be easy, but He'll help you through it."

He remained silent, so she got up and headed for the door.

"Hey," he called after her.

"Yes?"

"I'm sorry."

"I know you didn't mean it. We'll all . . ." her eyes brimmed over and she covered her mouth, barely managing to find her voice, "miss . . . him."

She turned and quickly left the room. Part of him wanted to go and apologize again, to comfort her, but he felt incapable of moving. He just sat there, trying to assimilate what she'd said. Could he ever allow himself to feel all the losses?

After a while, he got up and went to his suitcase. It was empty now, save for one object: The small Bible Zachary had given him so long ago. He'd never read it, but he'd never wanted to throw it away, either. He sat down on his bed again, holding it in his hands.

Chapter 34

In the Gulf of Mexico

Alex Dubois had been recalled to the Strategic Underwater Fibertronic Center in the Gulf. His superior, John Klost, told him this would happen occasionally, and that sometimes it would be at Kressman's specific request. It didn't necessarily mean trouble.

He took slow, deep breaths and tried to relax while he sat behind the beautiful desk in his immense office. Although night had fallen on the surface world above him hours ago, the lighting in his office mimicked late afternoon.

The phone rang, startling him. He quickly leaned forward in his seat and spoke into his microphone. "Alex Dubois." His screen remained blank.

"This is Mr. Kressman. Are you free now?"

"Yes sir." Alex mentally snapped to attention.

"Good. John will come for you in ten minutes. Bring your files." The tone returned to the line.

After Alex hung up, he got a key out of his pocket and went to the locked drawer. He unlocked it, removed a yellow case, then closed the drawer and locked it again. The yellow case contained all the information he'd received from the psychics he'd contacted to follow Swordsman and other fanatics. He opened the case and quickly skimmed through the folders inside.

Soon Alex heard the tone of his door and saw John striding into his office. He placed the folders back inside the case before closing it and grasping the handle.

"Are those the pertinent files?"

Alex nodded. "Yes."

They walked out of his office together. This time, they didn't go back through the tunnel, but walked to one of the other portals of the great archive. Behind it was an elevator. When the doors opened, the two men walked down a long corridor which, unless Alex had confused his directions, lead to the area above the huge, upside-down pyramid in the ceiling of the Archive.

The corridor eventually opened into a large, round white room. Except for a few paintings on the walls, and a large, round hole in the center of the floor with a railing around it, the room had no other furnishings. On the far side of the hole, Alex could see the beginning of a circular staircase.

John walked around and started down the stairs. Alex followed.

They slowly descended through two long sweeping curves of the stairway into a very large, very dark room. Soon, Alex could barely see to follow. At the foot of the stairs, John stopped and pulled Alex to his side. The wall they faced flickered brightly with a movie of some sort.

"Just sit in that chair over there until he speaks to you," John whispered, pointing to the outline of a chair some feet away.

"Okay," Alex whispered back.

Clutching the yellow box closer, he moved to the chair. After he'd been sitting for a while, he started looking at the pictures appearing on the wall in front of him. At first he stared in shock, then horror as his stomach started to churn. The scenes of grotesque people doing all sorts of horrible things flashed before him. He saw riots, people beating, stabbing, and strangling one another.

Although the movie had no sound, the people often moved and chanted to an unheard beat, others opened their mouths wide in screams, their eyes flashing with fiendish delight. He turned away when he caught a glimpse of a man holding up an arm (unattached) and biting into it, but was drawn to look at the wall again by some compelling force within him. The cannibal scene had gone, but other things continued to flash by: Hitler. People—just flesh and bones— being thrown into mass graves. Warfare. Men and women weeping. Buddhist monks burning themselves alive. Young men blowing themselves up. Alex wanted to believe it was just a movie . . . not real. But he knew that the appalling images of blood, terror, and pain were real.

The pictures stopped suddenly, and the lights came on. Alex blinked.

Kressman sat about thirty feet away, reclined on a couch covered with pillows. He held a glass of something in his hand.

"Hello, Alex," he said, before taking a sip from the glass.

"Hello," Alex said, puzzled.

"I keep this in my archives and watch it occasionally. You see, it's easy for a man like me to get out of touch with the world so to speak. I have found most men of high achievement ended up badly because they paid too much attention to their own success instead of the problems at hand. This is how I remind myself of the suffering, the poverty, the hatred, the primitive forces still facing us. It's a graphic reminder, no? It helps me to push harder for knowledge and truth. . . . Can you understand that?"

Unable to speak, Alex managed a nod.

"Now, about your work." Kressman pointed to the yellow case.

Alex found his voice. "Oh . . . yes." He opened the case and pulled out the files, then stood and walked to Kressman with them. The closer he got, the more a strange sensation swept over him, like being drugged or drunk. Thoughts of the pictures he'd seen on the wall swirled around in his mind . . . but he needed to concentrate. Why was he here? *Oh yes. The files.*

Just as he stretched out his arm with the files, he remembered he must not touch his employer. He waited for the man to grasp the opposite side of the folders, then retreated back to his chair. Within a few seconds, he felt better.

Kressman opened one of the files and perused it. A look of displeasure came to his face. "What about this 'Swordsman' fellow?"

"As you can see," Alex said, "we've compiled quite a bit of data. Each fanatic leader appears to have his own method. This man has been working in an East-to-West pattern. He started on this side of the Mississippi River and has worked his way slowly westward since. He lingers in each vector for a while, then moves on. He's done this for quite some time, and my people are predicting he'll continue the trend."

Alex cleared his throat to stall for time. What else could he remember about Swordsman? "Also, we've discovered he doesn't make his decisions alone, but has trusted advisors he 'prays' with to help him decide on movements and policy. While it's doubtful we could actually get a person into this inner circle, we have teams working to influence the thinking of individuals in the group, and to alienate one or more of them.

"As you suggested, the best way to kill the man's following would be to have someone who knows him come forward and expose him to his own people. Then, with any luck, his followers would turn on him the way people turned on the evangelists at the time of the disasters." He pointed to the files. "We hope to do this with all the fanatic leaders we're tracking."

Kressman closed the files. "Good. Just be sure to consult John regarding any changes of status," Kressman said, before quickly changing the subject. "How is the campaign coming?"

"Well sir, per your instructions, I've delegated the job to someone who has given it a fresh angle. Her name is Linda Posner and she's the one who came up with the ads showing how 'all good things can *find you* when you have a code.' It's a think-positive message. Figures showed an increase of 7.2 per cent after the campaign started," Alex said, realizing the figure was disappointing. "Although it was a bit short of the goal, distribution of the book *Changing Times, Time for a Change* is having a very positive impact. A dramatized video of the book will be available next week, and we expect it will do even better. New figures will be out in a few days and I'm certain they'll reflect a strong upsurge. The campaign, along with an exposé of fanatic leaders, will achieve what we need."

Kressman looked at him. "Don't fail me, Dubois."

Alex went cold inside. "I'll do my best, sir."

###

The following day, still dazed, Alex made the return trip to Dallas via the new fast rail train. That evening, when he sat at home with Linda, he didn't refer to the movies or the files. He only mentioned the discussion he and Kressman had about her work.

"Was he pleased?" she asked eagerly.

"Well, yes . . ." He stared at the food on his plate. Rare beef. He couldn't touch it and pushed it away. "He was happy we'd made progress . . . but there is still a lot to be done."

"Oh," she said. "You're not going to eat that?"

He exhaled. "No."

Linda pulled his plate across the table and he looked at her. Her puffy face told him she must have packed on at least five pounds recently.

"Are you pregnant?" he asked.

"Yes." She stuffed a large bite of the meat into her mouth, "But I'm getting rid of it tomorrow."

He thought for a moment. "Are you sure you should? After all, they're asking non-contaminated couples to have children."

"You sure didn't mind me ditching the last one," she shot back. As soon as the words came out of her mouth, she regretted them. Why had she even brought it up? She quickly fought to shove sorrow, hurt, and anger out of her mind. Curse that Michael anyway.

"That was his," Alex said, "this one would be mine."

She gave him an angry stare.

"But, of course, it's up to you," he trailed off lamely.

"You bet it is, and I'm doing it. My work is too important for this and I'm just not suited for motherhood. I only like other people's children. . . . You want your milk?"

"No." He left the table and went to his study.

After a few minutes, she got up and stood in the doorway, looking in at him. "You're not going to get all sentimental and sappy about this are you?" she said, pouting. "I thought we were going to have a fun relationship with no jealousy, no strings. I just got away from someone who wanted everything and gave nothing. I don't want that again."

He didn't look at her. "Do what you want, Linda," he sighed as he opened a book. "I have so much to think about, I really don't need a child either."

"Well, as long as you understand my feelings in the matter." She felt confused. He'd agreed with her too easily. Was her grip on him getting tighter or looser? Did she care? She shrugged and went back to the table.

Chapter 35

A suburb of Atlanta

Little Jessica Newsome laughed for the first time in many months. When he heard it, her father stopped walking down the hall and opened her door. Looking into her bedroom, he could see his little girl sitting on the floor with a stuffed lion— her constant companion since Edwina left them.

"Hi!" he said to her.

"Hi!" she said back.

He came in and closed the door. "You seem happy today," She nodded her head yes.

"How come?" He asked, seating himself next to her on the floor. "Is it your lion's birthday?"

"No!" she giggled.

Deana looked in. "Time for supper," she said before walking on down the hall. She descended the staircase thinking about how tired she felt. Tired and fed up. She'd been taking care of Jessica and the house the majority of the time since they'd gotten rid of Edwina. Several maids had come and gone, but none of them seemed to satisfy the diverse needs of the Newsome household. Little by little, Deana ended up moving most of the things from her studio to the house. Now she had to settle for squeezing in as much work as she could between cleaning and caring for Jessica. Exhaustion and depression had taken their toll. Did she have even one creative molecule left in her brain?

The Newsome's son, Leon Jr., having completed a special training camp, would be coming home late that night for the first time since the terrible incident with Edwina Grant. Both Deana and her husband had worked to maneuver Jessica back into a positive attitude toward her brother, but neither had mentioned his impending visit to her. Deana feared this might be a mistake. Later, as the three of them gathered at the dinner table, she considered how she might direct the conversation to the topic.

Before anyone spoke, Jessica bowed her head and said, "Thanks, Lord, for letting me be happy again."

Deana opened her mouth to say something but Leon spoke first. "She's not hurting anyone. If it makes her happy, what do you care?"

"But what if she did this in front of . . . people?"

"If you care to discuss this," he said, giving her a hard stare, "I'm sure we can fit it into the evening. Later."

Jessica, oblivious to the tension, ate her food happily. When she finished, she skipped out of the room.

Deana got up from the table and took her husband by the hand. "Come, I need to show you something."

She led him upstairs to Leon Jr.'s room and retrieved leaflets out of a desk drawer. "I think it's about time we discussed this," she said.

He glanced down at the leaflets promoting government training facilities for the handicapped. "These are all hundreds of miles from here . . . or anywhere, by the looks of it. No. We can't." He handed the leaflets back to her. "I have a bad feeling about it."

"What do you mean?"

"I just wouldn't trust the people in those places to take good care of her. You know how your son feels about her. If it's any reflection of how *they* would feel about her, who knows what they might do."

"Stop this 'your son' business!" she said angrily, "He's *our* son."

"Well, *our* son despises *our* daughter, so I'm not about to send her off to a place *he* recommends for her." Leon snatched the leaflets from her and opened the drawer to put them back.

Something in the drawer caught his eye. It appeared to be his own padplanner. It had been missing for months. Leon took it out of the drawer along with a simple messaging clip screen. "Hey, this is mine. What's it doing in here?"

He booted up the padplanner to make sure it belonged to him, and it did. Then he looked at the clip screen files. They contained detailed notes Leon Jr. had made about someone. Where the person went, what the person did, and who the person talked to on certain days. Soon, he realized the subject of the surveillance was himself. He handed the notes to Deana. "Look at this! He took my planner with my whole schedule in it! He's been spying on me!"

Deana sat on the bed and scrolled through a file on the clip screen. "I never would have believed it."

They heard the front door, and then footsteps on the stairs. Leon Jr. appeared in the doorway of his room, and for a moment they all just looked at each other. Leon Jr. quickly sized up the situation. He set down his duffle bag and stared defiantly at his father.

"I can't believe you did this." Leon Sr. said. "Like I'm some sort of subversive or something. I've not broken any law. Why would you do this?"

"Because you *are* breaking the law, in a sense. You are not operating for the common good. You've sworn to support the new system and the Global View, yet you hold many of their values in disdain. You don't attend a dome and you try to keep Mother from doing so. You want to cling to an antiquated lifestyle and you ridicule everything the new order stands for. You are a subversive."

Shocked, Deana exclaimed, "That's no excuse for what you've done, Lee. How could you do this to your own father?"

Leon Jr. shook his head. "You'd defend him at all costs. You help him stay in the darkness. I've tried to show you the way, but you must do something for yourself. Rid yourself of this man. Help Jessica to be a useful part of society."

His father moved close to him and spoke between clenched teeth. "Get out. You slimy little spy! Get out! You'll get that girl over my dead body."

Lee smiled and picked up his bag. "That, old man, could be arranged." He left the house without another word.

Although he hadn't finished with them yet, they never saw Leon Jr. again.

Chapter 36

Atlanta

Edwina Grant sat in the small room where she now lived. In the first days after her departure from the Newsome home, she'd stayed with a friend. A difficult search eventually netted her a job washing dishes in a soup kitchen catering to "cash" customers. She received little of the cash; but, as with the Newsomes, her pay included room and board.

She'd grown rail-thin and didn't smile much. Although she tried to face every day with the monumental faith it seemed to require, many times she knew she failed. Just going on seemed more than she could accomplish. The grief of being separated from Jessica continued unabated—a haunting pain that never went away. She'd given up all hope that she could somehow get Jessica back. And, as each day dragged on, bitterness grew like cancer inside of her.

Where was her Jessica today? She sighed before kneeling beside her cot. "Lord," she said aloud, "is this how it's all going to end for me? I know I've not been living like You want me to, but . . ."

A thought of the Lord's request to daily take up a cross came to mind and seemed to taunt her momentarily. Perhaps she'd been a fool. Perhaps she'd suffered all this for nothing. She trembled at the thought.

"I'm not able to go on anymore. Lord, there's nothing left in me that wants to go on." She struggled for words. "I feel so much pain over not seeing Jessie."

The Lord spoke to her inwardly, *I know, daughter, I know. But, who can take Jessie out of My hand now? Where could anyone take her that I would not be with her?*

Hot tears formed in Edwina's eyes and she lowered her face to the cot in front of her. "I know, Lord."

Silence hovered in the room. It pressed in . . . and exposed a thought she'd never dared to voice.

"There's something else, Lord," she finally said. "I feel so much . . . *hate* toward her family." A picture of Leon Jr. choking Jessie sprang into Edwina's mind and her heart began to race. "He's so evil, and he pulls his parents along in his wake."

The voice inside her said, *Am I not a just judge? Won't you let go of them and trust Me, Edwina?*

"Oh, God," she groaned as she wrestled with the thought.

The Lord spoke again, in a softer voice. *Are you willing to let go of them?*

Her once-lovely hands moved up to grasp the blanket in front of her, shaking as if she held an invisible foe. Emotions waged war for her thoughts. Anger, bitterness, sorrow, and fear all seemed to want to burst through to a last, untainted part.

She finally answered through clenched teeth, "Lord, it hurts so much. . . . Help me."

Do you want to walk with bitter memories and hatred, or do you want to walk with Me? The decision is yours. I won't make you forgive Leon Jr., his father, or his mother; but, can't you see how your unforgiving heart is drying up your life?. . . What do you choose, daughter?

Edwina's whole body shuddered—then relaxed. She let go of the blanket in her hands and wept aloud, "I choose You, Father. I release them. . . . I forgive them . . . and I choose You."

Chapter 37

Northwest of Dallas

Michael walked slowly on his way home from the funeral. He needed some time to think.

The ceremony consisted of a few people talking about Pete and several people talking about "eternal life." Michael didn't know what to think about eternal life. . . . He didn't like to think about dying at all.

He pictured the funeral with Sara and Noel crying quietly and putting a small, wildflower on the grave. After the ceremony ended, he told them to go on home without him. He needed to be alone and walked around the graveyard a while, thinking of all the families of the other people buried there. Did all these people really believe they'd live on in eternity somewhere?

He finally decided to go home and made his way slowly through the streets. While still a few blocks away, he smelled smoke, so he began looking on either side of the road for a camp or brush fire. Nothing. He looked to the sky to determine where the smoke might be coming from and spotted a column of hot soot pouring into the sky, rising from the general direction of the store.

He broke into a run, making his way past trash, bricks, and other debris in the road. Now a block away, he could see it. The tallest building on the block—the store—had smoke and flames billowing out every window and door. A crowd of people had gathered with buckets, but the fire had grown so large, they'd stopped trying to put it out.

Michael bolted frantically through the crowd, shouting "Sara! Sara!" He prepared to dash into the burning building when he heard her voice calling him.

She and Noel stood off to the side, both still wearing their good dresses, now torn and covered with ashes. Their sooty faces showed streaks where tears poured down their cheeks. He hugged them both and ground his teeth as they watched the building burn to the ground.

When the fire was nearly out, people started coming by to offer them a place to stay. Most of them recalled times when Pete or Sara had provided them with food or lodging.

Later that night, in a small patched-together little house with friends, Sara went over what happened.

"We'd just come from the funeral when we heard a noise in the cellar," she began. "I went downstairs and left Noel on the ground floor. When I got downstairs," she said to Michael, "three men were there, stealing the food. One of them had only one arm and was wearing badly cracked glasses."

"What?" Michael said suddenly. "I know who that is. He's very treacherous."

Sara continued, "There were four more men upstairs rooting through our things. They were sure we had money hidden somewhere. They never thought to look in our purses. Anyway, when they'd packed up all the food they wanted, they poured our lamp oil all over and set the place on fire. . . . Of course, by the time the troops got there, the men were long gone and the store was beyond saving. Bucket brigades and garden hoses just aren't effective on that big of a fire." Sara stared into space, completely cried out. Noel had already fallen asleep with her head on the table. The couple who owned the house got up quietly and hugged Sara and Michael before going off to bed.

"And I wasn't there to help you," Michael said.

Her eyes focused on him. "I don't think you could have stopped them by yourself. They didn't hurt us. And they would have set the building on fire anyway." She touched Noel's hair gently. "I need some time to rest and pray . . . so if you don't mind, we're going to take the other bedroom, and you can have the sofa."

"Sure." He couldn't think of anything to say. "I'm sorry, Sara."

"Thank you," she said softly before gently tapping Noel. "It's time to go to bed, baby."

As he sat alone in the little living room, he admitted to himself just how much he loved Sara. More than any woman he'd ever known. And she'd almost been killed because he hadn't been there. Even now, she surely didn't know how much danger she'd been in.

He had no idea if she cared for him any more than as a friend, but he could no longer hide how he felt about her. He wanted to stay with her as long as he lived. He fell asleep thinking about how he would tell her.

The sun was well up when he awoke. He sat up and stretched, then paused for a moment and looked around. The house looked a little brighter in the daytime with colorful pillows and handmade wall hangings, barely visible by candlelight the night before.

Looking down at his funeral attire, he realized this had become his only outfit. He heard a conversation going on outside, so he got up and went to the door. Once he opened it, he recognized the owners of the home, an older couple, standing on the porch and talking with several people he didn't know.

The man saw Michael and walked toward him. "Oh, I see you're up. Come back inside here," he said, stepping past Michael, "and I'll give you something." He smiled nervously as he walked to a cabinet. "Sara asked me to give you something."

He produced a large envelope from a drawer and handed it to Michael. He kept looking down, trying to avoid eye contact.

Michael got a terrible feeling. "What's going on? Where is she?" he demanded.

"Just read the note," The old man said before leaving the house again.

Michael quickly tore open the envelope and saw several things inside it. When he dumped them on the table, out poured a letter, a bundle of money, and a harmonica. He grabbed the harmonica and sank into a chair, clutching it tightly as he read the letter:

Dearest Michael,

After some very hard soul-searching, I've decided to take Noel and go to a refuge in the North.

It has been one of the hardest decisions of my life, but it is something I must do. If I delay even a day, I might not be able to go.

I've known for some time that you love me. Although I've tried my best to avoid it, I realize I care very deeply for you, too. But I couldn't stay here with you, even if you asked me to marry you—which I'm not certain you would do.

I must believe that God works all things to the good of those who love Him. The fire made me realize it's time to let go of everything. I know God will help me in this, if I trust Him rather than myself.

In the envelope, you'll find 400 blue bills. That is exactly half of what Noel and I have, and we both felt that you should have it. Also, we decided to give you Daddy's harmonica.

Michael stopped reading and looked again at the harmonica, flexing his jaw over and over.

It's obviously not worth much to the world, but I'm sure that it's worth more than pure gold to the three of us. I know you will treasure it. I hope it will bring you only fond memories of Daddy, Noel, and me. I don't know if you can play or not—but if you do, remember that it has only played songs to the Lord before!

I just went in and saw you sleeping. . . . You looked so peaceful and sweet without the looks of pain and anger that I see in your eyes when you are awake. God help you find peace.

Please don't try to follow us. The trip is very dangerous without a guide. (Don't worry, we have one!) I'm asking the Lord to keep watch over you.

love,

Sara

Michael folded the letter and put it back in the envelope with the harmonica and the money. He put the envelope inside his shirt and found his jacket. He left the house without a word to its owners and headed for the cemetery.

Stepping through all the trash and rubble, he thought it appropriate. He felt like refuse. No good to anyone. The object of some great cosmic joke. If there was a God, He was a cruel being. He'd taken away everything Michael ever loved. His family, Pete, and now Sara. Gone.

He wondered, *What incredible blunder have I committed to deserve such punishment? Haven't I refused the "mark"? Haven't I been good enough?*

As he reached the cemetery, he felt more peaceful. *Maybe I belong here,* he thought.

He looked down the gentle slope to Pete's grave site, marked only by a crude cross made of wood. Some teenagers stood near it. While he watched, one of them grabbed the cross and started pulling it up out of the ground. The others joined in, tugging on it and roaring with laughter.

"Hey! You! Stop that!" Michael shouted, running down the hill. Just when they looked in his direction the cross came up out of the ground, and they all fell back with it. Michael tried to close the remaining distance to the grave as fast as he could, but the boys got out of sight before he reached it.

"If I see you here again, I'LL KILL YOU!" he yelled after them.

He picked up the cross and stuck it back in place. He packed dirt in around it and then looked for a rock. He soon found one and used it to hammer the cross further down.

When he finished, he looked down at the grave and saw the two little flowers Noel and Sara had left—already dark and shriveled. He started trembling. Only a little at first. As he stood there, though, he began to shake more and more, then fell on the grave, sobbing. He could no longer control the grief which spilled out of him in wracking waves.

His hands dug into the fresh dirt. "God, if you can hear me," he cried, "Help me. I'm dying."

He had no idea how long he lay there and cried before he heard a man's voice.

"You okay, Mister?"

Michael looked up to see an old man holding a shovel, watching him. "I said, are you okay?"

Michael realized how crazy he must look, with his face and clothes all sooty and dirty, lying on top of a grave. He wiped his face on his sleeve and tried to straighten himself up.

"Yeah . . . I'm okay."

The man stepped closer. "No need to be ashamed, sometimes it's good to cry. Was that your dad?"

"I loved him like he was." He had to swallow to continue speaking. "I can't believe he's gone."

"I see he was a Christian—by the cross, I mean. That won't last long. Those awful people come in here and burn or break the crosses. . . . Crazy folks. Always in here at night, dancing and lighting fires."

"But why?"

"Don't know. Maybe they've got contaminated brains, or maybe they hate Christians, or maybe they hate God. . . ." He looked at Michael. "It don't really matter though, does it? God doesn't need a marker to know where to find him. Your friend is already there."

Michael stared at the grave and started to say, "Thanks, I know," but when he looked around, he saw the old man had walked some distance away to tend another grave. Michael brushed off his hands and clothes and spoke quietly. "I'll try to do right by the harmonica." He closed his eyes. "God, just tell me what to do."

From the moment he said the words, he felt his mind clearing. He would go and buy some clothes, a pack, and enough food for a couple of weeks. Then he would head north. He'd heard Sara speak of a place called a "refuge" before—she said she had friends living there.

Regardless of the danger, he knew he couldn't keep existing like this anymore. He might as well take the risk of going north and finding something to live for.

But first, he would have to go further south to get his supplies.

###

It had been a while since he'd been this deep into the city, and it seemed strange to be walking through such large crowds of people, all going to do certain jobs at precise times in particular places. He felt like a salmon going upstream.

He traveled into a section of the city with new buildings going up everywhere. And at sunset . . . lights. Instead of dark, deserted streets, paved walkways beckoned pedestrians to move around and shop. And in almost every window, a sticker that said simply, "we live."

A live billboard he passed caught his attention. A reporter on the large screen delivered the latest news to passersby:

> . . . . In an interview today, Housing and Energy Secretary Amber Knoll declared that the revitalization of a decaying neighborhood could be accelerated when the majority of occupants in that neighborhood became encoded. 'In such cases,' Knoll said, 'the majority always has the option to apply for relocation of uncoded individuals and then to place their neighborhood on the New Start Housing Program'—a top priority list for governmental improvements. . .

Michael moved away from the billboard and down the street. He began to notice a large number of Peacekeepers. Had they been there before? He didn't think so. They stood in groups of two or three on nearly every corner, one in each group holding the disk for identifying. Not liking this at all, Michael avoided walking near them whenever possible, and bought his supplies in small "cash" stores.

Everywhere he looked, advertising vied for attention. All of it started with, "Now available to coded consumers . . ." Other ads promoted coding itself: "Tired of being lost in the shuffle? Your code helps the good things in life find YOU!!!" One poster had a picture of a man in a recliner with a viewer a phone, and dozens of other things stacked around the chair.

Michael paused in front of it and grunted. "Good ol' Linda." He hadn't so much as thought of her in ages. . . . How ironic to think the idea for this very ad had come from his own mouth.

He stopped in front of a store window with dozens of viewer screens. On all the screens, a popular celebrity sat touching his temples, demonstrating a mind control method. In order to find some peace of mind, Michael had tried this (at Linda's suggestion) when they first came South. His counselor told him he needed to "clear out" his negative brain waves. Eventually, this same person taught him how to use the black box—therapeutically, of course, along with eating certain foods to build up his body and psyche. What a horrible abyss that had been!

Michael looked away from the viewers and shook his head. A sense of purpose had settled on him and he didn't want to lose it by digging up unpleasant memories and feelings. Turning to walk away, he bumped several people. He wasn't used to moving in such crowds. In fact, being pushed along in a stream of bodies made him quite uncomfortable.

He rounded a corner as rotating yellow lights began flashing on top of every pole. Speakers carried the voice of a woman saying, "Step to the side. Wait. Peacekeeper activity in progress. Step to the side. Wait. Peacekeeper activity in progress."

Everyone nearby slowed and moved closer to the building-side of the sidewalk before stopping. Obviously, the lights were a signal to stop. Michael slowed his pace and moved to the side, like the other pedestrians.

A voice called loudly, "That one!" A soldier grabbed his arm and shoved him through a small group of people to press him against the wall. He turned to see two uniformed soldiers looking on while a third frisked him. A swarm of watchers quickly gathered around them.

"What's this for?" Michael demanded.

"What's your name?" one of the soldiers, a tall woman, asked.

"Michael Gordon."

"Can you prove it?"

"My I.D. is in my backpack."

They allowed Michael to get it out.

"How do we know this is you?"

"What do you mean? How ludicrous! This is an official I.D. My picture is on it."

The yellow lights flashed as the crowd around them continued to grow.

"Anyone can make a card and put a name and a picture on it."

"You're accusing me of forging my I.D. before you even scan it?" Michael started to lose his temper.

"Just wondering why you don't have a code," she said, looking to the audience for support.

"Yeah! Only people with something to hide are afraid to be identified," a man in front chimed in. A ripple of agreement went through the crowd.

"We've had a pickpocket working this area," the soldier who frisked him added, "and it could be you. We have you on video, bumping people down the street there."

"This is ridiculous!" Michael shouted, "I haven't done a thing, and you're trying to insinuate that I'm a thief because I don't have a mark?" he quickly realized what he'd said and corrected himself, ". . . because I don't have a code."

As soon as the word "mark" came out of his mouth, he saw a glint in the eye of the soldier in charge. He wanted to punch himself. Why had he used *that* word? Only fanatics used that word!

"Maybe we should take a walk down to the station," she said, motioning the other soldiers to take him.

Just then, a soldier wearing an earpiece said, "They've caught the pickpocket on the next block. . . . It's a woman, and she still has the items on her."

The lead soldier gave Michael an icy stare as he pulled his arms free. "Well," she said, "it looks like you're off the hook. This time." She clapped her hands twice and held them up to the crowd. "Go on now! Show's over!"

Michael put on his backpack and swiftly moved away. The sooner he got out of the city the better.

He eventually got to a section without lights and stepped into the darkness before turning to look at what he'd left behind. Next to the first street lamp stood a billboard. It had a picture of a viewer on it. Mr. Kressman's face was in the viewer but his arm and hand appeared to be coming out of the screen and pointing down to the lighted world below. "Behold! We make all things new!" was the caption on the board.

The thought struck Michael; perhaps the time had come. He recalled the words he read in Zac's Bible the day Pete died.

> "Also it causes all, both small and great, both rich and poor, both free and slave to be marked on the right hand or forehead, so that no one can buy or sell unless he has the mark that is the name of the beast or the number of his name. . . . If anyone worships the beast and its image and receives a mark on his forehead or hand, he also shall drink the wine of God's wrath. . . . And the smoke of his torment shall go up forever and ever."

Michael glanced back at the billboard. "I always knew there was something about you I didn't like," he said, before turning north.

He walked throughout the night, stopping only for food and drink. When the sky began to brighten, he took off his starlight glasses and put them in his jacket pocket. He'd come farther than he thought.

An abandoned building seemed a good place to rest for a few hours. He took off his coat and shirt, knowing the temperatures would rise during the day. He leaned some old doors and other pieces of wood against a wall, then he threw old chunks of brick on top of it to make it look more like rubble. This way, he'd be less likely to be disturbed. He crawled under his new creation and used his coat on his backpack for a pillow.

During the heat of the day, it would be harder for sensors to find him. At night, his body warmth made him more detectable, so being awake during those hours would be safer. He had his starlight glasses—purchased from a man of questionable character—that allowed him to see in the dark. He'd keep walking north, staying away from fires or lights where people might congregate at night.

Chapter 38

Near San Antonio

"So why don't you have your I.D.?" the raspy voice asked again.

"You stole me out of my room," the man answered. "I don't, as a rule, keep my I.D. in my underwear."

Silence.

A bright light shining in his eyes prevented the man from seeing the face attached to the raspy-voiced inquisitor who had questioned him for hours. He heard a sound nearby, so he squinted in its direction, and said, "Look, I'm sure that if you go back to my room, you'll find my I.D., and we can straighten this out." And he knew they would straighten it out. Eventually. They always did. It was pretty much the same every time. He didn't think it would go on too much longer now.

The raspy voice spoke again. "So you're the one they make such a noise about, huh?"

The prisoner didn't respond.

"Well, you don't rate much in here. Just another detainee."

"That's okay," he answered, trying not to sound exasperated. "If you'll just have someone fetch my wallet, I can show you I am a legal migrant. I wasn't breaking any laws, to the best of my knowledge, so why are you detaining me?"

"This would all be simpler if you had a code," the grating voice said from a different part of the room.

"So I've been told."

"Look, Don," the raspy voice said to someone else in the room, "you've been here all night, I can handle this alone. Why don't you go get some rest before the meeting."

The other man spoke for the first time. "Yeah, I think I will go. See you in a few hours."

A door opened, and a dark silhouette of a man appeared in the rectangle of light, then disappeared.

Raspy spoke again. "So why don't you have a code?"

The detainee had grown weary under the broiling light. Hand restraints kept him from rubbing his eyes while he thought. "Because I love the Lord. You would have me renounce my allegiance to Him in order to get that code."

"So lie. Take a code, and then do what you want."

"I'm afraid He takes truth more seriously than you do."

The interrogator let out a scratchy chuckle. "Truth is relative. You need to do something to survive—you do it. There are no absolutes anymore."

"You *absolutely* sure about that?"

Another chuckle. "You're okay. . . . So look, I'm getting tired, and I don't think you're gonna crack under the strain and beg to get coded tonight; but I need to keep you here for a while longer. It would look bad if I let you out too soon."

The prisoner heard the sound of a chair being scooted closer. A pair of uniformed legs appeared right in front of him as the man with the raspy voice sat down. Their knees were almost touching, but he could not see the face lingering in the shadows.

"So," the raspy voice said after a short silence, "you're 'Swordsman,' eh? It must be nice to be anonymous."

Swordsman tried to focus about where the face should be. "I don't know who you are. If you have my I.D., you know who I am."

"So you think your God would make you die for him even though he supposedly died for you?"

"At least you admit it's coming to that. . . . He died for my sins, yes, but He never promised me my physical body would not see death. What we believe is that our souls, what you might call 'life essence' or energy, will live eternally in resurrected bodies with Him in Heaven. All we need to do is to believe and confess that, via His death and His resurrection, He became the door to an eternity in God's presence. To get a code, I would have to deny what He accomplished and who He really is."

"Seems to me," the raspy voice said, "all that gets you is trouble."

Swordsman continued to look in the direction of the hidden face. "Scripture says, 'I tell you, my friend, do not fear those who kill the body, and after that have no more that they can do. But I will warn you whom to fear: Fear him who, after he has killed, has power to cast into hell. . . . Everyone who acknowledges me before men, the Son of man also will acknowledge before the angels of God, but he who denies me before men will be denied before the angels of God.'"

"You don't believe in reincarnation or any of that do you?"

"No. If Jesus died for my sins, I don't need to come back and pay for them. Besides, if I could perfect myself, why would I need a Savior?" Swordsman paused a moment as if listening to something, then leaned forward. "Let me ask you a couple of things: Have you enjoyed this life? Would you want to do this all over again in other bodies that will get old, feel pain, and die?"

"I don't believe in any of that junk. When you're dead, you're just dead. Period."

"What do you gain by believing this?"

"Gain? Gain? Why do I need to gain anything? I just know what I know."

"But it seems to me," Swordsman said, shrugging, "you are a man in favor of survival. You advocated that I lie in order to live. Is that what you would do?"

Silence.

The prisoner continued, "Why? Because you don't want to die. Most people don't. And if your theory is right, then these might be your last minutes, ticking away even as we sit here. And when you die, it's just over. . . . But, if *they* are right," he nodded to where he had seen the door, "you get to do this all over and over again. And everything you've done here—even though you don't remember doing it—you'll pay for in the future! And, here's a scary thought: If there really are no absolutes and everything is relative, you don't know *what* you might be punished for in the future. What's right today, could be wrong in the future. The 'Global View' may end up being totally incorrect in the future, and you could end up paying for this in an incarnation as a dung beetle, or a beggar without feet in India. And you'll be caught in an endless cycle of sin and death, being punished in the next life, then dying again. Hardly something to look forward to.

"Then again, if I'm right, you don't get a second chance once you're dead. You had the power to decide your eternal destination right here. . . . Your theory hasn't benefitted you in this scenario either.

"But let's just apply all this to *me* for a moment," Swordsman continued. "If I die tonight, and your theory is right, so what? I gave it my best shot, I'm satisfied with the life I lived in Jesus. And if they are right, what's the worst that will happen to me? I get sent off to some extra dimension for a while as punishment for rocking their boat before I get reborn. . . . But if my theory is correct, I spend but a short while on this earth where no suffering can begin to compare to the glory awaiting me! So you see," Swordsman leaned back on his chair with a smile, "living for Jesus is the only thing that'll benefit me in all cases!"

"But if I have a code," the raspy voice said, "then it doesn't matter, does it?"

Swordsman leaned forward and whispered, "There is life in you yet. God is telling me so right now."

Silence enveloped them. The hands of the man with the raspy voice formed into fists before he cleared his throat and whispered back. "I have this friend. He's found a way to beat the system. It's gone on for so long that he's an established part of society. If he comes forward now, he'll lose everything—certainly his job. If he doesn't tell how he did it and get others in trouble, there will be prison, maybe torture. Maybe death. Any day they could discover him."

"Then your friend has a big decision to make," Swordsman said softly. "He will be forced to choose one way or the other. Living in constant fear can be worse than torture sometimes. Not a real appealing choice. Or he could choose to come forward, fess up, get coded, take his lumps, and start again. If he dies and there is nothing after, it won't matter. Or . . . he could risk it all and accept Jesus. He'd no longer be a slave to fear, thinking this life is all he's got. Nor would he feel trapped in the tyranny of doing it all over and over again. . . . Jesus said, 'For whosoever will save his life shall lose it; but whosoever shall lose his life for my sake and the gospels,' the same shall save it.'"

"I'll tell my friend," the raspy voice said, "and I'm sure he'll spend some time choosing."

Another silence followed, but this time Swordsman broke it. "If you dare to tell me your friend's first name, I will pray for him."

A face now came into the circle of light as the man leaned forward, a look of deep anguish in his eyes, and said, "Gene. My name is Gene."

Chapter 39

Dallas

Linda Posner dropped to her hands and knees in a frantic effort to locate a contact lens she'd dropped in the wooly rug near her sink. "Why does he insist on these stupid rugs?" she mumbled to herself.

"Aha!" she cried, finding the nearly invisible object. Linda rushed to the sink to rinse it, only to see it slip from her fingers and disappear down the drain. She screamed and beat her fists on the sink.

Alex Dubois came bursting out the door. He had a towel around his waist, half a face of shaving cream, and a large cut on his chin. He glowered at her for a moment before yelling, "What in the *world* are you shrieking about?"

Near tears, she looked at him. "I lost my contact lens in the stupid sink after I found it in that stupid rug of yours."

"Oh! Well! That explains it! *Everyone* screams hysterically when they lose a contact lens! *Terrific!* You made me cut my chin off over a contact lens!" He went back through the door and slammed it.

She immediately put her index fingers under each tear duct and wiped frantically. Crying would ruin her face for the whole morning. "Stop!" she commanded her reflection in the mirror. She pulled out a tissue and dabbed gently around her eyes as she peered at her own image. No puffiness yet. She closed the eye without the lens and inspected her face closely. Tiny lines continued to encroach on her soft skin. How depressing. She could only hope she'd be able to obtain plastic surgery as well as eye correction surgery in the near future. She'd heard such things had become available again . . . for people with the right connections.

Meanwhile, inside the bathroom, Alex finished shaving and inspected his cut. He got out the skin bracer and threw it on his face. The cut felt like fire, and he sucked air through clenched teeth to keep from making noise.

No wonder the old boyfriend let her go, he thought while he dressed. In the months since Linda moved in, the tension in his apartment had grown to an almost unbearable level. She'd become a constant source of irritation. Had he ever met anyone so conceited or self-centered? Her whole life revolved around acquiring wealth and beauty for Linda. And the more she acquired, the more aggressive she became. What a relief it would be to get away from her for a few weeks. He pulled on a long-sleeved white shirt and began to button it. Maybe in his absence he could find the time to write her a letter saying, "It's been nice, but goodbye." Of course, he didn't know how this would affect their business relationship.

He frowned. Business. He had so much to do. He even lay awake at night trying to figure it all out. How to get those fanatics out of the way. How to get everyone coded. He could see people polarizing between his side and the fanatics. The battle lines became more distinct by the day with the worst of the conflict yet to come.

Once again, he'd begun to have doubts about some of Kressman's tactics. He sighed. Maybe the end really did justify the means. Even so, Alex had been raised on a very strict code of ethics and justifying some of his own actions had grown difficult lately. In addition to running afoul of his religious standards, living with Linda cut across business and personal standards. What had come over him? He shook his head.

Maybe he would write that letter tomorrow. Perhaps it would start the process of setting things right once again. After all, how could he call others to a higher level of integrity with such a large chink in his own armor? Could he prove a man didn't have to be a fanatic to be ethical?

Perhaps he could still bring together the best of the old world with the best of the new. The future could be bright, but there had to be discipline in order to preserve it for all. Perhaps his own stand for morality could serve as a witness to the others of his own faith—many of whom held positions of importance.

He'd gotten fully dressed and needed only to tie his tie. He tightened the knot with an air of finality as certainty settled into his mind. Yes. He'd get rid of Linda. He'd begin cutting off his relationship with her as soon as possible without totally ruining their work together. He opened the bathroom door and washed his hands before approaching her.

"Linda dear," he said in a solicitous tone, "Please forgive me for my outburst. Come, sit beside me for a moment," he said, moving to the sofa.

She sat down, still pouting. "Well, okay . . . but you know how hard it is to get contacts anymore. And I hate doing without."

He ignored her complaint. "I just found something out last night and haven't had time to discuss it with you."

"What's that, dear?"

"Well, instead of being gone a few weeks, I may be gone for months. We're getting to the end of our deadline, and I'll have to spend every waking moment working on the job. Much of it may have to be done at the Underwater Center. Of course, you're free to stay here in my apartment, if you'd like."

Although she'd always hoped that, somehow, she'd be able to wheedle an invitation to the Underwater Center, the prospect seemed decidedly dim at this point. Still, there was an upside: She loved this penthouse. In fact, it was about the only thing she loved about Alex. And now, she'd have it all to herself.

"Oh, but I'll miss you," she cooed. "What will I do when I'm lonely?" She squeezed up against him.

He clenched his teeth, then tried to relax and sound casual. "Oh, I'll miss you, too. . . . But we can just keep busy, right?" He smiled.

She smiled back. "Right."

"Well, I guess it's time to go." He stood and helped her up as well. He gave her a little kiss on the forehead and a hug, then picked up his briefcase and left.

Chapter 40

Atlanta

The young man looked around the soup kitchen for a black woman who might be working behind the counter. He didn't see her there, so he climbed the stairs at the side of the restaurant and knocked on the second door to the left. When Edwina Grant opened it, he quietly said, "From David," and handed her a small scrap of paper. She unfolded the paper with a seven-word message: *Please come as quickly as you can.*

In another half-hour, she would have been gone. Obviously, her plans would have to change. She thanked the boy and sent him on his way before she dashed around her room, making ready to leave for the rest of the day.

After checking the contents of her large, cloth purse, she closed and locked her door, then quietly descended the stairs to the main floor. She stopped at the foot of the stairs and glanced beyond the counter into the kitchen where Isaac stood with his back to her, stirring a pot at the large stove. She held her breath and tried to glide quietly toward the front door of the soup kitchen.

Technically, she had the afternoon off; but Isaac always made a big deal of it when she went anywhere outside the walls of his wretched domain. If only she could get out the door while his back was turned. Her hand no sooner pushed the handle of the rusty screen door when she heard his voice.

"Going out to meet someone? That one is a little young for you, isn't he?"

Very little slipped by Isaac's attention. He'd seen the teenager going up the stairs and he wanted her to know it. Doubtless he'd also seen the boy leave within moments of arrival, but this fact he'd keep to himself. He loved to goad her. It was like a hobby for him. The needling never took on a racial tone since Isaac didn't seem to care about her color. Who knew what fueled his cranky temperament?

"I'm just going for a long walk," she answered, "maybe some window shopping."

He wiped a chipped bowl and set it on a stack of similarly damaged vessels. "Don't be out too late. I need you in here bright and early tomorrow."

Why did Isaac care so much about what she did with her free time, anyway? She stepped out the door and spoke over her shoulder, "See you later, Isaac."

Walking quickly away, she inhaled the muggy air as if she were in a cool garden and thought, *Oh, thank You, Lord. A few hours away from the hot kitchen, from boiled cabbage, from Isaac. If only I didn't need this job.* She rounded the corner in a stream of pedestrians and tried, once again, to frame her life in a better light. *I have a visible means of support and a legal residence which aren't connected to anyone else in the group. I have my own room and a bathroom all to myself. I have hot food every day. Besides, there are more important things to consider.* She quickened her pace as she thought about all the stops she'd have to make. *No time for any personal errands now. . . . I wonder what David needs?*

She continued to move toward a section of the city where a greater number of coded people lived and worked. Freshly painted buildings and solar-powered street lamps marked the turf of a burgeoning new society encroaching on the ruins of the old. Making a final turn, Edwina entered a street where the two worlds (coded and uncoded) fully interfaced, and she noted a "live billboard" on the corner of a building. At the top of the billboard, a digital clock displayed the correct time in hours and minutes. Under it, a glowing message read,

REMAINING TIME UNTIL CLOSE-OUT DATE:

Below those words, a digital clock, flashing a countdown of days, hours, minutes, seconds, and tenths of seconds rapidly sped toward the deadline: midnight of the night when money would no longer hold any value. The text sliding along the bottom of the billboard said,

TIME FOR A CHANGE?

On the right quadrant of the billboard, a giant television screen played a video clip from former First Lady, Edith Todd. Her words poured from the billboard speakers onto the street.

" . . . you know, It's more than technology. It's converting to a whole new state of mind. It's erasing all the old borders and throwing down all the old superstitions. We must, as the young folks say, 'stop being viral.' If there is to be lasting peace, there must be *one* society, *one* class of people, *one* hope, *one* currency. We must choose to *embrace* this future, not dwell on the dark past or cling to a self-centered now. . . ."

Shoppers bustled by, continually reminded that the truce between cash and cashless economies would vanish soon. The future would overtake them, whether they wanted it to or not.

For the time being, however, this stretch of road saw shoppers of *all* kinds, and the booming businesses catered to the resourceful. Customers here could use virtually anything to obtain what they wanted. Bartering was already illegal, but if someone was willing to trade superior goods to satisfy eclectic (or illicit) tastes, no real barrier stood in the way. For the time being, mammon, not government ruled. Would this ever truly change? As long as the merchants and customers were discreet, local government officials had thus far been content to take a cut and look the other way.

Edwina slowed as she passed by the front of a small store specializing in pre-owned goods and rare items. This was David's store. She took particular note of a rotary-dial phone in the window and her face softened. *Young people probably wouldn't even know what that is.*

Once she passed through the open doorway, she noted the familiar smell. The musty odor took her back to the old world, back to a time when people had so much "stuff," they stored some of it in attics. Thoughts of stockpiled Christmas decor-ations, winter clothes, chests filled with family quilts, childhood memorabilia, and old photos came to mind. There was no time to linger in memory lane, however, so she forced herself to focus. She scanned the store for other customers. A middle-aged woman stood near a bin containing folded sweaters, carefully examining a bulky blue cardigan. Another shopper picked her way through a table laden with shoes.

"Thanks for coming in," David, the shopkeeper, said from the back of the store.

Edwina turned to see him motioning to her, so she moved toward him, noting the tight lines in his face, the strain in his voice. "I'm glad to see you. My daughter acquired a purse you might like. She set it aside for you, and I have it in the back."

Edwina nodded, "Thanks. May I have a look?"

He led her through a door beside the counter in the back, and called out to his daughter. "Chase! Your customer is here!"

He'd stepped back into the store before his daughter, Chase, moved to close it; then she threw her arms around Edwina.

"I'm so glad you came."

Edwina felt a tremor running through the girl's frame. "What's happened?"

Chase couldn't hold back tears. "It's Grandma," she said, turning and moving down a narrow hallway. "Something is very wrong. We think she may have had a stroke."

Edwina fell into step behind her. "Did you contact Walter?"

Chase kept moving and spoke over her shoulder. "He can't come until late tonight."

The two women climbed a flight of stairs and passed through another hallway before stepping into a beautiful attic bedroom. Sunlight filtering through lace curtains illuminated a small, pale woman on the bed, propped up on several pillows. Chase lit a bedside lamp before she moved to the window and closed it. When she pulled a set of heavy drapes, the room became significantly darker, and the old woman tried to speak, but only garbled sounds came from her crooked mouth.

"It's okay, Grandma," Chase said. "I was just closing the curtains. I brought someone to see you, though. It's Edwina. She's come to help."

Edwina leaned over the woman on the bed. "Don't try to talk for a moment, Mae. Let me take your pulse."

Another elderly woman peeked around the partially closed door. "Is she here? Is Edwina here?"

"Yes, Aunt Ruth," Chase said, moving toward the woman in the doorway. "If you want to come in, you need to be quiet so Edwina can work."

Aunt Ruth took several steps then hovered a few feet from Edwina, leaning on a walking stick. After a short silence, she asked, "She's not going to let them take Mae away is she? We don't want anyone to take her away."

Chase slipped her arm around Ruth's waist and turned her around in an effort to ease her back to her room for a while. "No, Aunt Ruth. No one is going to take Grandma away. That's why Edwina is here. She's going to help Grandma."

###

Downstairs, David waited on several customers before his daughter appeared in the back of the store. One look at her face said the news wasn't good. She motioned for him to go upstairs. "I'll watch the store for a few minutes. You take a break."

He rushed upstairs and met Edwina outside the bedroom.

She spoke in a voice just above a whisper. "I'm afraid your mother probably has suffered a stroke. At this point, even Walter can't do much for her. It's up to God."

David turned his face to the wall. "Now comes the test. I thought it would be when we lost the store. . . . But this is so much harder. Edwina . . . if you don't want to get tangled up in this . . . I understand completely."

He didn't have to explain. She knew that if David took his mother to the hospital, they would not treat her without a commitment to have her Regenerated and coded. If he refused, or if he simply opted to keep her here and the government found out, he could face serious charges of "abuse" or "neglect." Any person assisting him could face charges—especially if that person gave medical help or advice without a government-sanctioned license.

But she also knew that Mae would rather die than be Regenerated and coded. In the dim light of the hall, Edwina could see David's shoulders heaving as he wept silently. She reached over and clasped his hand before she bowed her head. "Lord, we're in this together, and all we can do is lock our eyes upon You. We run to Your feet, Father, and say we cannot fix this. Help us."

David kept his face averted as he spoke, his voice thick with emotion. "We don't know what will happen, Lord, but we commit my mother and all things concerning her into Your hands."

Aunt Ruth joined them in the hall before all of them made their way back into Mae's bedroom.

###

Thirty minutes later, Edwina began the trek away from the shopping district and back into the decay of an uncoded, unwired, unattached world. Everywhere she looked, she could see leaflets that Peacekeepers had posted in recent weeks. It was just the latest effort in the government's continuing campaign to restrain the lives of uncoded people:

> FOR THE SAFETY OF ALL CITIZENS
> NEW LAWS HAVE BEEN ENACTED.
> IN CONTINUING EFFORTS TO DETER
> CRIMINAL ACTIVITY
> AND GUARANTEE GREATER SECURITY FOR
> ALL,
> THERE IS A CURFEW
> IN ALL UNINCORPORATED (UNLIT)
> NEIGHBORHOODS.
> THE CURFEW WILL BE ENFORCED
> FROM 9 p.m. EACH NIGHT UNTIL 6 a.m. EACH
> MORNING.
> BREACH OF CURFEW WILL RESULT IN
> ARREST AND INCARCERATION.

Edwina continued walking past the area of the soup kitchen, even deeper into a neighborhood filled with people who, for whatever reason, had chosen to live like this.

She found a four-story apartment building and scaled the dilapidated stairs to the top floor. The worn-out railing had given way in numerous places, so she stayed near the wall as much as possible. In apartment 4A, she examined a toddler with a bad cold before giving the child's mother a list of natural remedies and the name of a place that would barter for the items. At her next stop, Edwina examined a boy with Cerebral Palsy and discussed a few options with his family. She also informed them they had a credit at a shop not far away. David, the owner, just happened to have a good set of metal crutches, and plenty of clothes of all sizes. An anonymous brother or sister in the Lord had given money to David on their behalf, so they could go in and select the items they could use.

By the time Edwina made her way back to the soup kitchen, she'd walked several miles and seen two more people in need of care. The curfew siren would sound any minute.

Hoping to slip up to her room, she came in via the back entrance. The sound of running water at the sink told her she'd hoped in vain.

"I thought you'd never get back," Isaac said without any sort of greeting. "Come over here."

She made her way to where he stood at the sink, and he glanced at her as she approached. "Gone shopping all that time and you didn't come back with anything? I hope you had fun with your boyfriend."

"I told you I was just—" Edwina said before she saw his hand. "Oh! That's a terrible burn! What did you do?"

"Another flare up with the back burner of the stove." He shot her another sideways look. "Probably would have been more alert and gotten out of the way if I wasn't trying to do so many things by myself."

"Here," she offered. "Let me look at it."

"Don't make it worse, I don't need you to make it worse."

She carefully dried off his hand and examined both sides of it. Blisters and red skin surrounded a deep burn in his left palm at the base of his thumb. Knowing the "required" first aid kit in the dilapidated old kitchen would be empty, she said, "I have some—"

He pulled his hand away. "I have some ointment."

"No," she quickly answered. "Don't put ointment on that. This is a serious burn and your hand needs special attention."

"How do I know you won't make it worse?"

She stepped back from him. "Would you rather go back to tending this by yourself?"

"No," he quickly answered. "I just wanted to know what you'd do, that's all."

He reluctantly offered her the hand again. After she'd expertly cleaned and bandaged it, he cradled it up by his chest and said, "This better not get infected."

She put her hands on her hips, wanting to ask, *Is grousing your only means of making conversation?*

He kept his eyes on Edwina. Her body posture said she'd had just about enough of his remarks when something suddenly changed. Her face softened, and she gently put her hand on his arm. "You'll be just fine, Isaac. We'll need to clean this every day and put on fresh bandages, but you'll be just fine." Although visibly tired, she seemed confident in her assessment. "I know you'll be just fine."

He frowned. This was not the same woman he hired. The woman he'd hired was gaunt, downcast, and silent. But over time, she brightened and became friendly with customers. Many of the newer customers seemed to have some connection with her. Undoubtedly she met with them when she went out at night and on her afternoons off. He didn't like her traipsing about all the time, but he had to admit his business had improved with her there.

Edwina gathered her things and turned to go upstairs. "Good night."

"What are you doing here?" he asked.

She turned. "What?"

He moved the bandaged hand. "Not everyone can do this. People who can do this . . . work in hospitals. . . . And you choose to work in a soup kitchen instead?"

She looked out into the empty restaurant for a few moments, then straight at him. "I'm a follower of Jesus Christ. I work here in order to have a means of living—so I can help people who don't have codes. I meet with other Christians when I'm not here, and we pray for ways to resist the coming darkness. Harboring me may eventually get you into trouble." The curfew siren sounded in the distance before she said, "If you want to fire me, that's fine, but it's after curfew now, so I'd have to leave in the morning."

He scowled and waved his good hand at her. "Who wants to fire you? . . . But I don't need trouble. You'd just better keep that part of your life outside this building."

She said nothing.

"You're still young," he said in a thoughtful tone. "Why would you want to throw your life away like this?"

A sad smile came to her lips and she shook her head. "I didn't throw my life away, I gave it to God. A better question is, what are *you* doing here, Isaac?" She looked at her watch and said, "Don't you know that you only have 162 days, 2 hours, and fifty-nine minutes before you get a code or lose all this," she moved her hand to indicate their surroundings, "*and* all the money you've saved? Even if you're only passively resisting at this point, Isaac, you're resisting. What's *your* reason?" When he offered no answer, she said, "You're a Jew. Could it be that something in your history tells you there's a need to resist this?"

He shook his head. "My troubles will come soon enough. Just don't bring me any extra."

"Good night, Isaac. Keep your hand up above your heart when you go to bed and it won't hurt so much."

Chapter 41

A suburb of Atlanta

Leon Newsome Sr. sat at his desk, gripped with fear. In his hand, he held a letter he couldn't bring himself to open. The postmark showed it was from Outer Perimeter, Vector 202. The return address said, "Bureau of Training."

Clearly the letter came from the people who had Jessica. Would they say she was incapable, untrainable, or emotionally disturbed? His mind went back to how they took her.

Leon Jr. got the government to check on Jessica's "status." It wasn't long before they started hounding the Newsomes to have her sent off to one of their schools. Leon Sr. flatly refused. Then came threats about the stability of his job and other forms of harassment if he did not relinquish Jessica for "suitability testing" and future placement in "as productive a job as possible." Security forces increased surveillance of his daily life, questioning neighbors and coworkers about him. But Leon remained firm in his resolve. He wouldn't give up his daughter.

As it turned out, he lost all choice in the matter. A government worker showed up at the house one day. She had troops with her, and a letter of command which entitled her to take custody of Jessica. Deana stalled as long as she could, but eventually had let them take her after several unsuccessful attempts to call Leon at his office. The worker took Jessica with the assurance that the government intended only to test her, and that in-depth reviews would be forwarded to the Newsomes in a very short time.

But in Mr. Newsome's mind remained the fear that, somehow, they'd find a way to kill his daughter if she wasn't capable of doing whatever it was they wanted. And what if she displayed some sort of fanatical behavior in front of them? Deana was right. He shouldn't have indulged Jessie in her fantasies about God, heaven, and the like.

Although Jessica hadn't been prepared for this, she'd been surprisingly calm about leaving the home that had been her cocoon, and going with total strangers. She'd donned her own coat and hat, carried her own bags, kissed her mother goodbye, and left. The girl had been gone for ten long days and nights during which Deana tried to assure Leon everything would be okay. She repeatedly said that, perhaps, this was for the best.

Now, he held in his hands a letter from the people who had his little girl. He ran his fingers through his hair several times and just looked at the envelope. A letter. Not a computer-generated report to be read online, but a letter. An official document. Finally he ripped open one end of it and pulled out the letter.

He unfolded a single page, dated three days previously, and after the official headings and greetings he read:

> It is with deep regret that we inform you of the death of your daughter, Jessica Blair Newsome. During transport to our facilities, she became ill and was placed in our infirmary. She died in her sleep of natural causes. Another, more detailed account will be sent to you after routine investigations are completed . . .

Mr. Newsome would never know she'd actually been caught praying with other children; and that when the results of those prayers became evident, the parents of other children would soon be receiving similar notices of "an unfortunate accident" or "a sudden, fatal illness," as well.

Chapter 42

Atlanta

First Lieutenant Leon Newsome raced up the stairs as if a monster from a fathomless pit was about to overtake him. He willed himself to know no pain, to yield to no obstacle. Bounding up the final flight he bumped into another soldier, knocking the fellow off his feet. The young man shouted at Newsome to no avail. Nothing would stop him.

The first Lieutenant bolted through the stairwell door and into the hallway. Before he'd taken another two steps, First Lieutenant Tedrick Chalmers appeared at the other end of the corridor, speeding toward the same goal: the entrance of their shared quarters. Leon Newsome knew Ted could beat him in a sprint, so he poured on the steam. Neither man made any attempt to slow down as the distance between them rapidly decreased. Leon figured he had the advantage because he could grab the knob, throw the door open, and veer into the room. Ted would have to stop and change directions to get in.

Leon almost had his hand on the knob when they crashed in an all-out match of boots, knees and elbows—each man struggling to gain first entry into the room. Lee finally managed to get Ted off balance and shove him to the floor, before quickly grabbing the knob and leaning against the door. Ted caught Lee's foot and tripped him just as it opened, causing him to fall headlong through the doorway. The struggle stopped.

"Ha!" Leon cried before rolling over on his back. "First one in."

Ted stood up in the hall, an annoyed expression on his face. "You cheated with the countdown, Lee."

Leon stood up and stepped further into their small apartment-turned-barrack, rubbing his scuffed elbow. "Spoken like a loser."

Ted entered and quietly closed the door. Still out of breath, each man moved to his own side of the room.

Leon unbuttoned his uniform shirt then cast it at the foot of his bunk. "I wonder how long they'll keep us in this vector.

I'm bored stupid. Sure wish we could head out for a few days of hunting."

Ted pulled off his left boot before smiling at his roommate. "Sounds great, but it's doubtful we'll get up into the zones again any time soon. . . . Still got your souvenirs from last time?"

Leon laughed and began removing his own footgear. "You sure pay an awful lot of attention to my personal property. Could it be that's because I have more souvenirs than you do?"

"Just concerned for you," his roommate shrugged. "It's not wise of you to keep such things anymore. I ditched mine."

"Chicken."

Ted rose from his bunk and placed his boots in a locker. "I, my friend, am gonna be squeaky clean: the perfect example of a man they'll want to promote to captain in the Universal Legion."

Leon smiled and stretched out on his bed. "You know that promotion is mine, Ted. I bagged it a few weeks ago when I was chosen as Folson's prime liaison."

"You wish. There are still *plenty* of candidates," Ted said, heading for the shower, "I'm glad you made prime liaison. That way Folson and his staff can see how defective you are first hand."

Knowing it was coming, Ted managed to duck in time to let a boot shoot by and bounce off the wall. "Ooooo," Ted said without looking at his assailant. "Gotta watch that temper, soldier."

They both laughed when Leon missed with the second boot.

Within an hour both men decided to skip the mess hall in the fenced compound and cruise out in search of a place to dine for the evening, wearing their new "dress casual" uniforms for the first time. Slightly reminiscent of the flight suits Air Force pilots once wore, the one-piece outfits were black, silken, and custom fit. Only rank and the interlocking-triangle insignia of the Universal Legion on the collars adorned the suits.

After a twenty-minute walk, they settled on a busy restaurant near a renovated section of town. Through the window in the front, Leon could see the eatery had an Italian theme, with candles and red-and-white checkered table cloths. He could remember eating in Italian restaurants before the disasters, and while he wasn't overly fond of Itallian cuisine, the number of patrons waiting outside said the food must be good.

"First one with a table wins," Lee said, hurrying ahead of his friend.

The two soldiers pushed through the line at the entrance to the restaurant, getting looks of admiration from a few of the ladies, pained expressions from other patrons. The hostess moved to intercept them, but they brushed by her.

"We'll let you know what we want in a minute," Lee said.

The two men entered the main dining room and stood together momentarily while they chose their potential tables.

Lt. Chalmers moved closer to Leon and said, "You sure we should do this? Think of all the lectures we had this week about making sure we set a perfect public example."

Lee let out a sarcastic laugh and stared at his friend. "Deep inside, all these people want leaders they fear and respect, m'boy. The timid get nowhere."

A middle-aged man at a table nearby saw the two men wearing Universal Legion uniforms and quickly averted his face. He began to slowly spoon a bowl of soup. The mechanical motion of his eating fairly screamed, *Try to look normal!*

"I'll take that table over there," Lee said.

Ted nodded toward a small table in the corner where a pretty woman with dark hair sat. She noticed him almost immediately and smiled. "There's mine," he said.

Before the roommates parted, another Lieutenant from their barracks entered the room, walked straight over to the brunette, and kissed her before seating himself with her.

"Ohhhhh. Tough luck, my friend," Leon said prior to stepping toward his own table.

Knowing the middle-aged man could sense his presence, Leon simply stood behind him for a few moments. The man leaned closer to his bowl and kept eating. Leon drank in the power of it. He could almost taste this customer's anxiety.

The man jolted slightly when Lieutenant Newsome moved another step closer, letting his right boot strike one of the back legs of the chair.

"Excuse me, sir," Lee finally said in an overly loud, yet boy-scout friendly voice. "My friend and I are in a terrible hurry and we wondered if we could share your table."

Total silence enveloped the restaurant and most of the customers openly stared at the scene.

Peering into his bowl, the customer weighed his options. Chances were, the soldiers didn't really want to dine with him or to arrest him, they merely wanted his table. He didn't turn or look up to reply, "That's okay. I was just finishing up. You can have the table."

"Why, thank you, sir," Leon said, turning to Ted with a look of triumph.

The man put down his spoon and scooted out from the table. Without ever directly looking at the lieutenants, he moved out of the room.

Selecting a seat at the table, Lee slowly lowered himself into it while looking around at his audience. Most of the onlookers chose to resume their own conversations and meals, but the atmosphere in the place was decidedly tense.

Ted sat down and shrugged. "Intimidation wins over charm when it comes to getting a table I guess."

Leon brushed a cracker crumb off the table. "Nothing will stop me from getting what I want, Ted. I could have gotten a table from anyone in this room. If you start getting tender or sentimental, you'll never get anywhere."

After a moment of silence, Ted casually unwrapped the silverware from a napkin and asked, "Gonna go visit your parents while we're in this vector? Your house is only a couple of hours from here."

"What did you mean by that?" Lee asked.

Lt. Newsome had come back from his last visit home in a particularly malignant mood. Since then, he'd stopped talking about his parents completely. All signs pointed to a large breach in the formerly close relationship.

Inspecting his knife for water spots, Tedrick said, "What *would* I mean by it? I heard from my folks today and I just wondered if you'd contacted yours yet. How is your family doing these days anyway?"

Lee grabbed a menu off the table. "Stop sticking your nose where it doesn't belong, Chalmers." He tried to appear calm, but his mind rushed to the sore spot. *Dad cared more about keeping that stupid monkey than anything else! How could he have chosen her over me? He's getting what he deserves. . . . But what about Mom?* Unconsciously mirroring one of his father's nervous gestures, Lee raked his fingers through his hair while he pretended to study the meals listed before him. *Oh, get a grip and forget it! There's nothing you can do to fix it. Not now. Probably not ever. You did what was best. If Mom wants to stay with that loser, you can't help her anymore.* He flipped the menu shut and said, "Don't change the subject. You're buying dinner."

A contented smile came to Ted's face. *Just like being a sniper on a roof. He didn't even see it coming.* He spread his hands in an open gesture and said, "Not a problem, dear boy. When I'm Captain, the cost of a meal like this will be a trifle."

Leon seized the arm of a waitress passing by the table. "We want to order now."

Flustered and a little frightened, the young girl pulled away. "This isn't my . . ." she said before she looked up and saw the restaurant manager nodding to her and giving her a go-ahead signal. She got the small, plexiglass clip screen from her pocket and asked, "What would you like?"

"This will all be on one bill," Leon said before pointing to his associate. "He gets it. And we want it all from the organic menu. No substitutions unless you check with us first."

Within minutes of the order, she delivered hot food to the table, and the two men ate as other patrons dared to steal glances of the higher quality food the soldiers seemed to rate. The two Lieutenants ate and made small talk about new procedures and which men and women in their unit might be viable competition for the promotion.

They'd barely eaten half the meal, when Leon's interest started to wander. On their way into the restaurant, he'd vaguely noticed an open-air market across the street. Crowds of civilians flocked in and out of the market with cloth bags of goods they had either purchased or hoped to sell. Now lacking anything better to do, Lee sat watching the bustle of activity through the large, front window of the restaurant. He began to wonder how many of the people in the market were illegally bartering. Ted continued to drone on about a guy who lived a few doors down the hall from them.

Leon nodded in the direction of the crowds outside. "Look over there. Across the street."

Ted turned. "Yeah. It's a market. So?"

"So they sure do a lot of business. I wonder how much of it is illegal."

"The place is right downtown. Local cops and soldiers are everywhere. . . . Besides, why should we care what they do?"

Just then, something familiar caught Leon's eye. With heightened interest, he watched a slender black woman walk into the market with a cloth shopping bag. He knew this woman. "Meal's over," he declared dropping his fork on his plate and scooting back his chair. "I need to go now."

"I have to pay the bill first."

"Then pay it," Leon said, standing up, "I'll be over in the market."

Lee hurried from the restaurant and ran across the street. Once he got through the entrance of the market, his eyes urgently scanned the heads of the shoppers to see if he could locate the woman he'd seen from his table. He pushed his way into the crowd and kept searching.

Ted joined him. "What are you looking for?"

Vendors gave the soldiers disapproving looks when a few nervous customers moved away.

"I thought I saw someone I used to know."

"What's she look like?" Ted asked. While waiting for a reply, he noticed something. The burning rage in Lt. Newsome's eyes said this wasn't a search for an old flame or a childhood friend. "What's the deal?"

Lee let several shoppers pass by them before he responded, "Never mind. Let's get out of here." He quickly threaded his way out of the market with Ted in tow, then trotted back across the street to the restaurant. When they stopped, he could barely stand still, shifting his weight from one foot to the other, his whole demeanor reflecting a mixture of agitation and excitement. "Tell you what, Ted. I need some time to myself. I'll see you back at the barracks."

Tedrick shrugged. "Sure. Whatever. See you later."

Chapter 43

Near Dallas

Psychic Tony Bensen sat, legs crossed, fingers touching thumbs, humming the tones. After several minutes, he opened his eyes and said, "It's no use. I can't concentrate." He got up before stretching and breathing deeply.

He'd been following Swordsman's movements and attending the fanatics' conferences. Despite huge expenditures of his energy, however, he still hadn't been able to tap into the mind of Swordsman or have the slightest impact on the meetings. Equally as troubling, he couldn't seem to predict much about what might happen next. His concentration continued to grow spottier by the day. Perhaps his recurring nightmare could be blamed for this. Who could concentrate with so little rest?

He had to admit he'd never struggled so hard to accomplish a task. Yet, whenever he got near Swordsman, or stood within crowds of fanatics, it was as if he'd bonked into a wall he couldn't go over, around, or through.

His star-reader said this would be a bad year. He should have listened.

Every day for the past week, he'd gone through the same process. As the time to go to the conference drew near, the strain would increase, and he'd almost decide not to go. Then, he'd get a lid on his feelings and opt to make another attempt.

As soon as he stood in the midst of the fanatics, however, he'd feel his strength fading. Their collective drive, thus far, had withstood him. Worse, he sensed this spiritual force pulling on him, wanting his surrender! Increasingly, it called to him. If not for the dream, he might not have been able to resist it.

He sat down on the floor again, desperately needing to get himself under control. He hummed and hummed. Finally, after what seemed ages, he began to slip down into his inner, quiet place.

The next thing he knew, he awoke with a jerk. Hours had passed, and he realized he'd fallen asleep. And he'd had the dream again. He'd dreamed of walking up for prayer . . . of them finding out . . . of Swordsman reaching out to kill him.

He got out his phone and dialed the number. When the transmit tone sounded, he hesitated. He wanted to shout, "I quit!" into the receiver. Instead he found the courage to say, "The subject moves to the Old City section tomorrow, and I will be there. Message ends."

How would he do this? How could he do it and succeed? He'd spend the next day fasting. Yes. That would help.

He looked around his hotel room, and a thought occurred to him; his own apartment was near the stadium in the Old City section. Maybe he just needed familiar surroundings. How he missed home. . . . How he missed Joan. He wanted to see her smile. He wanted to hear her contagious laughter, her lovely British accent. He quickly packed his bag and set off for home.

By the time he reached his apartment, Tony knew he'd made the right decision. It felt so good to be going up the stairs to his own place, to Joan. He opened the door and looked around at all of his favorite things. Relief flooded into his heart when the scent of incense wafted into his nostrils. "It's me, dear one," he called out softly, setting his bag on the sofa and looking about. "Joan?"

When Tony entered his meditation room, he found her. He opened his mouth to speak before he noticed the man sitting in front of her with his eyes closed, meditating.

"*Joan,*" Tony said, a bit louder than he intended.

She opened her eyes and popped up to hug him. "Tony! You've come home!" Her response said she was genuinely surprised and happy, as opposed to startled and guilty. She embraced him before looking back to her guest. "This is Blake," she said, pointing to the man who turned to look at Tony.

"Hi!" Blake said, before quickly standing and offering his hand. "I've heard so much about you. It's great to finally meet you. Joan says you're one of the best telepaths in the country. Sure would like to get some tips from you."

Tony looked at him a moment before shaking his hand. "Sure. But I've been away a while and I really need some rest," he said, putting his arm around Joan, "so if we could do this some other time . . ."

Blake nodded and replied, "Oh, sure, man." He glanced at Joan and gave her a small wave. "I'll call you sometime." He picked up his things and left.

Without another word, Tony sat down on the floor and Joan sat down facing him. He studied her for a moment. She looked cheery—not any the worse for missing him. Something dark brewed in his soul.

"You're actually jealous!" she said before her smile faded. "And you look . . . really awful." She placed her hands on his shoulders. "Something's wrong," she said in a serious tone. "What's wrong?"

"You are getting too good at this," he said pulling away and trying to smile.

"Are you in some sort of trouble?" She moved closer.

"You know I can't discuss it. And I don't want to." He hardened his resolve to keep his secret.

"That's okay," she said and leaned over to hug him tightly. "I'm so glad you're home."

Sensing her affection, he relaxed again. "That's just what I need from you. No requirements, just love."

Later that night Tony awoke from the dream, shaking. Joan asked what was wrong, and he could feel her growing concern.

"Look, I'll be fine," he said. "I've just been under an incredible amount of pressure and I'm really tired. I know it's made me a little weird but I'll get over it. I'll feel better when I stop having the same bad dream over and over."

"Perhaps it's a warning," she offered. "Have you considered quitting the job?"

He couldn't allow himself to be intimidated away from this task. He rubbed the back of his neck. *I have to ride this out,* he thought, before looking at her. "I'm okay now. Go back to sleep."

He got up, went to the living room, and sat for a while, thinking, trying to be totally objective. Was his employer correct? Did the future truly depend on stopping these fanatics?

Years ago, Tony understood there would be a rough "Transition" to the new, global order. Each person would have to push through surface reality and grasp the power available to all, to discover the divine self. Society would go through convulsions as those less enlightened fought the inevitable, while novices experimented with personal divinity and decided whether to use their powers for good or for evil. It would *seem* like chaos. The Masters warned of this. Once humanity passed through Transition, however, once people "got it," the whole earth would be different, new . . . wonderful. The wealth of the world would be shared. War, poverty, pestilence, and ignorance would all eventually be banished.

There had been many convulsions, and millions had died. Implementors of the Plan now occupied seats of authority. War had been halted, but what else could be said about the New Age of Peace so far? Millions had made the choice to accept the Global View and more chose it every day. But did the occupants of all these wired communities feel satisfaction, or gladness, or relief? When Tony walked the streets in these communities, he most often sensed two things: the numb acquiescence which led to the decisions of some, and the greed/self-preservation which fueled the decisions of others. Were all these people still just in the beginning phases? To "protect" these citizens, armed soldiers occupied virtually every corner, ready to enforce the wisdom of the enlightened elite.

And what about the stubborn resistance of the fanatics, their insistence on keeping the one way? Tony's pulse quickened as he considered the issue. Was he helping the government abolish something dangerous and destructive . . . or was he helping those in power extinguish free expression? Hadn't he committed himself to bridging the gap between those with the Global View and the fanatics? Now he wondered if that was even possible.

Tony got up and stood near a window, leaning against the sill, searching the heavens. As clouds tracked across the sky, they moved away from a full moon. His eyes drank in its beauty as the issues swirled around in his thoughts.

Supposedly, the God of Swordsman would change the whole destiny of *anyone* who became "saved." This intrigued Tony. This being "transformed" by a mere decision wasn't as easy to laugh off as he first thought.

But, how could this work—this way of being made "right" without laboring for it? How could there be no reincarnation, no chance to relive, to personally repay? How could one's whole life be changed by merely admitting fault and then believing that someone else had blotted the stain away? Fanatics believed in only one life, one choice, one way, one escape . . . or one judgement.

Tony frowned as he considered it. *Am I a god with power to use as I will?* He looked up into the sky once again. *Or am I like the moon—with no light of my own, made to reflect the light of another? There really is no way to merge these ideas. The teachings of Jesus are either everything . . . or nothing. I am either everything . . . or nothing.*

He moved away from the window to a nearby bookshelf. On the second shelf, his eyes found it: the old Bible that Joan had given him as a gift. The book had been printed over one hundred years ago. He carefully slid it out of the collection of rare books and held it in his hands, letting his thoughts flow freely.

Over the years, I've tried to tell myself I "know" their Jesus, that I respect the man as a teacher. But, Swordsman is right about one thing: If Jesus really believed what He told people—that He was the only God, the only Way, the only Truth, the only true Life . . . how can I deny these claims, and honestly say I know him or that I respect him?. . . I'm not working to "widen the view" of the fanatics. I want them to forsake the Jesus they know, and find another one. A Jesus who will be content to take his place in a painting and leave the job of giving instruction to those who have attained greater wisdom.

Tony exhaled heavily and moved the book in his hand up and down as if he were weighing it. *Why do I care what the Fanatics think? So what if their Jesus has nothing to do with me?*

The central question finally formed in his mind: *But, is their Jesus real?. . . How I long to know.*

He opened the book and read aloud the first line he saw.

". . . he that cometh to God must believe that He is, and that He is a rewarder of them that diligently seek Him."

Chapter 44

Dallas

Before dawn, Tony Bensen crept into his meditation room and lit candles of varying size, shape, and scent, arranged on stair-stepped shelves. He seated himself on the mat in his favorite spot and took a deep breath.

He scanned the books on a nearby shelf and frowned. He had books in every room. Most of them were books on meditation, spiritual experiences, techniques, positions, postures, breathing, diet, pleasure, self-discovery . . . intended to help people actualize the power within, to extend self beyond the five senses, to achieve more. He'd written some of the books himself. . . . *All this information, he said to himself, but are there any real answers?*

Joan looked into the room and he turned around to smile at her. "I'm not disturbing you, am I?" she asked in her soft, British accent. "I figured I'd get up and squeeze some fresh juice for you. I didn't hear your music playing when I came by, so I figured you hadn't started yet."

She remained in the doorway, looking at him with so much affection that he found the courage to ask her a question. "When was the last time you were totally taken in by something or someone?"

She started to chuckle, then realized he'd asked a serious question. "Totally?"

He nodded. "Yes. I'm talking about this life, this world, the realization you'd been 'had.'"

"Why do you ask?"

"I want to know what it was that fooled you. Was it that you trusted someone who lied? Some bit of evidence which put you onto the wrong trail? Or was it that you *wanted* to believe a lie?"

"You mean, like believing in Father Christmas, only more recent?"

He nodded again. "Yes. Like that. I really want to know."

She looked at the floor before mentioning a subject she seldom discussed. "I suppose it was my brother. After our parents died, I felt so responsible for him. I wanted to believe he would turn out okay . . . that he'd be *good* at something, even if he was a bit quirky. But the only thing he was actually good at was robbing people. . . . Well, that and lying about it. He always had some story to make uneven things line up. They were always such interesting stories, you know— positively loaded with inconsequential facts. And he'd be *so* charming . . . I'd come away, convinced anew of his veracity." She leaned her shoulder against the doorframe. "But after a while, I realized that living with him was like living in an eternal maze. There were always new twists to the plot, new bits of information that, if I checked, didn't quite line up with the evidence. . . . And I finally realized all those interesting stories, all those little bits and facts were just distractions to keep me wandering in the maze." She sighed. "Looking back, I suppose I always knew it. . . . So I guess the answer is I *wanted* to believe the lies. I wanted to believe them because the truth was just too painful to face. . . . When I stopped wanting to believe the lies, the truth was pretty plain." She stood straight again and put her hands on her hips before asking, "Was my dreadful disclosure satisfactory?"

He attempted a smile. "That was pretty dreadful, wasn't it? But helpful, dear one. It was actually quite helpful. Thanks."

She started to move away from the door, but stopped and moved back. "Ummm," she said, a bit uncertain whether this might be the proper time. "I want to say . . . notwithstanding the things both of us have said about codes, *this* is the underlying reason why I haven't gotten one yet. I mean, if it's so 'right,' why can't the idea stand on its own merit—in a free market, so to speak? Why the hard sell? Why all the bits and facts that never quite measure up to the evidence?" She knew she might be treading on sacred ground. "Sometimes, when I look at Edith Todd on one of those live billboards . . . I feel like I'm watching my brother . . ." Her words trailed off as Tony's face drained of color. She'd said enough on the issue. Maybe too much. "I'll just go and make some juice then." She moved out of the doorway and closed the door.

Tony rubbed his face with his hands. *Should I go and talk to her? What can I say? That I'm working for the forces behind Edith Todd? That things in the global movement only seem* *askew? That things will get better soon?* He closed his eyes. *I have to figure it out for myself first.*

He turned once again to look at the books on his shelf and realized what he wanted, more than anything else, was the truth. He wanted to know it more than he wanted to be distracted by interesting facts, more than he wanted to be in a position to influence people like Edith Todd. He wanted to know the truth more than he wanted to be proven right.

With that decision, for the first time since he'd taken the assignment to follow Swordsman, he felt unblocked. Within minutes, he had a lead to follow. Would it be just another trail in an endless maze?

\#\#\#

By the time he left his apartment, Tony knew exactly where Swordsman would be at 8:00 a.m. He would follow Swordsman and watch him outside the confines of staged events. Would the private man be the same as the public one?

Tony hurried to a particular street corner and soon, to his great delight, he saw a lanky, dark-haired man striding down the street. It was Swordsman. Within moments, two men joined the spiritual leader and the trio began walking north. Tony followed them, hiding in clumps of pedestrians, keeping a sufficient distance to remain unnoticed.

They kept a good pace all morning, talking now and again, but rarely slowing down. At noontime, they stopped for lunch in a large, open-air restaurant where a man and woman joined them. On an impulse, Tony risked sitting at a table not far from the group.

What could he sense, so far? Emanating from the people accompanying Swordsman, Tony sensed deep affinity and respect for each other and for Swordsman. And what radiated from the man himself? Tony concentrated and felt a profound resonation. Was it faith, hope, love . . . or a mixture of all three?

Although not close enough to hear the conversation, Tony had an unobstructed view of the group. He could see Swordsman connecting with each person at the table, looking at each one, listening to each one, touching each one.

If we met under other circumstances, Tony thought, *wouldn't I like this man? Wouldn't I want to be his friend, his equal? How different he seems from those who hired me! An uncomfortable idea now took shape in Tony's mind. Has my fear of Swordsman come from a deeper insight into an evil thing in him . . . or is it a fear that something evil in me will be exposed?* He began feeling dizzy, then nauseous. There came a sudden, overwhelming impulse to go home. Tony put his hands on the table in front of him to steady himself. *No! I must follow him today. I must see for myself. I will not go home.*

The meal came to an end, and everyone at the table stood up. Hugs went round the group before the two men who accompanied Swordsman to the restaurant departed without him. Now, the couple walked with the spiritual leader, continuing the trek northward. Despite feeling unwell, Tony kept tracking them.

At mid-afternoon, they stopped briefly in a park to talk to a small group of people before pushing on through the remainder of the day. Again, Tony sensed and saw what he'd been feeling and seeing for weeks among these people. Genuine affinity . . . love . . . like one would have for close family members.

Tony rarely lost sight of Swordsman and his companions all day. When late afternoon came, they entered a crumbling neighborhood and continued walking.

Oblivious to the man following them, the married couple and Swordsman walked along broken sidewalks. The sun would soon set; but the area was familiar territory to the couple, so they didn't press their guest to hurry. Sensing he needed a few minutes of solitary time, they let him fall behind a short distance.

Grateful for a private moment, Swordsman had an inward conversation with the Lord as he stepped along, occasionally noting the direction his hosts walked.

Behind them all, Tony saw first the couple, then Swordsman, turn a corner, and he realized something: With the onset of evening, it might be easy to lose sight of his quarry in this unwired neighborhood. He felt an urgency to keep up, so he quickened his pace.

When he rounded the corner, the last rays of the sun greeted him on a street so long and straight it seemed to lead right into the golden ball of light, dipping down into the horizon. He followed along in the hot-orange glimmer reflecting off buildings and the path beneath their feet.

Nearly half a block ahead of Swordsman, the couple looked back to be sure their guest turned the corner. Preoccupied with seeing him, they passed a lone, adolescent girl leaning on the pole of a lamp which hadn't had electricity in years. The teen girl let them go by, waiting for a particular circumstance. When she saw an unaccompanied male coming down the street, she moved around the pole to face him.

Swordsman slowed his pace and blinked at the strange sight in front of him. At first, he thought it might be the evening-stretched shadows of other pedestrians briefly enveloping, then moving away from the small, teen girl standing before him. Yet, even when the shadows moved beyond her, the phenomenon continued—as if layers of dark smoke continuously poured out of her and slowly sank into the ground around her feet.

A terrible stench began to fill his nostrils. In addition, the closer he came, the louder he heard an agonized wail. He peered at the girl, somehow framed in a dark cloud, yet silhouetted against the glowing sun. Her skeletal form held up a small face with sharp cheekbones and deep-set eyes. Her mouth appeared closed, but the horrible cry continued and grew louder still.

Now only five feet behind Swordsman, Tony stopped walking as his mind unexpectedly exploded with a picture. He no longer saw his surroundings from his own perspective. He experienced the sensation of being enclosed in a giant hand and felt himself being drawn up to a higher vantage point. From here, he could see, hear, and understand *everything* below him. He could see Swordsman. He could also see what Swordsman saw, smell the stench, hear the awful sound . . . *feel* a mind-bending pain pounding through the girl's fragile body. Tony's mind screamed, *NO!* but the scene continued to unfold below him.

The girl eyed Swordsman briefly before saying, "I haven't eaten in three days. I'll do whatever you want, mister, just take me with you."

The howl emanating from her soul almost drowned out her voice. Swordsman had to take a step back from her in order to regain the ability to think clearly. *Dear Lord!* He desperately prayed in his mind, *What IS this? What has happened to this girl? What do You want to do?* Almost instantly, he knew this girl had been orphaned, then captured and held in a basement where she'd been enslaved for months . . . a place where unspeakable things had happened to her. He saw a terminal illness in her body—and deep inside this dying girl a beaten, smoldering soul begging for the pain to stop.

From above, Tony continued to comprehend and experience all of it as it happened, hearing Swordsman's prayer, then knowing the same things about this girl. He could see dark claws tearing at her mind and body, he could hear hissing voices taunting, tormenting, joining with the scream of her own soul. Overlapping all this, his own thoughts considered what could end such horrible pain. Before he could ponder it further, he became aware of a light so intense it bent around corners, filling every space, leaving no chink or crack where a shadow could hide. His whole life became bare and open in this light, and his entire being shuddered. Were it not for the protective hand around him, Tony felt he might perish in the brightness. Overwhelmed, he closed his eyes, yet he understood what he could not see. Coming from this light, he could feel a love greater than the ocean, rolling out, cascading toward the girl. This love was not merely a power or a force. This love had intelligence, cognizance . . . this love was a person . . . someone Tony dared not look upon.

As quickly as it began, the vision stopped. Tony jolted and found himself standing behind Swordsman.

Swordsman's gaze remained locked on the girl. He said, "You'll be fed, little one. But what you need, more than food, is for the howling to stop."

She swayed. "Yes. . . . You can hear it, too?" She put her hands on either side of her face and began to make a sound which echoed the pain within. She doubled over and fell to the ground, continuing to howl.

Tony stood there on the sidewalk, disconnected from the vision he'd experienced, realizing his own power and skill were no match against the darkness which would soon snuff out the life of this girl. His blood ran cold, but he couldn't move. It felt as if his feet had been bolted to the sidewalk, preventing him from running away from the horrible sound resonating through his body. Was something inside *him* beginning to make the same noise?

Several people pushed by Tony as a crowd of onlookers formed an uneven perimeter around the girl, like a broken fence around a haunted house. Each person feared what might be wrong, yet still felt drawn by sick curiosity to stand and witness the spectacle. What was the man near her about to do?

Swordsman began praying before his companions pushed through the crowd to stand near the girl. They bent down to lay their hands on her, but he said, "Don't touch her yet. God is doing something and these people need to see that **He** is the one who does it. Stay near her and pray with me." He bowed his head and said, "Be merciful to this child, Lord, for she is faint. Oh Lord, heal her, for her bones are in agony. Her soul is in anguish. Turn, Jesus, and deliver her; save her because of Your unfailing love. She is worn out from groaning; all night long she has flooded her bed with weeping and drenched the place of her sleep with tears. Her eyes have grown weak with sorrow; they fail because of all her foes. In the name of Jesus Christ," Swordsman said, raising his head and opening his eyes, "*Away from her, you spirits of death, for the LORD has heard her weeping!*"

The crowd stepped back when a loud shriek came out of the girl. She went silent and limp on the sidewalk. Swordsman squatted down, tenderly moving matted hair away from her face. "Thank you, Jesus. You have set her free" He motioned to his friends who now leaned close to her. The woman placed a tender hand upon the girl's shoulder and she awoke as if from sleep. The teen slowly sat up and Swordsman took her hand, saying "The sound and the sickness are gone now, little one. Do you want to meet the One who set you free?"

She nodded. Even skeptical onlookers stayed to listen.

"The One who set you free is the Lord Jesus Christ. Long before you were born, He left all his riches in Heaven to come to earth as a man, so that He could adopt you and me into His family. He took on a body of flesh and bones just like ours. He lived the blameless life you and I could never live, and He took the penalty of death due to all people. Jesus—the One who created the whole universe—came down here so that He could die in your place and mine. He did it so we could come to live with Him and Father God in Heaven. . . . Only Jesus has the power to set a soul free—like what just happened to you. Only Jesus can open the way to real life . . . eternal life. All we need to do is admit this and ask Him to be our Lord, our big brother, our guide while we walk this earth, until it's time to be with Him in Heaven. . . . Do you want to meet Him and accept what He has done for you?"

She focused on his words, unaware of the crowd around them. "Yes." She put her hands on her stomach. "I . . . I don't hurt. I believe you. I accept Him."

Tony stared incredulously over the shoulders of the people in front of him. The light had moved through this girl and swept away the darkness. A transformation took place, not through lifetimes of struggle, but on the spot, *here,* in a moment. She'd been given liberty . . . even the liberty to say 'no' if she didn't want to know the One who had so miraculously set her free.

Swordsman helped the girl to her feet before smiling at the crowd and saying, "Since you're all here . . . anybody else want to meet Jesus? Anybody else want to pray? He's willing to meet you right here, right now . . . "

Tony found he could move and he stepped back. He needed time to process all of this. What should he do now? What *could* he do now? He stepped back a few more paces, bumping into several pedestrians. He put his hand on his forehead. *I must get away and think.* He turned and hurried away.

###

The sun had set by the time Swordsman and his friends finished praying with people in the crowd. The curfew sirens would sound soon. Before finishing their journey, they'd take the girl to a home where she would be fed, clothed, and sheltered.

Chapter 45

The border to the Northern Zones

Michael Gordon stood on the edge and stared. He'd finally reached the zones. During the night he'd had to stop traveling and take shelter from a large electrical storm. By the time it blew over, a growing light on the horizon said dawn would come soon.

Tall, razor-wire fences, strung to barricade the way north, had blown down in several places. He looked out at the great expanse of wasteland, wondering if he dared enter. Even in the dim light, he could see a bright orange crust covering most of the ground. Obviously a contaminant of some sort. He hesitated, considering just how dangerous it might be to walk across the crust. It probably wouldn't penetrate his shoes, but what about fumes or dust rising out of it?

He'd have to move soon if he wanted to get out there. He'd been told troops patrolled the zone's edge twenty-four hours a day. It might be a matter of minutes before they came by to fix the breaks in the fence. He debated another moment, then walked forward a few steps. The crust was hard as rock. He took a few more steps.

In one place, a patch of thinner crust broke like ice, exposing buff-colored soil beneath. This wouldn't do. They'd see his footprints. He looked for the darker, harder patches of crystals to step on, walking at a brisk pace, but not running for fear of breaking the crust.

Later that morning, Pvt. John Louis found the breaks in the fence and saw a couple of footprints in the thinner crust. He didn't go for a closer look. He wasn't crazy. He'd heard enough to be scared stiff of the orange crust.

He also decided not to tell anyone. If they found out he'd left his post during the storm, he'd be in big trouble. They might even make him search for the nut who ran out there. No. He'd just fix the fences and forget it. When broken, the orange crystals grew quickly, so within hours, the crust would fix itself. No one would ever know.

By mid-afternoon, Michael felt safe enough for a brief stop. The crust had given way to sand and then to soil, rocks, and eventually plant life. He sat down on a rock in the shade of a tree, too tired to go on. He had to rest. The shade felt so cool after being in the sun, and soon he fell asleep.

Michael awoke with a start. People with torches stood over him, staring. They didn't look like Sammies. In fact, their clothes looked pretty ragged.

One of the men stepped forward. "Hello, friend. Sorry if we frightened you. You gave us quite a jolt, too."

Michael slowly straightened up and drew his backpack closer. He remembered putting his knife in it and regretted it.

"It's okay!" the man assured him. "We're all friends here. I'm Friend Robert." He pointed to himself and then to each of the others. "That is Friend Leah, Friend Susan, Friend Barbara, Friend Fred, and Friend Stuart. Feel welcome to come and sup with us."

Michael felt threatened; but he didn't think he had much choice. "Thank you," he said, rising to his feet.

A woman grabbed his backpack before he could get a good grip on it.

"Friend Leah will carry your burden for you," Robert said.

After a few minutes of walking, they came to a clearing with large stones set in a circle around a fire. About twenty other people had gathered there, and as he looked at them, Michael noticed something: More than half of them had no right hand. The hair stood up on his neck. Could this be a colony of escaped convicts?

Prisoners received a special chip—not one of choice, but one which identified them as criminals. Similar to the chips of soldiers, it emitted a tracking signal which could be picked up at much longer range than ordinary codes. After escaping, many convicts had their right hand cut off to avoid capture or positive identification, fearing that if they merely removed the chip, a poison believed to be imbedded with it would disburse a lethal dose into their bodies. . . . Michael hoped they weren't the type of criminals who murdered people.

Soon, he smelled the large pot of food cooking and Michael felt his stomach rumbling. Everybody else took some, so when they offered him a plate, he accepted. Before they ate, they stood in a circle, and Friend Stuart said a prayer.

Perhaps, Michael considered, *I've been wrong. Could these be Christians? Is this a refuge?* An inner sense told him, *No.*

They all sat and ate. Michael cautiously downed the contents of his plate, then turned down an offer for seconds.

At the end of the meal, everyone sat and talked for a while, trying to engage Michael in small talk. This only increased his uneasiness. He considered it strange they had no desire to know who he was or where he'd come from. Of course, they did have his backpack . . . and his I.D. and his money, and his food . . . and of course, his knife. He considered possible means of escape.

Friend Stuart stood and held up his hand for silence. "Friends!" he called, "It's time to share about Brother Beanly.

Michael noticed it wasn't "Friend Beanly," but "Brother Beanly."

Friend Stuart continued talking. "We have a new Friend in our midst tonight as well as a Friend who has decided to stay."

They all looked from Michael to a man about five people down on his left.

"So we've decided to share about Brother Beanly."

A general sound of approval went through the people.

"As you all know," he said, "the disasters weren't the end of times forecasted by many, but a warning to all True Believers to mend their ways . . ." he looked around the circle. "It was at this time that Brother Beanly stepped out of the void to guide us. To teach us. To reveal the Vision to those of us who would follow."

As he spoke, various people from the group said "Yes!" or, "Amen!" The number of voices grew, and the intensity of their responses rose, as Friend Stuart got louder.

"It was revealed to Brother Beanly that the contamination was *from* God. It was a means of purging and purifying True Believers . . . a way to separate the sheep from the goats . . . a way to give ultimate redemption to even those who were deemed lost if they would surmount the obstacles . . . if they were willing to rid themselves of the evil code, or maybe even the temptation to take it. He gave us the purging power of the Feast!"

"Yes!" shouted many of the people, some of them rising to their feet and lifting their arms. Michael looked at them as they stood, and it began to dawn on him. They had cut off their hands as some sort of ritual. He felt sick.

"And," Stuart shouted, "if one can partake of the Feast, one can commune with God! Bring on the Feast!"

Two women came forward, holding a large, wooden platter. They stood in front of Friend Stuart with it. Michael scarcely dared to look, fearing the plate contained human hands. He breathed a small sigh of relief when he saw it didn't. Friend Stuart reached down to the platter, picked up a chunk of something and held it up.

At first, Michael couldn't make it out, but once the firelight illuminated the object, he finally recognized it as a piece of the orange crust he'd walked on all day. They started gathering around it, each person taking a bite. Within seconds, each partaker fell on the ground shaking and jerking.

That was it. He didn't want to see anymore. Michael bolted from his place and ran as fast as he could into the nearby trees. He grappled in his pockets and whispered a hasty "thank God" when he found his starlight glasses. He put them on and immediately could see his way between the trees. Several people from the camp picked up torches and pursued him.

Michael ran faster and faster but still heard their voices behind. "Come back, Friend Michael!"

I should've waited till more of them had eaten their feast before running, he thought. He kept going, dodging branches, weaving between the trees.

"We're all Friends!" The voice sounded closer.

He turned for a split second to see torchlights advancing from behind. He crashed right into a tree and fell down. Stunned, but not hurt as far as he could tell, Michael jumped up and started to trot forward again. Within seconds, he became aware of another noise. A loud roaring sound. A waterfall.

Michael barely caught himself on a tree branch at the edge of a long drop onto wet rocks. He looked back, panting. The torches moved still closer. They'd catch up if he didn't hurry.

He ran among the trees along the edge, hoping to find a way to cross the gap to the other side of the falls. The voices sounded nearer again. His lungs burned, and his legs ached more with each step. "If you're there," he gasped, "Lord, I need—" He caught his foot on a downed limb and started to fall.

Someone caught his arm and pulled hard. He felt himself being yanked into a huge crack in the trunk of a tree. Once inside it, Michael looked around to see who or what had pulled him in. He prepared to fend off an attack from a large man or a wild animal, but a quick look told him he was alone inside the hollow of the tree. His mind leaped about for an explanation. For a moment, he considered jumping out to face the friends rather than some unknown creature.

His pursuers drew near once again. Certain they'd hear his ragged breathing, Michael covered his mouth.

They moved not far away, and their torches cast dancing light and shadows everywhere. He again looked around inside his hiding place to see who or what had placed him there. Seen through his starlight glasses, the firelight made the space as bright as day. . . . No one, nothing was there.

Michael turned back to the opening when a sound warned him of someone's approach. A brilliant light flooded the crack in the tree. Not the light of the hunter's torch but a steady, brilliant blue-white glow, completely filling the space and shining all around him. He took off his glasses and could still see it.

Several of the friends stood right next to his hiding place now. Surely they saw this bright light, or at least the enormous crack in the tree. But they just stood there and talked.

" . . . maybe he fell in the canyon," one man said.

"Well, I could have sworn I saw him run this way, but I don't know how he could get away so fast in the dark," said another.

"Oh well. We're missing everything. Let's go back."

The voices receded.

Michael sat in the tree for what seemed like hours, watching the steady glow of the light. He'd been afraid to walk through it at first, then took it as some kind of warning not to leave the tree. Finally, it dimmed and disappeared. Now he wondered if he'd imagined the whole thing.

He tried to pull himself up, and a pain shot through his right shoulder and arm. *Well at least I didn't imagine being jerked into this place,* he thought, rubbing the shoulder gingerly.

"Thanks," he said, looking up.

Noting the sun would soon be rising, he left the tree and walked for a couple hours, continuing to follow the edge of the canyon in hopes of finding a way across it. Once he'd gone a sufficient distance from the Friends, he hid in some leafy bushes to sleep.

Hours later, he woke from his sleep and looked around for a moment to be sure no one was nearby before stretching or making any noise. He could hear the buzzing of insects and the rush of water through the nearby canyon.

His stomach rumbled, and the sound of all that water made him realize he was thirsty as well. He had no idea which things in the wild were edible and which things were poisonous. He'd have to go without until he found something he recognized as food. Meanwhile, he kept walking. The walls of the canyon had gotten shallow, so he hoped he'd find a place to cross over to the opposite side.

Soon, he found the spot he'd been searching for. He scrambled down the bank to the river. He was so thirsty, he no longer cared if the water might be contaminated. He got down on his stomach and drank. The cold water tasted sweet.

He stood and started to wade out, then stopped and checked his pockets. He could lose the few things he had left in the water if he didn't secure them somehow. He had a comb, his starlight glasses, four coins, and Pete's harmonica. Hardly the makings of a survival kit.

He looked at the harmonica, happy he hadn't put it in his backpack. He took off his shirt, placed all of the items in the middle of it, and tied them up. Then he threaded his belt through the knot in the shirt and buckled it tight.

He was ready. Just when he got knee-deep in the rushing water, he noticed a tree trunk coming his way down the middle of the river. The thought occurred to him he could use the trunk as a flotation device and glide down the river with it—catching a free ride for as long as he wanted. If he got tired, or neared rough water, he could swim ashore.

He waited a few moments for the log to move closer, then swam out to catch it. Now immersed in the cold water, he wondered how long he could stand it. The current took him east, and somewhat southward. Not the most desirable direction, but he wanted to put as much distance between himself and the friends as possible.

The sun neared the western horizon when he decided he'd have to get out before he froze to death. His teeth chattered loudly as he swam for the nearest bank, hoping he could make it. His arms and legs had gone numb. He reached the shore and crawled up a few feet from the river's edge.

A steady wind blew. Weakened by the cold water, he crawled into the cover of some nearby trees. He'd have to find some way to start a fire if he wanted to live through the night.

How did the Boy Scouts start fires? Friction. Would it really work? It would have to. Plenty of twigs and dead grass had piled up around the trees where it had snagged during a flood.

Michael collected some of the material and packed it around a hole in a large piece of bark he'd found. He put a stick in the hole and rubbed it furiously between his hands, just the way he'd seen people on survival shows do it.

He checked for warmth with water-wrinkled, trembling hands. Barely warm. He tried again and again. He'd about run out of energy and turned blue with cold when he saw a little smoke rising from the pile.

"Come on, come on . . ." he said, the sight of the smoke giving him new strength to move his hands back and forth. After a flicker, the kindling was ablaze. He quickly put more twigs and branches on the fire, and it grew larger.

He knew he'd be a sitting target with the fire going, but he didn't care. He figured he'd rather be shot while sitting by it than freezing to death.

It took an hour for him to stop shaking. He felt his shirt, now dry and warm from the fire, and put it on. Before long, he fell into a deep asleep.

At first light, he awoke. The fire had gone out. He looked at the river and wondered if there were any fish to be caught. How would he catch them without tackle? Then he realized something. "Oh no," he moaned. "I got out on the wrong side."

"Hello there!" a man's voice called out from the opposite bank of the river.

Michael's gaze shot over to the far shore where several men stood in a group.

"Hello!" the man called again with his hands cupped around his mouth. "Do you need help? We saw your fire last night."

Michael looked them over. They weren't in rags like the friends, and they didn't appear to have any weapons.

Another one of them spoke. "There's an area of rough water then some falls! In less than half a mile! We wouldn't advise traveling on the river!"

Michael thought for a moment. He could go no further alone. "I'm looking for a place called a refuge!" he called over.

They all looked at each other, then turned to address him again. "Stay put. We'll throw a rope across to you! The current might be too strong to swim if you're tired!"

Tired wasn't the word. Half dead was more like it.

He called, "Okay! Thanks!" and sat down while they uncoiled some lengths of rope and tied them together.

One of them made a lasso and started swinging it overhead. He made bigger and bigger circles with it and finally let go. It fell short of the bank and quickly sped away. He hauled it back in. Next they tied a good-sized stone to the end, and a larger man swung it round and round before flinging it across the river. It landed only a few feet from the shore, and Michael lunged for it.

"Tie the rope under your arms!" the man shouted. Michael started to do so when he remembered his things by the fire.

"One moment!" he called. He tied the rope to a tree branch and then took off his shirt. He made the bundle again and secured it to his belt. Then, he tied the rope around himself and waded into the stream. It seemed even colder than the last time, and his teeth started to clack together almost immediately.

The men on the other side hauled on the rope. All but one. When Michael was only a few feet away, he noticed the empty right sleeve of the man's shirt, dangling by his side.

Oh no, he thought, *not again.*

They dragged him onto the bank.

Chapter 46

Strategic Underwater Fibertronic Center in the Gulf of Mexico

Alex Dubois poured himself a glass of water and looked at the tiny pill. The words he'd overheard just that morning echoed in his head. *"What kind of parent would let their kids live in squaller anyway? Gwen told me they'll all lose their children if they insist on staying uncoded. It's about time. Why should we continue to let them pollute the minds of the young?"*

A slight tremor went through Alex's hand. He took the pill and drank all the water.

"Use those often?" John Klost said.

Alex whirled around in his chair. Had he been so preoccupied that he didn't hear the tone of the door?

"Oh . . . just for a nervous stomach . . . occasionally," Alex lied.

"Men in our position do face a lot of stress, but I thought you were attending the Mind Enrichment sessions developed for employees." John said in an admonishing tone.

Alex tried to smile. He hated the Mind Enrichment courses. All Kressman's people just raved about them—perhaps because those who didn't attend the meetings weren't Kressman's employees for long. Although the breathing, "deep conscious-ness," and positive mental projections relaxed Alex while he participated, the more he attended the sessions, the more he noticed something in himself and in the others that gnawed at him: a self-absorption which reminded him so much of Linda it scared him.

As he followed the instructions to look deeper and deeper within himself, there came an increasing sense of emptiness he could neither fully describe nor completely erase. It was as if termites had been set loose in his soul. Beneath his skin, they silently ate away at him, slowly eroding his faith, his confidence, his reason for existence. The cumulative effect? His mind and his will had no truth, no structure on which to rest. He feared that one day his facade might collapse altogether and expose all the rottenness underneath. How could he stop this sense of being devoured? John would say he needed more Mind Enrichment. . . . No, his pills did the same thing. They numbed his mind and gave his soul the illusion of soaring–without elaborate ritual. He'd given up all hope of stopping the termites.

Coordinating the psych-war against fanatic leaders in the western vectors had been an ordeal. Although he'd never believed the tactics would work, he'd been put in charge of the project, and would soon have to bear the brunt of Kressman's disappointment at the lack of any real progress thus far. As if this weren't enough, Linda got promoted to a high-profile job reporting the news on TV. When it happened, John informed Alex that he'd have to reassume the reins of the coding campaign.

How could my life get any worse? He asked himself, then answered his own question. *I could be forced to attend Mind Enrichment sessions.*

He pretended to look at a painting on the wall of his office. "I try to make time for M.E. sessions but, the past few weeks have just been so crammed with work, I haven't had time to go. I've virtually lived in this office since you gave me the new government policy statements to start incorporating into the campaign." He could hardly wait till this project was over. Maybe he would take a vacation then.

John gave him a once-over. Was Alex so dense he didn't know all his secret walks and black-market pill purchases had been recorded? It would be addressed—later. Right now, he needed to get to more important topics. "What have you got for the coding campaign so far?" he asked.

Alex got out a clip screen and handed it across the desk. "Well, these are the layouts of ads we released to the general public regarding the end of *Phase One: Withdrawal of the Blue Bill System.* Until the banks stop recirculating blue bills, we'll continue to run them." He cued up the series of advertisements put up on billboards and posted on government buildings and banks. Some of the ads were comical, some had a reassuring tone, some had a more urgent appeal. All encouraged encoding now, offering a temporary relaxation of the 20 percent surcharge on blue bills being converted to credits in a new account, and a chance to win one of 5,000 fully wired apartments in revitalized neighborhoods.

"Here's what we have regarding *Phase Two*," Alex said, sending a command which opened another file on the clip screen. "It's less hype and more explanation of what happens when the blue bills are gone. . . . We'll start posting this information by the end of next week. Soon, we'll even have live billboards in the unwired neighborhoods. I figure we'll have a huge jump in numbers when that happens."

The majority of the ads had a more serious tone. Some gave basic information about the options—or lack of them—for anyone who had not converted by the close-out date. Uncoded individuals needed to realize that, soon, all types of "money" would be valueless. If people waited past the deadline, they could end up losing all assets when bills and taxes couldn't be paid.

"That's as far as I have gotten." Alex sat back in his chair. "Even though I see the necessity of all this, I can't help wondering how far the fanatics will carry it when close out comes, and they lose everything. How many would actually choose an archaic belief over the essentials that enable them to live?"

"That's where *Phase Three* comes in," John said. "They'll pay for all the trouble they've caused."

Alex's stomach lurched. John had made veiled statements before, but now he displayed open hostility toward fanatics. The obvious glee John took in thinking of *Phase Three* made Alex sick. Strong measures might be necessary, but implementation of them would bring Alex no pleasure whatsoever. He never wanted to see anyone hurt. Wasn't that his purpose in staying with this? The Global View stood for peace and brotherhood without all of the hypocrisy of western "religion." He wondered if Kressman knew what a hateful man John Klost was.

"Well," Alex replied, "I'm trying to make this the most convincing campaign of my life. If we can reason with them, there's no need for anyone to suffer."

Chapter 47

Somewhere in the Northern Zones

Michael just lay there in the mud, his feet still in the river, too cold, too tired, and too hungry to run or even to put up much of a fight. He asked himself, *How in the world could I have been so stupid as to make this trip?*

The man missing an arm rushed forward. "Isn't your name Michael?"

"Word sure travels fast out here," Michael said. But when he looked closer at the man's face and eyes, there was something familiar about them. The man had a full beard and quite a mane of hair so Michael couldn't really be sure.

"It's *me!*" the man said with a huge grin, "Albert! Dr. Donner. Don't you remember me? Your brother came to the hospital once, and you—"

"Oh yes!" Michael exclaimed with a bit of relief, "I remember." The doctor had always been good-natured and intelligent in the past. Despite the missing arm, it seemed unlikely he'd have become part of a dismemberment cult. He glanced around at the others, relieved to see everyone else in the group still had two hands.

One of the men helped Michael get up, another offered him a blanket, saying, "Get this around you. Are you hungry?"

"I haven't eaten since night before last," Michael said. "Is this really the refuge?"

"Yes. . . . But come. We'll eat first and talk later."

After a fifteen- minute walk, they arrived at a cabin. Judging by its appearance, Michael figured it had been built before the disasters. Maybe it had belonged to a hunter. Inside the cabin, a big cast iron pot hung on a hook over a fire and the whole place smelled of stew. All of them crammed around a crude trestle table and sat on stools. Michael had four platefuls of food before he stopped to catch his breath.

After they ate, several of the men scooted back from the table to allow more elbow room. One got up to tend to the fire, and another collected the dishes and stacked them in a wooden washtub.

"Is this the best food I've ever eaten, or is it that I'm so hungry?" Michael asked.

"Probably both," Albert surmised.

"I haven't had fresh beef in years."

"It's deer, actually. But it's good meat and the vegetables are fresh."

The others didn't say much, and Michael sensed they were checking him out. *I must really look bad,* he thought, *although I certainly couldn't be very dirty after all that time in the water.*

"So this is it." Michael finally said. "This is the refuge."

"Well, you are on part of a refuge," the tallest man said. "Why did you come?"

"I came for two reasons . . . I wanted to know if God was really . . . alive, I guess. I figured that, if He didn't exist, if He didn't help me, I'd probably perish—but I had to know." Michael looked at them.

"What do you think now?" Donner asked.

Michael bit his lip while he framed a truthful response. "I don't claim to understand everything, but I believe He does exist." His eyebrows came together. "And, although I don't know why, He did help me." He paused to pull the blanket tighter over his shoulders, then said, "The other reason I came was to find someone. Her name is Sara." He didn't see any recognition in them. "She came with her sister, Noel, from Texas. They're both Christians. When their father died, looters burned their store and left them with almost nothing." Michael saw a possible flicker of recognition in one man's eyes. "They would have come with a guide a week or more ago."

Silence followed, but he had the feeling they probably knew something. Perhaps they wanted to keep the girls safe from harm. Michael tried a different tack.

"They're friends of mine. . . . Look, I have their father's harmonica." He started to unwrap his shirt and show it to them before he realized how ridiculous he sounded. "Anyway, they're Christians. And the older one, Sara, is very special to me. Please, just tell me if they are safe."

Albert Donner leaned over and confided, "We're not trying to be cruel to you. I've already broken with tradition and said my real name. I said yours, too. Each person living here is en-couraged to use only his or her first name, and even to change that if they wish. This way, if we are ever taken captive, we can't be forced to locate anyone the government might be looking for. If this Sara and her sister are here, and if you stay, I'm sure you'll see them. But, you must understand, this isn't the only refuge. They're scattered all over the north. She could have gone to another one; or she could have been here and moved on. Many people do that. All I can do is promise we'll look into it," he said, before going back to the topic of Michael's trip. "So how long have you been traveling?"

"I don't know. I've lost all track of time. . . . I'm sure it is not as long as it seems. Two weeks maybe."

"Where did you come from?" A man in a dark flannel shirt inquired.

"Northwest of Dallas," Michael answered.

Another man leaned forward and asked, "How'd you get across the Red River?" they asked, referring to the first barrier he had to cross. "And then, how did you get over the fence?"

They all seemed interested in his answer.

"Actually, getting by the fence was easier than getting over the Red River. A storm blew down the fence. I found a place where no one was watching, so I ran for it. Actually, I walked. I was afraid of breaking that orange crust."

"How did you find us?" the man near the fire asked.

"You found *me*," Michael answered. "If you hadn't called to me, I'd have just kept on going, I guess. I ran into some people upstream on the other side of the river. They called themselves 'friends' and worship some guy named Beanly or something . . ."

All of the men exchanged glances. He'd impressed them.

"How did you get away from them?"

"Well, they were feasting on the orange stuff—they actually eat it you know—and I ran out of their camp. It was night time but I had these starlight glasses here, so I could see in the dark. I almost fell into a canyon, though. Then something happened to me." Michael hesitated. Would they believe him? "They were just about to catch me. I was winded, and my legs were beginning to cramp when I tripped and started to fall. Someone, or some *thing,* grabbed me and pulled me into a dead tree. It about scared me to death. I didn't know who or what was in there but I couldn't see anyone. And then, when the Beanly people came near, a bright light shone around the crack I'd been pulled through. The people stood right next to it without ever noticing the light or the crack in the tree! Even after they left, the light stayed there almost all night before it disappeared. . . . I know it's hard to believe, but I swear I'm telling the truth. When the light was gone, I crawled out and walked along a canyon until I could get to the river. Then, I got into the water and held onto a log as long as I could. When I got out, I managed to start a fire for the night; and then you found me."

With his stomach filled to capacity, Michael soon realized how tired he was. He could hardly keep his eyes open. "Could I lay down for a while?"

"Certainly. You can change into some different clothes, then you can take that bed over there." Albert pointed to one of the beds pushed against the wall of the cabin.

The men talked quietly and Michael fell sound asleep. When he awoke again, only a small fire burning on the hearth illuminated the room. One man sat at the table with his feet up, watching the fire. The rest appeared to be asleep.

"What time is it?" Michael said in a hushed voice.

The man turned to look at him, and in a soft, southern drawl replied, "Maybe four in the morning."

Michael moved closer and sat in a chair. "Wow," he said, scratching his head. "That means I've slept for nearly a whole day."

"Happens to lots of people their first night here. Most of them are exhausted from the journey and haven't had much food or sleep along the way. Add to that, when they get here, they feel safe. After they eat, it usually isn't long before they zonk out for a while." He smiled. "You went out within sixty seconds of hittin' that cot. You were sleepin' like the dead, so we just let you rest. You can go back to sleep if you'd like."

Michael thought about it. "No. That's okay. I've slept enough for now. Can I ask your name?"

"Daniel."

"You already know mine. Michael."

"Glad to meet you."

Michael pulled his chair closer to the fire and, uncharacter-istically, started talking. Perhaps he felt like he needed to give an account for himself, or maybe the time had come to uncork some of the things he'd bottled up for so long.

In either case, he began to unburden himself, and his host just let him talk for nearly two hours.

He spoke of moving from place to place with an abusive, alcoholic father; and of his younger brother, Ben, who died of AIDS at the age of twenty-six. He told how he lost his mother, father and sister to the plague, each within hours of the other. He recalled the bitter cold winter that followed, and being forced to serve on a death squad, hauling away the dead. After surviving all this, he had to go through quarantine—twice.

"When they finally let me migrate, on the way south, I met this girl, Linda. We made the journey together and eventually decided to share an apartment. At first it was like hiding from the storm together, but even after time passed, I couldn't seem to get on with my life." Michael said, watching the flames.

"When I was young, getting drunk or stoned was just something to look forward to. But as my life got worse, I started drinking more, just to stay sane. At least that's the way I saw it at the time. I straightened up for a while, when Ben was dying. But after all the other stuff happened—I had no peace. There was no place to rest, no place where all those memories weren't tormenting me. I started using a black box and doing crazy things just to . . . escape." Michael thought a moment. "Do you know anyone named Zachary? I suppose you can't say. He's the only family I've got now, and I sure wish I could talk to him."

Daniel took a metal rod and poked the logs in the fire. "I was raised in a Christian home. I never did any drugs or anything like that, but once I stayed out real late and came home crawling drunk. I figured my parents were going to beat me for sure. But they both cried. My mom and dad just stood there and cried. I'd have preferred gettin' beat. I never got drunk again. Of course, after all we've gone through in the past few years, my entire childhood seems like a nice story . . . too good to be true. I can't fathom how idyllic it was, or how little I appreciated it. If not for my faith in the Lord, I don't know how I would have survived the disasters. . . . Didn't your parents teach you anything about God or anything?"

Michael shrugged. "Well, my parents went to church sometimes. Now I know there's a difference between some of the 'church' people of my past and real Christians; but, back then I didn't understand. Anyway, my parents didn't much care what I did as long as I didn't get into trouble with the law or expose them to shame like my brother Ben. He found a relationship with Jesus before he died—and he tried to tell us—but, by then, none of us wanted to hear about it."

Michael recalled the peace and forgiveness that radiated from Ben in his final days . . . given his brother's circumstances at the time, it made no sense at all to Michael. And what about now? Perhaps now, he had a glimmer of understanding.

Daniel could see the world outside the window beginning to brighten, so he tapped Michael on the arm. "Let's get goin' before the others get up hungry." They stood, and he went to dig around in a bag. "A cool front came through last night. You'll need a warmer shirt. Here," he said tossing one to Michael.

When they stepped outside, they could feel a slight chill in the air. Michael found it pleasant enough, since he had on warm clothes and wasn't wet.

They gathered large pieces of wood from a stack and went behind the cabin where they found a stump with an axe sticking out of it. Daniel split a few logs and then asked Michael if he'd like to try. Daniel made it look easy, but Michael found the task required a certain amount of skill.

Daniel laughed at Michael's futile attempts at hacking up a log. "Careful, or you're going to cut off your foot! Put your foot over there," he said, pointing to a spot. "You keep trying, and I'll go get breakfast," Daniel said, walking toward the trees.

After he split a small stack of wood, Michael carried it around to the front of the cabin and stacked it; then he took some inside. Just as he put it on the fire, Daniel returned with a small piece of meat and a bag of eggs.

"Where did you get all that?"

"We killed a deer day before yesterday. We cleaned it and took most of it back to the village to be dried. The rest we wrapped and kept in the river so it would stay cold."

"Is that water safe?"

Daniel grinned. "Seeing as how you've already soaked in it like a tea bag, does it matter?"

"I guess you're right."

"But by way of comfort, as far as we know, that water is cleaner than it's been for decades. It wasn't near any contamination, and now there's nobody up north to dump in it."

The other men awoke when Dan started cooking the food. As they ate, Michael thought this must have been what it was like on farms when he was small. Now, with the government distributing all the food, few people saw produce like this.

"How'd you get to live here?" Michael asked between bites. The men looked at each other and Michael realized that he'd asked something they didn't want to discuss.

"Well, Michael," Dr. Donner said, clearing his throat, "there are lots of things we won't explain right now. If you stay, we'll tell you anything we know the answer to. For starters, though I guess I should introduce you to everyone. You fell asleep before we got around to names." He went on to introduce Michael to each man around the table, adding a funny comment about each one.

The rest of the meal was filled with friendly conversation. Keenly interested in the current events down south, the men asked Michael about all the latest news. He filled them in as best he could.

When they finished, the dishes were cleaned and put away before each man went to his things and returned with a book. Each man's book looked different, but showed signs of wear and tear. Michael knew they were Bibles.

Daniel looked at him. "You're welcome to stay for our study if you'd like. You might think that all of us up here just sit around day after day just praisin' the Lord and readin' our Bibles."

The other men laughed.

"It would be great if we could do it, but somebody around here has to plant crops, keep the living quarters in repair, watch our perimeters, and cook if we want to be of any help to the people God sends our way. We're God's hands and feet. But each of us needs a little time to just rest and renew, too. That's what we use this cabin for. . . . You can go for a walk if you'd like, or I have an extra Bible if you want it."

Michael suddenly realized that the Bible Zac gave him was in his pack. Gone forever. He sat down and Dan got a Bible for him.

"We're going to be starting in Acts chapter eight today, starting in the twenty-sixth verse . . ."

They all turned pages, Dan helped Michael find the right place, and the man they called Charlie began to read.

Chapter 48

Atlanta

Edwina Grant stacked the dirty bowls and handed them to Donny, the new dishwasher at the soup kitchen, before consulting her watch. Ten minutes before six. But, wasn't the time ten-to-six the last time she looked? She unlatched the band and held the watch to her ear.

"Did it stop running?" Isaac asked.

"Appears so," Edwina said sadly. She ran her finger over the scratched crystal as a picture of George's handsome face, smiling at her from across the table in their first apartment, came to mind. *"Do you like it?"* he asked. *"I promise you, 'Wina, when I finish my internship we'll have more money and I'll buy you real jewelry."* In the years that followed, he bought her beautiful jewelry, even a better watch—but this was the one she treasured. This watch and her wedding band were the only pieces of jewelry she still owned. All the rest had been sold in the hardest months after the disasters. She slowly closed her hand around the broken timepiece.

"I have a friend who may be able to repair it," Isaac offered.

She didn't know what surprised her more. The fact that he'd just used the word "friend" to describe another person, or the possibility that this person could fix her old watch. Since she didn't respond, he expanded on the original statement.

"He's been repairing clocks and watches since before you were born. I could ask him to look at it, if you'd like."

The time she'd spent tending the burn on Isaac's hand these past few weeks had earned her several small glimpses of the man inside the crusty exterior. She nodded. "I'd appreciate that."

His face relaxed from his normal scowl into a sad-yet-tender look. "My Sophie had a locket," he said. He moved his thumb about an inch away from his index finger to indicate the size and then held the inch up to the middle of his chest to indicate precisely where Sophie wore it. "The locket wasn't very special looking, but it was her mother's . . . and she wore it till the day she passed."

The sound of a bowl shattering on the floor startled both of them, and they turned to see Donny standing over the wreckage. Isaac's tender moment vaporized in a puff of hot steam.

"You think I'm wealthy? You think I have nothing better to do with my money than replace all the things you break?"

"No sir," Donny said, bending down to pick up the scattered shards.

A customer came to the counter to buy some soup and a slice of bread so Isaac left the area to complete the transaction. Edwina picked up a few of the fragments by her foot and got Donny's attention. "It'll be okay," she whispered. "Just try to be careful."

Their employer returned to the back of the kitchen intending to continue his rant, but Edwina stepped into his path. She nodded toward a customer in the dining room. "That man in the corner shared his soup with a friend, so he should return two spoons with the bowl."

He looked out over the counter to take note of the customer and grunted.

By her reckoning, he still needed a distraction or two, so she said, "It's probably well past quitting time now, so I'll be going." Next, she reached over and carefully touched a large, empty pot on the stove. "And this is cool now, so you might want to have it washed before the stuff in the bottom dries up."

Isaac placed several dirty utensils in the pot and lifted it off the stove. On his way past her, he shot her a disapproving glance. "You going out for the rest of the evening?"

Weeks ago, Edwina decided he could terminate her employment or keep her on, but he wouldn't intimidate her when she wanted to leave the premises during her hours off. She clasped her watch back on her arm before looking up. "Yep. I'm leaving you."

He started to speak, then stopped. How could he say it? Last night, he'd noticed a man standing across the street from the restaurant, and something about this guy didn't add up. The man didn't look gaunt and apprehensive like most of the people in the neighborhood. He was muscular, confident . . . catlike. The stranger lingered across the street, casually observing each person stepping out the door of the soup kitchen. He tarried until after the restaurant closed, occasionally glancing into the windows, as if waiting for someone in particular. Finally, he left. Could this stranger have been casing the place to rob it? No. Some inner sense told Isaac the man wasn't a robber. He was hunting. The question remained then: Whom was he stalking?

Once again, Isaac looked at Edwina, opened his mouth and closed it again. He stood there, holding the cooking pot, his body shifting around as if the words he wanted to say had to crawl up from his feet to get out of his mouth. The young man at the sink stopped washing dishes and looked at him.

When he realized Donny was watching him, he said, "You want I should stand here all night holding this pan for you?"

The boy took the pan and quickly set about washing it, so Isaac turned his attention back to Edwina. He frowned as he tried to formulate something specific to say.

This wasn't his standard I'm-mad-that-you're-leaving expression, so she finally asked, "What is it you want to say?"

He settled for shaking an admonishing finger at her and saying, "Stay out of trouble." Then he moved closer and spoke a bit softer. "Be careful."

Was this his way of expressing father-like concern? She smiled. "I'm not going far, and I'll be in a house with friends. Besides," she said, "I'll have all those new billboards to light the way." She started walking toward the stairs but stopped and turned. "It will be a few minutes before I'm ready to leave. Would you like to come and spend the evening with us? I'd wait for you to finish up. You might enjoy yourself."

He turned away. "I should have so much free time. There is too much work to do around here."

Twenty minutes later, Edwina left the kitchen and began walking down the street. She noted the crowd at the corner and slowed as she passed the group, all staring up at one of the new billboards installed in the neighborhood during the past week. The messages on these billboards were different from the ones Edwina had seen in neighborhoods where coded people lived and worked. These ads, with small injections of "news" aimed specifically at uncoded individuals, shone brighter-than-life and played night and day. Even during curfew hours, they infused the message of the Global

View into the very atmosphere of the neighborhood. The billboards had a voice, and many wondered if they had eyes as well.

When she passed it, Edwina could see a dark-haired lady on the screen. Tears ran down the woman's face as she spoke. "I guess the final straw for me," she said, "was when I broke a tooth on a small rock that was in our beans. And, I realized I just couldn't go on like that. I mean, what was it all *for* anyway? I realized just how *foolish* I'd been and how much I'd hurt my family," she wiped her face. "That's when I got my code."

The picture switched to a scene outside a new apartment complex, but the woman's voice continued. "I didn't even know that when I got my code, I was automatically entered into a contest for one of five new apartments in this vector— but I won!"

The scene showed the woman, a look of awe upon her face, entering her new home. "I feel . . . just like a princess in a fairy tale now . . ."

Edwina frowned and kept walking.

###

Hours later, Isaac found himself wandering around in the empty kitchen, wondering when Edwina would return. He fiddled with the bandage on his hand while he worried about her lateness.

The curfew siren sounded, and he looked at the door. She'd never stayed out past curfew before. What should he do? He walked to the door, then changed his mind. He paced for thirty minutes before something occurred to him: Perhaps the floor needed sweeping. After getting his broom, he opened the back door and swept his way into the alley. Once outside, Isaac gave the broom a few more strokes before he looked down the alley. Both ways. He didn't see her.

He went inside, locked the back door, and walked through the dining room, still carrying the broom. He opened the front door to the restaurant and repeated the same procedure. No Edwina.

Isaac went back inside, stuck the broom in a corner before perching on a barstool at the counter. He stared into the kitchen, and his mind went back to a moment several months ago when he was looking out his bedroom window. A shaft of light from a window next door briefly illuminated a small group of men who were out walking after curfew. No, it was a man from the neighborhood being escorted down the street by strangers. Strangers who were muscular and somehow out of place. In the coming days Isaac heard the neighbor had "disappeared," but he never told a soul what he'd seen. Why get involved in such things and be labeled a troublemaker? What could one person do about any of this? Perhaps the neighbor and his companions really were skipping town. He grunted and reminded himself that he'd never liked that man anyway.

Isaac stood up. Why was he thinking of this now? Because Edwina reminded him that all this was similar to things he knew from the past.

His thoughts echoed with his mother's voice. *"They said they would make a perfect world. They took people away. One at a time in the beginning, but they got bolder once most people were too afraid to protest. Eventually they came for my whole family, they came for everyone in our synagogue. I alone survived,"* she said with tears. *"Look here, Isaac, and never forget what you see. . . . Here is the number they put on my arm. . . ."*

The tattoo on his mother's arm left an indelible mark on Isaac's soul. As a child, he had often dreamed that his arm held the number. A number which symbolized his people's near extinction. . . . Would anyone who witnessed such things and kept silent escape judgement for it?

"I must go and find Edwina," he said, and walked back into the kitchen. He grabbed a button-up shirt off a hook and pulled it on over his multi-stained T-shirt. If he was going to be arrested for being out after curfew, he wanted to look like a decent man. He left via the back door, still hoping to see her hurrying down the alley, but a quick look told him he'd have to venture farther away if he had any hope of seeing her. By the time he got to the corner, he figured he knew where she'd gone. He lived in this neighborhood too, and meetings of that sort didn't go unnoticed.

###

A block away, Edwina and three other adults knelt on the floor in the front hallway of a home. Their captors, armed with stun pistols and wearing hoods, stood at either end of the hall. She heard one of them say that "others" were en route who would escort "the prisoners" to an unknown location.

Edwina placed her hand on the floor so she could lean on her arm and ease the pain in her knees. The masked man standing nearest the front door stared intently at her fingers for a few moments before he deliberately stepped on them.

She straightened up, and tried to flex her hand before her captor grabbed it, yanked it behind her back, and fastened a restraint on it. He reached around and did the same with her other hand, interlocking the two restraints, and then pulling them extra tight. Edwina cried out in pain, and the other hostages reacted in protest.

"Go ahead and try something," he said, pointing the stun gun right at Edwina. "I'm just dying to use this on her again."

He'd been quiet up until now, letting his partner do the talking. When he finally spoke, Edwina realized why. She knew this voice! It was Leon Newsome Jr.! How she wanted to blurt it out . . . but she knew that saying his name might turn the *possibility* of death for the other prisoners into a guarantee of it.

He nudged her with his boot. "Come on, you're a real fighter for the cause, aren't you? You've probably saved lots of defective specimens around here."

"Please, can't we talk about this?" the prisoner by the name of Paul said. "We're not putting up a fight. Please untie her. Tie me up instead."

Leon looked at Paul and kicked Edwina in the hip. "Does it upset you when I do this? Wanna try and stop me?"

The other hooded man spoke. "Hey, take it easy. I just got a transmission saying they're on their way in. I'm not carrying her, so unless you want to, you'd better make sure she can still walk."

Leon hesitated, shoved her in the back with his boot, sending her to the floor. She couldn't use her hands to stop the impact, and she felt her cheek split open. She sobbed in agony.

"Just wait. It's not long now, monkey lover, till you get the full treatment," he said.

###

Isaac approached the house with great care. He stopped and listened. The home stood dark and quiet, like all the guests had gone their separate ways and the family inside had gone to bed. Was this even the right house? Then, he heard a loud cry. With his heart pounding, he crept toward a window near the front door. A small opening in the curtain allowed him to see into the dimly lit hallway.

###

With her face still to the floor, Edwina managed to say, "She's not a monkey. She's got the same blood in her veins as you do. The only difference is that she's right with God."

Her captor stepped back, both surprised and furious. Part of him wanted to wait until later, to let her have a hope of getting out of all this—and then reveal his identity to her and let her realize there was no hope at all. The other part of him just wanted to kill her now. He settled for pointing the stun gun at her and pulling the trigger. The shock sent her into convulsions When the violent contractions stopped, she said something, but Leon couldn't hear her. He moved closer, placing his right foot inches away from her head. "*What* did you say?"

Edwina mustered all her strength against the pain and moved her head so it rested on his boot. "I . . . forgive you."

Leon lost all control and began beating her.

###

Isaac stepped away from the window in horror. What could he do? Before he could consider the matter fully, he heard a sound down the street. He stepped into a hedge and squinted in the direction of the sound. A group of people approached. Were they coming to help take Edwina and the others away?

He heard Edwina crying out again and his legs trembled. What could one person do? What could anyone do? His vision blurred, and he thought he might pass out before he saw a flicker. He strained to focus and saw it again.

"Yes," he whispered before he stumbled out of the hedge. He ran as fast as his shaking legs would go and started yelling at the top of his lungs. "FIRE! FIRE! OVER HERE! FIRE! HELP! HELP! THE HOUSE IS ON FIRE!"

Within moments, people ready to put out a fire (before the whole neighborhood burned down) rushed outside and ran to the house where Isaac stood, still shouting, "FIRE! FIRE!"

Soon, virtually all the people from the block were there, with more on the way as the word spread. Men rushed past him and up onto the porch. They tried the door. It was locked. Several of them looked back at Isaac and asked, "Where's the fire?" While one man banged on the door and shouted. "Paul! Virginia! Wake up! Your house is on fire!"

Several people ran around to the back of the house. Neighbors dragged garden hoses into the yard and a great crowd formed as they all prepared to fight a fire. A crowd of witnesses. Isaac looked at them and wondered what to do next.

###

Inside the house, they were all surprised to hear someone shouting outside. Leon and his companion knew their confederates wouldn't make such a racket. This was supposed to be a clandestine operation. Within a minute, knocks and calls at windows and doors all around the house told them they would no longer be able to slip away unnoticed.

Chapter 49

Atlanta

Col. Folson liked working during late-night hours. After 6:00 p.m., he got so much more done. He began typing an answer to a letter from Gen. Chang when the prompter for the intercom on his desk chirped with a message from his assistant. He hit the save button on his screen then touched the light on the intercom. "What is it?"

His aide sounded unsure. "Uh, yes, Colonel. Lt. Chalmers is here to see you. His appointment isn't until tomorrow, but he says it's urgent."

"Send him in," Folson responded.

Tedrick Chalmers entered the colonel's office in full uniform with his hat under his left arm and a briefcase in his right hand. Once the assistant had closed the door, Tedrick seated himself near the desk, with the briefcase on his lap, and waited to be addressed.

"I only have a few minutes. You have something new to report, Lieutenant?"

"It's bad, sir. Worse than we suspected. I believe Newsome is running rogue operations—capturing civilians for his own purposes."

"His own purposes? What kind of purposes?"

Ted looked around the drab green walls of the office and sighed. "I feel I should have been more vigilant, sir. I mean, when I first came to you months ago, I'd heard some disturbing rumors, but I had no idea just how sick Newsome really is. He has such a capacity to appear every inch the solid soldier."

The Lieutenant looked deeply troubled. "On several occasions, I heard him talk about 'hunting' and how much he missed it. He joked about how 'intelligent creatures' were the most fun to track and kill. I didn't take his meaning at the time. Lately, though, he and several officers with rough reputations have been hanging out together, going out in the middle of the night, that sort of thing. One time, he came back with blood on his clothes, and, when I asked him about it, he said he and his friends had gone to a fight club and sat in front-row seats. Since then, he often returns wearing different clothing than what he was wearing when he left." Ted touched his own forehead before saying, "In hindsight, it all adds up. I guess I haven't wanted to believe someone in the Legion could be so twisted."

"Twisted?" the colonel asked. "What have you learned?"

Ted opened the briefcase on his lap, donned a set of gloves, and extracted a flat, rectangular box. The metal container had an overlapping lid, like a cookie tin. "I found this in a secret compartment at the bottom of his locker—along with this," he said, reaching into the case again and removing a nonstandard-issue, eight-inch boot knife. "I assume forensics can prove both of these items are his."

Col. Folson leaned away from the objects on the desk. "You shouldn't have brought that box in here. What if it contains some sort of contaminant?"

"Actually, sir, without thinking, I already opened the box. I'm only using gloves now to keep from putting my fingerprints all over it. I know what's inside the box, sir. It's not any sort of weapon or immediate threat to us."

Folson kept his distance from the box. "What's inside?"

The lieutenant put his gloved hand on top of the box. "It's fingers, sir. People's fingers. I've heard of combat soldiers doing this sort of thing before—a sort of revenge thrill. But given the problems we face, and the need to convince civilians of what we stand for . . . " he shook in disgust, "we just don't need this sort of thing to cast a shadow on the Universal Legion."

Chapter 50

Atlanta

All eyes locked on Isaac, all movement stopped, all talking ceased, and he looked around the large gathering. He knew most of these people, but noted several strangers standing at the very back. Were they new to the neighborhood . . . or had they come to help the masked men inside the house?

"Actually," he finally said, "I lied."

"What were you *thinking?*" a man nearby shouted. "You could be arrested for this."

A chorus of grumbles circulated through the crowd. A few of the people started to walk away.

"Wait!" Isaac said. "The reason I shouted 'fire' was that it was the only thing I could think of to get all of you here so fast. Listen to me! There are criminals inside the house, holding Paul, Virginia, Edwina and Caleb hostage—and beating them up!"

Everyone looked up at the home, wondering if cranky old Isaac had simply lost his mind.

"Ask yourselves," he pleaded. "'If everything is fine, why haven't Paul and Virginia come out and asked us about all this noise?' Why haven't they shown themselves? It's because they're being held at gun point! Go ahead. See if anyone lets you in. One of us can do *nothing* against these criminals . . . but all of us together can make sure they don't get away!"

A man on the porch called out. "Go get lamps! Somebody run to the substation and see if we can get the cops here!"

\#\#\#

When two police officers finally arrived, the growing mob outside the house had lamps and crude weapons. After making voice contact with someone in the house, one of the officers was permitted to enter through the front door. Leon and his partner had already dragged the hostages into the livingroom, taken off their hoods, and stowed some of their gear before letting one of the cops in the house.

Once inside, Officer Watts found himself in the midst of a confusing situation. He wanted to clarify the information they'd given him. "So, you say you're soldiers? And you were in the process of arresting these people? I'll need proof that you're who you say you are."

Leon ran his fingers through his hair. "See, there's the sticky part. This was a covert operation. Nobody should have ever known we were here." He stepped a little closer to the cop and lowered his voice. "The new Citizen's Security Act gives us the authority to search, seize, and arrest in any jurisdiction. We can prove to you that we're Universal Legion, but the Legion Secrecy Act says you can't load this into your data base. Insurgent forces could pirate the information and use it to set ambushes against those of us who are fighting for public safety."

Watts looked at Newsome and thought, *Are you a typical agent of global superiority or what? You think you can do anything you want without consequences. We get to look like inept or corrupt fools when you do one of your secret activities and then slip back into your dark hole.* His blood pressure started to rise as he wondered how many more times he could say, *"Your husband is missing? Oh. . . . Well he must have just run away to escape some bill collector. . ."* Watts ran his tongue around in his mouth as though his thoughts had an actual taste. *Makes me sick. Women drool all over them while the rest of us have to work in these neighborhoods and put up with crap like this every day with no thanks whatsoever.*

###

In the living room, Edwina struggled to flex her hands. The wrist restraints allowed almost no circulation to find its way into her fingers. She had a large bump on her face from where she hit the floor and shooting pains where Leon had kicked her. In addition, every muscle, joint, and nerve of her body still felt jangled from the repeated, stun-induced convulsions.

"Are you going to be okay, 'Wina?" Virginia asked her.

Leon's partner came into the room. "No talking. If any of you says as much as one word to the cop, we'll make you sorry you were ever born when he leaves. You understand me?"

Moments later, the policeman leaned into the doorway of the living room and looked at the prisoners on the floor. He'd seen them around the neighborhood. Word had it that the black woman did medical treatments on the poorest residents. Given the respect the locals gave her, he figured it was true. Even known desperados in the community seemed to leave her alone as she roamed about. His gaze drifted to the couple nearest the window. They ran a small store. The other guy was relatively new, and Watts didn't know much about him.

None of these people were "criminals" as far as he knew, although they had been organizing house gatherings. He knew this bit of information because several leaders from nearby domes had complained about the situation. They said house meetings were "confusing" the undecided masses on the issue of coding. All Watts could think at the time was that he had larger problems to solve than house meetings. His substation was undermanned in a neighborhood where robbery, rape, and murder were common occurrences. As far as he could tell, blocks with meetings were generally quieter. Would he be in trouble now for having ignored this group?

###

While Watts occupied himself looking at the prisoners, Leon leaned back against a wall in the front hallway and tried to think. This had gotten way out of control. Would he and McCauley be able to convince their superiors they'd discovered a cell of dangerous subversives? Since this happened before the other soldiers got here, wouldn't it be wise to keep them out of it?

He could say that he and McCauley originally intended merely to do some recon, but while they were here, they discovered an imminent threat which required immediate action. He raked his fingers through his hair and thought, *Yes. I can say I was about to send McCauley back to tell the C.O. when it unraveled. We can go directly to the colonel. He knows me.* Lee punched his own leg in frustration. *This certainly isn't what I hoped for, but it'll have to do. McCauley and I can work on a simple story. We won't get elaborate* *and we won't get tripped up. As long as the story is a good one, the colonel will let it slide. And it's not like the monkey lover or any of the others will have a lawyer or get a trial. It's our word against theirs. . . . It's a good thing Ted got sick at the last minute and didn't come along. The fewer people in on this the better. Besides, he'd say <u>anything</u> to get the promotion away from me.*

The policeman stepped back into the hall and looked at Leon. "What are you charging them with?"

"Engaging in a conspiracy to start an uprising is the most serious charge I can disclose to you at this time. Trust me, you're better off with them out of your precinct."

The cop's instinct said something didn't quite gel here. "What evidence do you have?"

"Again," Leon said with a superior tone, "this was supposed to be a secret operation, and I'm afraid that most of the details are sealed. But if you want evidence, just look outside. Many of those people are their followers, and you can see they're nearly in riot mode already."

Officer Watts sighed. "Yeah. I'm afraid that if you try to remove these people now, there *will* be a riot."

Leon went to the window and chanced a peek outside. "We'll need you to clear the entire block around this house and the access to Simpson Street so we can get back to the Legion compound downtown."

The policeman shook his head. "You may have an army behind you . . . but all I've got is two guys. One of them is holding down the station while Gil and I are here. Unless we get orders from higher up, we wouldn't be able to call out more men before dawn when the new shift comes in."

Leon's partner, McCauley, spoke up. "All those people outside are already guilty of breaking curfew. If you ask them to leave now and they don't, that's non-cooperation. They're massed in an unauthorized group of more than twenty-five people, and that's a possible conspiracy for rioting."

The "unauthorized-group" law, enacted during the disasters, was rarely enforced these days. Police agencies had to walk a fine line between keeping order and being perceived as armed persecutors.

Officer Watts rubbed his eyes and exhaled loudly. "I'll see what I can do," he said and exited the house.

When he stepped outside the front door, the entire crowd fell silent. He frowned when he saw a man in front of the mob holding a table leg with a large bolt sticking out the top of it. He pulled his partner to the side of the porch.

"These guys are with the Universal Legion," Watts said in a low voice. "It was a covert op and someone blew it. They want to be able to leave with their prisoners, but I told them I don't think we're going to be able to clear this crowd without backup." A man ran around from the side of the house and stepped in front of the crowd. "I got into the back of the house! I heard the whole thing! The strangers inside are Universal Legion! They want to arrest Paul, Virginia, Caleb Smith and Edwina Grant!"

"On what charge?" demanded several people in the group.

Officer Watts stepped to the center of the porch and held up his hands. "Listen folks. You're all breaking curfew. The soldiers inside—"

"Those soldiers inside are acting like criminals," Isaac said. "They wanted to take innocent people away in the dark of night. Tomorrow, if we asked, you would have said these people ran away on their own. And who knows what would have really happened to them? Next it will be me," he said, then pointed to others in the group, "or you, or you, or you." Tears formed in his eyes. "I'm a scared old man, but I know we can't let them do this right under our noses and say nothing. If we all stay here, it will be hard to explain how we all ran away. . . . How many of you have gotten help from one of the people in that house? You know they wouldn't harm anyone, and they haven't committed any crimes! . . . I don't know about you, but I have a friend in there, and I will not leave until they let her go or take me, too!"

###

Inside the house, Newsome and his partner wanted to hear what happened outside, so they cracked open one of the windows by the front door and stood near it to listen. When they heard someone had been in the house, McCauley ran to the back rooms to make sure no other intruders had remained. Afraid he might lose his prisoners, Leon roughly dragged them back into the hall. Once there, Edwina tried not to think about the wracking pain in her body. *Oh Lord,* she prayed inwardly, *Virginia and Paul and Caleb and I knew this might happen. Into Your hands I place my life, Father.*

Could she hear someone talking to the crowd outside? Her eyes grew wide. Was that Isaac's voice? *What is he doing here?* she asked herself. She felt consciousness slipping away. *Before it's over, before he has to meet You face to face, help dear Isaac to know the truth. Accomplish the highest good out of this.*

###

On the porch outside, Officer Watts pulled his associate off to the side and whispered, "Get on the radio and ask the commander to call me on the emergency channel. Maybe he can call whoever is in charge of these soldiers and fill them in on the gravity of the situation."

###

In the Universal Legion Compound, Col. Folson pressed the earpiece of his phone tighter against his ear. "A police commander told you *what?* . . . Two of *our* men? Are you sure?"

The captain on the other end of the line winced. He hated to be the one to break the news to the colonel. "Yes sir. The man said he couldn't give us their names but says they identified themselves as Legion officers. He went on to say, and I quote, 'If you want your men and their prisoners, you'd better come and get 'em. We didn't create this situation and we're not going to attempt to fix it,' end quote."

The captain could just picture the veins popping out on the colonel's neck as he heard the voice barking over the line. "Who might have given our soldiers orders to go into this neighbor-hood?"

"Didn't you, sir?"

Col. Folsom's voice became low and lethal. "Let me ask you, Captain, if I had given the orders, do you think I'd be asking you who did? I want answers from you, not questions. I'll call you back with instructions momentarily."

In his office, the colonel hung up his phone, then had his aide recall Lt. Chalmers immediately. When the Lieutenant returned, Folson asked him, "Can you tell me the location of Lt. Newsome at this very moment?"

Ted frowned. "No sir. He and Lt. McCauley went out earlier this evening. He said he wouldn't be back till late. I wasn't made privy to their plans, but Newsome did wear his regular boots this evening—something he doesn't do if he's just going to dinner. I hope there hasn't been any sort of trouble."

Folson looked directly at the Lieutenant. "Could he be running one of his 'operations' tonight?"

Chalmers thought a moment before nodding. "You know, sir, I think it's possible. He was in a euphoric state all day and he wouldn't say why."

The colonel swore inwardly before picking up his phone and punching in a number. "Capt. Jackson, I'm going to get you the I.D. numbers of two soldiers. Tell security to run a scan of the compound to locate them." He clenched his jaw as he waited several seconds for a response.

"Sir, they aren't in the compound."

Col. Folson closed his eyes for a moment and considered his options. *If I order a track on them, our computers will automatically flag the action and notify superiors.*

The colonel cleared his throat and said, "Jackson, do a level two tap into the metro area and see where they've walked."

Within seconds, the captain responded, "They went west before they dropped off the grid."

Folson couldn't avoid it. "Get an uplink to tracking and find them," he said. "In addition, I want a complete scan of the compound *now*. If any soldiers are AWOL or have signed out of the compound since eighteen hundred hours, I want to know *who* they are, if they are listed as on- or off-duty, and *where* they are. This is a top priority."

Chapter 51

The Northern Zones

Every sound seemed magnified. The cold water in the river created a constant, gurgling melody as it rushed by. When he knelt on the bank, Michael heard the scrunch of smooth river stones shifting under his weight. Water dripped down from his hair and his beard with a tapping noise. Several other men stood in a circle around them while Albert and Daniel knelt with him and prayed.

Michael considered how quietly it started. There had been no church service, no shouting, no crying, or any of the other things he associated with people getting "saved." The steps leading to his decision had slowly accumulated over time, so that the culmination of it seemed quite tame.

After he made the decision, however, while he stood in the river, something like a spiritual bomb detonated inside him, blowing away the accumulated sorrows of a lifetime. Why hadn't anyone told him it would be like this? Maybe they had. In his mind, a picture of his younger brother, Ben, briefly flashed. Yes, Ben *had* tried to describe the joy, the hope . . . the peace that passed understanding. At the time, though, Michael just thought Ben had lost his mind. And what about Zac? . . . Yes, he'd tried to describe it as well. And Sara. And Pete. He'd written each of them off with one excuse or another. Yet now, here he was, saturated by the river on the outside, and filled to overflowing with clean, new joy on the inside.

Dan gave Michael a Bible, and he grasped it tightly in his hand.

"Keep in mind," Daniel said earnestly, "the same Jesus who saved the first believers has saved you. The same Spirit who filled the early believers is inside you now. And, when they got filled, those ordinary men and women spoke in other languages, worked miracles, and were filled with boldness to tell others about Jesus." Dan pointed to the book in Michael's hand. "That Bible you're holdin' says this is God's promise, even for believers in far off places and in future generations, and that the manifestations of this promise will cease only when the Perfect has come."

Michael's thoughts went back to a day when he peered into a house from the window to see and hear the people inside praying and singing in such a curious way. He'd been so drawn by it.

Daniel spoke again. "But God doesn't hold people in bondage, Michael. He won't force anyone to receive anything. He doesn't want passive slaves. He wants sons and daughters who choose His ways with their mind, will, and strength. Do you *want* what God would give to you?

Michael looked at all the men. "I want as much as there is."

###

Two hours later, they all realized they needed to get going. They'd lingered at the cabin trying to answer multitudes of Michael's questions, but they'd have to do the rest of their talking on the road back to the main encampment.

Michael helped them pack up the gear in the cabin before they all began the trek to the village. As they walked along the remnants of an old road, he still felt almost as if he could float. Would the sensation ever stop? Yes, they told him. It wouldn't be gone forever, though.

Walking along the road, Michael saw everything with new eyes. He noticed the gently swaying trees bordering the road, the tall grass and other plants taking up residence where ancient asphalt had buckled and crumbled over the years. Occasionally, he could hear the trickle of a nearby stream. *The sky is just so blue!* he thought. *How awesome.*

Before coming here, he'd always pictured this part of the country as an endless, flat prairie. Actually, the men told him, south-central and eastern parts of the former state of Oklahoma were hilly, almost mountainous in some places, and filled with lakes, streams, and rivers.

Even though the countryside they passed looked lush and inviting, the men asked Michael not to wander far from the group. Wild dogs—decedents of domestic animals left behind during the great exodus south—traveled in hungry packs and could take a lone man down. Troops, and robbers also crossed the area occasionally, willing to take advantage of any defenseless person traveling solo. Staying in groups whenever possible was the wisest idea. He thought about his trip to the refuge and realized how dangerous it had been. He'd probably been protected from harm in more places than just inside that hollow tree.

Once most of the other men from the cabin became involved in smaller, private conversations, Michael asked Albert and Daniel, "What will I do now? Will they let me stay in the refuge for a while? Where will I go when I leave here?" Not wanting to ask again, but unable to suppress his burning need to know, he asked, "Will anyone tell me where Sara is?"

Daniel and Albert nodded at each other before Albert spoke quietly.

"We're not trying to keep you in suspense. We're pretty sure she and her sister did arrive here."

Michael's heart soared until Daniel added, "But, if they are the two women we remember, they left."

Michael stopped walking. "Where would she have gone? How will I ever find her?"

Daniel put a hand on Michael's shoulder, gently urging him forward again. "That's why we didn't want to say anything, even after we knew you weren't a nut or a spy," he said in a confidential voice. "We're just not sure of the facts. Others in the village will have more details, though. We'll find out and see what can be done. Try not to worry. God is good."

Michael kept pace with the others, no longer "floating," but wanting very much to keep a grip on his surge of faith. The God of the whole universe had come to live inside him, like a living flame. Surely He would help. Many of the others here had probably endured great trials and still served God. He eyed Albert's empty sleeve.

Albert saw the look. "No, I never accepted the mark," he said. "I wasn't thinking that," Michael said, embarrassed. "I mean, once I found out you were a Christian, I didn't think that anymore. I was wondering if . . . someone had tortured you."

"No," he said, shaking his head.

Daniel and Michael kept quiet, waiting to hear the rest of it.

"I must confess," Albert said, "I planned on getting a code. I didn't want one particularly, but my supervisors informed me they'd terminate my employment if I didn't get coded. My job, real food, and my lifestyle meant more to me than any god or government. Until then, being a doctor had exempted me from living with less. When my employers threatened my job, I had to ask myself if I wanted to become one of those uncoded castoffs wandering the streets, finding it harder and harder to locate each meal, getting squeezed into nasty living quarters, being refused medical attention."

All the other travelers fell silent, listening to Albert's tale.

"I was only a day away from getting a code when I got called to the scene of an accident. A little girl was pinned under a steel beam. Rubble held some of the weight off of her, but she couldn't be pulled out. We got quite a few people together to lift the beam while I pushed her out from under it. Trouble was, the beam shifted and fell, crushing my arm beyond repair. Once they got me out, they took me to surgery, and my arm had to be amputated.

"After the operation, getting a code was a moot point for me. I was a right-handed surgeon with no right hand. Of course, I could still get a code but even with a code, how would I live? Being a doctor was all I knew . . . it was all I ever wanted to do. All the advice I would've given to someone else in my circumstances meant nothing to me. . . . I secretly planned to commit suicide."

Albert stopped speaking while they pushed through a high stand of grass where the road had been entirely eaten away. Once they found the road, he picked up the thread of his story.

"Again, I came within a day of doing something to seal my fate. But a man came to visit me and said he felt God directing him to talk to me. He'd been a patient of mine in the past and hadn't known my arm was gone until he saw me. He encouraged me and he asked if he could pray for me. From the moment I let him do it, I felt different. I somehow felt . . . hope. A week later, I committed my life to the Lord and I've been helping save lives ever since, but," he added with a smile, "rarely in a medical sense."

"So how come you guys get to live out here with no harassment?" Michael asked.

Albert looked at Michael. "If you went south today, could you live there with no harassment?"

"Well . . . no. Not really. I mean, there are ways of avoiding troops and government systems, but it's a hassle." He recalled some of the unpleasant brushes he'd had with troops because he had no code. "Regardless of what you do," he said, "they can still get to you at times."

"There you have it," said Albert. "No matter where we are, they can find ways to get at us. . . . So why are we still here? Why haven't they dragged us all away? All we can figure out is that God wants us here or we'd have been rounded up by now. Maybe He's got them thinking the fewer fanatics stirring up trouble in the cities, the better. Maybe they've got their hands full with resistance in the south and armed rebels further north. It's possible they're watching us by satellite. For whatever reason, or combination of them, so far, our confrontations have been small. We know it won't last forever, though. We expect to see troops coming over the hill one day."

Michael looked ahead at two men who had rifles slung over their shoulders. "Will you fight when they come?"

Albert got a somber look. "It's something we've all thought about and prayed about. We finally decided not to decide. Throughout Bible history, and beyond that, God has seen fit to warn His people in times when danger was coming near. Sometimes He led them to battle, sometimes to run, sometimes to stand and see Him win the victory. And, sometimes, He asked them to bear witness to their captors . . . or their executioners. If we are His people, we have to trust Him. He will tell us what to do when our time draws near. We're praying for the wisdom and the strength to do whatever He asks of us."

Albert slowed down to reach out and pull some leaves off a tree. He rubbed them between his fingers before inhaling their fragrance. "Right now, I for one am grateful to have come to this place and met these people."

Michael's eyebrows came together. "What about contamination? I thought almost all the land up here was poisoned."

"Even though several large areas of land and water up north and east were contaminated," Albert answered, "that doesn't make the entire North untouchable. Where do you think your food comes from? When you are in the city, I mean."

Michael shifted the pack on his back. "I don't know. I guess I always thought of them growing huge amounts of food on a few small uncontaminated pieces of land with radical new farming methods, or in covered greenhouses . . . or perhaps buying food from other countries."

Albert opened his hand and watched the leaves fall to the side of the path. "Guess again. Remember the wheat famine during the disasters? The crops from genetically altered seeds crashed, and the loss of the crop almost starved us all. Now, just like us, the government is growing old strains of seeds out in the open—the regular way. We've had some of the biggest scientists in the country, who are Christians now, pass through different refuges, and they've found little wrong with the land or the water. In any case, I believe the Lord would protect us even if there was some contamination."

Michael stopped walking. "Isn't that what the Beanly people say?"

Daniel jumped into the conversation. "No. There's a fundamental difference. They *seek out* poison and willfully eat it. We believe God allowed us to survive the disasters for a purpose. We try to avoid contamination but have faith He will protect us if we are forced to eat it or ingest it accidentally. There's a difference between 'testing' God and trusting God."

"Isn't it amazin' though," one of the other men chimed in, "that there is almost exactly a ten-mile strip of one kind of contaminant or another along the entire border to the zones?"

"Amazing," Michael answered. He thought about the orange crust he'd walked through—how, after a certain point, it disappeared.

They crested a hill and stood together for a moment. Below them stretched even rows of cultivated plants near a cluster of tents and small cabins.

"There it is," Daniel said with a sweeping motion.

As Michael looked down at the little village, he wondered how long he'd stay. How soon would be able to find out about Sara?

###

After several days, Michael finally pieced together all the available facts concerning Sara's visit to the refuge. She and Noel *had* come, intending it as a resting point on their way to another refuge. They would have stayed longer, but rangers came and warned the residents that government troops might be looking for two women who had recently crossed the border.

Civilians detained by troops for "questioning" were rarely seen again. Guides hurriedly took Sara and Noel north, using an unusual route to protect their safety.

By now, who knew where Sara and Noel had gone? A letter from Michael could be forwarded to their intended destination, but no one could be certain she'd receive it. The message had to be carried on foot, through wild country, to a woman who could've changed her destination and even her name. In order to have any hope of a reunion, Michael needed to stay put.

Days passed, and Michael begged God to see her again. At first he felt as if he could expect to see her. But as weeks passed, he began to think he might be alone for the rest of his life and aspired to reconcile himself with the possibility. In the midst of it all, he tenaciously held onto the belief that God knew the desires of his heart and would do what was best.

Chapter 52

Near Houston

The ex-Reverend Ike Bointon sat on the ratty couch in his room. Stuffing erupted out of torn cushions, and stains of various colors vied for attention on the faded pattern in the upholstery. He sipped the hot lemon water carefully and held the cup with two hands. His clothes hung on his frame due to enormous weight loss.

He heard a knock at the door, but stayed on the couch and called, "Come in."

A man, resplendent in red robes and matching cap, opened the door before looking around, unsure of his location. He hesitated, not certain if he knew the man on the sofa. "Ike?" he asked, tentatively.

"Hey, Joe!" Ike called. "Come on into the castle here! . . . Want some hot lemon water?"

Joe entered the room, making every effort not to look shocked. This pathetic man in this horrible little room had been a classmate in seminary. They'd graduated together at the top of their class. They'd both been assigned domes at the same time. Both had done well. That is, until something went wrong.

The guest smiled nervously. "I was thinking about you all last week, Ike, so I decided to look you up."

"And that's not so easy these days, is it? I've been relocated twice, due to the 'New Start Housing Program.' Can't let the uncoded riffraff stay in neighborhoods getting wired anymore. But I make do," Bointon said, with a melodramatic wave of his hand. "Would you care to sit down?"

Joe found an unpainted wooden chair and slowly sat in it, fearing it might collapse.

"You look like a cross between a Hare Krishna and a cardinal in all that stuff," Ike snickered. "Is this what the best dressed Ring Masters are wearing these days?" He used the name non-believers hurled at dome leaders.

"You really are bitter, aren't you?"

Ike took another sip from his cup before responding. "What did you expect? You certainly didn't come running to champion my cause when they accused me. Was that supposed to be a humbling experience? I borrowed a few lousy bills, and they canned me! *Me!* My Circle had more than doubled since I started."

"Don't kid yourself, Ike, you didn't 'borrow' the money. If you'd been missing any more than four thousand, they wouldn't have cared about the scandal it would've caused, and you'd have been sent to prison for sure. And since we are assassinating characters here, you weren't doing so hot in your dome either. You were losing potential Circle members to the fanatics. You were slow in implementing the incorporations. And to top it all off, you had a chance to make it all good and you refused it!"

A harsh laugh escaped Ike's mouth. "You mean get coded and go to 'retraining'? So they could wash my brains and then let me be an assistant to the leader in my dome? Why should I have to buy a demotion? They thought I'd hop on it like a trained dog. Not me," he said, defiantly.

"You'd rather live like this? What's your job now? Cook? Dishwasher? Litter-picker-upper? God, look at you, Ike!"

Ike paused a moment and straightened. "He did. And he threw me away. I am a self-made man, Joe. I was when I was on top and I am now. I can play the game but I bend my knee to no one. Even now I still have my pride. Don't kid yourself either, Joe. You paid for those robes. With your life."

Joe stood, the rustle of his garments making the only sound in the room. He walked to the door and turned to Ike as he opened it. "I can see you don't want any help. Pardon the intrusion. It won't happen again. . . . You can't say you weren't given a chance . . . " He fixed his cap. "You know, you might as well have become a fanatic," he said, closing the door between them.

Chapter 53

Atlanta

In a room the size of a walk-in closet, the fading, green glow of a chemical light ebbed on the verge of going out. Edwina Grant pulled up into a fetal position and began to cry.

Oh Lord, she said in a desperate, inward prayer, *please don't let the light go out.*

Her injuries continued to mend, but the fear of being left to rot, alone, in total darkness began to press up against her like wind-driven snow. She let herself cry for a while before she sat up on her mat and scooted over so her back could rest against the wall. She wiped off her face and tried taking long, slow breaths.

She could still see right *now,* couldn't she? Yes. She could still see the dim outline of a seatless toilet bowl in the far corner and the wrinkles in a crumpled blanket at the foot of her sleeping mat. What would she do when she couldn't see them anymore?

"Think of something else," she said aloud.

How many days have I been here? She remembered reading scientific studies involving people living for extended periods with no sense of day or night. They might sleep for an hour and think they'd slept for eight. . . or stay awake for thirty hours thinking they'd only been up for a normal day. What little food she got seemed to come at odd intervals. But then, how would she know? She had no means of measuring time.

This will certainly hinder anyone from being able to give interesting tours of the place in the future, she mused. *They won't be able to show people hundreds of scratches on the wall and say, "See? This is where she spent the early years of her imprisonment, marking each passing day."* While she pondered these things, Edwina separated a clump of hair at her left temple into three locks and began braiding it. Once again, a number of strands came away in her hands. *The tour guide may have to settle for something like, "This is the small rug she managed to weave from all the hair she lost while she was here. . . ."* She managed a smile before starting another braid on the other side of her head.

What was the last thing she remembered happening before waking up here? A large number of troops showing up at the house where Leon held her and the others hostage. She recalled the crowd outside getting louder. After that, someone drugged her. She had no memory of being transported to this place, no idea how far she might be from the room she called home . . . from Paul, and Virginia . . . and Isaac. Where might *they* be? What would happen now?

Edwina stopped braiding her hair and took several slow breaths. *No matter what, Lord, I am Yours.* Lifting her hands upward, she continued praying, *We've gone through too much together for me to quit now! You've been with me through everything else, and I know You will see me through whatever lies ahead. Even,* she hesitated. *Even if the light goes out, I know You will be the Light to my soul. Thank You, Lord, for sharing this place with me. You are Lord of Heaven and Earth . . . You are my Father and I am Your daughter. All the time I have left on this earth is Yours. Please help Isaac, wherever he is. Watch over Paul, Virginia, and Caleb . . .*

She heard the *clank* of a heavy lock in the distance. Remaining perfectly still on her mat, Edwina stared in the direction of the door as footsteps echoed along the hall outside her room. Without warning, bright lights sprang on and she had to cover her eyes.

A soldier unbolted the door and pulled it open before issuing a command: "Get to your feet and come with me."

She felt around for her flip-flops and slipped them onto her feet before she crawled off the mat toward the door, squinting with all her might. Finding the doorframe, she held onto it with her left hand and rose to a standing position. When she let go, the soldier placed restraints on her wrists and grasped her right elbow.

"This way," he said, nudging her to the left.

The unrelenting light continued to dig at her eyes as she limped along. The sound of her plastic flip-flops slapping her feet with each step reverberated in the windowless corridor. Where was the guard taking her?

Her first memory of this place was still hazy. She could vaguely remember being taken down—was it *this* hall?—for a brief doctor's visit. She recalled fearing the encounter might involve some sort of torture or interrogation, but the female doctor asked her no questions. She examined all cuts and bruises, applied ointment on the cuts, and sent Edwina back to her "room."

Could this trip be a follow-up visit? After all, she thought, *they wouldn't want me to have any active infections or untended wounds when they . . . do whatever it is they're going to do with me.*

A sentry opened the door at the end of the hall, allowing Edwina and her escort to pass through it. Instead of turning left, as they had on their previous trip, the soldier took her to the right and led her through a labyrinth of hallways with pipes along the ceiling, then into an elevator.

She could open her eyes most of the way now. *Trust the Lord,* she told herself as they entered the lift. The guard pushed the button for the second floor, and her focus expanded to an old placard above the buttons.

Welcome to the Pleasantree Hotel
Enjoy your stay with us!

Then it occurred to her. *The Pleasantree! That's only a few miles from the soup kitchen! I'm downtown.* Until now, it was as if she'd been in an endless free fall, not knowing a single solid fact about her status. Somehow, being able to put a pin in a mental map, knowing her precise location, gave her some comfort. *No matter where I go Lord, You are with me, You will watch over me.*

The elevator doors opened, and they stepped out into a wide corridor with a row of windows above eye level along the left wall. Edwina peered through the windows into the darkness beyond and wondered what time of night it might be.

The soldier prompted her to move down the hall. Along their right, stretched a long span of empty wall, interrupted with an occasional door. Rectangles of bright patterns in the otherwise dingy wallpaper testified to missing artwork.

"Stop here," he said when they came to a set of glass doors. The sign above the door said "Conference Room 111."

Another sign at the left said, "Maximum Capacity, 120 persons." When Edwina looked inside, however, she could only see five people gathered at the far end of the room, seated at a large wooden desk and skirted tables on either side of it. An older woman sat at the desk with two men sitting at the table on her right, another two on her left. Each of them wore a charcoal-colored shirt with a Nehru-style collar and buttons down the left breast. No insignias, pins, or labels adorned their attire. All of them sat facing a solitary metal chair placed ten feet from the front of the desk. The woman behind the desk looked toward the door, then motioned to the soldier escorting Edwina.

"Inside here," he said, pushing the door open.

Edwina breathed faster as he led her to the solitary chair, then commanded her to sit in it. *Didn't I know it would come to this?* she asked herself. *Yes. Yes I did—but Father, You say that when we are called to give an account for ourselves, the Holy Spirit will give us the words to speak. Father, here I am. Don't let me fail.*

Edwina sat down, suddenly aware of her outward appearance. She looked down at the crumpled gray dress and the white plastic shoes a soldier had given her in exchange for her own clothes when she visited the doctor. Next, she remembered that she had two straggly braids in her hair! Edwina momentarily closed her eyes. *Regardless of how I look, let me glorify You, Lord. Help me to be a witness.*

"Edwina Marie Grant," said one of the men at the table on her left. "You are charged with multiple counts of providing medical advice without a licence, providing medical services without a licence, illegal bartering, establishing means for others to illegally barter, the corruption of minors, organizing and participating in insurgent assemblies, soliciting co-conspirators, conspiracy against authority . . ."

Edwina listened to the charges. While they all seemed to relate to her Christian walk, notably absent were any words specifically mentioning her faith.

Her accuser continued, ". . . breaking an established curfew, inciting a riot, resisting arrest, and inciting civil disobedience. Who will present your plea?"

"I will," said a man at the table to Edwina's right. "She pleads guilty to all charges and—"

"Wait!" Edwina interjected. "I've never even seen this man before. . . . And I don't plead guilty."

"Ms. Grant," the reader of the accusations said, "you have a right to representation. But your intermediary must be someone familiar with the charges, the applicable laws, and our procedural rules. Therefore, Mr. Goze will speak on your behalf."

Edwina fixed her gaze on the slender, gray-haired woman behind the desk and said, "I have my own advocate."

The woman behind the desk spoke for the first time. "We can't allow a delay. There is no time to call in outside representation. Do you want Mr. Goze to present your plea?"

Edwina cleared her throat and answered, "No. My advocate is already here with me."

The woman looked up at the ceiling and exhaled the words, "Very well," before adding, "let it be noted that the defendant refused court representation against our advice."

The two assistants, one seated next to her accuser, the other near her would-be representative, spoke in unison while they typed on small keypads. "Duly noted."

Mr. Goze asked, "And what does your imaginary advocate plea for you?" before adding a sarcastic, "Feel free to translate if we can't hear his or her imaginary voice."

Edwina looked at each of the people facing her. "Some of these charges are entirely false. I have neither condoned nor incited violence of any kind. I have corrupted no one. I am not a 'conspirator,' I am a follower of Jesus Christ, which as far as I know, is not against the law. I didn't break curfew and I didn't resist arrest. As for the other charges . . . you will have to decide whether or not it is wrong to help others in need."

The words were barely out of Edwina's mouth before the woman behind the desk stated, "We find the defendant guilty on all counts." Her next words took on the monotone cadence of one who has memorized and repeated a statement so many times it has lost all meaning. "We are given the task of preserving the peace, of punishing those who pursue the ways of intolerance and violence. I, therefore, sentence you to a minimum of fifteen years at a labor camp. Take her away."

Edwina blinked. Was that it? No evidence, no witnesses, no questions . . . no chance to say why she helped others? "Wait," she said.

The soldier reached for her arm. "It's time to go."

"Excuse me," a male voice resonated from the back of the room "but I have an urgent communication regarding this case. May I approach?"

The woman sitting as judge nodded. "You may."

A tall, blond man in a Universal Legion uniform walked up to the desk, handed a clip screen to the judge and said, "From Colonel Folson, ma'am."

Edwina's escort awaited further instruction while the judge silently scrolled through the text on the screen, then handed it to Mr. Goze, who quickly scanned it before passing it to the prosecutor's table.

The Legion officer stood perfectly still. Even while technically "at ease," the man's physique conveyed the fact he could easily spring in any direction, slash a few throats, and have his knife back in its sheath in a matter of seconds. His demeanor said the court's acquiescence was a mere formality. After allowing them a few moments to peruse the document, he said, "The authorization number listed there should be entered on your records for future reference."

After duly noting the number, the judge offered the clip screen back to the officer. "As always," she said in a frozen tone, "we are but servants in the cause of justice."

"Yes, ma'am," he replied, as he took the device from her. Next, he turned to address the soldier near Edwina. "The prisoner is now in my custody. You're dismissed."

The soldier exited the room, holding the door for the Legion officer and Edwina.

After the door closed, the judge looked at Mr. Goze and said, "I don't know why they made us waste our time with her. They make a mockery of the whole system when they interfere."

Mr. Goze cautiously looked around the room before speaking in a low voice. "Actually, I see this as a lucky stroke. We did our jobs and we have an authorization number." He paused before adding, "All of us have seen the unexpected demonstrations outside the compound the past week. I heard yesterday that similar problems have erupted in other vectors."

The others nodded.

"Mark my words," he said, "dangerous situations are developing and the fallout from them is yet to come. If something isn't done soon, the fanatics will get completely out of control. . . . Maybe the Legion is going to make a public example of her. Maybe they're going to . . . convince her to implicate others. Whatever happens to that woman, the Legion will be listed last in the chain of custody. I for one," he said brushing his hands against one another, "am glad to let them have her."

###

The Universal Legion officer took Edwina down several floors and through a tunnel to another building. Within minutes of being found guilty of numerous "crimes" and sentenced to a labor camp, she found herself sitting comfortably on a sofa in a well-appointed office. She wondered if she might be dreaming when the soldier removed her hand restraints and offered her some herbal tea.

"No . . . thank you," she said.

He pulled a bottle out of a small refrigerator. "Some cold water then?"

She stared at it, thinking, Just like the old days. Imagine that. A refrigerator. Bottled water. . . . I am thirsty. She felt uneasy about taking it, so she shook her head. "No, thank you."

A man with graying hair, brown eyes, and a Colonel's insignia on the collar of his uniform entered the room. The officer near Edwina stood at attention until the Colonel addressed him, saying, "You're excused, Captain."

Once the captain left the room, the Colonel seated himself in a leather chair near her. "I'm Colonel Folson."

Edwina nodded but said nothing.

He frowned and shifted around in his chair. "Despite the fact that you have broken a number of laws, Mrs. Grant, we've looked into your case and see a few complications."

"Complications?" she asked.

Folson cleared his throat. "I've been told that one of the men involved in your case, Mr. Newsome, may have bypassed a few procedures in his haste to arrest you."

Edwina looked incredulous. "Would these be the procedures that involve charging me with a crime and not letting me respond before he bound my hands so tight it cut my wrists? Despite the fact that I offered no physical resistance, he repeatedly kicked and stunned me. You can call it an 'arrest' if you want to, Colonel, but if people hadn't disrupted Leon Newsome's plans, I don't think there would have ever been a record of any arrest. . . . Or is this the way 'arrests' are always handled when the public isn't around to watch?" Edwina spoke softly, but firmly. "Is this what everyone in my neighborhood has to look forward to?"

Folson's hands tightened for a moment, then relaxed on the arms of the chair. "I want you to know that Mr. Newsome's actions were those of a rogue individual. He doesn't represent the standards of the Universal Legion or the Global View. . . . To publicly demonstrate the truth of this statement, we're prepared to suspend your sentence."

Edwina's pulse quickened. "In exchange for what?"

Folson wanted her to understand his point. "We're not the monsters you think we are. The world would be nothing more than a lump of charcoal floating through space if global forces hadn't taken charge. While some personal liberties have been lost, most people would say it's a fair exchange for the peace and safety we have achieved. If your superstitions didn't make you so blind, you'd see that we are striving for the greater good, Mrs. Grant. Regardless of what you believe, we will be releasing you today. You will be free to work and live in the neighborhood you have chosen—*provided* that you cease from illegal activities, and that you make no false accusations against the government regarding the actions of Mr. Newsome."

Edwina thought a moment. "You keep saying Mister Newsome. Is he a civilian now?"

"Mr. Newsome has been sentenced and will not be getting the second chance we are giving you."

Could this be true? How would she ever know? She decided to focus on more important issues. "Were my friends taken as well? If so, where are they now?"

"The people with you in the house were released six days ago, but they will be arrested and stand trial if there are any more demonstrations or threats to the public welfare."

*Any **more** demonstrations,* she thought. Obviously, a lot had happened while she was being detained. "How long have I been here?" she asked.

"Today will make eleven days."

"Why was *I* held for so long?"

"We wanted to make sure your wounds didn't need further medical care."

"And you wanted to make sure I got a trial," she added.

Colonel Folson sat perfectly erect, a man accustomed to being in control. "Make no mistake about it, Mrs. Grant, you have been convicted of serious crimes, you have been sentenced to fifteen years in a labor camp—but from this moment on, your sentence will remain suspended, as long as you keep the conditions we've set."

Edwina could hear her own pulse. Could they truly be offering to set her free *without* the stipulation of getting a code? If so . . . why? Could it be that greater numbers of the uncoded populace were waking up and openly resisting?

###

Several floors above the room where Edwina sat, a prisoner waited, shackled hand and foot to the rear wall of the cell, his mind racing with so many thoughts that he couldn't sleep. He looked over expectantly when he heard the cell door open, then let out a sarcastic laugh when he recognized his visitor. His heavy chains made a soft clunking noise as he sat up and said. "I knew you wouldn't miss the opportunity to gloat before they carted me off."

Tedrick Chalmers entered the cell and assessed his former roommate. "You look a little thin, Leon. Better eat your breakfast when it comes. They won't have anything nearly as good in the prison up north." He smiled. "Certainly, you won't be getting anything off the organic menu."

Leon spat on the floor. "You thieving, back-stabbing swine!"

Ted shrugged. "I warned you. You were just so busy being smug you didn't hear me. You thought you were better. You thought you were smarter."

Leon wiped his mouth. "I am."

His visitor looked around in pretended horror. "To think, all this time, I had a brilliant serial killer in the bunk next to me! And such a proud one at that. He kept souvenirs." Ted changed the topic to that of his most recent victory. "You know, your mother took it real hard. Your father, on the other hand, just gave her this real icy stare and left the house." Ted couldn't resist a sigh of satisfaction. "She was a real basket case though. Being the one who had to tell her was tough. . . . I may have to go back and see if there's anything I can do to comfort her."

Leon spoke quietly. "Don't think you're going to get away with this, Ted. No matter how long it takes, I'll keep working at getting free . . . even if I have to crawl all the way back through the zones to get you, I'll find you. You'll beg me to kill you before I'm done with you."

Ted calmly inspected a fingernail. "Well, if it's any time after next week, make sure you're looking for Captain Chalmers, okay? I doubt you'll get the chance to stalk me, though. McCauley will be going to the same prison and he's not too happy with you. If you hadn't picked him for your little raid, he'd still be in the Legion, still be out and about. If he gets loose before you do . . . well, let's not worry about that, shall we? You'll have enough of a problem once the other prisoners realize you were in the Universal Legion." Leon's old roommate turned the palms of his hands upward and shrugged. "Personally, I want you to live, so you have time to appreciate the fact that I beat you." He leaned forward—close enough to be just out of reach—and stared down into the eyes of his foe. "I beat you, Newsome. In every way that counts."

Enraged beyond words, Leon stood up and strained against the chains until his whole body shook, a loud, growling noise escaping out of his contorted mouth.

Ted took a casual step back and smoothed his uniform before consulting his watch. "Well, just look at the time. Must be going. I'm meeting the others for breakfast downtown." He moved back to the door. "Guard? I'm all finished here."

Leon started screaming. "I WILL get you! I WILL!"

The door between them locked before Chalmers spoke over the din, "Watch your back, bro. That's the best advice I can give you."

Chapter 54

Little Valley Refuge in southwest Missouri

There wouldn't be any lessons today. In fact, packing up the camp would occupy everyone's time for the next few days.

Sara looked around at the refuge and felt a bit sad to leave it. From the moment she'd arrived, she'd been able to pick up her long-standing friendship with Rosa and Ricky who welcomed her so warmly. Within days of their arrival, she and her sister, Noel, both felt very much at home within the community. Noel loved working among so many other young adults, and Sara could resume the career she loved so much: teaching. Although still grieving for her father and missing Michael terribly, looking at the eager little faces of so many children at the refuge comforted her.

She and Noel had found a resting place. But this would soon change. Ricky and the others had known for some time a move would be necessary. None of them felt they should spend another winter in this place for a multitude of reasons. Then the people of the camp got a warning from the Lord: They needed to pack up and move on. The direction of their move, they believed, was to be southward, back into Oklahoma. Making preparations and storing food for such a long trek would take time and careful planning. Given the number of children and old people in the refuge, the journey might take as long as a month.

The work had taken on greater intensity when messengers arrived two days ago with disturbing news. An entire refuge in Missouri had been raided and no survivors had been found. The missing might be in hiding . . . or they could be on their way to labor camps.

A little voice intruded on her thoughts. "Miss Sara?"

She turned to see her favorite student approaching. "What is it, Daisy?" she asked, embracing the little girl and smoothing her long, dark hair.

"Mama says I can be your helper today."

"Oh, what a fine idea," Sara responded.

Looking at Daisy, it amazed her to think the little girl wasn't actually Ricky and Rosa's biological daughter. She had the skin tone, hair, and eyes of Rosa and little Angela . . . and a certain shine in her smile reflected Ricky.

"Come on then," the teacher said. "We have to help Dr. Bill pack up his dental tools today."

###

Just above the camp, hidden in the trees, Ricky and Rosa approached "the tank," a survival bunker which had provided so much for them in the past year. Ricky pushed the hidden clasps off with his foot and slid the lid to one side before descending down the ladder with a wind-up flashlight lashed to his wrist. Once he'd reached the bottom, he called to his wife and she began her descent, closing the lid behind herself.

By the time she reached the bottom of the ladder, he'd lit two more lights and was winding up a third. When he finished, they stood together and looked around the first chamber.

"We'll take most of the protein packs with us," he said. "We'll leave those two containers of rice . . . and two containers of beans. They'll keep well and they'll be good nutrition for whoever finds them."

Once they decided what to take from this room, they moved to a second chamber and selected more items, moving them back to the first room. Before they climbed the ladder, they moved to a bookshelf at the far end of the room. Ricky removed several books from the right side of the middle shelf. Using a blade from his pocket knife, he pried on a small chink in the surface of the wood until a six-inch square of the veneer came loose, revealing a hollowed slot in the wood underneath. This was the only addition the group had made to the chamber—a secret hiding place for messages. This way, should they lose contact with others, the message would say where the group intended to go from here.

Rosa pulled a single sheet of paper, folded in quarters, from her pocket and handed it to her husband. He set it in the slot, then closed the hollow and replaced the books.

"There," he said. "I told Jason and the others to look here."

The couple faced each other, sensing something tragic, yet not wanting to say it. Jason, Troy, and Jen had gone with the Rangers on their mission to rescue slaves from labor camps. Each of them knew the risks, but felt the Lords' leading to go. Since then, however, Rosa had been unable to shake a deep sense of foreboding. Seeing tears glistening in Ricky's eyes only confirmed what she hadn't dared to voice. She broke down and covered her face, barely managing to ask, "Do you think they will ever make it back here? Will they survive?"

He put his arms around her, and she could feel the spasms in his rib cage as he silently wept. They held each other tightly and just let themselves cry.

When he could speak, he said, "We've been here before, haven't we?"

"Yes," she replied.

"God called them away, but we will see them again. We *will* see them again. One way or the other. . . . Lord," he prayed, "please give us all strength and hope. Help us all to finish what You have called us to do."

Down in the camp, Sara and Daisy helped Dr. Bill and his wife pack up tools and supplies in the dental tent.

"I think I would hate this one," Daisy said, holding up a tool used to scrape along the roots of teeth.

"Me too," Sara replied, curling her lip.

"Worse things happen if I don't use it!" Bill countered. "Just wrap it like I told you, and we'll all be happier in the long-run."

The tent flap flew open. Amanda leaned inside and called out. "Messengers are coming! Where are Mama and Papa?"

Bill quickly stepped outside the tent to confer with Amanda, then returned to say, "We'll stop to see what news the messengers have."

Within minutes, almost everyone from the refuge had gathered around the canopy. The last to show up, Ricky and Rosa, arrived only moments before the messengers.

Three people, a middle-aged man traveling with a teenager, and a lone man in a tattered Ranger uniform were led to the canopy and invited to sit down. All of them gladly sat down and removed wide-brimmed straw hats before they were given water and fruit.

The ranger had come from the north and just happened to encounter the other messengers at a river crossing only ten miles away. Everyone from the refuge waited patiently, knowing the messengers had traveled many miles.

The ranger sorted out three, folded pieces of cloth from the others in his pouch and handed them to Bill. "All of these," he said, "were forwarded on through River Bend."

The messenger handed a bundle of cloths to Bill, saying, "One letter is from Five Forks, two are from Lakefront, and two have been forwarded on from cities south of the border."

Bill took the messages from the two men and inspected each one for specific markings or names before he read them aloud. "This one's for Kate," he said, handing the woman with dark hair her message. She hurriedly moved away with her prize.

"This one's for Ricky and Rosa! Bet it's from Jason," Bill said, handing it to Ricky with a hopeful look.

Rosa pulled closer to her husband. "How long ago was it written?" she asked quietly.

"More than a month ago," Ricky replied after opening the document and scanning it. The somber look on his face didn't improve much until several children gathered and looked expectantly at him. He moved the letter to look down at them and gave them a wink. "We'll all sit down and read it when Dr. Bill is finished passing out the letters."

"And, this one's for everybody," Bill declared, holding up a letter. "We'll get to it in a minute. The next one is for . . ." He stopped, puzzled, then looked at Sara. "I think it's for you."

Sara pointed to herself. "Me?"

"Yes. I think so."

Noel put her arm around her sister. "Who would know that you're here?"

Sara didn't answer, but held out her hand for the folded piece of cloth passed to her.

Noel stayed close. "Who's it from? Who's it from?"

Sara opened the message and looked at the signature before her legs gave way and she found herself sitting on the ground. "It's from Michael."

#

Ricky and Rosa's clan gathered on the grass outside their cabin to hear the letter from Jason. Ricky sat in the doorway of the cabin, Rosa sat on the ground nearby with twelve-year-old Mary who helped corral the toddlers. Amanda had temporarily disappeared with a letter from Luke Norris.

Ricky cleared his throat as he squinted at the scrawled words. "This is what Jason says:

> *Dear Family:*
>
> *We've made it safe into Illinoy. We try to make as many miles as we can every day. Stopping only for short breaks. The weather has been good. Usually we eat while we're walking. Troy and I mostly travel with that guy Bob Ulman's group, so we're out in front a lot of the time. Jen is the general medic and she camps with Sam's group. We spoke to her tonite and she says HI to everyone. She wants Mama especially to know she's making it okay even if it's not as nice as getting to see her friends every day. She says she's sorry she's been too busy to rite. . .*
>
> *Ricky looked up at his wife, and she nodded.*
>
> *Bob Ulman is doing better all the time. The other guys in the unit really raz him about being a Christian now, but he's taking it pretty well. I also saw Norris today and he said he was riting a letter to Amanda.*
>
> *Several young girls sitting together said, "Wooooooooooooo," before Ricky gave them a look which quickly silenced the silliness. He continued reading,*
>
> *This trip is really different from when we went south. We don't see other people and we travel at night a lot more. The food is okay but not as good as you guys have. Troy and I are thankful they did some trades with you before heding out, or else all we'd have are rations.*

We want the kids to know how much we value their prayers. We feel them. Don't stop! We won't be able to bring you any toys from this trip but we really hope you'll pray for us every day. We pray for you, too, and hope to see you in the spring. Be good for Mama and Papa.

Love,

Jason

"How will they find us if we leave, Papa?" Daisy asked urgently.

Other children either echoed the words or looked concerned.

"Not to worry," Ricky answered, trying to look each child in the eye. "We made a plan with them before they left. We made a way to leave them a secret message saying where we went so they can find us later."

"Oh," Daisy said, breathing a sigh of relief. "That's good."

Rosa stood up and hoisted little Daniel onto her hip. "Okay everybody, we have a little time before lunch. Older children need to go be helpers, the rest of you guys," she said, tickling Daniel, "come with me and Mary!"

Ricky stayed behind at the cabin. Another page of the letter contained more material for Ricky and Rosa, but not for the children. Ricky would read the rest to himself, then let his wife and Amanda read it. He sat back against the doorpost and silently continued through the letter Jason had penned more than a month ago.

P.S. FOR RICKY, ROSA, AND AMANDA ONLY—

It gets harder to keep track of time. Alltho the seenery changes I forget how many days it's been sometimes. We also probably won't get to send you any more letters soon, but we're glad that Major Tam is sending a man on a mission that will take him thru your area so he can deliver these letters. If we succeed in this mission, it will probly take quite some time to return.

A late-summer breeze sprang up, sending leaves skittering by his feet and down an alley between the tents. Ricky stopped reading and thought for a moment. Once they rescued some slaves, they would divide into smaller groups, and head south. If they hurried, they could get out before winter weather set in. Would they succeed? Ricky went back to reading the letter.

> *We found something vary upsetting a few days ago. Sam and her partner came upon a cave. The mouth of it was intentionaly sealed from the outside, so we opened it, thinking it might be a secret stash of weapons, ammo, or food. Inside the cave were the bodies of more than 40 men, women, and children, who'd been left in there to die. They had no clothing or jewelry.*

> *I had almost forgotten how I felt when they tried to kill us in Oklahoma. God gave us such a good rest in the little vally, it healed my heart from my past. But seeing those dead people made it all focus for me. How could someone do such a thing? It has only deepened the resolve of me and Troy and Jen. We do not want revenge, but we must at least attempt to do the right thing. Our time of rest in the vally is over, we must go forword.*

> *I want, more than ever, for Jesus to come back soon—but if He is delayed I promise you and Him to spend my life well. I realize now I could never repay you and Rosa for the sacrifices you made to reach me, but I'll try to serve Him till I shine.*

Ricky got up from the doorway and tried to clear his throat of the giant clog forming there. He walked to the mat that he and Rosa shared and knelt by it before he read the last words.

> *I want you to know I'm happier than I've ever been. I know I'm doing what God wants me to do. There is no greater joy than this. You are all in my prayers.*

> *Your son forever,*

> *Jason*

"Oh Father," Ricky said in an anguished voice. "Now I know how You must have felt."

Chapter 55

Five Forks Refuge in Oklahoma

Having worked the first part of the night watch, Michael slept well past sunrise. When he awoke, he could hear the refuge buzzing with morning activities: the irregular cadence of someone chopping wood, the distant song of children, the happy chatter of two women as they hung laundry nearby all wafted into his tent with a light breeze.

Wanting a few moments alone before socializing, he got dressed and walked through gardens, fully ripe and bulging with the summer's harvest. Soon, he found a small clearing and sat in it. He shed his wide-brimmed hat and allowed the sun to fall full on his face. Soaking in its welcome warmth, he took a deep breath and closed his eyes to pray. It had been months since he'd sent a message to Sara, addressed to her last known destination. There had been no response yet; but he spoke to the Lord about her every day. He continued to hope that, one day, he'd at least know she and Noel were safe.

All too soon, a man's voice broke into his silence. "There you are!"

He turned to see Albert Donner standing nearby with a large grin on his face.

"I've been looking all over for you," Albert explained.

Michael rubbed his eyes. "Hey Al. What do you need?"

"A whole group of visitors has arrived and we need extra vegetables for meals. Could you help me out?"

Michael stood and stretched before he picked up his hat. "Sure."

The two men walked toward one of the vegetable patches where they could dig some potatoes, then pick tomatoes and squash. They passed tall stalks of corn and started walking down one of the rows of tomatoes before Albert stopped.

"Oops," he said. "Forgot the baskets and the trowels. Tell you what, you start with the tomatoes, and I'll run back to get the tools."

Al seemed entirely too delighted about not having trowels and baskets. Michael watched his friend disappear down the row, nearly dancing his way out of the field. Pushing back his hat a bit, Michael asked himself, *How could anyone be so cheerful in the morning?* Shrugging, he figured he might as well start picking.

Since he had no baskets, he decided to stack the tomatoes in piles at regular intervals along the rows. He came to the end of a row and knelt down to unload tomatoes out of his shirt tail, placing them on the ground.

"Here," a woman said, handing him a basket.

"Thanks," he answered without looking up. He started piling tomatoes into it before he froze.

"Hello Michael."

On the other side of the corn, Albert and Daniel waited anxiously, until they heard Michael's shout.

"Sounds like they found each other all right," Daniel said, slapping Albert on the back. "Good work!"

Some of Albert's smile faded. "Speaking of work, I think we'll have to do the rest of the veggies alone."

Michael had jumped to his feet with a loud whoop, catching Sara up in an embrace. Elation washed over him as he held her tightly. When reality crept back in, he needed to verify the data. Was he dreaming? He set her down and pulled off her hat to inspect her face, to touch it, to be sure a counterfeit hadn't shown up. Once the hat came off, he saw the large bruise covering the area from her chin to her right cheek bone and a small shiner around her right eye.

"You're hurt!" he said. "Are you all right? What happened?" he asked with concern.

Sara let out a small groan as an unwanted picture flashed in her mind: She wanted to help set up camp two nights ago and offered to cut down a few small saplings so tents could be erected. After noting her inexperience, someone told her the task would be far easier if she bent each small tree over, held the top of it down with her *left* foot, then chopped through the base (as close as possible to the ground) with the axe in her right hand. This worked well on the first two trees. She felt like a pioneer woman!

Only two saplings remained when she decided to chop down the larger one—a springy six-footer. By the time she wrestled it down, she'd forgotten all about positioning and felt victorious when she got it under her right foot. Someone asked her a question. She looked up to answer, then went back to work. As her axe found its mark, Sara realized she'd gotten it all backwards and chopped the wrong end of the trunk. Instead of separating the base of the tree from the ground, she'd cut completely through the end near her foot. The little trunk shot up with a vengeance and smacked her so hard she saw bright sparks for several seconds. Bill and Ricky tended her injury, trying not to laugh, telling her to be thankful. If she hadn't managed to turn her head, it might have damaged her eye or broken her nose.

She refocused on Michael. "Uh . . ." Sara finally managed to say. "I had a minor accident."

"What happened?" he repeated.

She felt her face grow even hotter. "I was attacked by a tree."

He looked mildly amused. "What?"

She shut her eyes. *So much for the romantic reunion.* This was worse than the gum on her shoe thing and she knew Michael would burst out laughing when he heard it. She looked up at him and pleaded, "Can we not talk about it right now?"

"As long as you're okay," he said, bending closer to her. His heart flipped around in his chest. *Now what?* Although he'd longed for this moment, he'd never planned much beyond it. *She's traveled all this way. Surely this means something. . . . Will we have to start out as friends again? When can I tell her how I feel?* He gently cradled her face in his hands and softly kissed her eye, then her bruised cheek. She made no effort to retreat. Before he realized it, words escaped right out of his heart. "Sara, I love you, and I– "

Without warning, a young girl fell onto the ground, right behind Sara. The startled couple turned to see two sets of hands reaching out to grab the fallen girl and yank her back to a hiding place behind several tall plants. Before Sara or Michael could respond, three barefooted girls ran down the next row, wildly giggling, probably bursting to tell everyone what they'd just seen and heard.

"Ohhhhhhhhhh, those girls!" Sara said, feeling yet another rush of embarrassment.

Not recognizing the children, Michael asked, "Who are they?"

"They're three of Ricky and Rosa's girls. They must have followed me out here. We'd better go soon."

When Michael and Sara arrived back at the main camp, Michael was surprised to see scores of newcomers putting up tents. Sara led him to Ricky and Rosa's tent. After introductions went around, the girls who ran out of the field were told to come forward.

Red-nosed and teary-eyed, they apologized for not respecting Miss Sara's privacy. Then they gave Mr. Michael the same apology. Seeing them cry made Sara want to gloss it over, but she knew they needed to learn a lesson, so she graciously said she forgave them. When they finished, Rosa sent them off to do extra chores as punishment for leaving the camp without permission. For their conspiracy against Miss Sara, the normally inseparable friends wouldn't be allowed to associate for the remainder of the day.

Once the girls left the tent, Ricky and Rosa stood near Michael and Sara while a gaggle of younger children chased each other around the tent.

"I'm sorry we're getting off to a bad start with you, Mike," Ricky said, "It's just that the girls are at the age where boys and romance are of extreme interest. Honestly, most of the time, they're sweet kids."

Sara nodded and Michael shrugged; neither spoke.

After the lesson they'd just doled out regarding privacy, Rosa didn't dare to appear nosey about any details of Sara's reunion with Michael. Although Sara would surely share when they got alone, Rosa felt like she might pop from the suspense. Michael looked very much the way Sara described him: tall and lanky, tan, with sun-streaked hair, brilliant blue eyes. Rosalinda shifted the toddler on her hip and turned her attention to her friend's face. Sara looked scared, embarrassed, and happy all at once. Were the two officially in love now?

"I need to go and eat some breakfast," Michael said, before shyly glancing at Sara. "Would you like to have breakfast with me?"

She nodded.

Rosa opened her mouth, then closed it and settled for a wave.

"See you later," Ricky said.

Once the couple had departed, Rosalinda leaned near her husband to whisper, "What do you think? You think he proposed?"

Ricky grinned widely. "You assume *he* did the proposing? *You* proposed to *me,* ya know."

Rosa's jaw dropped. Several children in the tent stopped what they were doing and looked at him. While uncertain of Papa's exact meaning, Mama's reaction said his words were important.

She finally sputtered, "Enrique Ruiz! I did no such thing. You take that back!"

He laughed. "Let's just think a moment here. If I recall correctly, you said something like . . ." he looked upward, searching for the precise words, before he spoke in a higher pitch. "'I love you and I don't know *how* I could live if you moved away without—'"

Sara stuck her head back in the tent to ask a question. She'd heard a strange voice inside the tent, but assumed Ricky was entertaining the children. Seeing the look of distress on Rosa's face, however, she came to the sudden realization she'd entered at an awkward moment and began a hasty retreat. "Oh, I'm sorry! I'll come back later."

Rosa quickly caught her by the sleeve and pulled her into the tent. "No. That's okay. Come right in. What do you need?"

Ricky knew just how far he could tweak Rosa and still remain in her good graces. Satisfied that he'd reached the limit, he gave her a delighted wink and a peck on the cheek before stepping toward the opening in the tent. "Gotta run, *mi amor,* be back in a few minutes." He exited with two toddlers in tow.

Wanting to jolt the remaining children's minds onto another topic as soon as possible, Rosa turned to them and said, "Amanda is right next door helping Mrs. Cooper! Go and tell her I said you could help, too."

The delighted children ran from the tent.

"I really only wanted to find out if I could help you later," Sara said, wincing. "Should have announced my presence first, huh?"

"It was nothing . . . really." Rosa leaned close to her friend and changed the subject. "Please promise you'll tell me what happened later."

Sara smiled and wiggled her eyebrows. "Only if you promise to do the same."

###

For the first thirty-six hours after her arrival in the camp, neither Sara nor Michael could sleep. They stayed up for Michael's night watch, sitting in the center of the camp, keeping the fire going, serving food to watchmen, passing on messages when necessary. They sat on large stones near the fire, having a non-stop talking marathon. They cried and laughed, never more than ten feet apart. After sunrise, still hungering for each other's company, they talked through the following day. By the time they finally parted to rest, Sara had also confessed her abiding love for Michael.

During the next week, Ricky, Rosa, and the other visitors at the refuge made plans for their continuing migration. Michael and Sara made plans as well. As another day drew to a close, the two sat together in a large, wooden swing under a tree near the center of the camp.

Someone in the refuge had used a new formula to make a fresh batch of soap that day, and its strong, clean scent drifted through the air along with wisps of smoke. Michael and Sara's swing creaked back and forth. They could hear bits of conversations as people walked to and fro, the snap of burning wood, and the chirping of crickets. The nearby fire gently lit their faces as they sat without speaking for a while. Sara wanted to pull in every sound, smell, and impression . . . to remember this sublime moment for the rest of her life.

They caught sight of Ricky and Rosa passing by with several small children. Just as the family disappeared from the firelight, Michael could see Ricky slipping his arm around Rosa's waist.

Michael turned sideways in the swing, disturbing its rhythm, then pushed the ground with his foot so it would resume its gentle sway. He studied the woman he'd traveled so far to find. For a moment, he felt the pain of that day long ago when he realized she'd taken off into the wilderness with her sister and left him alone.

He took her hand and said, "I would have proposed to you the next instant I saw you."

"I was afraid you might. It's the reason I wanted to get away." She leaned forward and spoke softly so he would be the only one to hear her words. "I was in so much pain and I cared so deeply for you. I don't know if I could have resisted."

His face mirrored his confusion. "But, you said you loved me. Didn't you *want* to marry me?"

She looked him in the eye as she spoke with conviction. "It would have been wrong for me to marry you with the hope you'd change something so fundamental as your relationship with God. After promising to take you as you were, could I then set out to convert you? Could I compromise? Could I pretend it didn't matter to me? No. Every single day it would have broken my heart that the most important thing in my life meant so little to you. It might have been a life of regret—for both of us."

He could see the sorrow in her face as she continued. "Just as bad, what if I had refused to marry you but stayed around, holding out for a change in you? It might have caused you to fake a relationship with the Lord just to please me, or made you resent Him as an obstacle between us. Either way, I could have ruined your chances of an honest relationship with Jesus forever." She squeezed his hand. "Michael, I can't think of anything that would be more horrible than claiming I love you while leading you to miss the most important thing in life. You had to belong to Jesus—unconditionally—first."

Michael's face softened and he said, "You gave this a lot of thought, didn't you?"

She nodded. "And prayer."

He thought about the angry man he used to be, the dark outlook, the hopelessness that often engulfed him. Words couldn't express all he felt, but he knew she was right.

For the first time, something occurred to her. "You know, I think Daddy realized this would happen. He knew you'd get saved. He sensed we would end up together."

She watched a slow smile appear on Michael's face as he considered it.

He agreed before the smile disappeared. "I wish he could have been here to see it, to give you away and all."

Sara looked up at the open sky above them. "I have to remember he and Mama are in a place of no sorrow . . . and that they'd truly want us to be happy on our day" She let her gaze rest on Michael again. "I want to be happy on our day."

"Me too," he responded. "I'm happy and honored and sad all at once."

She nodded.

"I'm sad about something in particular, Sara."

She tilted her head slightly. "What's that?"

He let go of her hand and brushed her cheek with his fingers. "I'm . . . I'm so," he stopped for a moment. "I'm overwhelmed by the gift you're giving me. . . . I'm blown away by the fact that you waited. To tell you the truth, it never occurred to me until a few months ago that *anyone* waited anymore."

She looked down and he moved closer.

"What an incredible gift you're giving me . . . look at me, Sara. I know I don't deserve it. I want to tell you and the Lord that I'm sorry I didn't wait for you." He took a breath. "I'm so sorry I don't have the same gift for you. Nothing I have can match—"

She put her hand over his mouth. "You're a new man. That's your gift to me. The new Michael. I love you so dearly."

He put his arms around her and she rested her chin on his shoulder a moment before she spoke again, "I love you, but I must go now and get some sleep." She got up, but he grabbed her hand and held onto it until she sat beside him again. "Michael Gordon," she said in a groggy voice. "You wouldn't deny me a good night's sleep before our wedding day, would you? I'm all talked out . . . and after tomorrow, we'll have the rest of our lives together!"

"Please. Stay a little longer."

She laughed softly.

"Please don't leave me," he said more seriously. "Just stay right here beside me. Don't go, not for a few more minutes. Please?"

"I'll look all rumpled and tired on my wedding day."

"S'okay by me." He squeezed her hand tighter. "For better or worse . . . rumpled, wrinkled, bruised, whatever."

"Are you going to let go of me?" she asked.

"Nope. You might evaporate in the dark. I don't want to let go for at least, oh," he said, pretending to look at a wristwatch, "a week or two."

She closed her eyes. "Just one more minute Mr. Gordon, that's all you get. I need to go back to the tent. All Rosa's girls have a big morning planned for me."

"Okay. Just a few more minutes," he conceded.

A cool breeze swept through the camp while the swing rocked back and forth. They were so tired that they both fell sound asleep.

Several hours later, a commotion and a light woke them. They bolted out of the swing. When Michael sensed danger, his instincts took over. He stood in front of Sara and held her behind him with his left hand.

Something appeared to be on the other side of the cabin in front of them. They saw flashing lights and heard a voice.

"What is it, Michael?" she said in a loud whisper, trying to look around his shoulder.

"Standing on the roof," he whispered back, not taking his eyes off the glow.

A male figure stood on the cabin with his back to them, presumably facing people on the other side. "Hear me! Hear me!" he shouted several times.

People in the camp would be awake and moving toward the figure by now. Michael motioned to Sara to come alongside him. They started to creep around the side of the cabin before he grabbed her arm again and urgently pulled. She looked at him. He put a finger to his lips to signal quiet, then pointed up to something in the darkness above them. She could barely make it out at first. She forced her eyes to focus and saw a fat, black disk, only about two feet in diameter, hovering about fourteen feet off the ground, just behind the cabin.

Michael had seen something like it once before, a couple of years ago. It had chased a group of people and terrorized them with all sorts of sounds as it mowed them down.

He signaled for her to go get other people. She nodded and crept away.

"I bring you great tidings," the being on the roof announced.

Michael straightened up and looked at it. It looked like a man, or an angel, with a shining aura. The arms moved up as it spoke. "Has not the whole sky been filled with signs of the Return? . . ."

Indeed, several times in recent weeks, the night sky had shown them fantastic displays. On some nights, bright lights moved about the heavens. Other times, it seemed as if the stars themselves were falling. The residents of the camp had chosen not to be alarmed by these things.

"The Christ has come," the being on the rooftop continued. "The Holy One to whom we all shall sing in unity and love . . ."

Daniel, Ricky, and two other men appeared around the side of the cabin. Michael signaled for silence as they approached, then pointed to the disk. Daniel reached down and grabbed a hefty log out of a stack.

The voice continued, "I have blessed you, says the Lord. Listen now, my children, and receive my words. Do not provoke me with unbelief as Israel did in the wilderness during the days of Moses. Listen to my voice and I will give you instruction: Do you not seek to be unified with me? Then know that all is God and God is all. The Christ has come to reign and dwells . . ."

Daniel heaved the log. When it struck the disk, a loud *zing* shot through the air. The figure disappeared, and the sound stopped as the disk crashed to the ground. Michael and the others gave the object a few more good whacks to knock off a few protruding instruments.

A crowd with lanterns quickly gathered around it. "What is it?" echoed around the group.

"Some sort of hologram-projecting device, it looks like," one woman said. "We'd better take it to Karl. He'll make sure *this* bird never sings again."

"I'm told things like this are appearing elsewhere," Ricky said. "The messages they bring have the same theme."

A small man in the front with graying hair spoke up. "Then there is no time like the present to recall the words of Jesus. He said 'If anyone says to you, "Look, here is the Christ!" or, "There he is!" do not believe it. For false Christs and false prophets will appear and perform great signs and miracles to deceive even the elect if that were possible. See, I have told you ahead of time. So if anyone tells you, "There he is, out in the desert," do not go out; or, "Here he is, in the inner rooms," do not believe it.'

The old man let his eyes sweep over all the people standing around. "Even though we can readily see this 'visitation' was a technological fabrication, we may not always have physical evidence to help us discern the origin of a message. Paul the apostle warned us, saying, '. . . even if we, or an angel from heaven should preach a gospel contrary to that which we preached to you, let him be accursed.'

"Hold onto the Word of the Lord and never let anybody compromise it, no matter what they look like, or who they claim to be." The man looked at the people, especially the ones he knew were new believers. "The return of Jesus, the one true Christ, will be an unmistakable event for all of us. And, there's a really simple, foolproof test that'll work every single time you think it might have happened: According to scripture, if your feet are still on this earth," he said, pointing down, "if your body," he placed his hands on his own chest, "hasn't been instantly transformed to a glorified one, and if you don't see all the believers from all of history with you and Jesus in the air . . . then Jesus hasn't returned."

Michael had noticed this guy before—a quiet, industrious sort of fellow. Each time he'd seen the man, Michael couldn't shake the notion he knew him or at least had seen him somewhere before. Now, it suddenly dawned on him. Hearing the man speak at length finally triggered the corresponding picture of a television evangelist from the past. The man had actually been convicted and even done prison time for his crimes before the disasters happened. Michael leaned over to Daniel and whispered, "Hey, isn't that Cliff Ed—"

Daniel quickly shook his head to stop Michael, then whispered back. "His name is Joseph. Just Joseph."

Everyone started walking around to the front of the cabin.

"Well," Michael said quietly, "Joseph sure isn't the man he used to be."

"Amen!" Daniel said, "God's grace is a wonderful thing isn't it?"

A few men began dragging the disk away, and everyone else walked to the front of the cabin. Sara rejoined Michael, looking a bit shaken.

Rosa could see the expression on her friend's face and took her by the hand. "I know," she said, "I know you're wondering if this should change your plans. Don't let it."

Ricky stepped closer and stood next to his wife. "She's right you know. We can't let the enemy or fear decide what we do with our lives. The Lord helped you find each other, didn't He?"

The couple nodded.

"Do you feel you have the Lord's approval to get married?"

They nodded again.

"Is tomorrow the day for it?"

Michael took Sara's hand before they looked at Ricky again and both said, "Yes."

Ricky beamed at them. "Then let's get ready for a wedding!"

Michael reluctantly let Rosa take Sara out of his sight with the promise that, when he saw her again in a few hours, they would become man and wife.

Chapter 56

Mr. Kressman stood in the control booth, watching the link-ups and monitoring the transmission of the "angel" at the refuge.

It suddenly went silent. The technicians fiddled with settings and called out to other terminals.

"What's wrong?" Kressman barked as he jumped forward. "What is going on?"

"Transmission stopped. Imaging shows that someone struck the—" one of the technicians said.

"I know that, *you idiot!*" he bellowed. His eyes bulged and he started shrieking at the top of his lungs, "I have spent millions on optics, satellites, and *technicians,* and I want to know why you didn't plan for this contingency!"

Every person in the room now shook in his presence. He wasn't accustomed to failure, and all feared the penalty for imperfection in handling one of his projects. Certainly none of tonight's fiasco had been *his* fault. Wasn't the angel delivering the message one of the most beautiful animations ever generated? Hadn't he placed scripture-sounding quotes in the message? Hadn't he even thought to make it appear as if the peculiar celestial phenomenon were advance confirmation of the message?

So far, almost everything had gone as he designed it . . . billions of people had come under his dominion. And yet, there remained remnants of fanatics in almost every country. They refused to submit. Even when shipped to camps, imprisoned, enslaved, kept from communication with each other—even when "accidentally" contaminated, or slowly terminated, they still clung to their God. Worse still, some of the remnant had found the will to begin a viable resistance movement. As much as he wanted the whole world to see the fanatics surrender to him, their progress in attracting new followers made any further delays unwise.

Once he'd left the control booth, he comforted himself. Although things would have to proceed more quickly than he'd planned, he'd by no means played his final card, had he? He took a deep breath and calmed himself. Within months, he would tie up all the loose ends and everyone would see what he could do. After that, who would be able to doubt him?

Chapter 57

Five Forks Refuge, Oklahoma

All of the visitors and most of the residents of the refuge gathered in the main area of the camp. The afternoon sun shone brightly between soft clouds sprinkled across the sky. Ricky stood facing Michael and Sara. Next to Michael stood Daniel. Beside Sara stood her sister, Noel, and her dear friend, Rosa. All the others stood or sat on the grass in a circle around them wearing their best or cleanest clothing. In the absence of cake, the smell of fresh-baked sweetbread filled the air.

"Today," Ricky said, "we have the great joy of gathering together with our Father, the Almighty God, to see this man, Michael, joined with this woman, Sara, in holy marriage.

"Some might ask, 'Why anyone would marry at such a time as this? If the time is short, wouldn't it be better to devote all our energies to service?'

"I would simply answer this way: Jesus should be the one who determines where our journey takes us, not the shortness of the hour—or *any* circumstance. . . . This is our witness. It is precious to God. It is a living example for the children around us. . . . It's what the whole world needs to see.

"If you never feel the Lord's call to marry, know that He walks with you, that He delights in you. Let no one belittle your sincerity or your purity.

"But know also that marriage is not a frivolous thing or a mere stop-gap measure to keep people from sin. God created marriage in perfection. He made the woman for Adam in the garden, and Jesus still plans on coming for His bride. Until that time, let each of us trust God to direct our time upon this earth.

"And so we come to celebrate the union of Michael and Sara. It isn't something they take lightly or without God's counsel. They will be joined together today as a sign to all of the hope and love that Jesus has placed within them."

Ricky looked at Michael. "I was told years ago that I would only *begin* to understand God's great passion, His willingness to sacrifice all, His enduring love for *His* bride, when I married the woman He chose for me—my Rosa. How true this has been for me, and I know it will be so for you, my brother. You stand here as a symbol of Christ, and God's command to you is to love Sara as Christ loves the church, being willing to lay down your life for her."

When Ricky turned to address Sara, she let go of her sister's hand, moved a step closer to Michael, and placed her hand in his. They looked at each other as Ricky said, "Sara, today you stand as a symbol of the Bride of Christ—pure and blameless in the sight of your beloved, having waited faithfully for this day. . ."

Ricky, Michael, and Sara each spoke in turn while the members of the small community looked on, some remembering their own vows, some wondering if they would ever be given in marriage, others merely reveling in the joy of a dear friend. When the couple kissed, the whole assembly applauded.

Chapter 58

Waco, in the former state of Texas

Ex-psychic Tony Bensen stood in a hotel room, staring out the window, watching the dawn break in the east. Choosing to forsake his life as a telepath, he would now lose his only source of income, his only claim to fame, his identity really. He would lose them all, but he didn't care.

He couldn't believe it. He hadn't slept all night—yet never felt better.

His mind went back to the moment last evening when Swordsman asked everyone to bow their heads and pray.

He'd actually done it. He'd actually bowed his head and silently prayed for salvation. The moment he'd admitted his need and surrendered his will, it felt as if a huge burden sloughed off his back and fell away.

He hadn't openly confessed his new-found faith, though. How could he discuss his life or what he would do now without disclosing information about his job and betraying his employers?

And what about his job *now*? He'd left all that he was in the stadium. There would be no turning back. What should he do? He'd simply cut communication with his employers altogether. Like closing one door and opening another.

Would Joan notice the difference when she saw him? He hoped she would ask him what had happened to him . . . so he could share it with her. If only he could communicate to her how it felt to escape the weight of Karma or living at the whim of some dark spirit. How could mere words describe the joy of knowing his past, along with his original "fate," had been cast away forever?

Chapter 59

Dallas

He asked himself, *Do I have the courage to do this?* It had only been four days since he'd secretly prayed. Four days since Tony Bensen had left his life as a psychic behind.

In the first hours after this life-altering event, he thought he could merely walk away. . . . But in the days to follow, he became convinced he couldn't just slink off into a corner somewhere.

He recalled the Bible passage he'd read last night: *"And there shall be signs in the sun, and in the moon, and in the stars; and upon the earth distress of nations, with perplexity; the sea and the waves roaring; Men's hearts failing them for fear, and for looking after those things which are coming on the earth: for the powers of heaven shall be shaken."*

He'd read the words minutes before stepping outside and witnessing a huge display of fiery lights in the night sky. Doubtless Kressman and others in the Global cause would soon find a way to put an advantageous "spin" on the phenomenon, but Tony felt certain these were signs from God. . . . Regardless of the cost, the time had come for him to speak. He closed his eyes. *Yes. God is giving me the courage to do this.*

Tony now stood in front of the unimposing building and took a deep breath. He'd only been here once before, but remembered it well. He mounted half a dozen stone steps and stopped short of the front doors. An oldie moved from his post beside the doors, and in a lifeless voice asked, "Yes?"

Tony's heart broke and he blurted out, "What have we done to you?" He'd not yet thought about oldies in this new light. He looked into old man's eyes to see if any spark lingered inside. The world's vain pursuit of endless youth had produced this: a lifeless shell of loose skin and sinew.

"What?" the oldie asked blankly.

This hardened Tony's resolve. "I wish to speak to Mr. Alex Dubois, please." The oldie moved back to his little work station, pressed the lighted square on his monitor and turned a microphone toward the visitor.

Tony leaned forward. His voice cracked a little when he said, "Alex Dubois, please."

A computer-generated female voice came out of the speaker. "State your name and business."

"Tony Bensen. It's about 'Cat Walk,'" he said, using his code words.

Seconds later, the doors snapped open. Tony's heart swam around in his chest as he walked through them.

"Follow me, please," a tall, bearded man said before leading Tony to a sterile-looking little office where he sat for fifteen minutes before Alex Dubois appeared. When Alex closed the door, Tony stood and they shook hands.

"Good news, I hope," Dubois said anxiously.

Tony's amusement at Alex's choice of words eased his tension somewhat. "Oh, *definitely* Good News."

The two men sat on either side of a small, laminated table.

"So what is it? The good news I mean," Alex said, smiling expectantly.

"Jesus Christ died for the sins of the world."

The smile on Alex's lips faded a little. Was this a joke? "I must admit there's probably some humor here, but I'm a busy man. What did you come to tell me?"

"That's it."

"What's it? What do you mean?" Alex could feel his whole body tightening as confusion crept toward anger.

"Let me be succinct," Tony said. "I need to tell you about the people you've had me spying on. . . . You're sadly mistaken if you think they'll be forced into eventual submission. Like you, I started this job thinking they were misguided—that I could help get them on track. . . . But it's not going to happen. They know the truth."

Alex let out an exasperated sigh; then, without an ounce, of enthusiasm he said, "Right. Hallelujah. Someone else has found 'it.' A 'Get-Out-of-Hell-Free' card." He closed his eyes and a now-familiar burn started in the pit of his stomach before he looked at Tony again. "*Don't you get it?* Your beliefs, my beliefs, their beliefs—are just supposed to help people live better. *All* the great minds of today agree. Ask them. It doesn't matter. *It's all the same.*"

"Really?" Tony asked. "And just what have the people of the Great Global Vision accomplished with this idea? How many people have 'chipped in' so far? Did they sign the Notice because they thought it was the right thing to do, or because they feared what would happen to them if they didn't? Tell me, what *are* the plans for those who refuse?"

Alex's anger flashed. "People *have* to get in the same grid. Things won't *work* unless we're all in the same grid. Agreement is in everyone's interest. It's our duty."

Tony leaned forward and spoke with conviction. "Don't answer me with catchphrases. You know you're on the wrong side of this. You've had proof I'm speaking the truth."

A wave of nausea hit Alex when, against his will, his mind locked onto the scene he'd witnessed with Kressman that one night . . . all those scenes of abominations and horror. They'd haunted his dreams. Even now, some of them flashed boldly in his mind.

"This is ridiculous," Alex said loudly, then collected himself to speak in a stern, but composed manner. "Certain things *must* be done to ensure the survival of humanity. You've let yourself become as deceived as those fanatics are."

"No. I see more clearly every minute." Despite the danger he sensed, Tony looked directly into Alex's eyes. "I resign, Mr. Dubois. I resign from this job. I resign from all of this. I want something all the religions of the world combined can't give me, something I couldn't have earned in a thousand lifetimes: Pardon for every mistake, every failure, every trespass, every debt. . . . I want Life. I want Jesus."

Alex touched a lighted area in the surface of the table. "Send a guard, please."

"It doesn't matter if you kill me. At least I've confessed it to someone now."

Alex's face reflected the disgust he felt. "What do you mean, *'kill'* you? I have no intention of killing you. Your delusion has made you paranoid. Let me be succinct: You're crazy."

A guard opened the door and stood at the ready.

"Take this man away," Alex said flatly. "Don't hurt him. Just get him off the property."

###

Later, Alex began to wonder if he should inform Kressman; or at least call John, and ask for instructions. But the more he considered it, the more he worried. Was it possible they'd do something to Tony? And, if they did . . . who would be right?

He changed the settings on the computer. All future messages about "Cat Walk" operations would be routed solely to him. He selected the option to be awakened, if necessary, with any new communications. In addition, he'd brief the other psychic on Tony's identity. This man could report if he sensed or saw Tony making trouble.

As night fell, his stomach continued to knot, and his head throbbed. Perhaps he could slip away for an hour and obtain more medication. The mere anticipation of getting some pills gave him a bit of a lift. Yes. He'd get through this. There was no need to assume the worst. As long as Bensen remained content to just disappear from the scene, Alex would say nothing.

Chapter 60

25,000 feet above the Earth

As his plane descended through the clouds to its final destination, the mind of James Hart raced with anticipation. The movie version of his book, *Changing Times, Time for Change,* was now being widely distributed to domes and other venues across the inhabited zones. Media mogul E.E. Kressman was so pleased with the results that he invited James to attend a "special event of global significance." Even after a fourteen-hour jet ride, the thrill of being secretly whisked away for the meeting still made him giddy.

What an honor this is! I wonder what will happen next! James tried, once again, to quell any expectations of receiving an award or special recognition during the "gathering of the world's finest minds from the government, the military, and the press."

He took a final sip of his bottled water as he calmed himself. *There are lots of other reasons he might invite me here. . . . Maybe he's putting together some sort of think tank . . . or a new, global media system. . . . I certainly hope I won't be expected to make this trip on a regular basis. Not here.* James peered through the small window next to his seat, and tried to reason away any lingering fears. *Surely, the danger of radiation must be gone, or Kressman himself wouldn't be spending time in this place.*

For the past couple of months Kressman had been in seclusion. There were no television appearances, no interviews, no sightings of the man. Speculation about his health and possible whereabouts had grown. Could he have some debilitating disease? Despite reports to the contrary from his personal aide, John Klost, rumors persisted.

During this same period, people around the globe saw strange lights in the sky, almost on a nightly basis. The world's information centers acknowledged the existence of the lights but denied that the sightings were of high-flying jets or of space debris burning up in the atmosphere. What could be happening on such a large scale? Many people began to think the lights had mystical significance. After several weeks of increasingly spectacular shows, however, the phenomenon stopped. Then came the rumor that E.E. Kressman would be having an exclusive conference with "key" people from around the world. While not specifically mentioning the gathering, the media began broadcasting that Mr. Kressman would soon be releasing information of major significance to all people.

James held onto his seat as the aircraft landed. Could he ever have imagined being here? The plane rapidly taxied to the terminal and stopped before an attendant appeared and informed him of the correct, local time. James advanced his watch and collected his personal items as he prepared to deplane.

Hot, dry air enveloped him when he stepped out the door. He lingered a moment at the top of the stairs, looking around the new airport. As if in honor of his arrival, lights sprang on against the backdrop of a setting sun.

In the distance an entirely new city—a model city, with every building wired, every walkway lit—waited for the eyes of the world to take in its perfection. He tried to take a mental snapshot of the image, then started down the stairs. He felt like springing down them and dancing when he got to the ground. It was all so fantastic!

The attendant brought his luggage around and handed it to him.

"Here, Mr. Hart. Please go into the door ahead of you there," she said, pointing at the one straight ahead. "Someone will meet you presently."

When he opened the door, he found someone waiting for him.

"Mr. James Hart? I am Hans," said a blond, well-built man. James noted Hans wore the sleek uniform of the Universal Legion with a triangle insignia on the shoulder. "I am to take you to the conference with the others. Could you please be seated until they are all here? It will only be a few minutes."

"Surely." James felt a little disappointed. Somehow, he'd thought he would be alone, the celebrity in the limo . . . but now realized there must be some sort of group.

One by one, others came in. Some he recognized as reporters, some he didn't know. James heard Hans speaking to two of the other guests in different languages before he walked to the door at the other end of the room and said, "I think we are all ready to proceed now. Will everyone follow me?"

The group exited the building and walked down a ramp which emptied onto a sidewalk. Hans let everyone gather on the sidewalk and indicated they'd be waiting for a ride.

Soon, they could see a large vehicle, rather like a trolley car, quietly moving toward them along the tracks. The driver of the thirty-passenger car brought it to a stop in front of them. There would be plenty of room for Hans and his flock of fourteen. "Everyone into the car, please," he said. "I will give you some information on how it works while we travel."

James found a seat toward the back of the car before Hans came around with a pamphlet containing a description of how the vehicle worked, how fast it could go, and how many cars the average system could support. James tucked it into his pocket for later. He didn't want to miss any of the sights in a *City of Tomorrow*. Someday, all cities could be like this. Today, however, it was one-of-a-kind.

Soon they reached the edge of the city, and James watched the multitudes of people walking well-lit streets. Most of the pedestrians stopped to wave and shout something. Had they been coached to do this for the out-of-town guests? They all seemed to be chanting the same small phrase over and over again. James turned to a woman nearby.

"Do you hear that? Do you understand it?" he asked her.

"I hear it, but I don't understand the language," she said, moving to the seat next to him.

He offered his hand. "My name is James Hart."

"Nancy Mills." She shook his hand and smiled. "Glad to meet—you aren't the James Hart, are you? The one who wrote Changing Times, Time for a Change?"

He nodded.

Her tone became much more excited. "How nice to meet you!" She eyed him for a moment. "You're different than I imagined you."

"Oh?"

"I imagined you . . . older, more . . . worn looking, I guess."

James laughed. "And taller, right?"

She laughed, too. "No. I meant that as a compliment," she tried to correct the impression, "I guess I said it in the negative. What I meant was that you're much younger–"

Hans interrupted their conversation with an announcement. "We are now arriving at your hotel. All of you will have an hour to freshen up and eat something if you wish. Then we will need to travel to the meeting."

Nancy got up and moved back to get her things on the other seat. "In any case," she said, "it's been an honor to meet you, Mr. Hart."

The car came to a halt, and they all disembarked, facing a compact garden in front of a small hotel. Hans told them the specially-selected plants around the hotel used a minimum of water while adding coolness and oxygen to the air around them. The garden, he said, represented the economy, ecology, and beauty to be experienced in the future.

As they walked into the building, James noted how quiet the group had become. It was almost as if they were all having a religious experience, needing a space of silence to assimilate everything.

They entered a utilitarian lobby containing several dark-green couches and a table holding various kinds of food and drink on their left. On their right, three floors of small cubicles formed a semi-circle facing the open area. The entire front wall and the door of each sleeping cubicle were solid acrylic. Open to public view at the moment, each identical room contained a twin bed, a night stand, a small closet, a door in the rear (presumably to access a toilet and shower), and a full length curtain which could be drawn for privacy. . . . Functional and attractive.

Each of the travelers hurried to an assigned room to wash and change in the allotted time. Most of them managed to gather in the lobby again before Hans returned. Overwhelmed by the spectacular sights and filled with anticipation, no one touched the food on the table or dared speculate about what they might soon see or hear.

The trip to the meeting seemed much like the ride to the hotel. People lined the streets, and James assumed the crowds had come out hoping for a glimpse of Kressman. Veneration for him in this part of the world took on devoted fervor.

Upon arrival at the stadium where the meeting would be held, the travelers saw thousands of people gathered around it. Soon, the trolley stopped, so James and the others could be transferred to small carts which would take them through a special entrance.

The U-shaped stadium looked as if it would normally hold about 40,000 people in tiered bleachers; but for this occasion, rows of seats filled the floor, facing a large stage at the open end. Behind the stage, empty land stretched out into the darkness.

James and his group followed a hostess to the rows of chairs on the floor. She gave each of them a wireless earpiece to wear, promising a full translation of any speech not given in their native tongue.

James guessed his seat was in about the 50th row of chairs and that there were about 50 more rows behind his. He assumed other "invited" guests would occupy all of these seats. He smiled and thought, *so much for the award idea.*

He settled in and watched a number of guards and several cameramen move about on the raised platform. On either side of the stage, attached to tall towers, stood huge video screens.

Men and women continued to pour into the stadium filling not only the chairs on the floor, but the bleachers as well. *So much for the think-tank idea as well,* he said to himself.

James glanced at his watch and looked around the inside of the stadium again. Almost every seat was now occupied.

Perhaps only a few more minutes now, he told himself.

Within seconds, a hush fell on the entire assembly. James looked around the stage but saw no signs of movement. The two large screens remained dark. What triggered the almost eerie quiet in the audience? Everyone sat still, as if watching, or listening to something.

He tapped his earphone. *Maybe mine is broken.*

A wave of sound started in the stands and grew louder. A chant. Soon, most of the people were repeating the same words over and over. James recognized the phrase as the same one he'd heard in the streets. He looked to the man on his left and said, "Do you have any idea what they're saying?"

"Yes." The man answered with a thick accent.

"Translated simply, they say, 'He lives, we live.' I don't know if you say something like this in your country or not.

This man means a great deal to us. We have lost so much here, but because of *him* . . ." Before he finished, the man's eyes went up, and his mouth dropped open.

A flash of light streaked overhead, and James looked up. A collective gasp went through everyone before stone silence fell upon them once again.

A large triangular object appeared, then hovered in the sky above the stadium before it began a slow descent. Covered with lights of brilliant hue, it slowly rotated while gravitating closer and closer. It made no discernable sound, but soon, an unpleasant sulfur smell permeated the air. Many people covered their noses and mouths with clothing or handkerchiefs.

The object slowed, then hung over the open land behind the stage. The viewer screens on either side of the stage lit up as cameras began filming the arrival of the craft. James briefly considered the lack of terror or turmoil he would've expected as people actually saw for the first time what so many had both feared and hoped to see for so long. It was as if a revelation long hidden in their memories sprang to life. They'd been prepared for this moment, they all *knew* what this was, and they felt no fear. All eyes shifted back and forth between the actual ship and the pictures of it on the large viewers. No one in the audience saw the small black disks hovering far above the stadium in the night sky.

A beam of light shot to the ground from the base of the craft. Another intake of breath came up from the crowd as the viewers showed a man descending rapidly through the beam and alighting on the ground.

The chant started up again as the cameras zoomed in closer to see the man who now walked toward the stadium. It was Mr. Kressman. As his face came into view on the screens, the crowd became almost frenzied. When he came out onto the stage, he raised his hands for silence. The crowd quieted before he turned and put his right hand toward the craft hovering in the sky.

James felt the hair on his head rising as if there were a static charge in the air. Was it happening to others? He couldn't move.

Without warning, a loud noise shattered the air around them, and the triangle of light shot into the dark sky in a brilliant smudge of light. James felt as if all the energy had been pulled out of him. He fought for consciousness. Kressman's voice sounded in his mind. Or did it come from his earpiece? He couldn't tell if others experienced the same sensation. He seemed only to be able to focus his thoughts on the words he heard.

"Beloved!" the soothing voice echoed, "I cannot describe the elation I am feeling at this moment! It is good. It is good! *It is good!* Concentrate on it, concentrate on it . . . open your minds to it . . . *It is good . . . It is good.*"

The words seemed to undulate rhythmically in James' head, making him relax still further.

". . . I have come to you tonight with a message of major significance for all those of our beloved mother, the Earth. You will not understand it all now. Don't struggle to understand it all. Just surrender. Surrender and know that in the future, you will be used as prophets and teachers to the people of your own nations! *We shall unite and become one! We shall declare it unto the stars. We live!*

"For two months now, I've been in communication with beings who have long waited to make contact with us. They have remained distant until now because they have been restrained until the ordained time. That time is almost here. They have asked me to relay to you their desire to see Earth whole once again. They have witnessed the destruction taking place and have heard the cries of so many for life . . . for justice . . . and for peace to flow into the hearts of all humans.

"There have been and still are divisions among the people and I stand here tonight with the message that these divisions will cease. I have taken up the cause of the world. I am destined to bear the message of light to the world. As different leaders and others receive the light into their minds, I will use them as well.

"Those who oppose the message are hereby given notice. The time of conversion is at hand!

"Meantime, my beloved, go forth as my child! Soon you will be released to tell what you have seen and heard. You will be my witnesses to the ends of the earth! Let expectancy be in the hearts of all people! Let us wait for the reality of it all! *Hope is not dead . . . for we live!*"

The speech actually lasted for perhaps as much as an hour. James lost all sense of time and couldn't fully remember all he'd heard. But when it came time to leave that stadium, he felt more alive, more invigorated than he could ever recall feeling. In fact, everyone he saw looked animated, surrounded by an aura of light. Truly, this had been a life-changing event. Nothing would be the same again.

He spent one night at the hotel, then journeyed back to America, ready to share the vision with the world, ready to receive the "visitations" he'd been promised.

Chapter 61

Along the border to the zones

Michael stopped singing for a moment. Did he hear another voice singing along with him? He stood still. No. No one was there.

He started walking again, listening to the sound of his own footfalls in the tall grass. For the next few miles, he hummed now and then, but sensed an increasing need to be mindful of the noise he made.

With the exception of an occasional scrabbly tree in the distance, foliage diminished until mostly dirt and rocks filled the landscape before him. An out-of-season heat wave made it oppressively hot, and he gradually moved slower and slower, trying to remember not to sing snatches of the tunes playing in his head. He rested at noon, eating only a few dried fruits and a piece of bread.

Before he and his fellow travelers split up earlier in the day, the guide told Michael he was within a day of the border. He needed only to keep walking south. The others would walk further east before going south. Sure enough, just after sunset, he reached the top of a small hill and, looking toward the horizon, he saw the first beginnings of the city in the distance. He unrolled an extra-long sleeping bag and sat on it, watching the first winking lights in the distance come on, then lay back as darkness crept over the sky above him.

Aware that the heat radiating from his body made him increasingly visible at night, he got up, opened the end of the bag, and crawled into it. The cloaking material, used for the outer layer of the sleeping bag, made annoying crackling noises. He understood the need to remain hidden from infrared devices, so he tried to ignore the irritating, crispy sound accompanying his every movement. He said a small prayer and thought about what he would do in the city.

Although he felt confident about his first trip away from the refuge, the sight of "civilization" gave him a sinking feeling. Until recently, believers in the zones had probably suffered the greatest personal losses. Now, however,

Christians in the south might soon face their own life-or-death issues. In cities, the squeeze to get a code and meet standards of productivity (in order to justify one's "drain on resources") brought greater abuses every day.

An underground network was already forming to establish means of survival and protect those who were elderly or disabled. Should some of these people be taken to refuges in the Northern Zones? Should believers in the refuges attempt to come south and stand with their counterparts against oppression? Should communities on *both* sides of the border be maintained to ensure that a remnant survived?

Refuge leaders decided to write letters to their counterparts who labored among the network of small groups meeting in homes and secluded places within the southern regions. Some of these leaders remained stationary while others acted as emissaries, migrating from place to place, openly sharing the gospel in public and secretly transmitting information along the growing underground. The letters which Michael and others carried were invitations to meet face to face, to pray and seek God for the steps that should be taken next.

The letter Michael carried was to be hand-delivered to a man known as Swordsman, an emissary who traveled from place to place. Would this man be where weeks-old information said he'd be? If not, Michael had only a week to find him.

He rolled over in his sleeping bag, and the harmonica in his shirt pocket dug into his arm. He pulled out his only remaining possession from the city. He couldn't see it in the dark under his blanket, but turned it over in his hands as he thought of Sara. Precious Sara. His wife. This was the first time she'd been out of his sight since they'd wed. Afraid to leave her at first, he'd finally decided if he couldn't trust the Lord to watch over her, his faith wasn't worth much.

Michael was a prime candidate to go to the city because he'd recently been there and would be less likely to commit an error and draw attention to himself. He missed Sara, but found comfort in the hope they'd soon be together again. He heaved a sigh and put the harmonica back in his pocket before falling asleep.

The next day, he located the remnants of an old highway he'd been told to find and walked along it. The sun boiled down from above, and the stained yellow soil on either side of the asphalt showed no signs of any plant life. In the heat, the road seemed to evaporate into the distance, disappearing into dancing wavy lines, melting skyward. By late afternoon, he needed to stop. Seeking shelter in the shadow of a rocky outcropping over a dry riverbed, he crouched down and waited for daylight to recede, taking small sips of water from a skin slung over his shoulder. At dusk, he heard angry voices echoing down the riverbed. Crouching down, he crept back toward the road. Just beyond a small rise, he saw a large tractor-trailer rig parked on the pavement. The trailer behind the vehicle listed to one side.

There were no private vehicles, and even government transports with internal combustion engines were a rarity. Michael hadn't seen a large truck like this in ages.

"It's not *my* fault they can't get new tires for these old pieces of junk," one man said, kicking the wheel.

"Well, it wasn't *my* idea to take a short cut!" another man's voice answered back.

"Just shut up and hurry! We're late already!"

Crawling closer, Michael realized the trailer behind the truck was full of cattle. He knew immediately what to do. He swiftly glided up to the far side of the trailer, then slipped over the back gate. Somewhat concerned about the newcomer, the cattle shifted around and mooed, causing the truck to fall off the jack.

"I *told* you to take the cows out first, stupid!"

"Right! And what were *you* going to do? Herd them around in circles with your belt until I was done? If you had a brain, you'd take it out and play with it."

"Why, I ought to–"

"Never mind," the first man said quickly. "We can't afford to waste any more time. I only need to tighten the lug nuts here."

Soon the truck started bumping down the road with Michael in the middle of all the animals. He got sandwiched occasionally, but otherwise felt grateful for such an easy means of crossing the border.

Within minutes they approached the checkpoint. Michael bent down. The driver produced shipping orders and the truck rolled on.

As soon as the truck drove through a dark area, Michael jumped off the trailer and found a place to hide until daylight. He needed to avoid troops who patrolled more heavily at night. He no longer had an I.D., and if they checked his records, they'd see he hadn't been registered anywhere in the city since he lived at Pete's store; and then he'd have to answer all sorts of questions.

When daybreak came, Michael stepped out of an alley and started walking. Despite the fact he'd hardly slept all night, he knew he must determine his exact location and how far he needed to go to reach his destination. He entered the first large store he found and kept an eye on the cash check-out line. Cash customers, in general, used money because they had no codes. A man soon came up to the front and paid with blue bills. When he exited the store, Michael followed him.

"Excuse me," he said, stopping the man. "I'm new in this vector and I'm looking for a friend. He's staying near the Broad Street Auditorium. Do you know where that is?"

"You're miles from it," the man said. "You'll need to use Central Avenue. It's about two blocks that way." He pointed to his left. "Then follow Central south till you get to Broad Street. Go right, west, when you get to Broad Street. You'll see signs for the auditorium after that."

Chapter 62

A suburb of Dallas in the former state of Texas

Joan threaded the wire earring through her left lobe, then leaned back to survey her whole face in the mirror. In particular, she studied her dark brown eyes. She'd always considered them one of her best features . . . but now, she wondered about them. Did they reflect the fear and emptiness she felt?

She focused far beyond her own reflection as she thought about the transformation she'd witnessed in Tony. It both intrigued and intimidated her. Tony Bensen, internationally known psychic . . . the man she loved . . . had changed.

Admittedly, Tony's cultivated aura of mystery was part of her initial attraction to him. But once she fell in love with him, she longed to see more than mere glimpses of the person beneath the public persona. She'd worked at gaining his trust for a long time, yet nearly gave up all hope of it happening when Tony took his most recent job.

As he became entangled in a mammoth spiritual struggle, he spent more and more time away from home. Whenever he made his way back to their apartment, his demeanor was distant and distressed. She watched helplessly as the formerly confident, unshakeable Tony moved to the edge of a total breakdown. She closed her eyes and recalled the pain and sorrow of those days.

A soft knock at the door brought her back to the present. She heard Tony's muffled voice ask, "Are you ready, dear one? It's almost time."

Joan made a conscious effort to relax before answering, "Just another moment, please!"

Once again she peered into the eyes of the woman in the mirror and asked herself, *Do I really want to go to this meeting with Tony?* After a short pause, she realized she was holding her breath while she awaited her own answer. This made her smile and dispelled some of her apprehension. *Is he as nervous about me going as I am?* she wondered. *Why am I so afraid?. . . Because everything has changed.*

She recalled his bright eyes on the night he returned from his last trip. He told her what had happened. . . . He said he'd given his life to Jesus and he wouldn't be a psychic anymore! He said he didn't know what he'd do, but he wanted to live for God. . . .

Joan's pulse quickened as she considered, *What does all this mean? What will happen to us now?*

Tony knocked on the door again. "May I come in?"

"Yes," she responded.

He opened the door and moved to her side before he knelt down and looked up at her. "I know you're probably nervous." He held completely still, allowing her to search his eyes before he said, "It's okay. I understand."

It came rushing back. She remembered why she'd agreed to go with Tony and hear about his new-found faith. . . . She'd spent so much time wanting to reach the real Tony . . . and now, she could see him. He was transparent, unguarded, and looking back at her—the Joan inside—with genuine love. . . . His eyes reflected deep water now. Didn't she long to experience that depth in her own soul?

She took his hand. "I'm ready to go now."

Chapter 63

Linda stood in front of the camera and looked at the cameraman. "Have you got a good angle on that?"

"Yeah. Wanna look?"

"No." She didn't want to distress the tight fabric of her new dress. Because Linda found herself more and more in the public eye, she'd become very aware of her appearance. She smoothed out the material at her waistline, inwardly smiling with satisfaction. All those hours at the gym had paid off. "Does my makeup need a touch up?"

"You're gorgeous already," he said in a monotone.

The lights came on, and a woman standing off-camera counted down, "Three, two, one," before pointing to Linda.

Linda put on her serious-reporter look. "Good afternoon. This is Linda Posner, standing across the street from the Broad Street Auditorium, where a group of fanatics has been holding a convention."

A lock of her newly-cut platinum-blond hair blew down over her forehead, but she ignored it and continued, "As you know, today is also our Unity March and the Universal Legion will be coming by in just a short while." A second gust of wind swept the lock of hair downward, where it tangled with her eyelashes. She struggled not to blink wildly as several strands of hair found their way into her eye. "We've been told there have been threats of trouble between the two groups. Some sources have reported that the fanatic leaders said, 'we won't have that godless rabble near our meeting.'"

She casually brushed the disobedient lock to the side of her forehead. Another puff of wind blew it back into her eye. "Preparations for the parade are complete, and both sides of the street along the route are jammed to overflowing with people who are anxiously anticipating the appearance of the Universal Legion."

The camera panned the sidewalk behind Linda while she spoke. She quickly scooped the hair off to the side, then smiled broadly as she became the center of focus in the lens again.

"The women of this vector have been waiting for months to get their first glimpse of these magnificent specimens, and those lucky ladies are about to have that dream fulfilled. We now switch back to regular programming and will return when the parade begins. This is Linda Posner, live outside the Broad Street Auditorium."

The lights went down while she held the gaze of the camera. As soon as the red indicator light went off, she stormed back to the chair where the remote make-up woman stood.

"If you don't get this piece of hair out of my face," Linda said in a low but deadly tone, "I will personally see to it that you never get another remote job again!"

Chapter 64

Michael hurried down the street. He'd stopped to rest during the day and overslept. He knew the meeting would have started by now but hoped to get there before it was over.

Once he got within sight of the auditorium, he encountered a large group of boisterous people, mostly women, obstructing the way. He pushed forward between them only to find his path blocked by ropes and barricades.

"What's going on?" Michael asked the woman to his left.

She eyed him up and down and smiled. "Unity Parade. You know."

"Oh. Yes. Unity Parade," said Michael, clueless as to what she meant. He looked down the street in the direction everyone else seemed to be turned.

He could hear a faint throbbing sound in the distance. At first, he wasn't sure he heard it at all. Then it sounded like a steady beat of drums, and it grew louder. Soon it began to sound like thunder, pounding over and over again. Lights went on a block away, and he could see a blond woman in front of a camera.

"What's that sound?" Michael said loudly to the girl next to him.

"Where have you *been* lately?" she asked. "It's the Universal Legion. They've been on viewers every day for weeks. I've been dying to see them in person. Oh!" She shouted, pointing down the street, "Look how gorgeous they are!"

Now Michael could see them. Soldiers. Marching around the corner. More and more of them. Michael's mouth dropped open as they approached. The noise became almost deafening as the female spectators began to scream at the top of their lungs.

The men coming down the street wore skin-tight stretch-satin uniforms of varying hues, arranged according to color. Each man had black boots and two black batons. As each one took a step, he stomped his boot, let out a shout, and clacked the clubs over his head. And at the end of each row, two men with large drums pounded out the cadence. There were hundreds of them—each one perfect, beautiful, in prime physical condition.

The sound got so loud Michael could feel his sternum vibrating with it. He tried to back away from the noise, but the crowd packed up against him and all of *them* pushed to get forward. He couldn't think or breathe it seemed. He yelled at the top of his lungs. He couldn't even hear himself.

Chapter 65

Inside the auditorium Tony Bensen sat and prayed quietly as Swordsman spoke. He'd heard the pulse of the Legion outside, but it finally receded. Now only the voice of Swordsman could be heard.

Tony prepared to stand up and walk forward. Swordsman spoke about the life Jesus lived on this earth. How a mere man couldn't have controlled the events in His life to make them fulfill hundreds of prophecies written about him centuries before his birth. How His suffering, the method of His death and even the actions of those at the foot of the cross fulfilled these prophecies. Swordsman read Jesus' promise of a literal return for those who believed in him. He stressed the need of every individual to accept the sacrifice of Jesus in order to receive that promise. The time had grown too short for putting things off.

Tony felt he could no longer keep silent about himself. He had to walk down and publicly confirm it. Regardless of the cost.

There. He heard it. The call to come forward. Some of the people started singing a beautiful song. Tony stood.

What if they rejected him or said he couldn't be saved? Was this the fulfillment of his dream? It didn't matter. He had to go. He'd gotten half way there before he felt a tap on the shoulder.

"Wait for me," a small voice said. He turned to see Joan behind him.

Chapter 66

Michael came through a doorway in the back of the auditorium just as people began singing a hymn. He didn't know the words, so he just closed his eyes and stood still, soaking it all in. The worry over being late left him. The sorrow of being apart from Sara, the bone-weariness of his long trip, and the fear of failing at his task all departed. Soon, his spirit began to soar again, the way it had that first day. He'd taken almost every intoxicating substance known to man, and drunk rivers of alcohol, but this was far better. The experienced presence of God was overwhelmingly sublime. *How could anyone NOT want this?* he asked himself.

Swordsman's voice rang out over the speakers.

"As these people come forward to make a commitment, I want everyone to pray a scripture from Ephesians, chapter six, with me. . ."

Michael's eyes snapped open. He recognized the voice. *Could it be?* He focused on the figure standing on the stage and started walking down the stairs, slowly at first, then faster and faster.

". . .Therefore," Swordsman continued, "let us take on the whole armor of God, that we may be able to withstand in the evil day, and having done all, to stand."

"*Zachary!*" Michael shouted at last.

Swordsman stopped speaking. No one had called him by that name in so long. He looked up the stairs to see a man running toward him, and a jolt ran through his whole body. "*Michael?* Is that *you*?" he shouted.

He jumped off the platform and sprang up the steps. They hugged each other tightly and wept unashamedly as the crowd looked on. It was several minutes before Zachary could even speak to tell what had happened, and when they heard, the entire auditorium of people got to its feet and cheered.

Later, Zachary went among the people as he always did after a meeting. He noticed a couple kneeling together and knelt in front of them saying, "May I join you?" They nodded. He grabbed both their hands and prayed for them.

When Swordsman stood and offered a hand to help him up, Tony felt a sharp jab of recognition. Instead of a threat, though, this was an offer of kinship.

"I'm sorry," Tony said, taking his hand and standing.

"About what?" Zac asked.

"I followed you for months, reporting your movements to the government so they could get something to use against you. . . . I also tried to interfere with your thoughts telepathically, to alter the course of this movement."

Zac's eyebrows shot up in surprise. After a few moments of thought, he asked, "And you renounce all of this now?"

"Yes."

"Are you willing to abandon telepathic connections, speaking with spirits, pursuing altered mind states, or seeking empowerment by anyone other than Jesus Christ alone?"

"I renounce it all. I only want Jesus."

"Then you are a new creature in Christ, and I welcome you as a brother." Swordsman embraced him. "God bless you and . . ."

"Joan," Tony said, slipping an arm around her waist. "Soon to be my wife. . . . Do you perform marriages?"

"I'm forbidden to do it by law, but I do have a friend who'll most certainly be happy to marry you elsewhere."

Hours later, Zachary and Michael stood on the roof of the auditorium looking out at the lights of the city, its brightness now rivaling that of the days before the disasters. The warmth of the unusual heat wave had disappeared, and a shift in wind brought a chill to the air. The two men buttoned their jackets to stave off the cold.

Michael took in the view below as he recalled his brother's childhood penchant for locating the highest lookout spots. "Still finding any way you can to get up on the roofs of buildings, eh?"

Zac chuckled. "Yeah."

"Are the meetings always like this?" Michael asked, leaning against a railing.

"Often. I wonder how Jesus must have felt, with people never letting Him alone, always pressing in to touch, to see, to hear. I'm only out there a few hours, and I'm totally drained."

After a short silence, Zac changed the subject. "Michael, if you only knew how many times I have asked for this. To see you again. To know you know the Lord."

"Oh. That reminds me." Michael started to reach into his shirt to get something, then stopped and leaned closer to his brother. "Is this a good place to talk?"

Zac straightened up, stepped back from the railing, and looked around the roof. He motioned to Michael and they moved over to a water-evaporation tower rising ten feet beyond the level of the roof. The sound of fans and rushing water filled the air around them. "We're probably safe from big ears here," he said.

Michael produced an envelope. "Here. It's a letter from a man called Jonathan at a refuge called Five Rivers."

"Is that where you were? How did you get there?"

"I was at the end of my rope and just decided to go and see if I could sort out the God thing. Of course, another major factor was . . . it's a long story. Read your letter first."

Zac looked around and figured if he sat with his back to the large light on the corner of the roof, it might be sufficient for reading. He plopped down and folded his long legs, Indian style.

Michael sat facing him, but with the light in his eyes, he could only see Zac's silhouette. He couldn't help thinking aloud while Zac tore open the letter. "Just wait till Sara hears Swordsman is her brother-in-law!"

Zac suddenly sat up more, then straightened his leg to give his brother a little kick. "NO! You got *married?* Who's Sara? What happened to Linda?"

"Long story."

Zac leaned forward and gave him a soft shove. "Don't tell me I'm an uncle, too!"

For the first time Zac could ever remember, Michael blushed. He could see it even in the dim light, and it made him roar with laughter.

"No, no," he said, smiling sheepishly. "We've only been married for a couple of months."

Zachary watched Michael's expression, then thought of their dear brother who had passed away. "Can you imagine how much we'll have to tell Ben when we see him? I can hardly wait. Remember how *crazy* we thought he was? I'll want to apologize for at least a hundred years. . . . Have you thought about how much he prayed for us? How we're probably here because he prayed for us?"

A sad smile came to Michael's lips. "Yes. Read your letter."

Zachary studied the letter intently then let out a sigh. "It's true."

"What is? What's true?" Michael asked.

"For some time now, I feel the Lord's been telling me that I'm to go on a trip. The way the government is about to cut off all public venues for us, I knew it had to be soon."

"What does the letter say?"

Zac folded the letter and put it inside his left shoe. While he re-tied it, he looked at his brother. "Some of us are going to try to gather in the zones and speak face to face. It may be the last opportunity we have."

"Oh," Michael said, sadly. "I thought things were looking up for the movement."

"Who says they aren't? People like me have been used to spread the message, to help scattered groups of Christians find each other, to pass information along in the forming network. But we have to be willing to let God direct the flow, and the time has come for a change. People like me, the visible ones, will be increasingly restricted," Zac said, "but Jesus will increase."

"You really think so, Zac?"

"Didn't you hear the parade earlier today? It's only a glimpse of the future."

"Did I hear it? I thought I'd go deaf! I was outside, right on the street, when they went by. It's like the return of the Reich."

"That's just the corner of it," Zac said. "You have no idea how they're breathing down our necks. Just tonight, thank you, Jesus, we had a man come forward and confess he'd been following me for the government. . . . They've tried sending me beautiful women. When that didn't work, they tried sending beautiful men. I get death threats almost daily now. Renting this auditorium was the struggle of the century—and they informed me tonight that in the future only people with codes will be able to obtain permits or rent public buildings." Zachary reached over and put a hand on his brother's shoulder. "And if the Lord didn't work miracles we wouldn't even have made it this far."

Michael smiled. "I still can't believe it's *you*," he said. "My brother. Swordsman."

"Sometimes, it's incredible to me, too. C'mon," he said, rising to his feet and stretching. "I'll buy you dinner while they still take cash. You can tell me all about my sister-in-law."

When they stepped out of the enveloping noise of the water evaporator, the wind blew a sound across the roof at them. Michael heard it first.

"Isn't there a lot of noise down there for this time of night?"

Zachary frowned. "Yes. You're right."

The brothers ran to the opposite side of the building and looked down. Below them, people lay strewn all over the ground like dolls. In the distance, they could see a lot of commotion and hear shouting and crying.

"What's going on?" Michael asked.

"I don't know, but I'm going to find out." Zachary trotted toward the stairs.

Michael's mind started racing around the possibilities. "Wait, Zac. Don't go down there. It could be a trap for you! Let me go first!"

"They need help, Michael, and I can't run away," Zachary said.

When they exited the building, they saw a middle-aged woman sitting on the ground. She held a blood-soaked handkerchief against her head.

Zachary knelt down and asked, "What happened?"

"I don't know," the dazed woman said. "We came out and those fellas in the tight, silky uniforms . . . they were waiting out here and started hitting all of us with those clubs. Then lights came on, and there were all sorts of cameras, and . . . I don't know after that."

Zachary moved her hand. "Let me see."

A large cut stretched from the outside corner of her eye to her hairline. Zachary placed a hand on the cut, and prayed quietly. When he removed his hand, the cut had disappeared. He helped her up. "Go home now, dear. Don't stay on the street."

Once they'd helped her to her feet and she seemed stable, Zac started running to where a struggle continued. Michael caught up and ran beside him. When they neared the largest soldier wielding a club, Zac charged him, calling out in a loud voice, "*In the name of the Lord Jesus Christ, I command you to flee!*"

To Michael's utter amazement, the man stopped and looked at him and Zac, then beyond them. The soldier's eyes grew wide and he turned to run. Other soldiers followed suit, some of them dropping their clubs in their hasty departure.

Confused, Michael turned around for a moment. "What were they look–" He stopped talking when he turned back and realized his brother had moved some distance away to speak to the battered people gathering around.

Zachary held up his hands. "The salvation of the righteous is from the Lord; He is their refuge in time of trouble. The Lord helps them and delivers them; He delivers them because they take refuge in Him."

People started raising their hands and praying. The cameras had gone, the attackers had fled; and the people who remained, despite being beaten and bruised, started singing songs of praise. Michael looked at them. It was easy to love the Lord in a meeting or when things were going well, but only His own children loved Him in persecution. Sadly, Michael realized, it had only just begun.

Calm came to the group. People held hands and listened as Swordsman addressed them again.

"Each of you, stay in contact with the others of your group. I just now received word about a gathering of leaders from many areas. No matter what changes take place, hold onto each other and know the Lord is with us all."

A chorus of exclamations went through the crowd.

"The meeting will be soon, so keep praying that God will give us wisdom."

The people walked away in small groups and soon most were out of sight.

One man stayed behind, waiting in the shadows. Brian Johnson was the other psychic who had been assigned to follow Swordsman. He'd been quietly waiting and watching these many months, and it had finally paid off. Not only did he have information about Swordsman and a possible secret meeting, but about Tony Bensen as well.

Chapter 67

Atlanta

Edwina Grant enjoyed more than three months of "freedom" after her trial. The first few days of her liberation, she felt such gratitude to be out, to see her dear friends, to walk outside . . . it was hard to consider doing anything for which she might be rearrested. Couldn't she quietly *suggest* things to people? Couldn't she take a back seat and let others do the things that would put her in jeopardy?

Col. Folson wasn't kidding about the serious consequences of active resistance. When she returned home, she found Isaac's soup kitchen boarded up. Paul and Virginia had lost their store as well. Her friend David had to be spirited away along with his mother, her sister, and several other elderly people in order to protect them from being taken into government custody.

How could Edwina remain a quiet observer of these things? How could she ignore the desperate needs of her neighbors while an imposed ghetto closed in around all of them? No. She couldn't stop helping people, wouldn't stop talking, wouldn't stop encouraging people to band together, to love one another, to be strong . . . to resist the encroaching darkness.

She'd had time to comfort Isaac over the closure of his soup kitchen and help him see God's love in the midst of his loss. She'd had time to say goodbye to those she loved.

"Next!" the guard bellowed.

Edwina stepped up to the uniformed man behind a narrow counter. To her left, stood the entrance to the platform where all prisoners would be held before boarding a train. How far would she travel? A cold breeze swept through open windows in the building, and she shivered.

The guard demanded that she place her small bag on the counter, then added. "You can't take any non-issue materials on the train." He searched the bag, hoping to find any food she might have squirreled away for the train ride. After rooting around and finding nothing to eat, he eyed Edwina, and noticed her sweater. He returned to the bag and pulled out a cotton jacket. "You're allowed *one* outer garment," he said, holding out the jacket, "hand the sweater over."

The sweater had been knitted with soft, autumn-colored yarns, and was a gift from David's daughter, Chase. Edwina's hands closed around the front of the sweater.

"You can take it off," he said, letting his right hand rest on the butt of the stun gun strapped to his waist, "or we can take it off you."

She closed her eyes and began unbuttoning it.

"Hurry up."

She watched him set the sweater aside, then heave the rest of her belongings onto a stack of parcels, cases and bags behind the counter. He didn't look at her again, but said, "Move to the door."

She put on the coat while she walked to the door. Once through it, her life in the city would be officially over. In all likelihood, she would never walk down an urban street, own a book, listen to music, see a photo of George, or know open fellowship with other believers again.

A woman in uniform unbolted the door and opened it. Edwina could hear the guard at the counter yelling "Next!" The door closed behind her, and the bolt clanked. Overlapping the front of the jacket for extra warmth, she silently prayed.

My comfort in my suffering is that Your promise preserves my life. The arrogant mock me without restraint, but I do not turn from Your love. Your life, Father, will be the theme of my song wherever I go. In the night I will remember your name, Lord, and see Your light. You are my portion, Jesus, and I have sought Your face with all my heart; be gracious to me according to Your promise. Though the wicked bind, I will not forget Your love, I will trust that You make the path before me straight.

The voice of a young man interrupted her thoughts. "You're Mrs. Grant, aren't you?"

Edwina turned to see a skinny, teenaged boy with a wave of blond hair swirled around his head and soft, blue eyes. He couldn't be more than fifteen years old.

"Yes," she replied. "Yes I am."

The boy shivered as a chilly gust blew through the fence at the open end of the platform. "My name's Quinn. You probably don't remember me, but you came to our apartment house and tended to my brother, Jack, a few months ago. He has Cerebral Palsy."

The prisoners on the platform began huddling together, hoping to retain a bit of warmth. Edwina and the young man were soon engulfed in the mass.

She remembered his brother. "Oh yes. Is he okay?"

The boy nodded and shivered again. "Should be safe now."

Instinctively, she put her arm around him. "What are you doing here, Quinn?"

The few conversations going on around them stopped as people listened for his response. "Troops came to take away my brother, so my dad carried him down the fire escape. Just before they got away, I saw a soldier coming around the back of the building to catch them. . . . I grabbed a clay pot on the window sill and threw it down on the soldier. Her partner stopped to help her, so my dad escaped with my brother. The soldier was hurt but she recovered. . . . I got twenty years."

"*Twenty* years?" a man nearby exclaimed. "Most of us probably won't last the winter!"

The boy bit his lip and averted his gaze. What could Edwina say? New laws, enacted in the past year, allowed any child over 14 to become a "liberated entity." Any person over this age could apply to be removed from parental custody, could take a code, or be charged as an adult and sent to an adult labor camp. Edwina surveyed the crowd around her. Most of these people believed they would die soon. Standing among them, it was hard to resist being absorbed by their fear.

A memory came to her mind. Two weeks before her final arrest, she entered the home of a dear friend. The woman's daughter, only nineteen, hugged her tightly and began to sob. Edwina could still hear the girl's voice, echoing words God had already spoken to her heart: "The Lord would say to you, 'If you continue in this way, you will be accused by those who falsely claim to know Me. You will be delivered into the hands of your enemies and suffer. You don't need to do this to earn My love. You're My beloved daughter and no one can touch the treasure that is already yours. But if you choose this way, you will also take My words to a place of great sorrow, great darkness. You will bring hope and Light to many who have lost all hope. If you choose this hard way, it will be for the sake of others.'"

That night, God was saying that she could still choose to stop. She could take the offers to escape to different locations and work in secret. No one would blame her for wanting to find a safer place to be . . . not even the Lord. The choice was hers to make.

Another sharp blast of wind whistling through the fence brought Edwina back to the present, back to a train station filled with frightened prisoners bound for a labor camp. She hugged the boy.

"I want to tell you something, Quinn," she said. "God is here with us. He knows what it feels like to be betrayed, to be hated, beaten . . . to be totally alone." She looked into his eyes, and then at the crowd around them. "He has sent me to tell you that He hasn't forgotten you."

Chapter 68

Alex Dubois sat in his quarters watching his muted viewer, too tired to go on with the work he'd brought with him. Suddenly, Linda's face appeared on the screen with a small "recorded earlier" tag in the left-hand corner. Alex turned up the volume, sat forward, and watched intently as she spoke.

". . . and what began as a minor confrontation has mushroomed rapidly into a battle." The screen filled with scenes of soldiers hitting, shoving, and pulling people. Her voice continued as the camera zoomed in here and there on particularly violent outbursts.

"As earlier viewers heard, we had a tip there might be violence near a location where fanatics had gathered for a meeting. Then, as far as we can piece together, some Universal Legion soldiers were walking in the area when they were ambushed by the fanatics. It looks as if they have gotten things almost under control now, but as you can see, it's been a pretty nasty fight."

The picture switched to show Linda in the studio. "Well," she said, "that was the way it looked several hours ago. Our cameraman was forced to leave the area for his own safety, but our latest update says troops finally managed to subdue and disperse the mob.

"What we would like to know is: How long will these fanatics be able to roam around at will? Would they have attacked just *anyone*? Are we safe from them? We now return to your regular programming. I'm Linda Posner."

Alex switched off his set. What was Linda doing? And by whose authority? The tone sounded, and his viewer came on.

"Priority One. Eyes Only."

He punched the keys. "Priority One, go ahead." He placed his hand on the side panel and read the words appearing on his screen:

MESSAGE FOLLOWS . . .

Have made information breakthrough re Cat Walk. Agent Bensen has revealed identity/purpose to

Swordsman. Fanatics now planning surprise move of massive number of followers within days. Will keep tight surveillance unless ordered to stop. Will try to send messages via computer or contact link whenever possible. This agent still undetected. Johnson . . .

MESSAGE ENDS

Alex sat, reading and re-reading the message. What should he do? Soon he realized he couldn't avoid telling them. He'd have to do it. He punched the keys to send the report on to John Klost and Kressman. He felt certain Linda's "news bulletin" was a staged event. This had gotten out of hand. His screen flashed.

PRIORITY ONE MESSAGE:

Proceed to main building. You will be brought to me.
Kressman.

MESSAGE ENDS

Forty-five minutes after receiving the message, Alex Dubois stood waiting at the main building. He shivered; not with cold, but with fear. His stomach burned with an alarming intensity. A man met him and led him up to the roof of the building. Within moments, Alex heard a loud whistling noise and looked up, searching the skies. A helicopter. He hadn't seen one in years.

This must be really serious, he thought, *for Kressman to send a helicopter where it can be seen by civilians.*

While the chopper came down on the "X" on the roof, he fought the urge to throw up. The door opened, and he ran to the chopper thinking how much excitement it must be causing on the streets below.

As soon as the craft lifted off the pad, John Klost gave instructions to a small, shy-looking little man. He told the man to find and kill Tony Bensen. John assured him no real investigation would take place, so he could use whatever method he chose—but he must leave no witnesses.

Chapter 69

A prison in the Northern Zones

As the sun set, people lay down on cold cement floors. Beyond the bars, out in the open cell block, the skylights in the tall ceiling darkened, signaling the official end of day. He'd been separated from the other prisoners in his group and thrown into this cell with about a dozen strangers. The whole place reeked of human waste; and, although no children occupied the cell, he could hear a child crying in the distance. Several women in his cell huddled together and cried as well.

Jason scooted back against a wall and closed his eyes, too tired to worry if the other people in the cell might be real criminals. It didn't really matter, he had nothing left to steal. Did he regret coming on the ranger's mission? Did he still think rescuing slaves was a good idea? He tried to resist touching the gash on his forehead with his dirty hands and wondered where Jen and Troy might be. The rangers had split everyone into small groups to increase the chances at least some of them would get through. Had his friends fared better and escaped capture? Would any of the groups make it south with some slaves? Would they live to tell Ricky, Rosa, and the others what had happened?

"Are you Jason?" a man moving near him asked.

He considered the fellow. *What if the guy is a spy*? Did it matter? "Yeah. I'm Jason."

"Jason from the Little Valley Refuge in Missouri?"

"Why do you want to know?"

"Some of your friends were brought in almost a week ago. They saw you arrive."

Jason could feel all the ears in the dark cell, listening. "How do you know that? Where are they?"

"You might see them tomorrow. They've been tortured, bad. A woman in the group told others to pass the word to Jason not to admit that you know them. . . . The rangers with your friends put up a big fight and killed at least twenty blinkers. It'll make things worse for you if you say you know them."

Outside the cell, a soldier leapt out of the darkness to whack the bars with something metal. Everyone jolted with the noise. "Shut up in there!" he yelled.

The man with the message stayed nearby, so when the soldier moved away, Jason whispered, "What about the rangers with them? Did any survive? Are they here?"

"There's a few, but they look about like raw hamburger by now. You'll see. The blinkers will drag them out of the cells tomorrow and either torture them some more or kill them."

Jason's blood ran cold. He didn't want to hear any more. It now seemed likely they had all been captured, and were being housed in a prison built long before the disasters. A prison far from any refuge or civilization. Unless the soldiers could use them as some sort of resource, it seemed doubtful they'd be allowed to live.

Jason leaned closer to the stranger. "Do most of the people here work at a factory or a farm or something? Why are the rest of you here?"

The sound of an approaching soldier brought all communication to a halt. The trooper stopped and stood in front of the cell. Jason could barely make out his shape, but not which way he faced. He was still standing there when Jason finally fell asleep.

Chapter 70

At the border to the Northern Zones

Zachary approached the gate, and the soldiers straightened. He walked up to the lieutenant.

"What do you want?" The soldier tried to sound intimidating, but Zachary could see he was probably only in his early twenties and smiled at him.

"Good day, sir," Zachary began. "We would like permission to cross the border."

"What?"

"We would like permission to cross the border."

"*All* of you?"

"Well, actually, more are coming. We're not all here yet."

"What on earth for?" The soldier's eyes opened wider.

"We're having a conference."

All border outposts had been alerted to the possibility a number of fanatics would seek to enter the zones. The soldier just never believed it would happen. Certainly not at his gate. "Out there?" He said, pointing to the barren land on the other side of the fence.

"Beyond there."

"I'm sorry, you can't go out there."

"Is it illegal?"

He knew better than to answer the question. "That's not the point. I am charged with public safety and I cannot permit you to endanger yourselves by entering the zones."

"We're willing to take full responsibility for our own safety."

"No can do. You can't pass this gate."

"If you're unwilling to let us pass, I must ask you to radio for permission."

"It could take hours . . . or days," said the soldier, hoping this would end the matter.

"We'll wait."

The young man took off his helmet and scratched his head. He hated to think this fanatic could make him do anything, much less call his superiors. These people really were demented. Only this morning he'd read how a man named Bensen had no sooner become a fanatic then he'd killed two people: his girlfriend and a minister (or whatever fanatics called them). After doing them in, he'd committed suicide next to their bodies in a small courtyard. The girl had flowers in her hair so it was presumed they had just performed one of their primal rituals. The paper hinted it could have been some sort of death-pact. The article showed the most gruesome pictures. . . . What maniacs these people were.

The young soldier decided he'd have to call his superiors. They'd want to know about any gathering of this size.

"Wait here," he said. Fifteen minutes later he found himself speaking with the regional commander.

"What reason are they giving you?" the commander asked.

"To have some sort of conference," the soldier said.

"I'll get back to you," the commander barked before hanging up.

Outside, people sat on the ground or stood in small groups.

"What will we do if they say no?" Michael asked.

"They won't," Zachary answered.

Twenty minutes later, the young soldier emerged from the small station house and called to the sentries standing at the gate. "Open them!"

The guards ran to the center of the gates, hauled them open, then stood on either side with eyes straight forward as the people walked through. Later, they would do the same for the soldiers who followed.

Chapter 71

A prison in the Northern Zones

The barest amount of sunlight had touched the skylights in the main cell block when the soldiers started yelling and banging on the cells.

"Wake up! Wake up!"

Jason opened his eyes and remembered where he was. He tried to get up and realized he hurt all over. By the looks of the other prisoners, they felt the same. He got to his feet.

A fellow prisoner came close, and when he spoke, Jason recognized the voice from the night before. "We'll work until eleven. Then they feed us. Eat it no matter what it is. It's the only meal we get."

A soldier unlocked the cell door and stepped back. "Everybody out."

They poured out of the cell door and stood in the open area of the cell block with dozens of other prisoners who had occupied different cells during the night. At a signal, they proceeded toward a particular door at the other end of the room. When Jason got closer to it, he could see several soldiers standing in the hallway with stun sticks. One of them had been with the troops who captured Jason, three rangers, and the seven slaves traveling with them. They had executed Bob Ulman and the other two rangers before the two-day forced march to the prison. One of the slaves died on the way, the rest of them had been placed in separate cells.

As they reached the doorway, a soldier pointed to Jason's traveling companions, saying, "That one, that one, that one."

Once identified, the selected prisoner was pulled from the main flow and forced to stand to the side. Jason was the last one of the group to approach the door.

"And that one."

Rough hands yanked him out of line and shoved him against a wall. The soldiers told him to stand with the three adults and three teens he'd helped to rescue from a factory ten days ago. Next, soldiers escorted the seven captives away from the main group and into an interrogation room. The only other male prisoner besides Jason, a man in his forties named Jerry, looked even more frightened than the teenagers.

A tall, female officer with a crew-cut came into the room with four other soldiers and looked them over. "Which one of you wants to talk to me first?"

"I will," Jason answered.

"*He* was with the rangers!" Jerry blurted out. "He was with them. The rest of us are just workers. We'll work hard for you."

"We're *all* workers," a teen girl by the name of Lakisha added, "He's just from a different factory."

"We're all workers," two more prisoners echoed.

The female officer raised one eyebrow. She seemed amused. "Really? I guess we'll have to question everyone thoroughly to clear up this confusion." She moved closer to Jason. "And just what did *you* want to say?"

Jason looked at the other prisoners. All of them except Jerry bravely looked back at him. "I'm not a worker," Jason said. "We kidnaped them so we could take them south as trophies. Look at their legs and you'll see they've worn shackles for a long time. We picked them because we could see they were hard workers and we knew it would help to cripple your efforts in the north."

The officer turned to her soldiers. "He must be friends with ol' dead eye."

They laughed.

She pointed to Jason. "Arrange a reunion for our new guest," she ordered, before signaling that the other prisoners could be taken out of the room. One of the soldiers hit Jason with a stun stick, causing him to convulse and collapse on the floor.

"Time to join your pals!" his tormentor exclaimed. "Come on! Get up! This should be a happy occasion for you."

Jason looked up at the other prisoners being escorted out the door.

"Don't think you're off the hook," the officer said to them. "There will be more time for you to answer questions after work tonight."

The soldier with the stun stick threatened Jason with it again. "Are you gonna take a nap, or are you gonna cooperate?"

Jason got up on all fours, and then struggled to his feet. "I'm getting up."

Two soldiers fastened his hands behind his back with a strap before they led him to a cell filled with prisoners and opened the door. Although they'd been badly beaten, Jason recognized several of the people inside. One of them was Jen.

As soon as the door closed, she ran to hug him, "Jason! I'm so sorry you're here. You look dreadful."

"You don't exactly look your best, either," he said. "Sorry I can't hug you back. I'm kind of tied up at the moment."

Jen exchanged looks with some of the other prisoners. "Yes. They'll keep your hands bound for the first day."

"Where's Troy?" Jason asked, hoping his friend was still walking south. "Does anyone know where he is?"

"I'm over here," Troy answered.

The crowd of prisoners slowly parted. Jen grabbed Jason's shoulder and shook it to get his attention. When he looked at her, he saw her eyes had filled with tears. She shook her head no, and put a finger to her lips.

They had placed Troy on a small pile of clothes in the back of the cell. Jason moved swiftly to his side and knelt down before he realized what had happened. Someone had knocked out both of his dear friend's eyes.

Chapter 72

One of Kressman's estates

Alex Dubois peered into the fish tank, absently watching the brightly colored fish darting about. After the long trip by helicopter and all the hours by jet to Kressman's location, he'd just sat around and waited. For nearly three days, he'd waited. In a room without windows.

He'd gotten over being scared, then bored. Now anger took its turn. He'd been almost plucked up off the street and rushed to a faraway country for this dire emergency, then forced to cool his heels in this . . . little space. As each minute ticked by, he grew more aggravated.

He looked around his room once more, trying to think of something he could do to kill time, to keep from thinking about this demeaning situation. What was he anyway? A butler who must wait in the dark bowels of the palace until summoned? The tone sounded, and a small, olive-skinned man opened his door.

"Follow please," he said, before walking back out the door.

Alex had to sprint a few steps to catch up with him before he got away. He said nothing for the rest of the walk, but Alex could hear various sounds throughout the building . . . voices, music, and the whir of machinery. The man stopped at the bottom of a small flight of stairs and motioned for Alex to go up them.

At the top, he entered an open doorway leading into a large room. Three of the walls flashed with hundreds of small television screens, presumably lit with news and other networks belonging to his employer. After one sweeping glance, Alex's eyes gravitated to the huge desk with a shiny black top located at the center of a large expanse of empty floor space. Behind the desk sat Kressman.

"Good afternoon, Alex."

"Good afternoon, Mr. Kressman." He'd been furious only minutes ago; now, in the man's presence, his anger evaporated.

"I trust you've rested well."

"Yes, sir."

"I'm sorry I kept you waiting. I had so many urgent things to do after I sent for you and I've just now found the time to speak to you."

"That's quite all right, sir," Alex said.

"At least you got a trip out of it."

"Yes, sir. I hadn't ridden on a jet in years. It was a pleasant flight, too."

Kressman touched a flashing light on his desktop, then turned to look at the bank of television screens on the wall behind him. Nearly half of them seemed to be showing odd weather phenomena. Six of the screens in the middle abruptly changed picture, then simultaneously locked onto the same signal. Former First Lady, Edith Todd, appeared on all of them wearing a simple white blouse and a pin with Kressman's familiar triple-triangle insignia.

Although Mr. Kressman watched the image of Mrs. Todd, he made no attempt to turn up the sound. After a few moments, Alex thought he heard sounds. With each exhale, Kressman seemed to be breathing out words. Alex leaned forward to hear.

". . . women . . . vile creatures."

Surely, Alex thought, *he didn't say that.*

Kressman whirled around in his chair and said, "Now as to why you are here." He leaned forward and pressed another light in the desktop. The bank of screens on Alex's left instantly melded—like drops of water forming a larger drop.

Before Dubois could express his awe over the liquid merge, the single screen lit up with a world map. It reminded him of the maps used in strategic war rooms of times past. Kressman rose from his chair, and they walked over to the map. Alex could see hundreds of flashing yellow and green lights all over it, but Kressman pointed to the ones on the North American continent. "Since you left, fanatics have crossed into the zones at these points," he stated, indicating the yellow lights. "We have not disturbed them, but we have troops ready at some distance behind each major group," he said, now pointing to the green lights.

We have troops, Alex thought, glancing around the world at the multitude of flashing yellow and green lights. "So it's happening elsewhere?" said Alex, thinking aloud.

"I'm afraid so. Without much warning, they've gathered in large groups for some spur-of the-moment event. We don't know exactly what they're planning next, but we've let them begin their little game and we're ready this time."

Alex couldn't help but wonder how the fanatics could co-ordinate such a thing on a global level with no reliable kind of communication system. Then Kressman's words sunk in. "Ready this time?" he asked.

"Yes. At nine tonight I want you to arrange a satellite linkup around the globe. I've tried every possible way to incorporate these . . . people . . . into society. You know I have. But there's simply no more time. They'll have to make their final choice." Kressman seemed to straighten and appear taller.

Alex felt sick inside. What had he done? Certainly Kressman wouldn't kill all of them. What had become of tolerance? Even Kressman couldn't get away with this . . . could he?

A group of military men entered the room. They each wore different uniforms, but all had gold buttons and braids, so Alex assumed each was the commander of his respective forces.

Kressman eyed them for a moment. "Are you prepared? Have you considered all contingencies?" He waited while they each answered in the affirmative. He stood in front of the maps and asked, "Have you pulled in all extra possible reinforcements? Will weapons be fully functional?" Again, they answered yes.

"Good," he replied. "After our troops have finished their tasks and are at safe distances, I want the warheads used on the rebels in the unpopulated zones." He pointed to several locations, then turned. "Those in populated vectors will be easily rounded up when my announcement is over. Until then, avoid public bloodshed if at all possible. After my broadcast, those who are arrested can be executed—one by one—in front of their co-conspirators. And by all means . . . women and children first."

A salute was the unanimous reply.

A hint of a smile came to Kressman's face before he said, "Dismissed." They all scrambled from the room before he looked at Alex again.

Under the weight of Kressman's stare, he slumped into a chair. This had to be a nightmare. "What are you saying?" Alex managed to say. "We can't do this!"

Kressman shook his head. "Can't we? When it's over, you can wash your hands in one of those silly little bowls of yours—that will make it right, won't it?"

Alex's words tumbled out slowly. "You know it's not . . . the water. If the soul . . . isn't surrendered . . . to the higher principles . . ."

Kressman leaned toward Alex and spoke in that familiar, imperative-yet-soft voice. "And, what principles would those be? You live by *my* principles now. I own you. I own your soul. You've done exactly what I wanted you to do. . . . You've relinquished everything—even your own flesh and blood—in order to serve me." The satisfied smile returned. "And, when your job is finished, I'll let you know."

Chapter 73

A prison in the Northern Zones

Jason hoped his interrogators believed he knew nothing more about the rangers or their future plans. He'd been beaten unconscious and thrown back in the cell with the others. Jen tended to his wounds as best she could. She'd already used almost everyone's sleeves to keep re-bandaging Troy. A man tore off a remaining sleeve for her to use on Jason. Before she bandaged him, she ripped off a small portion to wet with water dripping from a rusty pipe in the cell, so she could clean the gash on his head.

Again, there had been no food for any of the people in the cell. They hadn't seen a scrap of food in three days. At least they'd untied his hands.

Jason crawled over beside Troy. "Hey, bud, how you doing?"

"Actually," he said, before clearing his throat, "I think I feel a bit better today. If I still had my wallet, I'd ask you to run down to the corner for pizza."

"Yeah? What would you take on your half?"

"Half? No, man, I'd get at least one all to myself. Loaded with pepperoni, sausage, black olives, and onions."

Jason's stomach made a loud noise. "Stop. My stomach thinks you're serious." He looked at the other people in the cell who'd gathered by the bars to confer with one another. Leaning closer to Troy, he said, "Be back in a second. Gotta go see what the meeting's about." He got up very slowly, then moved over to the group. "What's the deal?"

A man by the name of Frank turned and said, "They took most of the other prisoners away and they haven't returned. Maybe the soldiers are taking them back to farms or factories."

"Would they bother to do that?" Jason wanted to know.

"Maybe they figure these people will tell other slaves there's no point in escaping."

Everyone nodded. It made sense.

By nightfall, they knew the majority of the prisoners had been removed from the prison. Occasionally, a few soldiers roamed the open area of the cell block. Jason could see only one or two prisoners in several other cells, and Jen told him the remaining rangers were in a cell just out of their sight. They hadn't been dragged out for their daily beating for two days; but the last time she saw them, Major Tam, Luke Norris, and the female ranger, Sam—along with several other captured rangers—they were still alive.

The prison grew dark once again, and Jason wondered how much longer they could live without food. All of them sat in a circle around Troy and held hands to pray.

"Father," Frank began, "we gather tonight before You, not knowing what lies ahead, but confident You haven't left us."

After a few moments of silence, Jason said, "I had kind of hoped to be alive when Jesus came back. But, if You have other plans, Lord, I surrender to them."

"Yes, me too," others added.

They heard a small sound by the bars and turned to look. A soldier they could barely distinguish from the darkness beyond stood there. He didn't tell them to be quiet. He seemed to be waiting for them to notice him.

Jason broke the circle and crawled to the bars. "What do you want?" he whispered.

The answer came so softly, Jason had to strain to hear it. "I want . . ." the soldier said, then reached through the bars.

Jason flinched, thinking the man would grab him or strike him.

"I want," he repeated, "for you to know we aren't all like that. Not all of us are like cruel animals. Here . . . take it."

He realized the man had something in his hand. He reached out and grasped the dark, oblong object. A potato. Once Jason took it, the hand withdrew, then came back through the bars again, with another potato.

Frank crawled over. "What are you doing?" he whispered.

"Shhhhh," Jason answered. "Here, pass them on," he said, handing the potatoes to Frank.

The hand came through the bars again and again until each of the prisoners had a potato. When the last potato had passed through the bars, the soldier whispered, "Remember me when you pray to your God. Tell Him I didn't want to help them, that I *did* help you." After his last words, he silently moved back into the darkness.

Jason peered into the black void for a few moments before he scooted back to his friends. Jen said a blessing on the food, then told them all to eat very slowly and chew well.

###

When Jason awoke, daylight had come again. He slowly reached over and put a hand on Troy's chest.

"I'm alive," his friend said quietly. "Is the sun up?"

"Yes," Jason answered.

Others in the cell started stirring.

"Can you help me up?" Troy asked. "I'd like to try standing today."

Jen's face appeared on the other side of Troy. She and Jason had slept with Troy between them, taking turns tending to him and praying for him. "I think perhaps we should settle for sitting up a while," she said.

They helped him scoot back against a wall.

"Well?" Jen asked, "How is it?"

They could see the color draining out of his face before he responded shakily, "Well, maybe I'll just sit here a minute."

Soldiers entered the cell block, making quite a bit of noise. They went to several cells, collected the people in them, and took them away. No one came to Jason's cell or to the cell with the rangers inside.

"What's going on?" Troy asked.

"They came and took the other prisoners away. All of the ones they took today are old or look sickly. Most of them are women. That supports the theory they took the other slaves back to factories or work farms."

"What about the rangers?"

Jason frowned. "I haven't seen any of them. Maybe they're still in their cell, like we are."

Within a few minutes, Troy needed to lie down again.

"That was good, though," Jason told him. "Maybe tomorrow you'll be able to sit up for even longer."

###

By the middle of the day, they heard another racket. Jason and everyone except Troy went to the bars to see soldiers coming back into the building with the elderly prisoners. This time, one of the soldiers told them to put the slaves "with the other prisoners."

The cell door opened and they made room for the new prisoners.

"Where's Anne? Where's Anne?" one of the new prisoners asked the others who had been outside. They had each been assigned tasks, mostly loading up gear for the soldiers, but no one had seen where Anne had been taken.

About an hour later, one soldier entered the cell block with Anne. Probably in her seventies, she looked exhausted.

"Get back!" the soldier ordered all of them as he approached the cell. Jason and the others pressed to the rear of the cell, and he unlocked the door.

"They're going to leave us here to die!" Anne sobbed as he pushed her in and closed the door. "They're all leaving!" she repeated, falling to her knees and weeping. The women who knew her huddled around, trying to comfort her.

The soldier remained at the door and pointed to Jason. "You. Come here."

Jason looked at Jen and the others, then complied.

"Come to the door," the soldier ordered.

Jason's heart leapt about as he moved toward the door.

"That's close enough," the man said when the prisoner stood mere inches from it. "Hands on the bars."

Jason stared into dark brown eyes as he put one hand, then the other on the bars of the door—and something occurred to him. He knew this was the man who had fed them.

The brown eyes moved to the lock of the door and froze there for a few seconds. "I bet it will be the last time any of you hears *this* sound," he said, turning the key in the lock one way, then the other. He'd locked it, then *unlocked* it! "That's right," he said loudly, "you just stand there like an idiot and hold onto that door for a good long time." His eyes had fastened on Jason's again. "Maybe you'll get tired of doing it when we've been gone a while." With that, the soldier turned and left the building.

Jason stood, frozen in place, not daring to reveal what he knew until certain they were safe.

Chapter 74

A prison in the Northern Zones

Once they'd gotten out, Jason, Jen, and several companions rushed toward the rangers' cell. They found ten rangers there, four of them critically injured. Major Tam seemed closest to death. Sam, the female ranger, and her partner slipped in and out of consciousness. Luke Norris, although alert, could barely move. Much to everyone's dismay, the door of the ranger's cell remained locked.

Most of the freed prisoners disbursed throughout the prison to see if they could find food, and anything—pry bars, saws, or keys—which might free the rangers from their cell. Two men went outside to scout around. Reaching through the bars, Jason and Jen did what they could to tend the wounded while several of the older women rested nearby with Troy.

The prisoner named Frank returned with several sleeping mats he'd found in the soldiers' quarters. They stuffed them through the bars so the critically injured could be placed on them. An hour later, someone found a set of keys and brought them into the cell block.

They tried most of the keys before one of them finally turned in the lock. Jason swung open the door, and they brought the rangers out to the central cell block. The sun would set in less than two hours.

"What do we do now?" one of the women asked. "Should we try to get away tonight?"

Jen and Jason had already made personal decisions.

"Whoever feels able should be free to go," Jen said. "If you find food or help and you're not far away, then come back and help us. If you have the strength to keep going and you find no help, then keep going." She placed a hand on Sam's arm. "I'm staying here."

"I'm with Jen," Jason added. "No one can blame you for wanting to escape from this place. Get away if you can."

"Let's be practical," Frank stated matter-of-factly. "First of all, it'll be dark soon. Even those who can still walk wouldn't get very far. I think we should continue to scout around inside and outside for anything we can eat. In the morning, those who want to leave should leave."

Everyone agreed. During another search of the barracks, one of the women found a sprouting, ten-pound bag of potatoes in an old toolbox. Obviously, the soldier who stashed it there hadn't been able to retrieve it before the hasty departure.

Although remaining inside the prison for the night seemed an unpleasant choice, they all realized the building's roof and walls would keep them out of the cold winds and inclement weather moving through the area. The prison had no power, so they couldn't cook on any of the stoves. They settled for building a fire on the floor of the open cell block and cooking the potatoes over it, using a large pot from the kitchen.

"Would you like a sip of soup?" Jen asked Sam when the ranger opened her eyes.

"No," she managed to say. "Not hungry."

"You sure? It's warm. Just a little broth?"

She wanted to know about her partner. "How's Dolan?"

Jen sadly shook her head. "He's getting weaker."

"Why are you still here?" the ranger asked, closing her eyes. "Get away while you can."

"No, Sam. I was sent on this trip for you. I won't leave you like this."

In the firelight, Jen could see the slightest smile light Sam's face for a moment. "I know," the ranger said. "Made me mad at first. I knew God sent you after me . . . and I wanted so much to get away."

Jen rested on her elbow, near Sam's head. "You oughta know by now, you can't ever really get away from Him. He loves people relentlessly."

The ranger lifted her hand slightly and Jen clasped it before Sam spoke. "I don't know what to say. . . . It seems kinda late to surrender."

"No, it's not," Jen responded.

"I've done a lot of really bad things. . . ."

"It doesn't matter. God can wash you clean. He can do it right this minute, Sam. Jesus died to set you free. . . . He's been waiting your whole life for this! But, you obviously know what you need to do. You need to surrender. You have to let go of your old life and accept the one He's offering. Do you want to leave the guilt, the sorrow, and the burden of all that anger behind?"

Sam closed her eyes and exhaled deeply. "Yes, I do."

Jen began to pray with her.

Several feet away, Jason once again assessed Major Tam. The man's breathing became more labored as he slipped further into a coma. Jason prayed silently for him and for Dolan before he moved on to look at Luke Norris.

"How you feeling?" he asked.

Norris spoke through clenched teeth. "Like a truck hit me," his voice squeaked. "Several times."

"Do you think you could keep some soup down?"

The ranger opened his eyes and looked at the ceiling above them, no longer seeing any of his surroundings. Instead, he pictured Jason's foster-sister, Amanda, with a thick braid of strawberry blond hair draped over her shoulder. "I won't get back to the refuge to see her . . . will I?"

Jason didn't answer him.

"You'll tell her I loved her, and I always wanted the best for her, won't you?"

"I have a feeling," Jason said quietly, "we'll both see her at the same time."

Anyone who could eat or drink did so. Although they stayed near the fire, a terrible darkness grew closer each passing minute. With the soldiers gone, all the prisoners could freely talk, yet words became harder and harder to speak. Even the light of the fire became increasingly dim against the invading blackness.

"Jason?" Troy called out.

"Yes?" he said, sliding close.

"Help me sit up. I'd like to read the Bible out loud for a while."

Most of the people looked at the blind man with pity.

Jason noticed the stares, but smiled at Jen as he propped up his friend. The others didn't know what they knew. Troy had devoted the past two years of his life to memorizing the gospel of John.

By now, the silence and blackness around them could almost be touched. When Troy spoke, however, both began to retreat. "If any of you doesn't know Jesus personally," he said, "now would be a good time to hear and believe. . . . The gospel according to John, chapter one. '*In the beginning was the Word, and the Word was with God, and the Word was God. The same was in the beginning with God. All things were made by him; and without him was not anything made that was made. In him was life; and the life was the light of men. And the light shineth in darkness; and the darkness comprehended it not...*'"

The prisoners huddled together in the growing warmth, Jen sat between Sam and Dolan, holding their hands.

Chapter 75

Dallas

A huge storm threatened outside the television studio as Linda sat in the control booth, watching the monitors. Word had gone out to all stations: An important announcement, being broadcast from the other side of the globe would be coming through shortly and replacing all programming. Kressman's face appeared on the screens, and she turned up the sound.

After a short greeting, he began. "On November 18, 1978, over nine hundred people committed suicide in a South American jungle in some sort of religious ritual with the man who led them there. Since then, many other acts of religious fanaticism have resulted in the loss of many thousands of lives.

"I come to bring you the sad news of the last few hours. The religious fanatics, in some sort of united frenzy, have banded together to destroy themselves with a dreaded contaminant. Whether they just mean to kill themselves, or to take all of us with them, I do not know. Not only do we expect incidents in the Zones of some countries, but in the cities as well.

"In view of the possible world-wide scope of this disaster," the camera angle widened to show a group of people behind Kressman, "the leaders of the world have asked my assistance; and we are declaring an international emergency. We have only a short amount of time to rectify the situation. This we must do.

"I want to make this point clear: Law-abiding citizens have nothing to fear. We hope to have the matter in hand shortly. The first order of business will be to declare fanaticism—radical, fundamental Christianity—a dangerous, terrorist movement. Those found guilty of being fanatics or of assisting them in any way will be subject to extreme penalties.

"If any of you suspect someone of being a fanatic, please contact authorities. We can no longer afford to let these dangerous people roam the streets. Our safety—the safety of our children—is at stake. If you see a fanatic, don't risk talking to that person. Get away as soon as possible. They may already be walking the streets, ready to unleash deadly contaminants upon unsuspecting people. So, again, please contact the authorities.

"Of course, justice has been, and still is, our highest goal. I give my solemn oath to you that anyone who is taken into custody without resistance during this sweep will be given ample chance to prove his or her allegiance.

"Meantime, know your leaders have united in purpose and given me . . ."

Alex Dubois stood in the next room. He could hear Kressman's voice . . . that soothing voice, and he fought off the effect of it. He'd made a vow. He tried to strengthen it. He called up the images of Kressman laughing at him . . . declaring him damned . . . watching those revolting pictures and enjoying them . . . standing on the verge of annihilating multitudes under the guise of "justice."

Alex looked like a madman now. . . . His eyes darted around the room. He saw what he needed inside a wall-mounted display case. He tried the front door to it and, to his surprise, it opened. He reached in and grasped the artifact in the middle. The sword.

Kressman continued speaking on camera. Alex entered the room trying to fight the sedating sound of the voice. He slowly stepped toward the front of the room, holding the sword against his leg.

He inched closer and closer. Now he stood only ten feet away. Kressman, not even noticing him, kept speaking.

". . . this is all we need . . . in fact, it's been fulfilled right now. *It has come!* It has all been delivered to me. I am not a powerless creature from a book but *a great force to be honored!*"

Alex, burning with rage now, lifted the sword and ran. Before he could be stopped, the sword found its mark, splitting into Kressman's skull.

Kressman fell back on the floor amidst great confusion and screaming. The camera got jostled a few times.

"I've done it!" Alex shouted into the camera. "I've rescued you!"

###

Watching from a control booth thousands of miles away, Linda sat in a state of shock. Was that *Alex?* What was he doing there? What had he just done?

###

A large man near Kressman ran forward, grabbed the sword, and stabbed Alex through the stomach with it. With cameras taking in the entire scene, Alex fell to the floor. As he felt his life draining away, he couldn't believe what he saw. Mr. Kressman got up and walked to him amid all sorts of pandemonium!

We must both be dead, Alex thought.

Kressman bent down—only a large red scar on his forehead now. He put an arm under Alex and pulled him close before whispering, "Well done! You let me use you to the last! Now go and wait for me!"

They were the final words Alex heard before dying.

The announcer could hardly contain himself. His voice quaking with emotion while he described the incredible scene, witnessed live around the world. "I tell you. He is amongst us. Our God! Not only is he living after a mortal blow, but he just bent down to embrace and forgive the man who inflicted the wound! . . . I can't go on . . ." he cried into the microphone.

Chapter 76

In the Northern Zones

Michael sat on a large rock and rested. He, Zachary, and a few others had moved to the rear of the group when they reached the edge of the canyon. Many had descended into the canyon, but now darkness approached, and a storm gathered in the distance, so those still at the top stopped.

They'd walked for days, and everyone was tired. But now, as it got darker and cooler, Michael's energy level picked up and he wanted to get into the canyon. He didn't think he'd be able to sleep much, knowing Sara would be waiting. He prayed silently for a while before he finally fell asleep.

In the canyon below, Ricky sat with Rosa and their children. Although they'd traveled far, the tiredness left his body and the heaviness he'd been feeling for months left his soul. Whether they would live and go on, or perish from the earth was entirely in the Lord's hands now.

All these people had come to seek the Lord together and worship Him with all they had. Like other believers around the world, they wanted Jesus to come and take them away . . . but, like the others, he would say, "Thy will be done."

On the cliff, far above Ricky and the others, Brian Johnson lay down among those who waited for daylight so they could walk into the canyon below. Once he felt sure his companions had fallen asleep, he crept away some distance and tried to make mental contact with his telepathic partner, to let him know all of the people hadn't made it into the canyon by nightfall, but that he believed this would be the final destination.

Zachary fell asleep, but not before seeing a man creep away from camp. The same man who had been following him. He'd almost prevented the man from coming, but felt prompted by the Lord to let him come along. Zac knew the man was . . . wrong somehow, but decided to leave it in the Lord's hands.

Long before daybreak, Zac's eyes opened. He sat up and looked around. Some of the others had already begun to stir.

He got up and walked among the few who still slept, touching each one saying, "Wake up. It's time to pray."

He stood over the last man. He hesitated and inwardly prayed, *Lord, I know in my heart this man doesn't belong to us. Should I let him sleep?*

He heard the answer inwardly, "*No. Wake him.*"

"Wake up." Zac said, tapping the man's foot with his own. "It's time to pray."

Brian Johnson opened his eyes and looked around. It was still dark! He stood uncomfortably with the others who gathered together to pray. He could barely see them in the darkness. Soon, silence fell on them and continued for several minutes.

"I'm going down now," Zachary said abruptly.

The group began forming a line behind him.

"Wait!" a voice called out from the rear. "You want us to go now? It's *dark!* Someone could fall and be killed. The path is very narrow. Those are sheer cliffs!"

Zac couldn't see him, but knew who spoke. "In any case," he replied, "I'm going. Anyone who wants to stay, may do so."

The people started singing a song as they approached the edge.

Brian hesitated and then caught up, grabbing the last man by the arm. "Why are you following that insane man?" he asked.

Michael turned to look at Brian. "We're not following *him*. There's not one of us here who wouldn't do this with or without him. The *Lord* is calling, and we're going." With that, he turned and walked on.

Brian hesitated again, trying not to panic. *If they can, I can,* he said to himself as he walked shakily to the rim and stopped. A dark abyss yawned in front of him, with a two-foot-wide ribbon of rock leading into it. If only he had time to meditate and prepare for this. He took a deep breath and followed the sound of the singing. After a minute, he'd gotten near Michael again.

Michael continued to move smoothly along while Brian stiff-leggedly followed, clinging to any rock, branch, or twig sticking out from the face of the cliff. Soon, Michael got out of sight again, and Brian struggled to move faster.

He came to a large opening in the cliff—some sort of cave? His sense of foreboding grew when he peered into the pitch black opening. He feared something terrible lurked inside. Although everything in him wanted to halt his pursuit, Brian could hear the seconds ticking. The others would quickly get away if he didn't hurry.

He gathered all his courage to move past the opening. He took a step. He took a few more. When he reached the midway point in the opening, he saw it: a gleaming figure coming at him from within the cave. It had the features of a man, but was much larger and wore gleaming armor. The fierce countenance of the figure filled Brian with terror. He stepped back to avoid the huge glowing sword. Soundlessly, he vanished over the edge of the cliff.

###

Gerald woke up. He'd been Brian Johnson's telepathic partner throughout this project and had traveled with the group of soldiers following Brian and the Swordsman.

They'd set up camp when Gerald received the message from Brian saying some of the fanatics had stopped at the rim of the canyon. Satellite imagery confirmed Brian's message.

After all of the fanatics got down into the canyon tomorrow, the troops would move in. Gerald could hardly wait. Watching each of them squirm and beg to take a code was something he'd looked forward to for a long time. His participation might merit a commendation! Maybe he'd get to join the Universal Legion!

But a nightmare had awakened him. He sat up. . . . What a wild dream, he thought. Walking this tiny path into darkness and then seeing this glowing object and falling, falling, falling until he jerked and woke up.

Chapter 77

With blood-red eyes, the former Reverend, Ike Bointon stood and watched the attempted assassination following Kressman's speech. Awakened earlier by the sound of civil defense sirens, he ran out of his apartment. No longer owning a viewer, and not knowing his neighbors, he'd rushed to a nearby store to see the viewers in the window. Watching the replays over and over, he realized one thing: The Swordsman had been right all along.

He began to wander the streets, not knowing what to do. The sun hadn't come up, and the sky remained very dark with storm clouds.

Without thinking, he'd walked to the front of his old dome. When he realized where he was, he sat on the steps and wept.

A man came by and spoke to him, "Here, here. What's wrong?"

Ike looked up and saw Mr. Brentworth, a faithful ex-circle member.

"Oh! Rever– Mr. Bointon," Brentworth said, embarrassed. "What are you doing? Haven't you heard? It's very exciting . . . We'll finally get things under control now."

Ike searched the man's eyes. "You still don't understand, do you? You always were easy to fool. . . . You still don't get it. The fanatics don't have any contamination. They don't plan suicide. But as long as they continue to exist, they prove him wrong. He's going to kill them all."

A look came into Brentworth's eyes. He understood all right. "Okay . . . yes . . . I see," he said, backing up slowly. "Don't you worry now. Just stay right here. . . . I'll be back in a jiffy." Once he'd gotten a safe distance, he broke into a run.

Ike knew Brentworth would head for the nearest troops. He knelt on the steps to pray; then he stood, strode up the steps, and walked around to the side of the dome. After smashing in a window, he crawled through it and ran to a room in the basement. In the room sat boxes and boxes of unused books. He broke open a carton and pulled out a Bible. He held it for a moment and closed his eyes tightly.

"Jesus, I'm sorry. You tried to tell me, and I didn't listen. Forgive me. I believe You now. Help me."

Filling with energy, he grabbed two of the boxes, ran up the steps, and threw them out the broken window. He did this several times, throwing all the boxes outside.

He made one last trip down the stairs and looked around in a closet. He found a white robe and put it on. Then he found the supplies for the building upkeep. He browsed among the many containers of paint until he found one can of paint in particular.

"Crimson." He smiled. "Perfect."

He quickly opened the can and found a large brush. Dipping the brush into the color, he painted a huge cross on the front of the robe.

Minutes later, he walked along the street, passing out Bibles, putting them in doorways, mail boxes, anywhere they'd fit.

"*I am no longer ashamed!*" he cried to people walking by. He woke others in their homes. If anyone looked as if they'd listen, he shared his heart with them, then asked if they wanted Jesus as their Savior. He spent two hours on the street, giving out every one of the Bibles. Thirty people had prayed with him.

Mr. Brentworth helped troops track Bointon down, then stood and watched as troops fired seventeen bullets into Ike's body. The soldiers gave him the job of "guarding" the body while they cordoned off the entire street, "to avoid hysteria."

The sky remained dark, and a stiff wind began to blow down the street. Brentworth felt jumpy about being alone with a corpse. His back was turned when it happened. A deafening sound and a flash. He jumped with terror and whirled around.

The body had disappeared. Only a flashmark on the concrete remained.

###

Hundreds of miles away, at a labor camp in the Northern Zones, Capt. Sonya Bayson frowned. Lightning had struck the communications center the previous day, leaving the camp cut off from all communication. The last report she received warned all outposts to be on high alert. Terrorists had kidnaped a number of workers from several locations in what appeared to be a coordinated effort. Many of the workers and their captors had already been captured, but all stations in the zones were ordered to post extra guards until further notice.

Even if the rain stopped, it would be at least three hours before Captain Bayson could contact the outside world or receive messages. Being far from any other vestiges of "civilization" could be considered an extreme disadvantage, but Sonya Bayson wanted to see it differently. It was her opportunity to get results her own way.

The captain's aide knocked before escorting prisoner 14372 into the cramped office. Although the temperature in the office wasn't as warm as the captain would like, compared to the prisoners' barracks, it was balmy. The aide started to leave the room as the black female convict took a seat.

"Harrison," the captain said to her junior officer, "bring some tea."

Ignoring the woman in the chair, Bayson looked down at her desk and set some papers on a folder containing details about what she hoped would be her next assignment. She kept the folder on, or in, her desk at all times as an incentive. *Within two years, if things go well here . . .* she repeated to herself.

Prisoner 14372 sat in silence, waiting to be addressed before speaking. Within a few moments, Harrison reentered the room holding a tray with a teapot, two cups, two saucers, a creamer, a sugar bowl, two spoons, and a couple of cloth napkins. The rose-like scent of freshly brewed tea wafted through the room as Harrison set the tray in front of the captain, then departed.

Captain Bayson glanced at the woman in the chair before picking up the teapot. "I've been watching you," she said, as she poured the dark, amber-colored liquid into a cup. "I make it my business to know what's going on in my camp. It cuts down on the negative surprises. You've only been here a short while, yet I note that many of the other workers respect you. Care for some tea?"

Edwina Grant was soaked with cold rain and chilled to the bone. Even *holding* a hot cup of tea would be bliss. She inwardly prayed before answering, "Yes, some tea would be nice."

The captain poured another cup, then passed it across the desk. "As I was saying, I see you are held in high esteem by fellow workers. . . . Sugar? Cream? Sometimes, tea is my only link with civilization. Sorry, we have no lemons, though. Who knows if lemons even exist anymore."

"Sugar, please," Edwina answered.

Bayson passed the bowl of sugar and a spoon across the desk and said, "I'm relatively new here as well . . . and I've been waiting for someone like you. While this is a labor camp, and I'm charged with its operation, I see no reason for antagonism. It's plain and simple. As long as all of you work hard, my life is easier. If you produce more, my life is better. In turn, I could make *your* lives a bit better."

The captain took a sip of her tea, before continuing. "You prisoners would do well to consider my power over you. I can do anything I want, I can be as cruel as I want . . . or as nice as I want. We're out in the middle of nowhere, so who would ever know? I'm supposed to give all of you regular opportunities to mend your thinking and to sign the Notice of Allegiance, but I have few illusions about this. Hopefully, none of you has illusions, either. You should have no illusions about why you're here, or what it will take to survive. You should have no illusions about escaping, either."

Edwina cradled the cup in her right hand. "And you're hoping I will help you?"

"Precisely."

"Why would I do this?"

"Because you happen to be the right person in the right place at the right time. You're in a perfect position to help me, and I'll make it worth your while."

"My while?" Edwina asked. She set the cup back in the saucer on her lap.

"I told you, I make it my business to know what goes on in this camp. Inside these fences, I'm omniscient—I know *everything*. For instance, I know about your little gatherings with two or three people at a time. I know you had an opportunity to steal a knife last week and you passed it up—I know because I made sure you *got* that opportunity. . . . I also know that the woman in the bunk next to yours is in the early stages of pregnancy and you've been helping her."

Edwina said nothing.

"I have ways to solve that last situation," the captain stated. She waited for the full impact of the statement to soak in before continuing. "But I'm prepared to, shall we say, be less than all-knowing, in exchange for simple cooperation from the workers."

A thunderous noise shook the entire building as a simultaneous river of light slashed through the rattling windows. The light became so intense, that it momentarily seemed to melt away the walls and roof of the structure.

In the midst of the sound—was it music? A voice?— Bayson also heard a teacup shattering on the floor. It took her eyes a few moments to readjust. When they did, she found herself staring at an empty chair.

###

At that same moment, on a faraway prison floor, Troy and Jason looked up and started to laugh. They all started to laugh as the ceilings and walls became transparent and the sky unfolded before them.

###

Hundreds of miles from the prison, Michael neared the bottom of the steep path. He could see light glowing on the walls of the canyon. He could hear the loud peals of thunder echoing down through the ravine, and the sound of thousands of voices singing: "I waited patiently for the Lord; He inclined his ear to me and heard my cry. He drew me up from the desolate pit, out of the miry bog, and set my feet upon a rock, making my steps secure. He put a new song in my mouth, a song of praise to our God."

"Michael?" he heard her voice.

"Sara! He spotted her and ran to her. They held each other tightly as the storm intensified. They heard the voice and looked up as Sara cried, "He's here, Michael! He's come for us!"

The people in the canyon reached up, and their feet left the ground in a magnificent display of sound and light. As they rose upward they could not only see the One for whom they'd waited, but also Pete, Jessica, Edwina, Troy, Jen, Jason, Norris, Sam, and all the multitudes of those who had, in times past or present, faithfully awaited the same moment.

Romans 8:31-32, 35-39

What, then, shall we say in response to this? If God is for us, who can be against us? . . . Who shall separate us from the love of Christ? Shall trouble or hardship or persecution or famine or nakedness or danger or sword? As it is written: "For your sake we face death all day long; we are considered as sheep to be slaughtered." No, in all these things we are more than conquerors through him who loved us. For I am convinced that neither death nor life, neither angels nor demons, neither the present nor the future, nor any powers, neither height nor depth, nor anything else in all creation, will be able to separate us from the love of God that is in Christ Jesus our Lord. [NIV]

1 Thessalonians 4:15-18

According to the Lord's own word, we tell you that we who are still alive, who are left till the coming of the Lord, will certainly not precede those who have fallen asleep. For the Lord himself will come down from heaven, with a loud command, with the voice of the archangel and with the trumpet call of God, and the dead in Christ will rise first. After that, we who are still alive and are left will be caught up together with them in the clouds to meet the Lord in the air. And so we will be with the Lord forever. Therefore encourage each other with these words. [NIV]

THE END of Book 3

Thanks for reading my book! If you enjoyed it, would you take a moment to write a review for your favorite retailer?

Thanks again!

Terry L. Craig

EPILOGUE

When I first felt a call from the Lord to write this book, I was blissfully unaware of the raging controversy over the "rapture" or "catching away" of Christians. Since then, I have heard every imaginable opinion on the subject—some plausible, others having no scriptural basis at all. Sadly, most people with an opinion on the matter have become so attached to their point of view they will ignore even the Bible when it contradicts them. My goal in writing *SWORDSMAN* wasn't to set a timetable for the rapture or for "end time" events, but to speak to two groups of people.

First and foremost, I wanted to speak to people experiencing deep spiritual hunger. Until I was in my mid-twenties, I was part of this group. Remembering my own quest, my heart goes out to those who are genuinely seeking answers to life's most puzzling questions, and I pray this book will direct them to the Author of life itself: Jesus Christ.

Second, I wanted to encourage Christians to keep Jesus as the central focus of their lives and their witness to others. The truth is, we can't promise *anyone* that if they accept Jesus they will escape the horrors of persecution, or imprisonment, or plagues, or wars, or famines, or earthquakes . . . or that they will pass untouched through the everyday sorrows of this dark world. All we can honestly show them is Jesus, the One who promises to be our ever-present help in times of trouble, our Light in the darkness, the One who will never stop loving us, never leave or forsake us.

I sincerely pray that every person who reads *SWORDSMAN* will read the whole Bible and come to understand that salvation doesn't rest on a theory or time, but upon belief in Jesus Christ *whatever* the time. I also pray that you will keep His words in your heart: " . . . *I have spoken unto you, that in me ye might have peace. In the world ye shall have tribulation: but be of good cheer; I have overcome the world.*" [John 16:33 *KJV*]

About this trilogy

While each novel in this trilogy can be enjoyed as a single book, there is a continuing thread throughout the trilogy that readers will savor. If you have enjoyed *SWORDSMAN* but haven't read the first two books in this series, we invite you to explore the "history" of your favorite characters in *GATEKEEPER* and *SOJOURNER*.

About Terry L. Craig

Born in the Southwest, Terry has lived all over the US and spent many years living in the Caribbean. She's a people-watcher and a comparative thinker who is fascinated with words, art, and ideas. She has a passion to share spiritual life in a way that allows the reader to weigh the values of different ideologies from a non-threatening perspective.

Terry is a follower of Jesus, a wife, mom, and grandma who currently resides in North Carolina with her professional pilot husband (her lifetime love) Bill. The development of true friendships and healthy community life are high on her list of life's essentials.

Paperback copies of all of Terry's books are available at the publisher's website at (www.wildflowerpress.*biz*), or at CreateSpace.com, Amazon.com, and other fine book retailers.

Ebook versions are also available through Amazon.com, Smashwords.com, in the Apple iTunes bookstore, and other fine ebook retailers.

To learn more about Terry or connect with her:

Visit her author page on the Wild Flower Press, Inc. website at **www.wildflowerpress.*biz*** for links to her social media pages.

Terry L. Craig's newest series:

Scions of the Aegean C

Scions of the Aegean C, Descent into the Wilds Book 1 of the series.

More than a century after an entire colony of people crashed in an unknown world, both the written knowledge of the survivors and fragments of the ship they dismantled in their efforts to stay alive are decaying. As eyewitness accounts of the "Firstlanders" pass from living memory, alternate versions of the colony's history are taking shape.

Her parents paid the ultimate price for faith and love, but Shaye Penway will be known for the mistakes that cost her everything—and changed history.

Through the Land of Cloud and Leaf, Book 2

Into thin air . . .

After two young women vanish, an unprecedented reward for information is offered—but even their kidnappers don't know where they are. Three small objects found in the forest and decaying fragments of history may provide the only hope of finding them.

Shaye grew up with dreams of walking with the legendary Exiles in a place her people called *"the land of cloud and leaf."* But this may be more of a nightmare than the stuff of childhood fantasies.

The Exiles have managed to conceal their own existence for more than sixty years, yet they will risk discovery to rescue two women and lead them on a long and perilous journey to their settlement—and the offer of a new life.

NEXT in the series: *Under an Open Sky*, Book 3

For updates on the upcoming release of *Under an Open Sky*, check out Wild Flower Press, Inc. at:
https://www.wildflowerpress.biz

Other Books Published by Wild Flower Press, Inc.

The *Within the Walls* trilogy
by Stephanie Bennett

The Within the Walls trilogy chronicles the life of Emilya Hoffman Bowes Brown—technological genius, collaborator in the newest wave of "tek" enhancements to hit the market, and creator of virtual vacations. In Book 1, Emilya finds information that leads her on a journey to a community of dissidents who have chosen to live without technology, exposed to nature and the elements—something that was supposed to be impossible. As the trilogy unfolds, Emilya tries to understand the puzzle of these people in the wild, the way they live, and their use of words like "faith" and "soul." Aren't humans just biology and electricity?

- *Within the Walls*, Book 1

- *Breaking the Silence*, Book 2

- *The Poet's Treasure*, Book 3

The *Within the Walls* trilogy is available in ebook or print through most fine book retailers.

Passport for the Journey, 21 Day Challenge
by Tonya J. Brown

This travel-sized devotional/journal will slip easily into a briefcase, purse, or pocket. Each entry in this book can be read in a couple of minutes, but is enough food to meditate on the entire day—great for a personal devotional, or for use by a group as an opener for meetings. The content is written for Millennial Generation believers who are ready to embark on a new experience with God.

Available in print and ebook formats at many fine retailers.